Betrayed: Book Two
The Road to Redemption

Nicky Charles

Betrayed: Book Two - The Road to Redemption
Copyright © 2018, 2017, 2014 Nicky Charles
Createspace Revised Edition

All rights reserved. This book may not be reproduced or used in any form whatsoever without permission from the author, except in the case of brief quotations embodied in reviews. Please do not participate in or encourage piracy of copyrighted materials in violation of the author's rights. All characters and storylines are the property of the author. Your support and respect are appreciated.

This book is a work of fiction. Names, places, characters and incidents are drawn from the author's imagination and are used fictitiously. Any resemblance to actual events, locales, organizations, or persons either living or dead is entirely coincidental.

This book contains mature content and is intended for mature readers.

Canadian grammar was used in this book, hence you might notice some punctuation and spelling variations.

Edited by Jan Gordon
Line edits by Jennifer Moody, MoodyEdits.com
Cover Design by Nicky Charles
Cover Images used under license from Shutterstock.com
Pawprint logo Copyright © Doron Goldstein, Designer

Library of Congress Control Number: 2014908674
CreateSpace Independent Publishing Platform, North Charleston, SC

ISBN-13: 978-1499152920
ISBN-10: 1499152922

This book is dedicated to

DEBORAH DAVIDSON

She is a courageous fan who is battling ovarian cancer. She reached out to me through a fan letter stating she'd likely not be here to read this, the next book in the series, to which I replied, "Excuse me? *Not* be here for my next book! That is *totally* unacceptable." I promised her this would be 'her' book provided she kept fighting and she did!

I'd like to tell you a little bit about her. First, she's a wonderful person. She has a great sense of humour, a creative spirit (as shown through the beautiful bracelets she makes) and a love for animals that matches my own. Thanks to a suggestion from Jan Gordon, she's also a member of my 'street team'. Plus, she's Canadian and you can't ask for more than that, can you?

Deborah is still bravely undergoing treatment and fighting each day to beat the disease that is attacking her. Please, may I ask that everyone who reads this book pray for her or send healing thoughts her way.

"We love you Deborah. Never give up!"
Love and hugs from,
Nicky, Jan and all the ladies of TLS

ACKNOWLEDGEMENTS

As always this book wouldn't be possible without the help and assistance of a number of people. Jan, my friend, muse, editor and whip-cracker. Jennifer Moody who does my line edits. Jessica Stelluto who designs my covers. Janet Ramsey who creates trailers for each book as well as advance banners. Carmen Reyes and Kalia Conklin-Green who run the Law of the Lycans page. And, of course, all the members of my wonderful street team who promote my books.

I am truly blessed to have such an amazing group of people supporting me and my writing. Thank you, everyone!

Betrayed – Book Two: The Road to Redemption

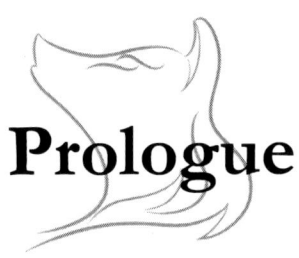

Prologue

Excerpt from The Finding:

Sam Harper tapped the table with a pen, eyes narrowed, mouth clamped shut in a straight line. Six months ago a meeting with Kane Sinclair had raised everyone's hackles and the memory still rankled. The arrogant son of a bitch had dared to claim the Chicago pack was inefficient and mismanaged. Ha! As if he knew anything about what went on in this city. The man had no idea; absolutely none!

And then there was the brother. Ryne Taylor had stolen from the Chicago pack; Cassandra Greyson had been a potential packmate. Both her land and money would have gone far to assist their beleaguered resources.

But instead of being grateful that the Chicago pack wasn't pressing charges against them, Kane, Ryne, and the Beta, Bryan—another pain in the ass—had pulled out the Book of the Law, using it to claim what wasn't theirs. And then Sinclair had the gall to leave mumbling about a takeover!

Well, it wasn't going to happen. The pack had met and agreed on a course of action. It wasn't ideal—they all knew it—but sometimes necessity drove you to take actions you never thought you would. For example, hiring 'Sylvia,' or whoever she was, to kill Leon Aldrich. It had gone against the grain to go to outsiders for help, but that damned Sinclair wouldn't leave them alone; constantly demanding reports and updates.

Sam snorted. Well, Aldrich was gone and at least they hadn't had to pay Sylvia. It was a small thing, but some days you took what you could get in the way of good news.

With the money saved, they could afford to buy some more help for the next problem looming on the horizon. Rumour had it Sinclair was sending someone in to check the pack out, but the intruder would have a surprise waiting for him. Sam took a swig of beer and leaned back against the wall, one lip curled.

There was a small faction of Lycans that were true loners or rogues. They were usually tough, mean and as deadly as they came, but they were also for hire. A meeting had been set up with one of them for tonight. On the off chance Sinclair's 'spy' came around, the Chicago pack would have the rogue in their back pocket and whip the intruder's butt, sending him back to Oregon with his tail between his legs.

A glance at the clock let Sam know it was almost time. A final swig of beer; a glance around the smoky, crowded bar... Yep, the usual crowd looking to start something. Well, good luck with that you losers, Sam thought. I don't take crap from anyone.

Shoulders back, chin up; look each person straight in the eye until they're compelled to look away. Sam smirked. I'm an Alpha, buddy. You don't stand a chance.

Almost to the door and... There it was, a hand on the shoulder. Some jerk always had to try his luck.

"Hey, baby. You got a cute ass." The man's liquor soaked breath was offensive as was the stench coming off his sweaty body. He tried to pull her backwards. "Wanna share—"

She jerked her arm back, elbowing the idiot in the stomach. As he bent forward, clutching his mid-section, she ground her stiletto heel into his foot, then pivoted around to deliver an uppercut to his chin. In a matter of seconds, the man was an unconscious heap on the ground.

"Anyone else?" Hands on her hips, she surveyed the men who were gathering around her. The assault was nothing new. She frequented quite a few bars and the human males always thought she'd be an easy target, not knowing what she lacked in size, she made up for with skill and speed.

When no one answered, she sniffed and turned, walking slowly towards the door at a leisurely pace. No hurried exit for her. She could see her reflection in the glass doors as she approached. Short, black hair spiked on top with a longer fringe almost hiding her eyes. She'd used black kohl liner to take further attention away from her eye colour. They were violet, a rare shade in humans and even rarer in wolves. Sam despised the colour; it was too girly for the image she tried to portray. Now, her black jeans and T-shirt, complete with leather jacket—*that* gave off the right vibes. Her heels were her only outward concession to femininity since they gave her some much needed height.

She was at the exit now. No one had made a move to follow her, not that she expected them to. As the door started to swing shut behind her, she could hear the murmur of voices and allowed herself a tight smile.

"Did you see that?"

"She flattened Phil in two seconds!"

"Just a mite of a thing, too."

"Hey, Phil! You okay, buddy?"

The sound of the voices faded as she walked down the street, carefully assessing the shadowed doorways. Pools of light from the street lamps brightened select areas giving a false sense that the street was safe, but Sam knew better.

Someone was following her. Not someone from the bar. This person had been waiting outside. Her rogue, perhaps? She wouldn't put it past the unpredictable beasts. Well, if he thought to get the better of her, he had another think coming.

The man was good, she'd give him that. His pace matched hers perfectly, but a prickling on the back of her neck, and the faintest shuffling sound gave him away. He had a slight limp and she wondered why. Wolves usually healed completely. Well, she'd ask him once she was done taking him down a peg or two for tailing her.

It wasn't that she needed help against Sinclair's spy, she was sure she could take whoever the bastard sent, but a male always seemed to impress other wolves more than a female, and creating an illusion was what this was all about. Smoke and mirrors. She'd been using it successfully for the past three years, it would work again—a faint frown passed over her features and she bit her lip—it had to.

Sam reached the corner and walked around it, then ducked into the first doorway she came to. This was the corner she was supposed to meet the rogue at. She chuckled thinking that this meeting wouldn't go quite as the man had planned.

The sound of his footsteps grew closer, but the tempo had changed. The man suspected something. Sam twisted her lips, impressed, but not ready to let him off. Muscles tensed, senses alert, adrenaline rushed through her as she prepared for a fight.

Chapter 1

Damien leaned against the brick wall, its rough surface lightly digging into his shoulder through a rip in his shirt. He was breathing hard, sweat trickling down his face, the still, heavy air doing nothing to help cool him off. With each inhalation, he took in the scents of the city; exhaust fumes, garbage, humanity. The back alley of one city smelled very much like that of another though this one had one significant difference. Lycans.

The she-wolf across the alley from him had her butt propped against the edge of a dumpster, her hands braced on her knees as she stood, half hunched, trying to catch her breath. The fight they'd just completed had been exhilarating as she'd matched him move for move. He'd barely needed to hold back; her speed and agility making up for what she lacked in size and muscle. Already, faint aches and pains were letting themselves be known, and no doubt in brighter surroundings he'd find a fine array of bruises decorating his body.

Grabbing the edge of his shirt, he gave his face a quick wipe, careful to keep one eye on his opponent. When Kane had described the petite female who acted as Samuel Harper's spokesperson, he'd made her sound ineffectual. Damien had pictured her as demure, perhaps carrying a clipboard and peering over her glasses. While it was true she might not look like much of a threat, the last few minutes had shown it wasn't wise to underestimate her. He wondered if Kane had set him up; purposely leaving out the information that the woman packed a lethal punch. Thanks, buddy.

Pushing off from the wall, he swallowed, wincing slightly at the pull of his dry throat and wishing he had a stiff drink. But there'd be time enough for that later. Instead, he focused on her.

"We done?"

There was a pause in her breathing and then he saw her nod.

"Yeah. I think we're done."

Had he really heard a hint of laughter in her voice? Damien eyed her speculatively as she straightened from her braced position. At some point their battle had moved from the street to the alley where they now stood. The faint light from a single bulb over the backdoor of a restaurant was the only illumination. It wasn't much, but he was still able to make out her features. Short, dark hair, a petite yet muscular build. An alley fighter—a damned *good* alley fighter—and a female. Who'd have thought?

"You put up a pretty good fight, Dante. I guess you'll do." She brushed some dirt from the legs of her pants and it gave him a much needed moment to consider what she'd said.

She'd called him Dante. The name had his mental warning bells ringing and not only because she obviously was mistaking him for someone else. He stalled for time as he tried to improvise a plan.

"Do what?" Wiping his mouth on the back of his hand, he noted the streak of blood from a cut on his lip. The woman had a wicked right hook.

"Act as our rogue." She looked up from where she'd been examining a scuff mark on her leather jacket and narrowed her eyes. In the dim light it was hard to determine the colour, but he could almost swear they were violet. "That's what we agreed on. You become a temporary part of the pack—a Beta, almost a co-Alpha—until we manage to convince Sinclair that there's no bloody way he can take us over."

"Right." Damien thought quickly, assimilating the new information. Sinclair. So she knew about Kane's planned takeover. "Just checking. I don't like having the rules changed once I start something."

"Once the job is done, we pay you the agreed amount and you head on your way."

"What does the rest of the pack think of this? Your current Beta? Won't he want to slit my throat for taking over his job?" Damien tried to fill in the missing pieces of the deal without revealing his hand.

She pursed her lips and he could tell she was weighing her words. "The Beta position is currently...vacant. We're a small pack...but strong." Her chin lifted as if she was expecting him to contradict her. "The problem is that Lycan society is too damned chauvinistic. Everyone takes one look at me and only sees a *female*." She spat out the last word. "I'm perfectly capable of running this pack, but Sinclair will use my gender against me. That's where you come in."

She was capable of running the pack? Damien held back a frown. This teeny weeny she-wolf wasn't the Alpha. He knew for a fact that *Samuel*, not *Samantha*, Harper was listed as Alpha in Lycan Link's books. Kane had said she was Harper's spokesperson and he'd somehow gotten the impression of her being more of a secretary or office manager than anything else. Perhaps she was a wannabe Beta and resented being overlooked? Damien filed that question in the back of his mind for later examination and focused on what she was saying.

"So, you still want the position?" She spoke as if she didn't care, but he could tell otherwise. This was important to her. A twinge of regret over deceiving her passed through him. He pushed it aside. Kane had sent him to do a job, to scout out the Chicago pack, find their weaknesses and report back on the best way to proceed with a takeover. What better way to gather information than to actually join the pack? It hadn't been part of his plan, but experience had taught him to grab whatever opportunity presented itself.

"Yeah, I'll take it."

"Good." She hid her relief well, only the barest change of inflection letting him know she'd been concerned. "Do you have your own transportation or do you need a ride to the pack house?"

"I'm good. I'll follow you. Give me half an hour and I'll meet you in front of that bar you just left." That would give him time to call Kane and tell him he'd made contact, as well as attend to one other pressing matter.

"Half an hour." She flicked a glance up and down the length of him and then walked away, her head held high, her stride confident. Usually people backed away from him. He raised one brow, impressed with her gutsiness.

As the sound of her heels clicking on the pavement faded, a voice spoke behind him. "She's a fine looking woman."

Damien didn't flinch. He'd known the man was there; the faint scent of lilacs—so out of place in a Chicago alley—had let him know a Lycan using a scent mask was in the area.

"That she is, Dante." He waited a moment before slowly turning. He had no fear of the man behind him though that had likely been Dante's hope. The Lycan stood just feet away. Grey hair showed at his temples and the lines on his face gave evidence to the hard life he'd led.

"Ah, Damien, my old friend. You're not surprised to see me?" Dante reached out to shake hands.

Damien flicked a look at the extended palm and chose to ignore it.

"The proverbial bad penny always turns up. Isn't that what they say?" Damien coolly assessed the man. Dante was an acquaintance from a life he'd thought he'd left behind and he wasn't sure what the man's appearance might mean. Coincidence or something more? "She planned on hiring you." He stated the fact and watched for a reaction.

Dante let his hand drop to his side and shrugged. "We were supposed to meet tonight to finalize the deal, to see if I met the requirements."

"And?" He cocked his head. "No cry of foul that I stole the job from you?"

"You were here before me." Dante shrugged again. "Our time working for Deirdre taught both of us to grab whatever opportunities came our way and, if we missed one, to move on. Anything else is a waste of time."

Something didn't add up. The man was too cool for someone who'd just lost a well-paying job. Damien nodded however. "Glad there are no hard feelings."

Dante extended his hand again. "Shake?"

Damien took half a step forward, reached his hand out and then smashed his knuckles into the other man's nose, following the move up with a strategic kick guaranteed to blow out an opponent's knee.

Dante hit the ground hard, blood spurting from his nostrils, a cry of pain escaping his lips.

"As you said, Deirdre taught us not to waste an opportunity." Damien looked at the man writhing on the ground, and casually taking a wad of bills from his pocket, dropped them on the ground beside the injured Lycan. "Sorry, but you wouldn't have passed Harper's test anyway. That should be enough to cover your out of pocket expenses."

"What the hell...?" Dante struggled to get up, anger contorting his face.

Placing his foot on the man's throat, Damien pressed down just enough to cause the man's eyes to widen in distress. "Just a reminder, this is *my* job now. *My* territory. Stay the hell out of it." He eased off the pressure and gave the man one final warning. "And stay away from the girl or I *will* kill you."

Shoving his hands in his pockets, Damien walked away whistling softly. Dante would know better than to show his face in Chicago again. If there was one thing Damien had learned over the years, it was to never leave potential enemies in doubt as to your intentions.

Sam sat astride her Harley, waiting for her new Beta to appear. She'd had reservations about taking a rogue into the pack but, after consulting with the others, it had seemed to be the best solution. He was younger than she'd anticipated; the experience he'd outlined in his emails seemed to belong to someone older. Most likely he'd exaggerated hoping to impress. An inelegant snort escaped her. As if.

The street was almost empty. A few cars passed by, a group of teens roughhousing. It was late enough that the majority of people had already headed for home, only a few hard-core revellers remaining in the various establishments that lined the streets. She tapped her fingers on the handles of her motorcycle, impatient to be on her way. It had been a long day and she was tired, not that she'd let anyone know. An Alpha had no weaknesses.

Sitting up straighter, she took a deep breath. Fall was almost upon them, but the unseasonably warm weather belied the fact. Heat and humidity made the air seem heavy to breathe and caused her clothing to stick to her. A cold shower or a cold drink; she'd take either of them right now if only she had the time.

A glance at her watch revealed it was exactly twenty-nine minutes since she'd left the rogue in the alley. Where the hell was…? The sound of an engine approaching stopped her mid-curse. A motorcycle pulled up beside her. Dante.

His bike matched him perfectly. Big and black. Powerful. It was an older model that had some signs of wear, but the engine purred like a well maintained machine should. Light from the overhead street lamp bathed them allowing her to see the dark stubble showing on his firm chin. His silvery blue eyes were topped by strong brows. There was a coldness about him, an 'I don't give a damn if I live or die' look. Men with that attitude were dangerous and it had her once again rethinking her decision to hire him. Was she bringing trouble into her pack? She hoped not.

A whisper of a breeze caused a lock of his black hair to fall over his forehead. It added a contrasting hint of vulnerability, as did his slightly fuller lower lip. Which was the real man, she wondered, an unexpected thrill coursing through her as she studied him. She gave no hint as to her interest, though, keeping her face impassive.

He flicked a glance at her wrist and Sam realized she still had her sleeve pulled back to reveal her watch. "Am I late?"

As she looked down, the numbers changed. Exactly thirty minutes. She didn't say anything however, merely letting her sleeve drop back into place and starting her engine. "Ready?"

He nodded and they set off.

Sam led the way, knowing the streets of Chicago like the back of her hand. She'd been prowling the city ever since she'd been old enough to leave the house on her own and knew every back alley and short cut. Of course, she wasn't going to reveal that to the rogue. He was an unknown entity and her knowledge of the city was an ace up her sleeve.

Instead, she took more traditional routes, winding her way past businesses and factories, abandoned lots and housing complexes. She could feel Dante's gaze on her, a distinctive twitch between her shoulder blades letting her know he was assessing her, no doubt noting the incongruity of a small woman manoeuvring a big Harley.

Too bad.

She loved the big machine, the idea of controlling so much power.

They paused for a traffic light and she glanced in her rearview mirror, catching Dante's gaze. He nodded, acknowledging the eye contact, his face expressionless.

Sam watched him, watching her. His gaze was intense, just bordering on being challenging. Then, slowly, he shifted his focus, his lids lowering as he slid his gaze down her body. Her muscles tightened. She could almost feel him touching her, trailing his fingers down her spine, lingering on her waist. What would it feel like to have him slide his hands around her, to pull her back against his hard body? Their earlier fight had brought them into close proximity and she was well aware that he was a fine physical specimen. Exploring him more intimately might be very rewarding.

The idea had tension coiling inside her as heat pooled low down in her belly. She swallowed hard, her hands inadvertently tightening on the throttle. The engine roared, the big machine throbbing with suppressed power between her legs. In the mirror, Dante locked eyes with her again. Was there an added heat in his gaze?

Sam broke eye contact and almost gave a sigh of relief when the traffic light changed from red to green and she had to concentrate on the road once again. Being attracted to Dante wasn't a good idea. She'd have to watch herself around him. Damn.

As they approached the neighbourhood that she and her pack called home, Sam lowered her speed and scanned the area. In its day, it had been a prestigious area, but time and changing economic fortunes hadn't been kind. The once grand houses were tired and in need of repair, many now converted into multiple family dwellings. In a way, it served as a kind of camouflage for her pack. A snooty neighbourhood might question the number of persons who came and went from her home, but here, no one noticed or cared. Minding your own business was the motto.

Sam swung her bike into an opening in a rusty wrought iron fence. The brick pillars that flanked the entrance were crumbling, the house number hanging crookedly from a rusty screw. She kept meaning to fix it, but there were always too many other jobs that took priority.

The driveway wasn't long. It curved around the front of the house and then along the side to the back. Years ago, this would have been the servants' entrance, but now it was the door they used most often given that the boards on the front porch were partially rotted.

Thankfully, it was dark, and Dante wouldn't notice the outward appearance of the pack house. That gave her time to establish herself with him before he started to form any kind of judgement. Some might think that a rundown house indicated a weak Alpha, but she'd prove him wrong. Economic hard times had nothing to do with her abilities as a leader. She wasn't the one who had run the pack bank balance into the red.

Compressing her lips at that thought, she turned off the Harley's engine and swung her leg over the seat. Dante parked beside her.

"We're here." Sam kept her voice gruff, her words clipped. Her momentary attraction to him had left her out of sorts and she wasn't about to hide the fact. Being a bitch helped keep the pack members in line, and they knew enough not to cross her when she was in a mood. Someone else could do the social niceties.

Betrayed: Book Two – The Road To Redemption

Damien sat astride his motorcycle, a dark cloud settling over him. Following Samantha had given him a perfect opportunity to study her as she controlled the massive machine she rode. The way she'd leaned into the curves showed she was sure of her abilities, the way her ass wiggled as she'd adjusted her seat at a traffic light revealed her love of creature comforts. It had caught his attention and reminded him of how her lithe body and toned muscles had felt against his when they'd been locked in battle. It had been ages since he'd experienced even a stir of interest in another woman and now guilt over that interest ate away at him. He scowled, damning her and himself.

Samantha didn't look his way after parking her Harley, merely heading towards the house. He knew she was expecting him to follow, but a perverse need to command her attention had him staying where he was. Besides, he was a rogue; since when did he do anything the easy way?

Her foot was on the top step before she paused and cocked her head to the side. Good. She'd noticed he wasn't trotting after her like some pup. He waited smugly for her reaction.

"You coming, Dante? Or have you seized up already from our fight? If you have, you're obviously the wrong rogue for the job and you might as well head on your way now." She spoke without turning, her tone hard. Even her hand remained resting lightly on the railing, no sign of it clenching in tension. Damien silently acknowledged her self-confidence. Turning would have meant she needed eye contact to enforce her authority. And her question was phrased to goad an answer from him. Smart girl.

He could remain silent, turn this into a battle of wills, but that wasn't his purpose. Some defiance was expected from a rogue, but he needed to stay within the pack's good graces if he was to carry out the mission Kane had sent him on. Going against his natural instincts, he answered her.

"Coming. Just admiring the view."

"View?"

Mentioning her ass in her snug pants would have been too cliché and, from the slight stiffening of her shoulders, he could tell that was what she was expecting. Instead, he kept things neutral. "The moon. It's full."

She glanced upward, but that was all the acknowledgement she gave the statement. "Hurry up. I still have things I need to do tonight."

Her dismissive tone irked and he compressed his lips to hold back a snarl. Why the hell had he agreed to do this job? Weeks of acting subservient to a slip of a girl and her ineffectual Alpha wasn't going to be easy. Did he really need the aggravation? Then he thought of Kane and Elise and sighed. He'd given his word and he'd stand by it…even if it drove him insane.

Damien shoved his keys in his pocket and grabbed his pack. No point in prolonging things any longer. "I'm ready. Lead the way."

He eyed the house as he climbed the steps, noting loose bricks and missing mortar. It was an old building, rundown and in need of some serious repairs. Once inside it was easy to see the same applied to the interior as well. It was clean but begging for a facelift.

"The pack office is over there." Samantha gestured towards the front of the house. "Common rooms, kitchen and dining room are all on the main floor. Bedrooms are on the second and third levels."

"Has your pack been here long?" He asked the question idly as he peered into the rooms they passed. Most of the furniture he saw had been elegant in its day, some were even antiques but much of it was long past its prime.

"We've occupied this particular house for over a century. Why?" Samantha shot a look at him over her shoulder, a mixture of defensiveness and suspicion lacing her voice.

"No reason. Just wondering." Damien shrugged and said no more. She seemed prickly and he could imagine it would be all too easy to get into a meaningless fight.

Betrayed: Book Two – The Road To Redemption

She led him to the second floor and then the third, the stairs creaking with age beneath their weight. Damien listened carefully, trying to detect how many other wolves might be in the house, but he only heard the quiet drone of a TV in some far off room. Nor was the air laced with a multitude of scents; a dozen wolves lived here at best. Strange. For a pack house of this size, he'd have expected more.

"You'll be staying here." Samantha opened a door near the end of the hallway and gestured for him to go ahead.

Damien brushed past and her scent teased his nostrils; leather and a touch of exotic spice. It stirred his interest, and his inner wolf perked its ears wanting to linger and test her scent again. *Too bad, boy; it's not happening.* He continued on into the room.

Trying to occupy his mind with practicalities, he glanced at his surroundings. The bedroom was a decent size with a double bed, dresser, table and chair. An old armoire filled most of one wall and windows flanked either side of the bed.

"You have your own bathroom." Samantha jerked her chin towards a partially open door. "Towels and sheets are on the end of the bed. If you're hungry feel free to raid the kitchen. Just follow your nose and you'll find it." Her tone was abrupt, her expression impassive save for a few lines of tension around the corners of her mouth.

Damien wondered what her problem was, not that he really cared. All he wanted was to be away from her and the uncomfortable awareness she stirred in him.

"I'll be fine." His words were clipped and to the point.

"Good, I'll talk to you in the morning." With one final assessing glance, she turned and left.

After pushing the door shut, Damien tossed his bag in the corner and checked the windows; old habits were hard to forget. The panes slid open with little effort and revealed that a branch from a massive chestnut tree was within reach, as was the downspout from the eaves trough. If need be, either could provide a means of escape. Satisfied, he shut the window, stripped and flopped down on the bed willing himself to rest.

Nicky Charles

The cross country drive from Kane's home in Oregon had been long and he'd pushed himself to complete it in as few days as possible. Hours on his motorcycle followed by a good fight had the old injury on his leg throbbing dully. Come to think of it, his other muscles weren't that happy with him either. When he'd left Smythston, he'd jokingly told Kane he was on the road to redemption. He hadn't expected quite these types of road bumps, though!

Being thirty wasn't all it was cracked up to be, he thought as he rolled onto his side and punched his pillow. Better than being dead, he supposed, though there were days when he questioned that. Another muscle twinged in his leg and he wondered if Samantha was feeling any aches and pains from their encounter. An evil side of him hoped she was. And with that he closed his eyes and tried to sleep.

Chapter 2

Sam stood at the far end of the hallway, listening to Dante move about his room. He'd opened and shut the windows and then faint rustling sounds followed. She assumed he was getting undressed and refused to acknowledge the visual that came to mind. He was a rogue she'd hired, nothing to get excited about. A thud indicated he'd flopped on the bed and was followed by slight protests from the mattress as he adjusted his position. Then silence. Cocking her head, she waited for five minutes until she was confident that he was settled for the night, before moving away.

Dante was on the third floor; it was hardly used anymore and therefore kept him away from most of the pack. Her inner wolf murmured its approval of her decision. It was suspicious of the man. More importantly, Dante's location kept him away from her grandfather and his querulous moods. Her mouth tightened as she thought of her patriarch, and giving a sigh, she headed down the stairs to the next level.

Her grandfather's room was at the far end of the second floor hallway—exactly in the opposite direction of Dante's. As she approached, telltale boards creaked preventing her from catching the old man by surprise. She snorted as, after the first squeak, the TV was suddenly turned off and the shaft of light disappeared from under his doorway.

She paused outside the room and shook her head at his attempt to deceive her before giving a light rap.

"Enter." His voice was gravelly with age and fatigue. It was well past his bedtime.

Sam pushed the door open and then leaned against the jamb, arms folded as she stared at the man in the reclining chair. "Grandfather, why are you still awake?"

"I wasn't awake," he began to protest, but when she raised her brow he paused and rephrased his statement. "I was dozing. Fell asleep with the TV on."

"Right." She rolled her eyes making no attempt to hide her disbelief. "You were waiting up for me."

He shrugged. "And if I was?"

Sam pushed off from the door frame moving to sit on a chair near him. "There's no need. I'm perfectly capable of carrying out a simple mission on my own."

He appeared about to protest but then changed his mind and gave a nod. "I trained you well."

"That you did." She lifted her chin slightly and straightened her spine.

They studied each other for a moment, the light from the hallway allowing her to see his thin silvery hair, the lines on his face, his faded blue eyes. There were no soft words or hugs between the two of them. That had never been Samuel Harper's way and, following his example, it wasn't hers either. He'd raised his namesake to be tough, resilient, to do her duty and show no weakness. She'd spent her entire childhood trying to live up to his expectations and, for the most part, she'd succeeded.

Finally, he grunted his approval of her and moved on to the real reason he'd stayed up. "Did the rogue show? Did he give you any trouble?"

"He showed. I tested him and he'll do."

"He'd better. Wasting money on a rogue." He snorted and shook his head before trying to push himself into a more comfortable position. "Once I'm back on my feet, none of this..." He began to cough, the results of a persistent cold he was still struggling to overcome. Sam instinctively reached out to help him.

"Let me..."

"No fussing! I'm not an invalid, you know!" His sharp tone had her freezing in place while her inner wolf shrunk towards the ground in the face of the Alpha's ire.

Betrayed: Book Two – The Road To Redemption

"Of course." She subsided, biting back the retort that had sprung to her lips. Age and an old back injury had left him mostly confined to his room these past years, but he refused to acknowledge he was no longer physically capable of running the pack. Instead, she served as 'acting Alpha' while he retained the official title. It irked that few knew she was really the one doing all the work and calling the shots, but short of publicly revealing his weakness there wasn't much she could do about the situation. Her time would come; it was just hard to be patient.

He sank back in his chair, fatigue and frustration showing in his face and his voice. "Keep the rogue in line. Don't put up with any nonsense from him. Knock him down the minute he starts to give you any trouble. Got that?"

"Yes. I know how—"

"And watch out for that bastard, Sinclair. He's sharp. He'll use every trick in the book to try to take our land, but don't let him."

"I have it covered, don't—"

"And remember to watch what you spend. Finances are tight right now and we can't afford—"

"I *know*, Grandfather. I'm well aware of the situation." Fed up, Sam cut him off and got to her feet. She didn't need him to tell her what to do. She'd been running the pack for years now. Taking a deep breath, she reined in her temper. He was old and ill and sometimes forgot she was an adult, not some young pup in training. Gentling her voice, she continued. "Don't worry, everything is under control."

He scowled. "It'd better be. I might get up tomorrow to check things out, so make sure you're ready."

"I will be." It was a threat he used often, but he never followed through. "See you in the morning."

He closed his eyes, effectively dismissing her. No 'goodbye' or 'sleep well' passed his lips. It wasn't his way.

Sam stared at him for a moment, once again struck by the conflicting emotions he evoked in her. He'd raised her and she respected him, loved him even, but there was always a distance between them, as if he was keeping his feelings firmly in check.

What would it have been like to have had a grandfather that doted on you? To have gone on trips to the amusement park or to have been pushed on a swing? From her earliest memory he'd 'trained' her to take over the pack. Kickboxing and bookkeeping; no dance lessons or parties with frilly dresses for her. Not that she'd have wanted to be decked out in pink lace but sometimes…sometimes it would be nice to get a word of praise for a job well done, to have some acknowledgement of all she'd accomplished. Unfortunately, it wasn't about to happen. Samuel Harper, Sr. wasn't about to let go of the reins nor was he going to change his ways.

Giving a sigh, she left his room, shutting the door quietly behind her. There was no point in bemoaning what she couldn't have.

The house was quiet, only the sound of her own footsteps and the ticking of the hall clock met her ears as she walked downstairs towards her office. It wasn't often that she had the house to herself; well as 'to herself' as possible with a rogue sleeping overhead and her grandfather in his quarters. Still, it was nice not to be constantly on call.

She'd sent most of the pack out for a run to celebrate the full moon, figuring it would keep them busy and out of the way while she sized up the rogue. A quick glance at the clock showed it would be several hours before they returned from the nature preserve they typically used. That gave her lots of undisturbed time to get some work done. She had bills to pay, correspondence to deal with and—she couldn't hold back the large yawn that overtook her—she desperately needed to get some sleep. Dealing with Dante in the morning would require her to be alert and on her toes. Pushing open the window, she let the warm night air spill in before settling down at her desk.

How long he rested, Damien had no idea, but at some point he realized he was hot. Too hot. He tried to push the covers off, to escape the warmth, but he couldn't. Heat surrounded him. The air was thick, acrid. It stung his nostrils and dried his throat. Smoke began to drift by, blurring his vision and stinging his eyes. What was going on? A fire?

Oh God.

No.

But even as he protested, a wall of flame appeared in the distance. He tried to run towards it, but his legs refused to obey his command. Lead weights seemed to be holding him in place. Panic filled him. He had to move. He had to save Beth! She was calling to him...

He struggled, fighting the unseen hands that pulled at him.

"Beth!"

Damien jerked into an upright position, his whole body shaking. He took in great gulps of air, staring about the room in a frantic search for something, anything, that would orient him. Surely, he was in his own bed, his mate at his side, her body swollen with his unborn child.

Yes, that had to be true. His sweet Beth was beside him. Couldn't he hear her gentle breathing? Detect her delicate scent?

He swallowed hard and inched his hand along the mattress, reaching out for the familiar warmth, knowing with certainty that it would be there. Any second now he'd feel the heat, encounter her soft flesh. A smile began to form on his lips in anticipation of that first moment of contact, but as he stretched his arm farther and farther, the smile faded. His hand found nothing. Panic began to rise in him and he splayed his fingers wider, searching, hoping... There was nothing to find.

The sheets were cold. The bed empty.

He was alone.

Damien closed his eyes and clenched the cotton material in his hand. His throat grew tight as he shook his head in denial, fighting against the emotion that welled inside and threatened to spill out.

It hadn't been a dream. His little mate was gone. His baby. Everything.

It was always the same. Waking up terrified, smelling the smoke, feeling the heat, hearing the sirens. He always hoped it was a nightmare, prayed that it was. Surely if he wished hard enough, what he wanted—needed—would become the truth. Wasn't that how it worked? Wasn't that the lie that all the movies and books and songs would have you believe?

A cynical laugh escaped him.

Cold, hard reality always arrived to kick him in the ass.

Letting his body fall back onto the mattress, Damien stared at the ceiling. They said it would get better with time, but what did they know? It had been three years since his mate had died and still the dreams persisted. True, he hadn't had one in months, but when would the torture finally end?

He tried to move and realized the sheets were tangled around his limbs, the sweat on his body making them cling all the more. The room felt hot and stuffy; apparently there was no air conditioning. With a sigh, he pulled himself free of the confining material then walked naked across the room, a patch of moonlight showing the way. Not that he needed guidance. The path to his backpack where he kept his whiskey was easy to traverse. He took the bottle from the bag, uncapped it then took a long swig enjoying the burn of alcohol as it slid down his throat and hit his empty stomach.

Another pull from the bottle burnt only slightly less than the first and he exhaled loudly before wiping his mouth on the back of his hand. He moved to put the cap back on, then shrugged and tossed the lid aside. Gripping the neck of the bottle he wandered to the window and opened it.

A whisper of a breeze stirred the curtains as the night air drifted into the room. It skimmed over him, drying the sweat that clung to his skin. Damien snagged a chair and sat down, contemplating the night sky with its dots of twinkling lights.

Experience told him there'd be no more rest for him that night so why bother trying to moderate his drinking? Instead, he'd spend the sleepless hours staring out the window, drowning his sorrows.

Lifting the bottle, he saluted the full moon. Somewhere out there Lycans were celebrating the celestial event. He wondered if Samantha was joining in the festivities. Was that why she'd been so abrupt with him? Had she been late for a pack run? And where did wolves go for a run in the heart of a city?

Damien tried to imagine her with her pack, running through the back alleys or perhaps a large park, playing with the other wolves, finding a mate... He frowned and his fingers tightened around the bottle, an uneasy feeling stirring within him at the image he was creating, though why he didn't know. What Samantha Harper did was none of his business.

He shifted his gaze from the window and noted his wallet sitting on the bedside table. Reaching over, he opened it up and stared at the lone photograph inside. Beth. He'd met her on a moonlit night such as this. She'd been beautiful and shy and had looked so lost. He'd fallen in love at first sight.

Slowly, reverently, he traced her features with his fingertip. It had been three years since he'd touched her, held her, pressed a kiss to her soft sweet lips. Some people had hinted to him that he should move on, find another mate. He shook his head. How do you love again when your heart is dead?

Melancholy threatened to overwhelm him again so he firmed his jaw and pushed the memory away. He couldn't afford to feel, at least not emotions. The smoothness of the floor under his bare feet, the heat of the whiskey in his gut... That was all he allowed himself. Only when he slept did it manage to escape. Sleep was not his friend. Unconsciousness however...

He laughed darkly and tilted the bottle, his lips forming around the cool glass. Drinking deeply, he wiped his mouth once again and slouched down in the chair. His right leg rested in a patch of light and he noted the scarred flesh. It was the only physical reminder of the fire that had almost claimed him. Everything else had miraculously healed or so the doctor had proclaimed.

Not everything, he whispered to himself as his fingers clutched the wallet in his hand. My body is alive, but my soul is dead. As dead as the child I never held, as dead as my love, my Beth.

Closing his eyes, he brought the whiskey bottle to his mouth and tipped his head back once more.

By morning he was numb. His Lycan metabolism prevented him from getting drunk on human whiskey, but numb was good. As dawn broke, he pushed himself from his chair and headed to the bathroom to shower. It wouldn't do to start his new job smelling like a brewery, and working for another Lycan meant it was hard to hide his drinking habit.

Kane had threatened to beat the crap out of him if he didn't stop, so he had...while he stayed with them. It had been Elise's reproachful looks that had really kept him on the straight and narrow. For a female Alpha, she was quiet, almost demure, but still managed to keep the pack members in line with her soft suggestions.

He chuckled. Samantha was a hell of a lot different from Elise, and from his Beth. Last night, he'd thought he'd have to rescue her from that creep at the bar. Instead, she'd wiped the floor with the man while not even breaking a sweat.

And then, when he'd followed her, she'd tried to ambush him. The resulting fight had been a draw, perhaps because he hadn't really wanted to hurt her, though he had a sneaking suspicion she, too, had been holding back merely wanting to test him. He grinned at the memory and shook his head. Yeah, Samantha was something different.

A banging on the door brought him out of his reverie and he realized he'd showered on autopilot. Wrapping a towel around his waist, he made his way to the door and opened it only to be greeted by his new employer's glowering face.

"Are you drunk?" She spoke bluntly, eschewing all the normal social niceties and barely gracing him with a glance before staring around the room.

Damien raised his eyebrows in surprise at her tone, then followed the direction of her gaze. The empty whiskey bottles lay on the floor by the chair in which he'd spent most of the night. "And good morning to you, too. No, I'm not drunk, only pleasantly numb."

"Good. We don't have time to waste waiting for you to sober up. If you're going to drink, do it on your own time."

"And when is my own time?" He leaned his hip against the nearby dresser and folded his arms over his chest.

"Whenever I say." She flicked her eyes over his mostly naked body, showing no signs of embarrassment. "Get dressed and meet me downstairs in the kitchen. We'll talk while you eat." Without further ado, she turned on her heel and left.

Damien straightened and pushed the door shut fighting to keep an unfamiliar grin from his face. God, she was a spitfire. And cool, too. He had no false modesty over his appearance. It was a well-documented fact that women still swooned over him, but she hadn't even batted an eye.

Drying himself off, he dressed and made his way to the kitchen at a leisurely pace despite the fact that he knew she meant for him to haul ass. Samantha Harper could bark orders all she wanted. He'd obey only when it suited him. And right now, it suited him to piss her off.

Sam tried to stop herself from drumming her fingers on the table top, but dammit how long did it take the man to get dressed in the morning? He was supposed to be a rogue, not some 'pretty boy' who styled his hair before he left his room.

She took another sip of coffee and reined in her temper. It could be he was testing her, trying to get under her skin. A rogue would do that. Well, she'd been in charge here too long for tactics like that to work.

Purposely, she assumed a leisurely posture; leaning back and propping her booted feet up on the chair beside her. She didn't usually wear her boots around the house, but felt she needed the extra height to make a point with Dante. From what she'd heard, he was an arrogant pain in the ass, but that's what she needed. Someone who exuded confidence, someone who would keep Sinclair off-kilter. With any luck she'd be able to bluff her way out of this whole stupid take-over scenario and avoid an outright fight.

Finally, she heard the sound of Dante coming down the stairs.

"Kitchen's back here," she called out to ensure he didn't start wandering around before she laid down the law. Start as you mean to continue.

The man sauntered into the room as if he had nothing to do for the entire day. He nodded at her, searched the cupboards looking for a mug and then poured some coffee. Still not speaking, he found milk in the fridge and added a splash to his cup, then grabbed a muffin from a plate on the counter.

Sam watched his progress. God, his body was gorgeous. She'd had a lovely view of it in his room. He'd still been wet from the shower. It had taken all her willpower not to allow her gaze to follow the tracks of the water droplets as they trailed down his muscular chest and abs before disappearing beneath the towel slung low around his waist. Now he was suitably clothed, but he was just as impressive to look at. The plain white t-shirt he wore clung to his torso, while his well-worn denims showcased his long legs and lean hips. She flicked her gaze to his face taking in his straight nose, and high cheek bones. His dark hair was still damp and slicked back from his face save for one recalcitrant lock that fell onto his forehead. For some reason she wanted to reach out and brush it back into place for him. Tightening her fingers around her cup, she ignored the impulse and studied the hint of scruff covering his lower face. It added to his dark and dangerous good looks. If she was looking for a lover, he was exactly what she'd have ordered.

However, it was a Beta she needed, not a fuck buddy. Unsmiling, she followed him with her eyes as he moved about the kitchen at a leisurely pace. Taking long, slow sips of coffee was the only thing that kept her from cursing him. That, and the need to prove that two could play this game.

Finally, after finding a plate and neatly cutting the muffin in half, he sat down across the table from her.

"Find everything you need?" She arched one brow.

"I think so, thanks." He took a bite of the muffin, chewed slowly, drank some coffee and then leaned back in his chair. "These are good. Did you make them?"

She snorted, her mouth full of coffee, and proceeded to choke. Damn the man! When she managed to catch her breath, she glared at him. "Do I look like Suzy Homemaker to you?"

Dante studied her for a moment, then shook his head. "No. My mistake. The muffins are still delicious though." He took another bite.

Sam barely managed to keep from gnashing her teeth. "Listen, Dante. I—"

"Damien."

She blinked. "Pardon?"

"You called me Dante. I'd prefer Damien."

"Why?" She narrowed her eyes.

He shrugged. "Does a rogue need a reason?"

"This one sure as hell does." She folded her arms and set her chin.

"Fine." A subtle change came over him, the cold deadly look she'd seen the previous night emerging, letting her know she was treading on dangerous ground. "I change names every few jobs. Sometimes my forms of employment aren't strictly...legal...shall we say? And leaving a continuous trail across the countryside can become dangerous."

Sam thought about it for a moment. It made sense. "All right, *Damien*, I'll fill you in on the particulars while you finish eating and then I'll give you a tour."

The hardness faded from him, his expression became almost affable. "Thanks, Samantha."

She cringed at the use of her full name. "Sam. Not Samantha."

He paused with the muffin half way to his mouth. "It seems to be a morning for changing names, doesn't it?" The corner of his mouth twitched as if he'd been going to smile and then changed his mind. Okay, he *was* trying to irritate her!

She forced her anger down, wondering if having him around was going to be worth the effort. The answer, of course, was yes. She'd do anything for her pack, even if it meant putting up with a pain in the ass rogue. Taking a calming breath, she spoke giving no indication she'd found anything perturbing about his behaviour. There was no way she was going to reward him with a reaction!

"Our pack has traditionally been known as the Chicago pack. No family name has ever been associated with it simply because one family—my family—has ruled it since its infancy. Our rights to this territory go back over a hundred and fifty years."

Damien's eyebrows rose at that statement and she smiled, pleased to see some show of interest on his part.

"Unusual. No challenges from outsiders?"

"No. It's been a straight line of succession from father to son. Unfortunately, we've had some setbacks in recent years." Sam hesitated, unsure of how much she should reveal this early in their association. "Suffice to say we're short of manpower and funds right now. But," she hastened to add, "don't worry. There's sufficient to pay you your full fee, provided you do as you're told and hold up your end of the bargain." She gave him a stern look.

"I'll keep that in mind." His face was serious, the teasing light that had faintly flickered in his eyes earlier was gone now, replaced with cool intelligence.

Good. Maybe he was only annoying first thing in the morning…or when he'd been drinking. She frowned recalling the smell of whiskey that had permeated his room. If she caught him drinking on duty, she'd have to rip him a new one. Setting her mug down, she proceeded to lay down the law.

Chapter 3

Damien followed Samantha—no, make that *Sam*—out of the kitchen for an official tour of the pack house. She'd held up well against his attempts to annoy her and he was impressed. He couldn't quite figure out exactly why he felt the need to get under her skin. This was a job and it would be better if he pandered to her more, got on her good side so she'd open up to him. Of course, kissing up too much might seem suspicious and he doubted he could do it for very long. He rubbed the back of his neck. Hell, he'd just play it by ear and see how things went; that's what he and Reno, his old partner, had always done.

She'd been blunt about her expectation of his behaviour. No drinking on the job. No fighting with pack members. No illegal activity. Interactions with the local humans were to be kept to a minimum. If any humans asked, he was a friend on vacation.

He'd nodded, raising no protest as he'd finished his meal. Pretty standard stuff.

"Dining room. TV room." Sam led him through the house and Damien looked at each with interest, automatically noting exits and inconsistencies in the rooms' structures. Old homes like this sometimes had hidden passages or trap doors. Useful information in a pinch. All the rooms were a good size, though there was evidence that the original floor plan of the house had been altered at some time.

"You've done some renovating, I see." He studied the floorboards noting how the wood changed halfway through the room. A wall must have been there at one point.

She made a non-committal sound. "Some previous Alpha likely thought they'd need more room for pack meetings."

Damien nodded and gestured towards the ornate tables. "And all the antiques? They don't seem quite your style."

Sam barely glanced towards where he was indicating. "Collected over the years. Apparently my grandmother enjoyed them, but I've too much to do to be worried about furniture."

"Some have been moved recently, I take it." Damien stared at a patch of darker flooring. Something large—a bookcase, perhaps—had once sat there, protecting the wood from being faded by the sun. Strange that it would have been relocated after so many years.

"What's with all the questions? I thought you were a rogue, not some sort of freakin' interior designer." Sam turned and planted her hands on her hips, a mixture of disbelief and exasperation on her face.

Damien held back a chuckle. Sam Harper didn't seem to have much of a filter between her brain and her mouth. "Rogue, yes. Designer, no. I'm just observant. I don't know a Chippendale from a Hepplewhite."

"A what?" She blinked.

"Chippendale and Hepplewhite. They were furniture designers. My mate liked antiques."

"You're mated?"

If she hadn't touched on a sore subject, the look on her face might have made him laugh out loud. As it was, he scowled and automatically drew his protective wall around himself. "Was. She died a little over three years ago."

"Oh. I'm…er…sorry."

"No need to be. You had nothing to do with her death." He stared at her, eyes shuttered and ready to fend off a barrage of nosey questions. She didn't ask any though and, after a beat, he verbally prodded her. "The tour?"

She nodded. "The office is this way." Sam headed towards the front of the house, her expression giving no indication as to how she felt about his abrupt change of subject. Not that he cared. He didn't discuss Beth with anyone.

Damien made no more comments as he followed her, only half listening as he mulled over something that had just struck him. When she'd asked about Beth, the searing pain that always appeared in his heart at the mention of his mate had only been a dull twinge. Given the night he'd spent, he'd expected his emotions to be raw, but for some reason they weren't. After all this time, the pain of Beth's memory was almost like a friend, a constant in his life that reminded him of all he'd lost. Why hadn't he felt it just now? Were his emotions dulled from his night of drinking? Had the well of grief finally run dry? No. That wasn't possible. His love for Beth would live forever. Hadn't her last words to him been 'never forget'?

"You with me, Dante?" Sam's voice intruded on his thoughts.

"Damien," he corrected automatically. "What were you saying?"

Sam rolled her eyes. "Pay attention if you expect to keep this job. Rogues are a dime a dozen."

Her tone of voice stirred his temper. He wanted to counter that the cost of hiring him would be a lot more than a dime, but he kept his mouth shut and merely raised a brow in query.

"I was explaining that the office is out of bounds unless I'm with you. No snooping in the files. No answering the phones. Stay away from the computer; it's password protected."

Damien leaned against the door frame and crossed his arms. "Then exactly what am I supposed to do as Beta? That *is* the position I was hired for, isn't it?"

Sam looked him up and down then snorted. "Act impressive. Be the 'big, strong, he-man' that everyone expects an Alpha to be."

She moved to brush past him, but he blocked the doorway with his arm. Even though he wasn't the rogue she'd hired, her casual dismissal of him rankled and he wasn't going to put up with it. Plus, he needed to figure out exactly what was going on with this pack. Kane had sent him here to gather information and pack hierarchy was a good place to start. "So why do you need me? Why not promote one of your own members to the Beta position rather than putting on an act?"

Sam glared at him. He could see the battle waging inside her and wondered if he'd pushed too hard. She clenched her hands into fists and he prepared himself to dodge a blow. Instead, she turned, walked over to the desk and sat on the edge. "Close the door."

After eyeing her for a moment, he complied. "What, exactly, is going on here?"

She exhaled loudly then pursed her lips and looked away. It was obvious she was reluctant to answer his question.

A second ticked by and then another. Damien hooked his thumbs in his belt loops and leaned against the door, ankles crossed. "Are you going to tell me or should I go looking for the Alpha? I assume Sam Harper is your father."

His comment had her snapping her eyes back at him.

"*Assume*. Ha! That's what everyone does." A bitter look twisted her face and she shoved off from the desk and strode towards the window. Pushing the curtain aside, she gestured at the street that ran in front of the house. "The whole world *assumes* an Alpha has to be a male. Even the humans out there, with their insipid paranormal books, have men leading every pack they write about."

Damien nodded. "And your point is...?" She scowled at him and an idea slowly began to form. "You? You're the Alpha of the Chicago pack?" He wasn't able to mask the incredulity in his voice. Kane had said she was the spokesperson.

"Acting-Alpha." Her chin lifted slightly and her eyes narrowed as if she were daring him to challenge her. "My grandfather has been unwell for some time, but he hasn't abdicated his title yet."

"And your father?"

"Died when I was four, though according to the stories I've heard, he was never interested in the position." A shadow passed over her face before she squared her shoulders and gave him a challenging look. "My grandfather raised me to take over the pack and I have. It's just not official on paper."

Betrayed: Book Two – The Road To Redemption

Damien gave a long low whistle. Female Alphas were rare and most often occurred when the Alpha died and his mate took over. To encounter one, even an acting one, this young was unheard of. "Samuel Harper. Samantha Harper." He nodded. "The similarity of your names helped you keep this under wraps."

"A fortunate twist of fate. Being his namesake has allowed me and my pack to stay off the radar. If anyone found out a 'female' was in charge we'd be deluged with takeover attempts or wanna-be Alphas trying to weasel their way in through mating with me." She returned to the desk, picked up a piece of paper and after glancing at it, threw it down again. "And we were managing perfectly well until Kane Sinclair started to poke his nose into our affairs."

"And my being the pack Beta is supposed to impress him?" Damien quirked a brow, wanting confirmation of what he'd begun to suspect.

She nodded. "You'll lend an air of 'male authority' to the image the pack administration presents if the chauvinistic old goats at Lycan Link start to investigate us."

"Which brings me back to my original question. Why not use someone from your own pack?"

A faint beeping sound interrupted and Sam glanced at her watch. "Sorry. I'll explain later. I have a meeting I need to attend." Damien was sure he detected a hint of relief in her voice, but let it pass. She crossed the room swiftly and he stepped aside so he was no longer blocking the door.

"You can finish exploring the house and the neighbourhood while I'm gone. Stay away from the north wing on the second floor – those are my grandfather's quarters. He's not well and needs his rest."

"I understand." He placed a hand on her arm to stop her. "Does the rest of the pack know why I'm here?"

"They do. I don't have to shield my packmates from the truth." She shrugged his hand off her arm. "You'll find we're a strong, resilient bunch."

"I'm sure you are," he murmured softly as he watched her leave. "But are you up to facing Kane?"

The doorbell jingled merrily overhead as Sam entered Marcello's Antiques and Collectibles. Its cheery sound was in stark contrast to the grim look on her face. She was supposed to meet with Mr. Marcello at ten o'clock and she was late. She hated being late. It spoke of carelessness and a disregard for schedules and order.

For a moment, she paused just inside the shop allowing her eyes to adjust to the dim lighting. The place was packed with collectibles and it wouldn't do to go blundering about. While her eyes grew accustomed to the darker venue, she took in the familiar scents of wood, leather, dust and age. After the bustling noise of the street, it was almost shocking how calm the atmosphere was; the quiet, steady ticking of a clock, the sound of a kettle simmering somewhere in the back. It was like stepping back in time, and she felt the tension begin to ease from her shoulders.

She'd lied to Damien when she claimed to know nothing of antiques; her grandfather and Mr. Marcello had been friends for years. She'd spent a great deal of time here as a child studying the cases of old jewellery and trinkets, trailing her fingers over ornately carved furniture while the two men had shared a glass of cognac. While she might not be an expert, she could usually tell if a piece was worthy of its price or not.

The old grandfather clock in the corner gave a whir and began to chime for ten o'clock. It was always fifteen minutes slow which meant she was fifteen minutes late.

"Keep your eye on the clock," her grandfather had drilled into her. "Once time is gone, you can never get it back again. An Alpha has too many responsibilities to be allowed to waste time."

He was right. The jobs were never ending, and the extra time she'd spent with Dante—Damien—meant she'd likely be behind all day.

Betrayed: Book Two – The Road To Redemption

The tension returned to her shoulders once again. Striding to the back of the shop, Sam brought her hand down rather more forcefully than necessary on the small bell that sat on the counter. The ting that rang out from it was demanding, reflecting her impatience. Faint rustling sounds could be heard coming from behind a curtained doorway and then it parted revealing Mr. Marcello. He was a short, round, Italian gentleman of indeterminate age.

"Ah, Miss Samantha. I was thinking of you only a moment ago."

She didn't cringe when he used her proper name. Mr. Marcello was an old-world gentleman who still clung to the ways of the past. Besides, he'd known her since she was a child. "Sorry to keep you waiting."

He glanced at a cuckoo clock on the wall and gave a negligent shrug; he never seemed to be in a hurry. "Barely past the hour. Nothing to worry about."

Sam disagreed with him but kept the comment to herself. "You sold the bookshelf?" She mentally crossed her fingers hoping Mr. Marcello's expertise at getting the best deal possible had worked once again.

"I did. It was a fine piece of furniture in excellent condition. I'm sure you'll be pleased with the price I was able to get for it." Mr. Marcello removed the bill of sale from his ledger and showed it to her.

It was an impressive sum, far more than she'd expected and the heavy weight that had settled in her stomach for the past week disappeared as she contemplated all the bills she could pay; there'd even be a tidy sum left over. She didn't let her relief show, of course. The pack's finances were a private matter. "Thanks. I appreciate you handling this matter discreetly for me."

"Not a problem. The selling of family heirlooms can be a touchy subject in the best of circumstances and given your grandfather's temperament…" He shook his head and made a face. "I recall about ten years ago…" Mr. Marcello launched into a recount of some incident and she nodded politely, not really listening.

The money from the sale meant she wouldn't have to touch the principal of their remaining investments. And if she could reinvest the interest and if the stock market would cooperate…

"— and so, I will write you a cheque and we are done for today, correct?" Mr. Marcello must have finished his tale for he was preparing to hand over payment.

"Cash. No cheques."

He smiled and inclined his head. "Oh course, how could I forget?" He put the cheque book away. "I'll be back in a moment."

Sam nodded and waited as the older man went to the rear of the store to where his safe was located. He wouldn't keep that much cash in the till. Too dangerous in this neighbourhood. Some might say it was also too dangerous for her to be walking down the street with that much money in her pocket, but she wasn't worried. Protecting herself wasn't an issue. Keeping her transactions secret was. Cash was harder to trace.

'Leave as few trails behind you as possible' her grandfather had always said. Not that it really mattered in this instance, but you never knew when a seemingly innocent act could become significant. At the moment, selling a few pieces of furniture wasn't a problem. No one noticed or cared that they were missing—no one except Damien, that is.

She frowned. The man hadn't even been in the house for twenty-four hours and he'd picked up on the missing bookshelf. She'd never noticed how the floor had faded, but he'd immediately homed in on it. Making a mental note to rearrange the furniture to hide the mark on the floor, she erased the worried lines from her face as Mr. Marcello reappeared.

He handed her a thick envelope and she opened it to count the money within.

"It's all there, Miss Samantha. After years of doing business together, you should know you can trust me." The shopkeeper tutted as if offended. He wasn't, of course, but he liked to pretend to be.

"I do trust you, Mr. Marcello, but I was born cautious." Sam turned her back towards the door in case anyone happened to come in and took out a few bills to examine. Counterfeit money wouldn't do her any good.

"You were not born cautious, Miss. Samantha. That is your grandfather's doing."

"Perhaps." She gave the man a half smile and slid the money back into the envelope. "All there and in order." Lifting her shirt, she tucked the envelope into the front of her pants and then pulled her shirt down over top of it. A quick glance in a nearby mirror revealed the envelope was unnoticeable. "Until next time." Giving Mr. Marcello's hand a firm shake, she strolled out of the shop and into the hot, steamy street.

A late summer heat wave had settled over the city and refused to leave despite the fact that it was September. The envelope tucked in her clothing stuck to her skin and crinkled softly as she walked. Not loud enough for anyone nearby to hear, but she was aware of it. She resisted the urge to readjust the package and continued on her way, pushing between the pedestrians, waiting impatiently for the traffic light to change so she could cross the street.

For some reason she felt twitchy today; that weird sensation that something was off, but you couldn't quite put your finger on it. She wondered if someone was following her—a mugger with a death wish perhaps—and ducked into a store, making a show of looking at a stack of used books, while surreptitiously looking out the window. Several pedestrians walked by, then a cop. A large man with a scar on his cheek caught her attention, but he didn't linger. Just to be on the safe side, she slipped out the back door and cut through the alleyway to the next street over.

It was a tough neighbourhood, but her determined walk and don't-mess-with-me face usually meant she was never bothered by any of the locals. In her boots, jeans and t-shirt, she looked like she belonged, and she did.

She'd grown up prowling the streets, getting into fights, making a name for herself with a certain segment of society. Her reputation was well known by the human population in this corner of the city. In her late teens, some had viewed her as being akin to a gang leader but she'd mellowed since then. Those who lived in the neighbourhood knew she wasn't interested in controlling the drug dealers, prostitutes or petty thieves. Indeed, she'd been known to step in when the criminal element was causing someone grief. Yet she wasn't a vigilante, either. Sam Harper was no Lone Ranger or Robin Hood.

Well, the humans could puzzle over her, but she knew her purpose. It was caring for her pack; ensuring the members were safe, fed and had a roof over their head. That's what an Alpha did and that's what she intended to keep on doing.

The twitchy feeling faded, so it had likely been nothing. Or maybe it had been the result of Damien messing with her that morning. Damned rogue; she hoped he wasn't going to be more trouble than he was worth.

Taking a final look around, she grasped the handle of the large door that gave entrance to the bank and stepped into the cool interior.

Chapter 4

When he'd arrived in Chicago the previous day, Damien had taken some time to explore the area around Sam's pack house. The exhaust fumes and masses of humanity present in a big city made it easier to move about undetected. Still, he hadn't lingered any longer than necessary, merely getting a basic lay of the land and locating his quarry. He'd been able to pick her out based on Kane's description of her, though he'd been surprised to see her mount a motorcycle and roar away from the pack house. It hadn't matched the mental image he'd formed of her and his interest had been piqued.

Originally, his plan had been to keep her under surveillance for a few days before attempting to make contact. Instead, he'd impulsively followed her last night and now found himself living in the pack house. Had anything ever fallen in to place easier than this?

Too easy, his wolf complained. *We need a challenge—a chase over rough terrain, perhaps—something to stimulate our mind and body.* The bland nothingness of their present existence was making the beast restless. *Last night's fight was interesting...*

Damien shook his head, sorry to disappoint the animal, but from what Sam had said, his job was simply to look strong and impressive; that didn't require much effort.

His wolf grumbled its discontent before lying down, resting its chin on its paws with a heavy sigh.

Damien concurred. The spark of interest he'd felt earlier in the day when talking to Sam had faded, leaving him with the flat dead feeling that so often permeated his life. Sitting down on a park bench, he popped open the soda he'd purchased and took a desultory drink, idly wondering how long it would take to get the information Kane needed.

It was almost noon and the sun beat down with unrelenting strength causing the air to shimmer above the pavement and the smell of pollution to hang in the air. The shade from the trees provided some relief from the heat, but sweat still trickled down his back and water condensed on the sides of the can he was holding.

The block of natural habitat he found himself in was surrounded by parked cars, brick buildings and the incessant hum that accompanied humanity. Cars and air-conditioners, conversations and sirens, a train rattled along a distant set of tracks. Not many wolves would have the tenacity to handle the constant noise of living in a large city. It was a far cry from the wilderness where song birds and the gentle stirring of leaves in the breeze were the norm.

For himself, it didn't matter one way or the other what his surroundings were. He'd kicked around the country enough that he could make any place home for as long or as short a period of time as needed. And right now, Chicago was where he'd hang his hat. He tried to spark some enthusiasm by recalling there was even the added bonus that he had an actual bed, rather than sleeping rough. That point didn't really cut it though.

After Sam had left, he'd finished exploring the house. It hadn't taken long, especially given the fact that it had been strangely empty save the sounds of life coming from the north wing on the second floor. Sam had told him to stay away and he'd decided to follow her orders…for now. That didn't mean that he hadn't done some intelligence gathering. Using the scents and sounds he'd determined two Lycans had been in that wing. One male and a female. Her grandfather and…his caretaker?

Carefully opening the doors of the other rooms he'd discovered there were six occupied bedrooms in the south wing of the second floor. And he seemed to be the only occupant on the third. Sam was being cautious, keeping him away from her family until she knew him better. Smart girl.

The walk around the neighbourhood had been uneventful as well. As he'd noted yesterday, most of the homes were older and had been turned into multi-family units. Some sat vacant, their windows boarded up and lawns overgrown. At the far end of the street, a few of the buildings were being restored; no doubt by developers hoping the area might transition into a chic, upscale location once more. Other than that, a corner store, a pool hall and bar, a pizza place and few other miscellaneous businesses were all he'd discovered. None seemed to house Lycans, though. That distinctive scent was only concentrated around the pack house.

The lack of pack members was definitely something he'd have to investigate further, but for now, he'd contact Kane while Sam wasn't around.

It only took two rings for Kane to pick up.

"Sinclair here."

"Kane, it's me." Damien relaxed, stretching out his legs and hooking one arm over the backrest of the bench. It was only around his old friends that he felt anything that even resembled a spark of life inside. Part of him craved that connection; the sense of belonging, of knowing that someone actually cared. It was rather like holding one's hands in front of a fire after being out in the cold; warm and comforting as the heat seeped in, causing nerve endings to prickle with returning awareness. Of course, if you lingered too long or got too close, you'd get burned and he couldn't risk that. His world might be cold, but he wouldn't get hurt. Blocks of ice didn't feel.

No, he warmed himself on the fringes of friendship, making mild enquiries about their lives, watching with interest and then withdrawing to safety if he felt himself getting too close. He wasn't hiding from life, merely keeping it at a strategically safe distance.

"How did Ryne's bonding ceremony go?"

"He was disappointingly cooperative." The discontent in Kane's voice was easy to hear.

"Really?" Damien laughed softly, knowing Kane had probably hoped to gloat over his brother as he finally bowed to tradition. Ryne had been unofficially mated to Melody Greene for some time but had never gone through a formal bonding ceremony. Upon learning this, Elise had quickly set out to remedy the situation and in less than twenty-four hours had managed to get Ryne to agree to tie the knot with Mel."

"Yes. From the way he was acting, you'd have thought it was his own idea."

"Typical." Damien smiled as memories of their younger escapades came to mind. "Ryne always did know how to turn the tables in his own favour."

Kane grunted in agreement. "So, what have you learned about the Chicago pack? I assume that's why you called."

Damien easily shifted into work mode, once again cool and unfeeling. "Not much new to report since last night. Sam is accepting me as the rogue she intended to hire and—"

"She?" Kane figuratively jumped on the word. "Harper is still hiding behind that girl?"

"Yes…and no."

"Explain."

"It seems that Sam Harper, Sr., has been incapacitated for some time and *Samantha* Harper is the acting Alpha."

"Acting Alpha? What the hell does that mean?"

"Exactly what it sounds like, I suppose. From what she's told me, she's calling the shots, running the whole place. Old man Harper just hasn't officially abdicated yet."

"That's ridiculous. A territory that size can't be run by a slip of a girl."

"Hardly a girl. Early twenties with a pretty good right hook." Damien wiggled his jaw. It was still tender from where Sam had slugged him the previous evening.

Kane snorted. "A lucky punch, no doubt. And you were always a soft touch around a good looking female."

"Perhaps." Damien didn't refute his friend's statement, but in reality being a 'soft touch' hadn't factored into the fight's outcome last night. Sam was a damned good fighter. She'd made a few mistakes but with some extra training… He jerked his attention back to what Kane was saying.

"If she's been functioning as the de facto Alpha for several years, and it's never been reported to Lycan Link, I might have a case against the Chicago pack. I'll have to check the Book of the Law, but this might be the wedge I need to start my takeover bid."

If anyone knew the Book of the Law, it was Kane. In the time that Damien had stayed with Kane's pack, he'd been impressed with how knowledgeable Kane was and the dedication he showed for his job. Of course, that dedication to the pack also meant less time for Kane's family. Damien hoped that the information he was providing would help his friend quickly win his claim to Chicago so Kane could get some balance back in his life.

A bit of movement at the far end of the park caught his attention and he realized it was Sam Harper. "I have to go, Kane. I'll be in touch." He put his phone away and turned slightly so he could watch Sam's approach more easily.

She strode along a pathway that cut through the park, head high, spine straight, hands tucked in her back pockets. Her stance pushed her breasts forward and Damien eyed them appreciatively before shifting his focus to her face. Sunlight filtered through breaks in the trees and, in those moments, highlighted her violet eyes.

Once again Damien was struck by how odd the colour was for a Lycan. No doubt there was a bit of Witch or Fae in her background.

Fae.

Beth had been part Fae, but there was nothing ethereal or fanciful about Sam. The woman seemed as down to earth and practical as they came.

"Damien." She spoke his name as soon as she caught sight of him and veered off the path towards where he sat. He didn't stand as she approached though he could tell by the look on her face she'd expected him to. And it wasn't that he didn't feel the pull of her authority. It was the inexplicable need to push her buttons that kept him seated. Both he and his wolf watched with interest to see how she'd respond.

Sam stopped a few feet away. He nodded and took a swig from his can of soda. The briefest hint of irritation passed over her face.

"Comfortable?" She queried.

"Yep." He nodded and then patted the space beside him. "Sit down and take a load off your feet."

Much to his surprise she did. And then grabbed the soda from his hand.

"Hey!" He protested, caught off guard by her move.

"Hay is for horses." She quipped. And bringing the can to her lips, she proceeded to take a long drink.

Damien watched as she drank, noting the faint movements of her throat as she swallowed, the way her lids half covered her eyes as if she were savouring the taste of the carbonated beverage. When she'd had her fill, she handed the can back to him and wiped her mouth on her hand. "Thanks. It's a scorcher today and I needed that."

He gave the can a shake. Empty.

Sam raised her brows as if she had no idea what his problem might be.

Giving her a dirty look, he crushed it in his hand and then tossed it in the recycling bin that stood a few feet away.

"And swoosh. Nothin' but net! A basketball star in the making." A soft, husky laugh accompanied her comment on his perfect aim.

The sound of her laughter caught his attention. So far, she'd shown about as much personality as a cactus in a desert; only her prickliness breaking through her bland exterior. He eyed her curiously.

"And you're a soda thief in the making. Ever heard of asking first?"

She shrugged. "Why? You're a member of the pack now. Pack shares."

He opened his mouth but couldn't think of a comeback. "Point to you."

"Naturally."

"Cocky little thing, aren't you?"

"Yep." She stretched her arms out so that her elbows were on the back of the bench and extended her legs out in front of her, crossing them casually at the ankles. Then she looked at him out of the corner of her eye. "You got a problem with that?"

He shook his head and felt the edges of his mouth curving upward, the action feeling almost unnatural. There'd been little to smile about in the past few years. Narrowing his eyes, he resumed a serious expression and studied the female beside him, wondering how she'd garnered such a response from him.

Something about her demeanour made her seem younger at the moment. The lines of tension around her eyes and mouth were gone. Mimicking her pose, he let out a long, slow breath. The sun had shifted and he was no longer in the protection of the shade. "Is it always this hot in your city?"

"In the summer it is, though usually it starts to cool down by now." She tilted her head back so her face was raised to the sun and closed her eyes. "I try to absorb as much of the warmth now as I can. Winter is a bitch here."

"You don't like the cold?"

"I don't mind it, but it's easier to move about in the summer. No tell-tale tracks in the snow."

Damien studied her full, red lips, noting how they were curved into a self-satisfied smile. "What are you looking so pleased about?"

She shrugged, eyes still closed. "A successful morning. I got a lot accomplished, dealt with a few pressing financial issues much faster than I'd thought and now I'm ahead of schedule. It's a beautiful day, plus, it isn't often I have time to sit and enjoy my territory." Her chest rose and fell as she inhaled deeply. "Smell that? Papa Tony's Pizzeria – he just took one out of the oven. He makes them with extra cheese for me. And the fresh tar? They're fixing the pot hole around the corner from the pack house; I damned near lost the front wheel off my bike in it last week."

Damien watched her out of the corner of his eye as he sniffed the air, sifting through the multitude of scents to find the ones she was describing. The expression on her face, the way she spoke; it was obvious Sam felt a deep connection with her territory. A breeze came by and the edges of her long front fringe moved slightly revealing more of her face.

Her bone structure was delicate. High cheekbones, a small chin, a fine nose with a hint of an up-tilt near the end. Her skin tones spoke of a French background, or maybe Italian...? His gaze rested on her lips once more; the lower one was enticingly plump and he wondered what it would be like to gently nibble on it or trace it with his tongue...

A truck's horn blared directly across from them and Damien jerked in surprise then growled. Sam snorted and sat upright.

"You get used to it after a while. Horns, sirens, train whistles – to me, they're like the bird calls the country packs have to deal with."

Damien scowled at the delivery van's driver who was now arguing with a cabbie over a parking space. He was inexplicably angry with them...or was he angry at himself? The way he'd been staring at Sam, contemplating kissing her... What was he thinking? He was here to do a job not ogle the local women. And since when did females catch his eye, anymore? Not since Beth had he—

"Come on." Sam got to her feet, thankfully oblivious of his wayward thoughts. "I'll treat you to a slice of Papa Tony's. Then you'll know what *real* pizza tastes like."

"Sure. That'd be great." Damien stood up and followed her, trying not to stare at how her jeans clung to her cute butt. He ran his hand through his hair, completely thrown off by his reaction to her. His inner wolf was equally puzzled by this new type of Alpha and cocked its head to the side while it studied the Lycan walking ahead of them.

~~~

Elise pushed open the door to the room she and Kane were using while staying at her brother-in-law's home. There was a celebration going on downstairs, but Kane had excused himself to take a call. That had been over half an hour ago.

Betrayed: Book Two – The Road To Redemption

Worried that something was wrong, she'd come looking for him.

Ryne's home was a sprawling old Victorian place built on a large property a few miles outside the small town of Stump River. The building had fallen into disrepair, but Ryne's pack was slowly returning the place to its former glory. This particular room had recently been finished and boasted an ensuite bathroom, comfortable furnishings and a spectacular view of the forest that surrounded the house.

Her mate presently stood with one arm braced against the window frame and, to a casual onlooker, he might look like he was observing the fall colours that were appearing on the trees. However, another glance revealed he had his cell phone in his hand and was focused on the conversation, not the view.

Elise leaned her shoulder against the doorjamb and crossed her arms, unashamedly listening in on the conversation. They were blood bonded mates. There were no secrets between them. As the trend of the conversation became apparent, she sighed. Pack business. Again.

Kane, seemingly unaware of her presence, kept talking. "That's right. I'm looking for information about Alphas abdicating their role or appointing an 'acting-Alpha' if they are temporarily incapacitated ... No. Not a Beta ... Are there any precedents? ... Uh huh ... Yeah ... Okay. Get back to me as soon as you can."

He ended the call and appeared about to make another, when she quipped lightly. "Must be a pretty important call if you don't even notice that I'm standing right behind you."

Kane gave a slight jolt and turned. "Elise!"

Obviously he'd been so engrossed in his conversation that he really hadn't registered her presence. It was a bit demoralizing.

Elise stepped into the room and trailed her hand lightly over the engraved wooden post that edged the footboard of the bed. She glanced at her mate out of the corner of her eye and gave a wistful smile. "There was a time when I'd never have been able to sneak past your radar. You'd have pounced and had me pinned to the bed within seconds of entering the room."

"Sorry. I was..." He held up the phone and shrugged smiling ruefully.

"I know." She returned his smile, but it was forced. Kane had promised to make this a 'work free' getaway. She parroted his all too frequent excuse. "You had a call you had to make. It couldn't wait. It was only supposed to take a minute, but it turned out it was more complicated than planned."

"Yeah." At least he looked uncomfortable making the admission. "The first one was from Damien. He had some information about Chicago—"

"The *first* one?"

He ignored her indignant statement. "And I wanted to get the ball rolling. I have John doing some research for me so that when we get back home I can start to act on the takeover."

"And, of course, you couldn't have done that later." She resisted the urge to put her hands on her hips, but couldn't keep her irritation from showing in her voice. "There *is* a celebration happening downstairs. Remember? Ryne and Mel had their bonding ceremony this morning? *You* officiated over it?"

His mouth tightened. "Sarcasm doesn't become you, Elise."

"And being abandoned at a party does?" She could feel the tension building inside her. This had happened so many times recently, Kane getting lost in pack business and forgetting his family obligations. "Kane, you promised me..."

He opened his mouth then snapped it shut. Taking a deep breath, he visibly forced himself to relax. "I know. I know." Keeping his eyes on her, he walked over to her and, placing his hands on her shoulders, he gave her a gentle shake then pressed a kiss to her forehead. "But I'm doing this for us. If you want us to have more time together—"

"If *I* want. What about you? Don't you want more time together?" She stepped back and tilted her head so she could see his face.

Betrayed: Book Two – The Road To Redemption

He was frowning at her comment, his mouth flattened into a firm line. At first, he seemed about to say something cutting in return but stopped himself. His features smoothed into a conciliatory expression. "Of course, I do. I chose my words poorly." Kane pulled her close and wrapped his arms around her, tucking her head under his chin. "If *we* want more time together, then a certain amount of preparatory work has to be done. We've discussed this."

His tone was calm and reasonable, almost overly patient as if he were talking to a recalcitrant child.

She bit back the bubble of resentment that welled within her. A fight wasn't what she was looking for today. There'd been too many of those recently. Maybe she was being unreasonable. After all, he hadn't been gone that long. And he *was* the Alpha…

"I know." Elise whispered the words into his chest feeling like she was being a shrew. He'd explained, when the idea first came to him, that taking over the Chicago pack would be work, that he was doing it for her, for their family. And she believed him…mostly. When it was all over, he'd have more time. He'd promised, and Kane Sinclair was a man of his word. Slowly, she ran her hand over his broad chest, feeling his warmth and strength. Beneath her ear, she could hear the steady beat of his heart. Kane was a good man, a wise Alpha, a loving mate and great father to their pups…when he had the time…

"Hey." He placed a finger under her chin and tilted her face up. Kissing her slowly, he whispered an apology against her lips. "I'm sorry. I should have left the call until later."

Elise stared into his amber eyes, seeing the contrition there, feeling it through their blood bond. "And I need to be more patient." She pressed a kiss to his mouth. He opened to her and the kiss deepened. A groan escaped him and he gathered her closer, sliding his hands down her back to cup her rear.

"Excuse me…"

A knock at the door had them both sighing and reluctantly pulling apart.

"Yes?" A faint growl could be heard in Kane's voice as he addressed the intruder. Elise twisted in his arms and saw Daniel. The young man looked a bit sheepish at having interrupted.

"Sorry to bother you, but Ryne wants everyone downstairs right now so he and Mel can cut the cake."

"We'll just be a minute." Elise tried to give the boy a reassuring look since he was eyeing Kane nervously. Little wonder given the fact that a low rumble was coming from the man. Daniel gave a nod and disappeared. She turned back to Kane and admonished him. "Quit growling. There was no need to scare him; he was only delivering a message."

"I know, but his timing was lousy." Kane gave her a last quick kiss before stepping back. "Ryne probably sent him here on purpose just to interfere."

"I doubt..." Elise paused. Knowing Ryne, that might very well have been the case!

Chapter 5

Sam kept Damien occupied by pointing out features of the neighbourhood and introducing him to some of the human population. She told them he was a 'friend' from the West Coast and no one questioned her, though a few gave a knowing grin no doubt silently including the words 'with benefits'. It didn't really matter to her. They could think what they wanted. She knew some speculated about her apparent lack of male companionship and that was fine. Let them speculate all they wanted about her sex life; it kept them from thinking about more important matters like the unusual makeup of the 'family' she lived with.

And speaking of family, Damien was going to start asking questions soon. Every wolf knew that the pack would want to greet a new member, learn its scent and determine its place in the hierarchy. She'd put him off this morning, but it was time to bring him up to speed before meeting the others.

As they entered the rusted gateway that led to the pack house, Damien reached out and adjusted the house number. It held in place for a moment before falling back into its usual crooked position. He cast a look at her, one brow raised.

Sam winced inwardly. Some might see that as a symbol of a poorly managed pack.

"Your porch needs repairing, too." He gestured towards the broken treads on the steps.

"It's on my list." She replied tightly, not mentioning that her 'to-do' list was a mile long and she was doing her best, but there simply wasn't enough time. It was her job and she took responsibility for any failings. An Alpha didn't make excuses.

"I'll fix it." There was no condescending tone to his words, just a gruff statement and steady look.

It made her uneasy, as if he could read her mind and knew that she'd often wondered if she'd be able to hold things together. While there was no way he could know that, she still answered guardedly. "Thanks. It'll help give you a presence around here, in case Sinclair's spy happens to be watching."

A look passed over his face, so fleeting she couldn't identify it, but then he nodded. "You have any tools?"

"Yeah. I have tools."

"Good. I'll get on it today."

"Interior design and home repair?" She relaxed enough to tease him as they rounded the corner of the house.

"I've had some experience working as a handyman. I repaired cabins at a fishing lodge once."

"Repairing a fishing lodge?" She scrunched her face in disbelief. It seemed a strange occupation for a rogue. Somehow she pictured him doing something more dangerous than pounding nails. His dark features, brooding eyes and sullen expression made one think more of a thug who'd pull a knife on you at a moment's notice. "You've got to be kidding me."

He shrugged but made no effort to elaborate on his statement so she let it drop. It wasn't as if his background really mattered. Still, she couldn't help cast one last speculative glance his way. Her rogue had hidden depths. Interesting.

As they reached the back of the house, Damien turned towards the door no doubt assuming they were going inside.

"Not yet. We need to talk in private first." She went to the far side of the house and grabbed the handle of an old wooden hatch.

"In the cellar?"

"Yep. Scared of the dark?" She tossed the question over her shoulder as she slid the door aside. It moved easily since she'd added a sliding track a few years ago.

"No."

Flicking the light switch, she nimbly descended the cement steps.

"If I had been, were you going to leave the lights off?" He followed her down.

"Perhaps." She shrugged. "Confronting your fears is the only way to overcome them."

Damien didn't reply. She wasn't sure if that meant he agreed or not, not that it really mattered. She was in charge and he'd do as he was told.

The temperature below ground was a pleasant contrast to the heat and humidity of the streets and Sam took a moment to enjoy the cooler air. The cellar had been excavated and extended over the years and now served as an exercise room though that hadn't always been the case. It was historical fact that, during the days of Prohibition, some members of the pack had originally made their money from the illegal liquor trade. Working as 'rumrunners' or 'bootleggers' as such miscreants had been called, the cellar had been used to hide the illegal beverage. As a child she'd often re-enacted the adventures, hiding from the authorities as she snuck her illegal cargo of penny-candy home from the corner store.

It was during one of those games that she'd discovered the trap door to a secret passageway that led to various rooms in the house. She'd never shared her find with anyone; it was often useful to be able to enter and exit the building without the others knowing. She chuckled to herself as she recalled some of her escapades.

Damien studied the bare light bulbs that hung overhead and the exposed floor joists from the house above. Nothing fancy, but it was clean with no cobwebs or mustiness. The walls had been whitewashed and several mirrored panels hung along the far wall, while the middle of the room was occupied by an array of workout equipment. Most of the floor was cement, though one area sported a set of mats for wrestling or sparring.

"Nice." He wandered over to a punching bag and gave it an experimental push.

"What I'm about to tell you goes no further. Is that understood?"

Damien turned to where Sam was leaning against a weight machine.

"Depends what you tell me." He propped himself against the wall and folded his arms. The expression that passed over her face made him smile inwardly. She wasn't used to anyone talking back to her and hadn't been expecting his response.

"What the —"

"I'm just being truthful. Would you really believe me if I agreed outright?" Damien gave her a level look.

Sam snapped her mouth shut and appeared to consider the point. "Perhaps not." She paused. "Are you always such a pain in the ass?"

"Pretty much. I'm a rogue, not an Omega that toes the line every second of my life. If that were the case, I doubt you would have hired me, would you?"

A reluctant grin spread over her face. "I think I like you. You're honest."

"I do my best." For some reason he was pleased to have made her smile again.

A chuckle escaped her before her expression sobered. "Truthfully, this conversation can't be shared. It might give Sinclair an advantage; being the weasel that he is, who knows how he could twist things around to his advantage?"

"Sinclair's a weasel? I thought he was a wolf?" The mental image that came to mind of Kane shifting into such a small animal had him struggling to keep from grinning. He'd definitely have to tell his friend about that next time they talked. Suddenly, it struck him that when he was around Sam the need to smile kept popping up. It had been years since he'd felt that sense of levity, three years to be exact. Ever since Beth… The memory of his dead mate wiped the joy from his heart. He had no right to be happy while she was dead. A cold empty feeling washed over him again and he focused an icy stare on Sam.

"You know what I mean." Sam scowled. "If I find out you've leaked the information, your employment will be terminated, you won't get paid and I'll beat the crap out of you."

Betrayed: Book Two – The Road To Redemption

"Seems reasonable." He carefully evaded answering the question. Lies were all part of the job, however, he avoided them as much as possible. You never knew when one could turn into a ticking time bomb.

Sam began to pace the room. "My pack is small, most members are getting on in age. The few of us that are still able-bodied find ourselves over-worked, our resources stretched to the limit. I have no one suitable to fill the Beta position. That's why we need you...temporarily. With Sinclair nosing about, Lycan Link is sure to get involved and a strong outward appearance is crucial." She paused by the punching bag. "We've gone through a few rough spots, but if the outside world would leave us alone, we can get back on our feet. All we need is time." She punctuated the statement by slamming her fist into the bag. It swung wildly, creaking on the chain that suspended it.

"Rough spots?" Damien straightened from his spot on the wall and caught the bag, holding it in place. He listened carefully hoping to pick up some information that would help Kane.

"My grandfather wasn't always wise when it came to finances. He made some bad investments and now we're...temporarily financially embarrassed."

The quaint turn of phrase seemed odd coming out of Sam's mouth and he raised a brow. "Bad investments...or was he a gambler?"

Sam delivered an unexpected roundhouse kick to the bag and Damien grunted slightly as he absorbed the energy from the blow. He had a feeling she wasn't pleased with his assumption and took it as a slur against her family. If she did, that was too bad. His job was to gather intelligence that would aid in a takeover bid and this bit of news just might do the trick.

An established pack being hard up for cash was unheard of. Lycan Link helped most with investment strategies and pack members usually pooled resources, the result being that a substantial nest egg accumulated over time. Given that the Chicago pack had been in existence for over one hundred and fifty years, it was hard to fathom how such a loss could happen. But, apparently it had. If the Alpha had a gambling problem, Kane could use the information to gain the upper hand.

"No. He didn't gamble. At least not in the traditional sense of the word." Sam compressed her mouth into a flat line then looked away, a heavy sigh escaping her. "Many members of my pack suffer from a genetic flaw. Infertility rates far exceed what might be expected in the average population." She flicked a glance at Damien. "There's less than a five percent chance that a mated couple will conceive and that the pregnancy will result in a live birth."

Damien blinked. To a species where family—pack—was everything, the inability to reproduce would be devastating. A memory flashed before him. Beth telling him she was pregnant, the glow of excitement in her eyes, the pride that had filled him. The fierce protectiveness he'd felt for her and their unborn pup. And the pain that still overwhelmed him when he thought of the child he'd never hold…

He controlled his reaction, no clenched jaw, no tightening fist. Sam would pick up on it and this wasn't the time to wallow in self-pity. The past was just that and he had a job to do. "And how does this relate to your finances?"

"My grandfather spent a good deal of money on research, trying to discover the cause and a cure. Several of the supposed 'experts' were nothing more than charlatans in my view. Now, the money is mostly gone and we're no better off than we were before. On top of that we've had some issues with other packs. A misunderstanding over the Finding clause got quite messy." Sam sat down at the weight machine and began to pull the weights.

Damien grunted, recognizing that she wasn't about to elaborate on that final point. He moved to a set of free weights. Choosing one, he began to do some arm curls. "So what's your plan now?"

"We carry on as best as we can. There are a few minor investments left. In time, we'll build up a reserve again. Then we'll look at our options for expansion."

"Why not join forces with Sinclair? From what I've heard, he has money—"

"No!" She let go of the handles and the weights fell down with a resounding clang. "I'm not giving up. I'm the Alpha here. The Chicago pack might be small, we might have our problems, but I'm not letting anyone take it from me." She rose to her feet and stalked towards him.

He'd definitely touched a nerve. Setting down the weight he'd been using, he warily watched her approach.

Her cheeks were flushed and her eyes seemed to spark with fire. "This has been *my* pack's territory for over one hundred and fifty years and it will *continue* to belong to us for the *next* hundred and fifty years."

Sam stopped directly in front of him. Damien flicked a glance at her clenched fists and then looked back at her. He could tell she was fighting to stay in control of her temper.

"Careful, Sugar. I don't take kindly to people taking a swing at me simply for making a suggestion." He narrowed his eyes as he issued the warning.

"Sugar?" As he'd planned, the name momentarily distracted her. "Why the hell would you call me that?"

"I thought you could use a bit of sweetening up." Damien struggled to keep the corner of his mouth from twitching up into a smile as he watched the expressions that flitted over her face. Outrage, bewilderment, anger. She finally settled on glaring at him.

"I don't need 'sweetening up'. I need you to shut up and can the crap talk about allowing Sinclair to take over my pack." She walked a short distance from him, exhaled loudly and combed her fingers through her hair. Eventually, she turned to face him, appearing calmer. "Sorry. I shouldn't have gone off on you like that. But how would you feel if someone suggested taking your pack from you?"

"I've no idea. I've never had a pack, not since I was a child." Damien shrugged, but he could feel a wall settling around him, locking out all feeling.

"Never?" She tilted her head and studied him. "What about with your mate? Surely, you must have belonged—"

"No. Not even then." He slowly clenched his fists as he recalled the plans he and Beth had made. Of how they'd strike out someday. Leave Lycan Link. Perhaps even join with Reno as his Beta.

"Oh." She appeared about to question him further and he lowered his brows, a slight growl appearing in his voice.

"The topic is off-limits. You don't want to discuss Sinclair taking you over, and I don't want to discuss my mate or my past. Understood?"

Sam straightened to her full height—what there was of it. Her chin lifted slightly, her shoulders went back. They stared at each other, a silent battle passing between them. He didn't look away and neither did she. Their surroundings faded into the background until all that remained was the force of their wills colliding in the space separating them. How long they stood there, he wasn't sure. Eventually, as one, they both nodded and the tension that had been crackling between them eased.

Chapter 6

Sam stood behind her chair at the head of the dining room table waiting for the pack members to file in. After their confrontation in the weight room, she'd left Damien to his own devices, stating she had work to do and would see him at dinner. As far as she knew, he'd spent some time in the cellar working out, and had then begun to repair the porch like he'd said he would. The sounds of hammering, and some random swearing, had drifted into her office. Perversely, she'd hoped that he'd hit his thumb with a hammer. The man irritated her. He challenged her authority, pushed her buttons. He stayed just this side of insubordination, and that was only because she was being lenient with him. Dammit, she needed him and couldn't afford to have him leave—after all, where would she find another rogue at this late date? But that didn't mean she was enthralled with his presence.

"Sam."

Hiram, Keith and Alyssa entered the room, each calling a greeting. At the same time, from the direction of the kitchen, Jonah entered carrying a steaming bowl of pasta; he was on kitchen duty, much to everyone's delight. Jonah was a trained chef and his meals were always delicious.

Jonah gave Damien a suspicious look as he set down the dish before making his way to his chair. He'd been against taking on a rogue, but had been outnumbered when they'd put it to a vote. Of course, he accepted the will of the pack, but it didn't mean he was happy with the fact.

Damien stood silently to her right. There were no signs of tension coming from him despite the fact that he had to have sensed Jonah's animosity. And the other Lycans who entered were unabashedly studying him as well. He withstood the scrutiny without any change in his breathing pattern, his face expressionless as he met each person's gaze with a steady look.

In each instance, it was the other wolf that looked away first, and through that simple act, Damien's authority was recognized.

It irked Sam, even though it shouldn't, and made her voice come out sharper than she intended.

"Listen up." The undercurrent of conversation ended and everyone looked her way. "Pack, this is Damien, the rogue we talked about. He's going to be our temporary Beta." She emphasized the word temporary and gave him a sidelong look to which he barely raised a brow.

General greetings were murmured and Damien inclined his head in response. Sam scanned the faces that surrounded the table. There was no tension, no animosity. Good. Giving a nod, she took her seat and everyone followed suit.

Dinner was fairly informal beyond the custom of everyone waiting for her permission to be seated. It was a throwback to her great-grandfather's day or perhaps even earlier. She'd yet to decide whether she wanted it to continue or not. It reinforced her position as Alpha, yet smacked a tad too much of the military for her taste. Oh well, she had more pressing matters to deal with than petty protocol and launched into giving Damien a brief introduction to the Lycans that were present. Of course, not everyone had been able to attend. A few were still on patrol and some held jobs at local establishments; their incomes were badly needed to help keep up with daily operating expenses.

As plates emptied and stomachs filled, Sam began to ask the various members about their day, whether it was pack business or, for the pup, his homework. Florence, who cared for her grandfather, gave an update on his condition.

Sam nodded and made notes when needed. She'd eaten quickly so as to be able to focus most of her attention on her pack. This was when she could observe them carefully, note if they had concerns or perhaps needed advice or encouragement. An Alpha should take a direct interest in the well-being of each member.

"Hiram," she quizzed the one wolf who had yet to say anything. He'd been picking at his meal and looked as if something was troubling him. "You were on patrol earlier today. Did you make contact with any shifter tourists?"

"One couple at the airport making a connection between flights. And three females—college students. They'll be staying in the area for two days." He hesitated and then added one final piece of information. "For some reason, I kept getting a feeling that there was one more Lycan in the area. Just the faintest whiff of a scent and then it was gone. Maybe I'm wrong…" He tugged his ear, a sure sign he was worried. "I'm not as young as I used to be and my nose could be failing."

"You're not that old," Sam chided gently, while taking in his greying hair and lined face. Hiram should have been retired from patrol, but given their small numbers she'd kept him on light duty longer than most packs would. It was good for his pride as well, thinking he was still contributing to the group. "It could be that spy Sinclair was sending our way. I'll check it out tonight. Good work."

Hiram grinned and tucked into his meal with more gusto than he'd been showing previously. Sam smiled inwardly, pleased she'd been able to boost his spirits. His daughter had left the pack last year, having met an outsider, and the older man had been in a bit of a funk ever since.

"Do you want me to go along with you on patrol tonight?" Damien spoke to her directly for the first time since the meal had begun. It had unnerved her a bit, how he'd seemed to be silently analyzing every word, every member. She'd never let him know that, of course.

"Good idea. It'll help create the illusion that you belong here. We leave as soon as it gets dark."

He gave a barely perceptible nod and resumed his silent meal.

Arrogant bastard, she silently decided. Was he thinking their dinner conversation was too mundane to join in? She turned away, resolving to set him straight on how he treated her pack once they were alone.

Crickets had begun their evening serenade and the wisps of orange and red that had stained the sky were fading into deep purple by the time Sam stepped out of the house. Damien watched her from his seat on an old porch swing. He'd repaired it that afternoon, tightening screws and oiling the chain. Now it glided silently back and forth in its shadowy corner.

She was dressed all in black again and he decided the colour suited her, though he doubted that was why she chose it. He didn't imagine fashion ranked high on her list of priorities.

"You ready, Damien?"

"Yep." He got to his feet, not surprised that she'd been aware of his presence. It was hard to sneak up on a Lycan unless you could stay downwind of them.

"Follow me." She set off at a brisk pace down the sidewalk, but his longer legs meant he had no problem keeping up with her.

The street lights were starting to come on, illuminating the parked vehicles that lined the road, but the neighbourhood was far from sleepy. Cars cruised past with music drifting through open windows. An argument could be heard coming from a nearby home while a baby wailed in the background. As they approached the intersection, various neon signs flashed advertisements for local establishments and the mumble of conversations created an indistinct hum. Papa Tony's pizzeria had a large gathering at the outdoor tables; good natured laughter and the occasional shout filled the air. A few of the patrons called out greetings to Sam as they walked past. She waved but didn't pause.

"Where are we headed?"

"Tonight was supposed to be Little Italy, but we'll go towards O'Hare instead. I can't cover the entire city in a night so I've laid it out in rotating sectors. If a patrol reports anything unusual, I bump that sector to the top of the list."

"You go out each night?" He'd decided some random small talk might yield useful information and tried to sound politely interested.

"Of course." She shot him a quick glance. "I'm the Alpha. It's my job to keep tabs on my territory."

"You could rely on your patrols."

"I could, and some Alphas might be lax enough to completely relegate the job. I know my patrols are competent and well trained. They know what to report, but it never hurts to have a second set of eyes on the job."

"True." Mentally, he applauded her dedication. So far, she seemed to be a perfect example of what an Alpha should be. Of course, that was only his initial impression. He'd bide his time and see what he could turn up that might be useful to Kane.

She turned down an alley and led him to a shadowed area. After testing the air and listening carefully, she gave a nod. "It's safe to shift."

"In the city? I'd have thought patrolling as human would be safer."

She shrugged. "We can cover more ground as wolves. And most people mistake a wolf for a stray malamute or a husky. Don't worry, we won't be running down the main streets."

"Back alleys all the way?"

"And along the train tracks. The right of way on either side will allow us to cut a few miles off the trip."

Before he could comment, the air shimmered and a small white wolf stood before him. Damien had a brief impression of fine bones and stunning violet eyes before it turned and began to lope down the alley.

He quickly shifted and followed, thankful that his own animal was more cooperative of late. His inner wolf and he had gone through a prolonged period of discord; the beast had been disapproving of some of the choices he'd made. As usual, the creature had been correct, though it had taken a while for him to realize it. His grief over Beth's death and the need for revenge had skewed his thinking. Thankfully, a Lycan's inner wolf was usually inclined to be forgiving and they'd come to some semblance of peace.

At the moment his wolf was focused on the fluffy white tail that was ahead of them. The animal was curious, intrigued even, by Sam Harper. *Alpha? And yet, not.*

"Yeah. I know boy. It's hard to figure out." Damien murmured his agreement. Something about Sam Harper sparked his interest, dragging him out of his usual apathy in a way that hadn't happened for ages. He wasn't entirely sure he liked the fact, either.

They travelled in silence, Sam leading him down back alleys, along railroad tracks and across abandoned lots. Occasionally, she'd pause and test the air before moving on following some mental road map. When they approached a busy main street, she fluidly shifted to human form, with barely a missed step.

"Impressive." Damien mimicked her shifting on the fly.

"An Alpha and its wolf should be as one, thinking and acting as a single unit." She brushed her hair from her eyes and stepped out of the alley and onto the sidewalk. After scanning the area, she turned right and began to stroll down the street.

He fell into step beside her. "You know, you sound like a textbook sometimes."

"A textbook? What do you mean?"

"An Alpha should do this. An Alpha should do that."

"An Alpha needs to know its—"

"There you go again. Don't you ever just talk?" He scowled at her.

She cast a glare his way before focusing her eyes straight ahead. "I've no idea what you mean."

"It's like you've been…indoctrinated." It irritated him, bringing back memories of a particularly annoying roommate named Quinten, at the Academy. The guy had read textbooks aloud every night until Damien had finally pitched him out the window.

"My grandfather trained me for this role from a young age. If you're going to be an Alpha, you have to act like one. Follow the rules day in and day out. It's not a nine-to-five job, you know."

Betrayed: Book Two – The Road To Redemption

Barely, Damien kept from rolling his eyes. How many times had Reno said something similar to him during those early days of training to be an Enforcer? Of course, Reno had been one of the biggest rule breakers of them all and they'd both often laughed at the irony of it.

The sights and sounds of Chicago faded as Damien thought of those long ago days. He and Reno patrolling together, hunting down Purists, instinctively knowing how the other would react in a tight spot. They'd been quite the team… Hell, more than that. One of the best damned teams Lycan Link had ever seen!

Damien shoved his hands in his pockets and wondered what his former partner was up to these days. Did he still spread his time between Lycan Link and the pack in Kolding's Pass? It was almost two years since he'd seen the man. Sadly, they hadn't parted as friends; barely even on the same side of the law. The broken relationship…hurt. Reno had been like his brother, and his disapproval—no matter how justified—had stung.

Noises coming from his right drew him from his melancholy. A group of young men had just exited a movie theatre and were rough-housing with each other, though from the looks of it, one member of the group was about to lose his temper. Damien instinctively drew Sam closer to him, wrapping his arm around her shoulders to shield her from the jostling men. His inner wolf went on alert as well, ready to defend the female at their side. Muscles tightened, a deadly calm sheathed his mind. He was no stranger to life and death fights and—

"What do you think you're doing?" Sam hissed the words at him and tried to push away, but he held her in place.

"Acting like a normal couple out for an evening stroll. A man protects his woman." Damien murmured the words through barely parted lips, keeping his gaze trained on the group. One of the young men noticed his attention and instantly stilled before nudging a cohort who had a similar reaction. In a matter of seconds the group had quieted down and was warily backing away.

Damien curled his lip as he watched their retreat then brought his attention back to Sam who was still protesting at his side. She was jabbing her elbow into his waist.

"We're not a couple! And if you call me 'your woman' again, I'll rip your balls off!" She shoved him again and this time he allowed his arm to drop to his side, releasing her.

He willed himself to relax, locking the dangerous half of himself away once more. "Sorry. It seemed like a good cover. Anyone who knows I'm staying with you will wonder about our relationship."

"Let them wonder. I walk alone. I take care of myself."

Damien shrugged. "Sure thing, Sugar."

"And stop the 'sugar' crap."

Irritation rolled off her and he chuckled, inexplicably pleased to have gotten that reaction. "Sugar crap? Sounds like some new brand of breakfast cereal."

"Cereal? Wh—" She snapped her mouth shut, exasperation oozing from her. "Will you be serious?"

This time he made no effort to control his laughter and it felt as if something had been released inside him, allowing the tension to flow from his body. "Only if you lighten up a bit."

"Me? You're the one who looked like he'd sucked lemons all during dinner."

"I was listening, trying to learn everyone's name. If you want me to be believable in this role, then I have to do my homework." He stopped and lightly touched her arm. Surprisingly enough, she actually paused and turned to face him. "I was impressed by the way you made sure Hiram felt like he was still contributing."

She studied his face for a moment seeming surprised by his comment, then shrugged and looked away. "He's had a hard time of it recently."

The light from the lamp-post caught her eyes, causing the violet to glow like some rare gem. Not thinking, he reached out, gently touching her chin and turning her face so he could see the colour more clearly. Amethyst surrounded by thick dark lashes.

"You have the most amazing eyes."

She scowled. "I hate them. Lycans shouldn't have violet eyes."

"I think they suit you." He brushed his thumb over her jaw. Something about her drew him in and stirred his interest. Before he could decide what it was, she jerked her face away from his hand.

"It won't do you any good."

"What won't?"

"Trying to get between my legs." She kept her face averted, seeming to be studying the traffic, but Damien was sure he heard an underlying tone of hurt beneath her hard response.

"I didn't think that's what I was doing." Truth was he had no idea what he'd been doing.

"No?" She arched a brow. "Just keep it that way, then. If I decide I need a lover, I'll choose one. Your job is to be my Beta, nothing else."

"Good to know." Damien shoved his hands in his pockets not sure what to make of her response. Not that it mattered. He wasn't looking for a lover and if he was, it wouldn't be someone like Sam. Beth had been soft and sweet, letting him lead the way. Sam would likely be issuing orders the whole time.

As if to illustrate the point, she jerked her chin towards a nearby nightclub. "We're going in here." The neon sign overhead proclaimed it to be Club Mystique.

He didn't question the decision, despite his instinctive aversion to being ordered about. Instead, he followed behind her like the good little Beta he was supposed to be.

Chapter 7

There was a long line of people waiting to enter the popular night spot. Sam pushed her way to the front, ignoring the deadly looks cast her way. The bouncer knew her and simply nodded and let her pass.

As the door opened, a throbbing bass beat rolled out of the club and spilled onto the street. The crowd began to surge forward and the bouncer moved to block the entrance with his body.

"He's with me." Sam inclined her head towards Damien, shouting the words so the bouncer would hear her over the music. She needn't have bothered. The look Damien gave the man had the burly fellow taking half a step back. A huff of laughter escaped her. Damn, she'd been lucky. Damien was one impressive rogue…provided he remembered his place.

The pass he'd made earlier—if it had indeed been a pass—had momentarily worried her. Fighting off males who kept their brains in their dicks wasn't a problem—she'd done it often enough—but it was annoying and interfered with her duty.

She wound her way through the crowd, heading for her usual spot at the bar and caught the eye of Tina, the bartender and her friend. Her drink appeared a moment later.

"Want anything?" She nudged Damien and he shook his head, obviously too busy scanning the crowd to even bother answering. Oh well, his loss.

He finally focused back on her, his jaw set in a look of disapproval. "Why are we here?"

"To dance?" She flicked a glance towards the centre of the room where couples were grinding to the music.

He snorted and she laughed.

"Right." She took a swallow of her drink. "Hiram was telling me about scenting a Lycan. I questioned him after dinner. It wasn't too far from here."

"He wasn't completely sure."

"No, but this is a popular hangout. Lots of our kind pass through." She shrugged. "It's as good a place to look as any other."

Damien nodded. "I'll wander around. See if I notice anything."

"Meet back here in half an hour."

She watched him leave, slowly sipping her drink and noting how the crowd instinctively parted for him. Yeah, he'd impress the hell out of Sinclair or any of the Lycan Link stiffs that might come nosing around. As he disappeared from view, she turned on her bar stool and casually gestured towards Tina.

The bartender nodded and began to make her way back towards Sam, clearing glasses and wiping the counter as she went along. It gave Sam a moment to appreciate the woman's garb. Thigh high boots, a short leather skirt, a black bustier and a choker chain necklace. It was topped off with rainbow coloured hair.

Sam grinned at the woman when she finally stopped in front of her, taking in the final touch to the costume, dramatic purple eye shadow and the liberal use of eyeliner. "Nice colours."

Tina cracked her gum and grinned. "I couldn't decide what I wanted today, so I went with them all."

"It suits you." She took a moment to marvel at the intricate filigree design that accented the outer corners of the bartender's eyes. Tina was studying to be a makeup artist. "Cool eye liner design, too."

"Yeah, I got a great mark from my instructor for it." She studied Sam's face. "You know, I'd love to do your eyes one day."

"I've told you before, that's not my style, Tina." Sam shook her head and grabbed a handful of popcorn from a bowl that sat nearby.

Tina gave a dramatic sigh. "I know, but I'll keep trying. Your eyes would be so much fun to work with." She glanced along the length of the bar. No one was demanding her attention, so she settled in to talk. "I'm surprised to see you here tonight. What's up?"

Sam raised her glass to her mouth and replied in a barely audible whisper. "Looking for information. Any new rumours? Hiram thought he scented a new Lycan in the area but wasn't sure."

Straightening, Tina wiped the countertop then glanced around. While the establishment was frequented by Shifters as well as Others, there were always humans about as well and discretion was needed. "There is one. One who is, yet isn't."

"And that means…?"

Tina scrunched her face, obviously trying to explain the feeling she had in words that a mere Lycan could understand. "You need to be careful. The wolf has two faces."

Sam frowned trying to make sense of what Tina was saying. The woman was one of the Others, part of the witch and Fae realm, and as such she was prone to insights about the future. Unfortunately, those insights tended to be vague, or perhaps it was that Tina had turned her back on her heritage and made no real effort to refine her skill.

Biting back a sigh of frustration, Sam nodded her thanks. "If you pick up on anything, let me know."

"Sorry." Tina tucked a pink lock of hair behind her ear. "I'm pretty sure there's another Lycan in the area but…" She shrugged. "Being a witch isn't an exact science."

Sam made a non-committal sound and downed the rest of her drink. Her grandfather would have a seizure if he knew she was consulting with one of the Others. Her friendship with the witch had often been a sticking point between them. *Non-shifters can't be trusted*, he'd growl while she'd argue back that the division between species was outdated. Having a witch as a friend could be useful…usually…if you didn't count the times when Tina's hexes had gone horribly awry. If only the woman would put more effort into developing her skills. Sam shook her head. Others weren't bound by duty like Lycans were and there was no point in trying to change them.

She pushed her empty glass towards Tina along with payment for the drink. "Thanks. If anything else comes to you—"

"I'll give you a call." Tina pocketed the bills. With a friendly nod, she returned to her bartending duties.

Sam turned her seat so she faced the crowd again and considered Tina's words. 'One who is, yet isn't.' Someone being deceitful? That was half the population of the bar right now. She watched as the women flirted and the men whispered promises they had no intention of keeping. She snorted and leaned back, resting her elbows on the bar behind her.

"Great music."

Sam turned her head to look at the young man beside her. He'd been there for some time but apparently only now had garnered the nerve to speak to her. He was about her age, short blond hair, average height. Cute, if you liked cute.

She nodded. "Yeah. Great." It was okay, good enough that her booted foot was keeping the beat.

"So…" He shuffled his feet, glanced away and then looked at her again. "You wanna dance?"

Sam flicked her eyes over the length of him and then slid from her seat. "Why not?" It gave her a chance to check out who was on the dance floor. Between the cheap perfume and body spray, a dozen Lycans could be in the room and she'd be hard pressed to pick up on their scent.

She led the way into the undulating crowd, found an open spot and began to move to the music. The floor reverberated under her feet, the rhythm persistent and pulsing as it attempted to wrap her in its spell, but her attention was on her own thoughts.

The Lycan Tina was sensing could very well be Sinclair's spy. And if the spy was already in town, then it was a good thing Damien was part of her pack. A spy would be looking for weakness, the inability to carry out the duties associated with owning a territory. That wasn't the case, of course. She had the city well under control, but if they saw Damien *and* her at the helm there would be no doubt in their chauvinistic little minds that the place was in good hands.

And speaking of hands... The man she was dancing with had pulled her close enough so that he was grinding against her butt.

"Hands off." She tried to step away. In response, he tightened his grip on her hips and nuzzled her neck. Giving her head a slight shake at the idiot's audacity, she grabbed one of his fingers and bent it back.

"Hey!" He immediately let go.

"I said hands off." She turned to stare at him, eyes narrowed, daring him to complain.

He snapped his mouth shut and appeared as if he'd like to back up even further if the dance floor hadn't been so crowded.

"Next time, ask before you maul." With that she walked away.

She pushed her way through the throng, scenting the air and studying those around her. A Lycan spy gyrating on a dance floor was totally absurd and thus a perfect cover.

Damien had caught sight of Sam dancing and had wondered what she was up to. When she nearly broke the finger of the male who was groping her, he'd given a mental nod of approval even though it was none of his business if she hooked up with random guys. Unfortunately, knowing it wasn't his concern hadn't stopped the scowl from forming on his face. His wolf hadn't appreciated it either, a low rumble reverberating in the beast's throat.

Now that she'd moved away from the mauler, his mood lightened or at least as much as it could, given the scum he was on the hunt for. The hint of lilacs that he'd detected in the air had him on alert. Sure, it could be perfume but... He sighted his quarry in the corner. Dante.

His hackles rose and he stalked towards the intruder, only the fact that they were in a public place surrounded by humans kept him from snarling.

"I thought I told you to stay the hell away from here."

Dante looked up from the drink he'd been nursing. "Nice to see you, too, Damien." He gestured towards an empty chair. "Have a seat."

"No."

"You really should, you know. We need to discuss…old times."

He hesitated and then slid into the chair. Old times with Dante meant Deirdre. The woman had been his 'handler' during his years working as an assassin. He'd turned his back on it though, walked away not caring that it meant a price was on his head. It still didn't matter, but, if Deirdre was going to kill him, it wouldn't hurt to know how and when.

"Drink?" Dante signalled for a waitress, but Damien shook his head.

"The days when we drank together are long gone, Dante. What do you want?"

"Just passing along some information."

"About?"

"Several things." Dante looked away, suddenly appearing disinterested in the conversation.

"You waiting for me to pay you?" Damien leaned back in his chair and crossed his arms.

"Depends on if you want the information." Dante shrugged. "If you don't, Sam Harper might be interested."

Damien shot his hand across the table and grabbed Dante's collar. "I told you to stay away from her."

Dante laughed, the sound coming out more like a wheeze due to the material twisting around his throat. "I really don't think you want the bouncer throwing you out, do you?"

Slowly, Damien relaxed his grip and sat back in his chair, his jaw tightly clenched; Dante's presence stretching his self-control to the very limits. One of his first assignments while working for Deirdre had partnered him with the bastard. Dante wasn't above stealing from the dead or saving his own hide at the expense of his teammates.

Betrayed: Book Two – The Road To Redemption

Taking a sip of his drink, Dante gave him a speculative look. "You seem protective towards Harper. Care to share why?"

Damien ignored the comment. "How much?"

For a moment, he wondered if Dante was going to press the issue regarding Sam but, typical of the man, the lure of hard cash took precedence.

"For my information? A couple hundred."

"Ha! You'd have to be selling me the code to Lycan Link's security system before I'd pay you that much."

"Just checking. You never spent much of what Deirdre paid you so you must have a nice fat bank account."

Damien narrowed his eyes. "I'll only ask once more and then I'll drag your sorry ass into the alley and beat the information from you."

"Fifty...for now."

His inner wolf bared its teeth and Damien barely held back the growl that rose in his throat. "You try and bleed me dry by delivering this one piece at a time and I'll break your fingers one at a time. Spill what you know now."

"Then it'll cost you a hundred."

"Fifty now. The rest if I decide your information is worth it."

Dante held out his hand and Damien pulled some bills from his pocket.

Once the money was tucked away, Dante leaned forward. "You were on Deirdre's hit list when you left."

"Old news, Dante. I knew that the moment I jumped ship." Deirdre didn't make idle threats, and, in the first few months, he'd had several brushes with her crew of assassins. The fact that he was still alive, a year and a half later, puzzled him. Her organization wasn't inefficient; he'd worked for them long enough to know their capabilities. He was curious if Dante knew why the hunt had eased off, but wouldn't give the bastard any satisfaction by showing an interest.

"True. But shortly after you left, something happened. No one knows exactly what, but she let a lot of us go."

"So that's why you're scrounging for jobs?"

Dante shrugged. "Deirdre paid me well. I became used to a certain standard."

Damien didn't doubt that Dante had been paid better than most. The man had even fewer scruples than the rest of the team and would take on any job. But Dante wasn't his concern at the moment. What did this news have to do with his own fate? "So...if she's closed up shop, I'm no longer on her hit list?"

"Perhaps. She didn't exactly close shop; more like scaled back." Abruptly, Dante leaned closer. He flicked a glance about the room and then whispered a question. "Do you have any idea what happened?"

"No."

"I'm wondering if it has to do with Stone."

"Elijah Stone?" Damien frowned. The name was whispered in hushed tones within Deirdre's organization. Supposedly, Stone and Deirdre had started the business together but, in his time there, Damien had never seen the man. In fact, he even questioned the mythical partner's existence. "Sorry. Can't help you."

"Hmmm." Dante rubbed his chin and his eyes focused on some distant point before he looked at Damien again. "I'd wondered if on that last day, you might have noticed something or heard something."

"Eaves-dropping was your specialty, not mine."

"Information acquisition." Dante gave a short dry laugh. "I thought you might have known more; Deirdre always did have a thing for you."

Damien shook his head. "More like she was pissed off that I didn't fall at her feet."

Dante shrugged and moved to stand up. "Well, thanks for the info—"

Damien shot out his hand and grabbed the other man's arm stopping him from moving farther. "Where the hell do you think you're going? I'm the one that paid for information."

"It was worth a try." The other man slowly sat back down, massaging the spot that Damien had grabbed. "Of course, if you want more…" He extended his hand.

"Dante, your information isn't worth shit. I'm not paying you again. I want a refund." Damien began to reach across the table, but Dante leaned away.

"All right. Don't start frothing at the mouth. I have more." He licked his lips. "Your old partner—Reno—he got the charges against you dropped. Official files list you as an ex-Enforcer, no mention of dishonourable conduct."

Damien raised his brows. That was unexpected news. His time as an Enforcer seemed like another lifetime. Since leaving Lycan Link and parting ways with Deirdre, he'd knocked about the country, taking on odd jobs here and there, spending time with Kane's pack now and then. He hadn't hidden, but he'd kept a low profile. Mouldering away in detention didn't appeal to him and, while he'd escaped the Trackers a few times, he'd known his luck wouldn't hold out forever. Plus, it would have been too hard on Reno to have to testify against him. Though why he worried about the man, he didn't know. Their final meeting in Grassy Hills hadn't gone well. The look on Reno's face—half accusing, half disappointment—had hurt, yet the man mustn't have totally given up on him.

Damn. Damien rubbed his neck, uncomfortable with the idea that Reno had continued to go to bat for him. He looked at the man sitting across the table from him. There was a speculative look in Dante's eye that put Damien's radar on alert. No way Dante was wasting his time delivering bits of good news.

"So beyond giving me an update, what 'old times' did we need to discuss?"

"Just a minute." Dante flagged the waitress who was passing by. When she stopped, he gave her a warm smile. "My friend here said he'd pay my tab; his birthday present to me."

"What?" Caught off guard, Damien was a split second too slow to react. Dante was on his feet, the waitress between them.

"I'll be in touch." With a salute, Dante slipped through the crowd.

Damien fumed and dug out some money to pay the waitress, but by the time he was done, Dante was long gone.

"Who was that?" Sam appeared at his side. She must have grown impatient waiting for him.

"An old acquaintance."

She sniffed the air and a sneer curled her lip. "He wears lilac cologne?"

Damien didn't bother correcting her. Dammit, he knew he should have killed Dante last night!

Chapter 8

Kane sat at his desk and stared at the backlog of work that awaited him. He'd just returned from Stump River and was now regretting having made the trip. The accountant needed to speak to him about an income tax problem, Lycan Link had sent three messages marked urgent, several pack members had requested personal meetings; the list went on and on. And that wasn't counting the items John, his Beta, had dealt with during his absence.

He sighed and opened up the first email from Lycan Link.

"Kane, wasn't it great to get away together? It was our first 'family' vacation." Elise breezed into the room interrupting his train of thought.

"What? Oh yeah." Their blood bond was tickling his brain, letting him know how happy she was. It was also distracting him from the message on his screen.

Elise perched on the edge of the desk. She swung her foot back and forth, a broad smile on her face. "I think we should try to get away with the kids a couple of times a year. Once could be to go see Ryne and Mel—I loved Stump River—and then another time could be something fun and educational for the kids."

"Uh-huh." He frowned trying to divide his attention between his mate and his mail. Lycan Link was looking at restructuring… "Yeah. A vacation for the kids. Good idea."

"And we need to get away by ourselves once in a while, too." She slid off the desk and stood behind him. "Time without the children interrupting or a pack emergency." Slowly, she slid her hands across his shoulders and down his arms. Then, a moment later, her breath tickled his ear. "Wouldn't that be great?"

High Council was considering… Damn, he lost his train of thought again!

"Elise." Kane shrugged her hands off. "I'm trying to read an important message from Lycan Link and you keep distracting me." He dragged his hand through his hair. "I've read this paragraph twice already and can't make heads or tails out of it."

"Oh." She stepped away, the smile leaving her face for a moment before returning, albeit not quite as bright as before. "Can I help you with anything? I know we were gone a week and things pile up."

He shook his head. "No. They're all things I have to do myself. If they could have been delegated, John would have taken care of them."

"All right." She shrugged and rearranged the pen holder on his desk. "I just thought I'd offer."

There was a hint of hurt in her voice and he closed his eyes, exhaling slowly before opening them again. "I'm sorry. It's—" The phone rang and he reached out to pick it up while casting an apologetic look at Elise.

"I know. You have a lot to get caught up on. I should have waited. It was just that we had such a good time and I thought we could spend the rest of the day together." She turned to walk towards the door but he stretched out his arm and grabbed her hand.

"We'll talk about it after supper, I promise."

She gave him a half smile and pulled her hand free, shutting the door firmly, both on the office and on the mental connection they had through their blood bond. He clenched his jaw knowing he was definitely in the 'dog house'. The phone continued to ring and with a sigh he turned to answer it. After dinner, he'd make amends.

As Elise left Kane's office, Jacob came barrelling down the stairs. The little boy did nothing quietly and was yelling for his father at the top of his lungs. "Daddy! Daaaadddy!"

Elise scooped him up and pressed his face against her shoulder. "Hush! Haven't I told you not to yell in the house?"

"Yep." He squirmed to get free. "Need Daddy."

"Daddy's busy right now with pack business. What do you need?"

"Gamma Helen go park!"

"She's going to take you to the park?"

He nodded. "I need 'mission."

"*Per*mission. Not 'mission."

"Yep! I go swing?" He grabbed her cheeks and turned her face so he looked her directly in the eye. So young and yet already exercising his innate Alpha instincts. Heaven help them all when he reached his teens!

The stairs creaked softly and Elise looked up to see Helen descending, her pace much slower than Jacob's had been. Helen was honorary grandmother to the children, the 'housekeeper' for the pack house and a general font of wisdom for anyone who needed a dose of common sense.

"Jacob said you were going to take him to the park?" Elise let the boy down and he began sliding along the polished wooden floors making some vague engine type noise. Obviously the long plane ride home hadn't tired him in the least.

"If it's all right with Kane and you. He's wound up and I thought maybe it would help wear him out."

"Good idea. He napped on the plane and probably won't want to sleep tonight." She reached down and grabbed hold of him just before he crashed into the wall. "I don't know where he gets all his energy."

Jacob pulled free and raced towards Helen. "Swings! Swings! Swings!"

Helen took Jacob's hand and headed for the door. "Leah is napping and I'll keep Jacob at the park for about an hour, in case you and Kane—"

"He's working." Elise made a face. "But thanks for the offer."

"Oh." Helen glanced at the closed office door. "Well, maybe a soak in the tub? I remember when my girls were little. Time to myself was precious."

"Thanks. I might do that."

She helped Helen buckle Jacob into his car seat and then waved as they drove off. It was a beautiful fall day. Warm sunshine streamed through leaves tipped with autumn colours while the sweet smell of drying grass drifted on the breeze. A perfect day for a walk or a run with your mate…if he wasn't working.

A sigh escaped her. They'd arrived home mid-morning and she'd thought she and Kane could spend the rest of the day together unpacking, reminiscing about their week away. *She* hadn't rushed off to check her emails, despite the fact that she'd only recently become co-owner of the Grey Goose. There was a lot to be done to revamp the aging establishment, but *she* knew planning new menus and redecorating the rooms could wait. Too bad Kane wasn't of the same mind.

Her inner wolf nudged her. *Pack comes first. Our mate is Alpha for a large number of wolves who depend on him. His duties are numerous and his time isn't his own.*

"I know that," she argued back. "All my life I've bowed to the needs of the pack. Father was Alpha, remember? He dictated everything I did, right down to who my mate would be."

And his choice was a good one.

"Yes, but…" She stopped unable to explain even to her own wolf. She loved Kane. He was a good man, one who'd been born to be a great Alpha. He took his duties seriously and had important responsibilities. And as a mate, he provided for her and the pups. That should be enough, shouldn't it? Surely, she was being selfish or unrealistic to expect more? Yet, there was no denying the feeling in her heart that something was missing lately.

This was the life we were born into, the way it has been for our people for centuries. The Alpha works for the good of the pack so that the members have all they need.

"But just because this is how it's always been doesn't mean it's right, that it can't change. And Ryne and Mel seem to have time for a family life."

Her wolf frowned and fell silent.

"See?" She felt a small thrill at winning the argument. However, that was short lived as she walked back inside. The low murmur of Kane's voice could be heard coming from the office. He was still on the phone.

She gave in to a childish impulse and stuck her tongue out at the door. Some might think being an Alpha's mate was an amazing opportunity, but at times it just sucked. The word 'Chicago' drifted out through the door and she crossed her fingers. The takeover couldn't happen fast enough.

~~~

"Yo! Damien!"

Damien glanced up from where he was hunkered down on the ground beside his motorcycle. Standing near him was a young Lycan by the name of Chris. He'd seen the boy at supper last night, but beyond hearing his name knew nothing else. The boy's appearance was revealing though. Cocky expression, slouched posture, ripped jeans, sleeveless t-shirt. Yeah. Damien knew his type.

He stood up and held his laughter in check as the kid automatically fell back a step losing some of his bravado. Being a good head taller than the young teen was going to make it easy to keep him in line.

"What can I do for you…Chris, wasn't it?"

"Yeah. That's me." The boy recovered some of his attitude and gestured towards the motorcycle. "Whatcha doin'?"

"After a cross country ride, it needs an oil change and a good cleaning." Damien glanced between his ride and the boy. "You want to help?"

Chris shrugged. 'If you need some. I mean, there's nothing else going on around here."

"Nothing to do? In a place as big as Chicago?" He tossed a polishing rag the boy's way and pointed at the chrome.

"I'm grounded right now, so yeah, it's boring."

"What are you in for?" He crouched down beside the machine again.

"Broke curfew. My mom got worried and Sam had to come looking for me. Man, was she mad at me." The boy rubbed his ear. Damien held back a smile. He could well imagine Sam grabbing the appendage and using it to drag the boy home.

"Not a good idea, pissing her off."

"You said it." The boy polished the chrome for a while before speaking again. "Will you teach me to ride this?"

"Why not ask Sam? She has one."

Chris made a face. "She said no. Said I'm too young."

"How old are you?"

"I just turned fourteen."

Damien raised his eyebrows. "Then my answer is the same as hers. But I can show you a few things about it, if you'd like."

"Really? That'd be awesome. Wait until I tell the guys at school—" He stopped mid-sentence and shook his head. "No. I guess I can't."

"Why's that?"

"'Cuz we're Lycans. And you're only our Beta for a while. And everyone says I have to keep a low profile." He spat over his shoulder. "Sometimes being a Lycan sucks."

Damien made a noncommittal noise. Something was bugging the kid. From personal experience he knew that sometimes you just needed the other person to wait while you got your thoughts in order.

They worked in silence, the sun beating down on them, and then reflecting back up off the cement driveway. Damien wiped a trickle of sweat from his brow; the shade had inched its way into the neighbour's yard and the breeze from earlier in the day had died down. He sat back on his heels and took a drink of water from the bottle he'd brought out with him.

In the distance the sound of traffic could be heard—cars, buses, a siren—the noises Damien had come to associate with the neighbourhood. Being a Lycan in a big city took on added challenges he'd never considered; sorting through the cacophony of noises and scents, learning to filter out the mundane from those that had meaning.

"Did you grow up in a big pack, Damien?" From the other side of the machine, Chris finally spoke.

"Me? No. There were about fifty members or so." He capped his bottle and got back to work.

"That's way bigger than ours." Chris made a face. "Were there any kids your age?"

"A few. And there was a pack not too far away that we'd meet up with sometimes."

"Jeez, you were lucky. There's no one my age around here." The boy rubbed harder at the bit of chrome he was working on. "Our pack's dying out, you know. Pretty soon there'll be no one left."

Last night, Damien had noted that there was only one pup at the table. Sam hadn't been kidding when she said fertility was a problem. The pack would be hard pressed to stay in existence for even one more generation at this rate.

"I've got human friends," Chris continued. "But you always have to watch what you say. Just once I'd like to be myself."

"That's understandable."

"You don't mind if I hang out with you while you're here, do you?" Chris flicked him a quick glance and then concentrated on his polishing. The too cool attitude of a few minutes ago had disappeared leaving a hopeful kid in its place.

Damien hesitated. He knew nothing about children except that he'd been one himself once. And the kind he'd been had always been in trouble, never really fitting in. He was about to refuse on the grounds that he wasn't going to be staying long, but something about the look on the boy's face had him agreeing despite doubting the wisdom of the move.

"Sure. Sam will likely keep me busy, but we can hang when I'm off duty…and when you've got your homework done." He added that last bit, recalling how Sam had reminded the youngster about school work when the meal had finished.

Mentally, he rolled his eyes. God, he couldn't believe he'd said that.

Chris had no reservations about it though, quickly agreeing and then launching into a long string of questions about how the motorcycle worked and what maintenance it required.

Damien did his best to answer, surprised at how easily he interacted with the kid. Was this what it would have been like if his child had lived? He and his son working on a motorcycle together, maybe going to a ballgame...

"Damn!"

"What's wrong, Damien?" Chris peered at him from the far side of the motorcycle.

"Nothing. Bashed my knuckle." Damien sucked on his injured finger and cursed his lack of concentration. The wrench had slipped as he tried to remove the spark plug.

"Christopher, are you bothering Damien?" A woman's voice called out from behind and Damien turned to see one of the pack walking up the driveway. From her appearance—a suit and briefcase—he assumed she was coming home from work.

"No, Ma. I'm not bothering him." Chris gave an over exaggerated eye-roll.

"That's your story." His mother—Damien recalled her name was Alyssa—frowned at him. "Besides, you're grounded for sneaking out last week and I bet your homework isn't done yet. I told you—"

"He's not bothering me." Damien got to his feet. "I asked him to help. Seemed to me that a little physical labour was a good way to pay his dues for the trouble he caused the pack. Better than sitting inside playing video games, at least."

Alyssa paused and then nodded. "I agree. If you have any other jobs for him, feel free to put him to work. Maybe if he's tired enough he'll stay out of trouble." She shot a look at her son. "I want you inside doing your homework as soon as you've completed whatever job Damien's given you."

"Actually, we're about done for the day." Damien wiped the blood off his hand with the edge of his shirt. "I'll be sending him in soon."

Alyssa stared at the blood and then back at Damien. A worried frown marred her brow and Damien wondered if the fact that he was a rogue concerned her. Might as well deal with her now, he decided. "I'm a rogue, but that doesn't mean I hurt children."

She stiffened and lifted her chin. "I never thought that for a minute. I was merely concerned about your hand."

He studied her for a moment finding no hint of a lie in her steady gaze. "My apologies. I've met with some prejudice in my life, but I shouldn't assume—"

"No need. I understand." She patted his shoulder as she walked past him towards the house. "Know that we're all glad you're here trying to help us save our pack."

Thankfully she didn't seem to be expecting a reply and went inside after giving Chris another warning.

As the door shut, Chris gave him a high five. "Thanks, Damien. That was smooth."

"Hmm?" He looked at the boy, still distracted by what Alyssa had said.

"The way you made Ma think me being out here was all your idea and part of a punishment. *And* she'll be okay now with us hanging out together. I wish I could think that fast."

"Comes with practice." The hero worship in the boy's eyes, along with the mother's words, made him feel guilty. "Listen, it's getting late. Let's call it a day and maybe tomorrow you can help me lube the chain."

"Great! Thanks, Damien!" The boy gathered up the polishing rags. "I'm glad you're here to help us fight that bastard Sinclair."

"Er...I don't think your mom would approve of you swearing."

Chris laughed. "No, but Sam does it all the time so what can Ma do?"

"True." He watched as the boy raced up the steps to the house. Strange, he'd always wondered what it would be like to have a pack welcome his presence. Only now that it was happening, he felt like shit.

Chapter 9

Damien tried to shrug off the feeling he was being watched. Millions of people lived in Chicago. At least a hundred were walking down this particular street. Somebody was bound to be looking at him from time to time. But it wasn't the feeling a casual glance would garner. It was more intense, as if someone were studying him, an itch between his shoulder blades that had both him and his wolf on alert.

A mugger? A crazed killer? Dante? None felt quite right.

Some might scoff that the gaze of a person had a feel, but over the years he'd honed his senses in ways that most other Lycans could never imagine. Of course, most other Lycans hadn't lived their life on the edge of society. Rubbing elbows with the dregs of the earth, expecting to kill or be killed at any moment. You didn't live long if you let your guard down. And he *had* lived, if it could be called living.

Dante had said there was no longer a price on his head, at least not one being paid out by Lycan Link. It allowed him to relax, maybe dropping to a nine from a ten on his personal alertness scale. It wasn't much, but he took what he could get. Lycan Link's trackers had been a bitch to outsmart, but he'd done it, much to the head office's chagrin. As for his most recent employer, Deirdre and her crew, who knew what was going on in that arena.

According to Dante, the woman had scaled back, but why? Something to do with the mysterious Elijah Stone? Or had business turned bad? Not likely the latter. Lack of clients had never seemed to be a problem. It was staggering, the number of people in the world wanting to hire assassins and bodyguards that asked no questions.

He'd avoided those jobs as much as possible, preferring to focus on his own personal vendetta. The Purists, the anti-Fae, those had been his favoured targets; scum that didn't deserve to breathe the same air as the innocents of the world.

Deirdre hadn't appreciated how selective he'd been in the jobs he'd taken on. Pissing her off hadn't bothered him though; their encounters usually had ended with her infuriated by him. Maybe it was one of her remaining men who was watching him tonight, either with orders to kill him, or bring him back so she could do the job herself. Good luck with that, he thought to himself.

A change in Sam's pace drew his attention, though he gave no outward sign. She'd been walking beside him most of the night but had suddenly dropped back for some reason. He gave a mental shrug. This was her territory, her patrol. He was just along for the ride.

The feeling of being watched faded; the sense of danger lessening. Had the 'watcher' grown bored? Or maybe he was getting paranoid. Things were too quiet and he was jumping at shadows. Yeah, right. And Sam wasn't giving him a once over right now either.

Sam slowed her pace as they walked down the street, letting Damien take the lead. There was no strategic reason for her decision beyond pure aesthetics; the man was gorgeous and she wanted to ogle him. There was something about the way he moved that oozed confidence and strength. It wasn't a swagger—that would have been a complete turn off—no, just an innate... She struggled to find the right word.

Sexiness?

Yeah, that worked.

Damien was sex on legs and she could spend hours watching him move; fluid, graceful, effortless. Muscle, bone and flesh perfectly formed and finely tuned, working in unison. Just looking at him made her aware she was a female.

Good thing their patrol was almost over for the night or she might've had to shove him into a dark alley and jump him. She chuckled at the idea, and then picked up her pace so she drew even with him again. Enough with the eye candy, she told herself. Get back into Alpha mode.

It had been an uneventful patrol which was the way she liked it. A few years back, she'd have found such a night boring, even a disappointment. In those early days, she'd been over vigilant, picking fights with young thugs, covering extensive miles each night while criss-crossing the city. Now she knew better. Her patrols were methodical, aimed at maintaining a sense of her presence rather than shoving it down everyone's throat. She no longer viewed all other shifters as a threat if they happened to pass through the area; she simply made sure they knew she was there and expected them to behave. There was no point in looking for trouble, it found you all too easily. Expending energy on pointless confrontations was…well…pointless. And human problems like car theft and graffiti weren't her concern, either. She had enough to do; as long as her family members were safe and there were no threats to her territory, she could let the small things go.

Damien, however, she wasn't sure about. She slid a glance his way, noting how his nostrils were flaring, his gaze darting about as if he expected an attack at any moment. Alert? Or looking for trouble? No doubt his life as a rogue was filled with more adventure than a simple evening patrol provided. Too bad. No matter how hot he looked, she couldn't afford to have him causing an unwarranted disturbance, not when Lycan Link might have her under observation.

"Something wrong?"

He gave a start, then scowled. "Nope."

Huh. A stellar conversationalist. Well, if he wasn't going to talk, then she would. The bio he'd sent her said he'd worked as a mercenary and specialized in information acquisition, whatever the hell that might mean. "So what did you do as a mercenary?"

"You don't want to know." A shuttered look came over him again, but she didn't let that stop her.

"Really?" She feigned a look of surprise. "You can read my mind and know that my mouth is moving without permission from my brain? That I asked a question just to fill the dead air space?"

The corner of his mouth curled briefly at her sarcasm before returning to a flat, uncompromising line. "I'll rephrase my answer. You might want to know, but I have no plans of telling you."

"Why?"

He didn't answer immediately, instead giving her an icy look. When she didn't back down, a muscle began to work in his jaw giving her the distinct impression he was waging some internal battle. Maybe debating what was greater; his desire to tell her to piss off or his need for the job. The job must have won for he sighed loudly and finally answered her question.

"When I finish an...assignment...that part of my life is gone and I don't bring it up again." He paused and then added, "It helps keep the guilt at bay." There was bitterness in his voice that caused Sam to bite back the cutting comment she'd been about to make.

"Okay, let's try this. You seem edgy. Have you done much patrolling before or was last night the first time?"

"Some."

Sam rolled her eyes. She stopped, grabbed his arm and spun him to face her. "Listen, Damien. I don't want to play damned twenty questions. I want to learn something about the newest member of my pack, my fucking *Beta,* for heaven's sake! How the hell am I supposed to know what skills you possess, if I can depend on you in a crisis, if I don't know anything about you?"

Damien's face clouded, his eyes narrowing to mere slits. She expected him to lash out, even readied herself for a verbal attack at the very least. Instead, he visibly reined in his temper. Curious. Did he need this job that badly? Sam tucked that tidbit of information away.

"I've done patrols both in urban centres and the wilderness. I'm good at picking up anomalies in the atmosphere; scents or sounds that shouldn't be there. I don't react rashly and I don't use more force than necessary. If there's a crisis, you can count on me."

"Thanks, that's all I wanted to know." Sam gave a nod and, without another word, continued on her way. She could sense Damien watching her, and managed to take a good dozen steps before he began to follow her.

With his longer legs, it took him no time to catch up. "What about you? Can I count on you?"

She smiled, appreciating how he came back swinging rather than being cowed by a simple tongue lashing. It wasn't often anyone stood up to her. "Yeah, you can count on me. I've got your back if need be."

He nodded. "It's been a while since I've had a partner I could count on."

"By choice or because of circumstances?"

"A bit of both." He shoved his hands into his pockets and his shoulders hunched ever so slightly, enough to let her know she was probing a sensitive subject. Fine. She'd let it go…for now.

Sam turned the corner and Damien followed. They were in a quieter area now. No night life happened on this stretch of street. Not far now; they'd be home in twenty minutes tops. She began to envision her bed. God, she was tired. Bypassing the full moon run the other night had been necessary, but she missed the opportunity to relax and let her inner wolf take control for a while. Being in charge day in and day out wasn't all it was cracked up to be. How humans did it, not having the tension releasing rush of shifting, she couldn't begin to imagine. Of course, they didn't have another creature living symbiotically inside—

Damien nudged her with his elbow and she instantly went on alert. She glanced at him, then followed the direction of his gaze.

The street was devoid of traffic, the storefronts in darkness, their windows staring blankly out at the empty sidewalks. There was no sign of life…except for the flicker of light coming from the back of the store they stood near. It was

Mr. Marcello's and everyone knew he didn't work late. For as far back as she could recall, the man had closed his shop at six and retreated to his upstairs apartment for the evening.

"Is it our concern?" Damien spoke in hushed tones.

She flicked a surprised look his way—apparently he knew when to fight and when to put differences aside for the sake of a job—and then looked back at Mr. Marcello's. Normally, she'd not get involved; human crimes were for human cops. But…

"Mr. Marcello is a long standing friend of my grandfather's."

"He knows?" It wasn't an idle question. Mr. Marcello's knowledge—or lack thereof—as to their true identity would influence how they'd proceed.

She shrugged. "He suspects, but has never asked; it's like the elephant in the room. Work under the assumption that he doesn't. I don't want a damned DC showing up on my doorstep." A Damage Control agent having to clean up after her would give Sinclair another weapon to use against the pack.

Damien didn't reply, only jerking his head to indicate she should take the alley to the back of the building. At first she bristled that he would assume control of the situation, but since it was exactly what she'd have done, decided to let it go. He could watch from the front, she'd handle the action at the rear.

As soon as Sam disappeared from sight, Damien double-checked that no one was watching and then began studying the shop's door and windows. The wire for the alarm system was easy to locate and…he visually followed it up and around the window…it was a dummy. Not connected at all, just there to give the impression of security to anyone who casually glanced at the entrance. Shaking his head, he used his pocketknife to lift the latch then tested the door. The handle turned soundlessly, but a wind chime was hanging near the top, designed to warn of anyone entering. Cautiously easing his arm in and around, he placed his hand over the chimes so they wouldn't jingle and slipped inside.

Betrayed: Book Two – The Road To Redemption

For a moment, he didn't move, allowing his eyes to adjust to the darkness. He could hear low voices coming from the back; no sounds of violence, though at least one voice was agitated. Moving carefully, he began to make his way to the rear of the store, searching the shadows for signs of movement, carefully manoeuvring through the maze of antiques and collectables.

Testing the air, he picked up the scent of furniture polish, wood, humans... And lilacs? Dante or was an actual potpourri being used in the store?

Adrenaline rushed through his system and he forced himself to stay controlled. Low, even breathing, silent measured steps. If Dante was back there, this was his chance to grab the bastard and rid the world of the man's sorry hide.

Damien inched even closer to the back room. It was separated from the main area by a half-drawn curtain. Through the gap, he caught glimpses of two men in profile. One—an older gentleman—was in a chair by a table, while the other was balancing his weight with his hand on the table, leaning forward in a menacing fashion. Yeah, it was Dante. He'd recognize the man's methods anywhere. Snooping, stealing, intimidating; all part of Dante's arsenal.

"You know more than you're telling me, old man." Dante hissed. "I know you were there. You saw it all happen. You wrote about it in this." An old leather-bound book came into view as Dante waved it about.

"Where did you get that?" The older man half stood to grab the book, but Dante moved it out of reach.

"You need to keep your windows locked, Marcello." Dante flipped the book open and scanned the pages. "This made for interesting reading."

"You have no right!" The man—Marcello—protested. "My personal journals are not for public consumption."

"Maybe yes. Or maybe no." Dante held the book open wide and shoved it in the man's face. "I found this. You ripped a page out. I can see the raw edges."

The old man's face visibly blanched. "Some cognac was spilled…"

"Right, and there's gold at the end of a rainbow." Dante snorted. "Never mind. I've pieced the whole story together and soon Harper will know of it, too."

"No!" The old man began to stand once more, but Dante shoved him back into his seat.

"Shut up and listen. If you want to keep this under wraps, then you'll have to pay for the privilege."

"Blackmail?" Marcello's face started to flush.

"Smart man." Satisfaction oozed from Dante's voice. "I'll take the first instalment now." There was a rustling sound, then the creak of metal followed by an angry snort. "Your cash on hand is suspiciously low. Do you have another safe hidden somewhere?"

Damien could hear items being shoved aside as Dante started searching, loud thuds as objects hit the ground; all background sounds for Marcello's protests.

"No. I've nothing else. I swear. I...I had to make a large payout yesterday and—" The man's voice was suddenly cut off and Damien could see Dante grabbing the fellow by the throat.

Time to make his move. Damien stepped forward just as someone—likely Sam—pounded on the backdoor.

"Mr. Marcello? Are you all right? It's Samantha. Let me in!"

Dante swore, shoved Marcello aside and turned to exit the room only to skid to a stop when he realized Damien was blocking the way.

Damien curled his lip and barely held back a low growl. Both he and his wolf were anticipating making Dante pay for his sins. Dante, however, wasn't nearly as eager for a confrontation. He spun around and grabbed a wooden chair, then rushed towards the door.

Mr. Marcello moved to stop Dante at the same time Damien leapt forward. The two collided and in the few seconds it took for Damien to right the older man, Dante had made it to the door. As Sam burst into the room, Dante brought the chair crashing down on her head. Sam gave a startled cry, staggered and Dante pushed past her, disappearing into the alley.

"You okay?" Damien barely waited for Sam to nod before heading out in pursuit of Dante. What the bastard was up to, he had no idea, but it couldn't be anything good.

Once outside, Damien glanced left, then right. There was no sign of his quarry, though the faint scent of lilacs at least gave him an idea as to which way to head. Dante had headed towards the street, damn him. The man was too clever for his own good. If he'd kept to the back alleys, Damien could have tracked him as a wolf, but on city streets, he had to stay human.

The trail was easy enough to follow; the scent of lilacs might dissipate quickly but the sound of Dante's running steps were obvious enough that even a pup could have tracked him. The man was opting for speed over stealth, heading towards the main street, likely hoping to get lost in the crowds; the main streets of a large city were never empty no matter what the time of day or night. Damien picked up his pace, ignoring the pain in his leg as his feet pounded on the concrete.

There, straight ahead!

He could see Dante only two blocks away, standing at the corner. The man had stopped running for some reason. Had the coward decided to fight like a Lycan? Damien clenched his fists in anticipation only to skid to a shocked stop as he watched a city bus pull up and Dante climb onboard.

Fucking hell and damnation! He watched the man take a seat then turn to salute him through the window before the bus pulled away. Damien kicked a nearby garbage can in frustration. Dante had eluded him again.

"I'm okay, Mr. Marcello. Really." Sam reassured the elderly man yet again as she finished putting pieces of the broken chair into a garbage can.

"But—"

"He hit the doorframe, not me. I only yelled because I was so surprised." Sam hoped Mr. Marcello wouldn't think to look for damage to the woodwork; with any luck she'd be able to add a few marks before the idea popped into his head. "Oh dear, look at all the books he knocked down!" As planned, her comment distracted the man and he began to try to restore order to the other corner of the room.

Sam gave her shoulder a surreptitious rub. Being hit by a chair wasn't at the top of her list of fun ways to spend the evening. She wondered if Damien had caught the fellow and, if so, what he was doing with him. Hopefully, he was dragging the bastard's ass back here so they could call the police. It made her blood boil to think that a two-bit thief would pick on a sweet old man like Mr. Marcello.

"Did he manage to get much in cash or jewels?" She began to help Mr. Marcello straighten the room.

"Er...no." Mr. Marcello paused. "There wasn't a large sum in the safe."

"That's good." Sam narrowed her eyes, not sure if the older man was lying or just nervous. Likely the latter since there was no point in lying about a simple robbery. "Did you hear him breaking in?"

"I heard movement down here and came to investigate." He tightened his hands on a book he was holding. "Miss Samantha, did you hear what he was saying to me?"

"No. I started pounding on the door as soon as I got here. Why?"

He seemed about to speak, then shook his head. "Nothing. Just...thank you."

Damien returned empty handed. The thief had gotten away, much to her disappointment, and Mr. Marcello didn't want to make a report to the police for some reason. Since there was nothing else she could do about the matter, she let it drop. While she considered Mr. Marcello a long-standing friend, almost a member of the pack, he was still a human and she shouldn't allow herself to get too involved.

After making sure all the doors and windows were locked, she and Damien left with assurances from Mr. Marcello that he was perfectly fine after the ordeal and didn't need anyone to stay with him.

"This is the first time that anyone has ever tried to rob Mr. Marcello." Sam commented as they walked back to the pack house.

"Robbery? Is that what he called it?" Damien gave her a sharp glance, relieved she wasn't asking about Dante. He'd been expecting her to make some comment about why his 'friend' was at Marcello's, but obviously she hadn't recognized the man. She'd only had a glimpse of him in the dim light of Club Mystique, and tonight, he'd been charging at her with a chair. Not the best of conditions for making a positive identification.

"Well, yeah. What else would you call it when someone breaks in and tries to steal your money?"

Damien grunted, his brow furrowed. Obviously, Marcello hadn't told Sam the whole story and, due to the scent mask, Sam hadn't realized it was a Lycan roughing the man up. Dante was planning on blackmailing Marcello over something the shopkeeper obviously didn't want Harper to know. But which Harper? And what exactly was the secret? And how did Dante know about it? Of course, Dante had a knack for discovering every secret out there, though how he did it was a mystery.

Marcello's problem really wasn't any of his business, Damien decided. He was here to find evidence against the Chicago pack to prove their leadership was unfit. And unless Marcello was keeping a secret that could prove that, there was no need to get involved. Of course, he'd never know if the secret was significant or not unless he uncovered it and that meant tracking down Dante. His inner wolf thumped its tail. Hunting Dante was an immensely appealing prospect.

Chapter 10

Sam drummed her fingers on her desk as she contemplated her newest pack member. Damien had been here for three days. During that time he'd been a model Beta, going on patrols with her at night, assisting her when she installed better locks on Mr. Marcello's windows. He helped around the pack house by doing much needed repairs. He'd even taken Chris under his wing which removed one of her main headaches; the boy had grown up surrounded by adults and kept trying to act like one. The Academy would be a good place for him in a few years if she could find the money to sponsor him; with the way his grades were, she doubted the boy would qualify for a scholarship.

Something about Damien made her think he'd been at the Academy. He might be able to provide her with some information…or not. The man wasn't very forthcoming. That was likely the rogue in him. Social skills usually weren't their strong point.

He was good at verbal sparring, though. She grinned as she thought back over some of their conversations. It was fun to push his buttons and see him lose his brooding expression. And he gave as good as he got. Battling wits with him was…interesting.

The only real complaint she had against the man was that he had a habit of going off on his own with no warning, only to return a few hours later looking as if he'd like to rip someone's face off. He never mentioned what he'd been up to, merely disappearing into the cellar and then reappearing some time later covered in sweat and in a more pleasant mood.

If he'd been an established pack member, she'd likely let it slide for a while, but Damien was a newbie and her Alpha instincts were on alert. As soon as he returned from his current jaunt, she planned on confronting him.

Nicky Charles

Almost on cue, he appeared. Through her office window, she could see him coming down the sidewalk. His stride was long and fluid yet the set of his shoulders conveyed his mood even before she could make out his face. She watched him run lightly up the steps; the front door was used more now that he'd repaired them. He disappeared from her view, but she could hear his booted feet thudding on the porch and…the front door slammed shut. She leaned back in her chair, rather smug that she'd pegged him so quickly.

In her mind's eye, she watched him walk towards the kitchen, grab a bottle of water from the fridge and head out the back door towards the cellar, all without saying a word. As usual, he'd returned pissed off and she was about to discover why.

She logged out of the email she'd been answering and pushed her chair back with carefully controlled movements. Anticipation of the confrontation had her adrenalin already starting to pump. It wasn't that she was hoping for a fight, but the memory of their first brawl played through her mind. Confronting someone who matched her skill level didn't happen often and she was looking forward to the competition.

Taking her time, she headed outside and around to the cellar, allowing him to settle into his routine before she descended into the exercise room. At the most, ten minutes had elapsed. Not long, but sufficient that a fine sheen of sweat was beginning to form on his skin. He'd stripped off his shirt, the discarded garment lying on the floor beside his bottle of water.

The weights on the machine made a staccato rhythm as he lifted and lowered them, his rapid breathing punctuating the chorus. For a moment, she paused at the bottom of the steps, admiring the flexing of his muscles, the look of intense concentration on his face. Being an Alpha didn't make her immune to the sight of a ripped male.

"You need something?" He growled the words, his brows lowered. Of course, he'd been aware of her presence.

"Yeah. I do." She stepped into the room and stopped in front of him, her hands planted on her hips.

"Spit it out, then." He released the weights and leaned forward to wipe his face on his shirt.

"Where were you?"

He stilled, the material still covering part of his face. Slowly, he finished drying himself before letting the t-shirt fall to the floor.

"And if you say 'out', I'll kick you in the nuts."

Damien cocked an eyebrow, but for once her verbal jab didn't bring a curl to the corner of his mouth. Funny, she hadn't realized how much she looked forward to seeing that flash of amusement on his face. Instead, he grabbed his water bottle from its spot on the floor. After a long drink, he replied. "I had things to do."

"Such as?"

Swinging his leg over the bench, he stood up and walked to the punching bag. "None of your business."

She followed him. "I'm your Alpha. Everything you do is my business."

"No. You're not my Alpha. I don't have an Alpha. I answer to no one." He punched the bag and it swung towards her.

Sam punched it in return, sending it swinging back towards him. "You answer to me. While you're here, you're my responsibility. Book of the Law, Section 5, paragraph nine."

He held onto the bag. "'*An Alpha is responsible for all Lycans residing in his territory, even if those Lycans are not members of the pack. The Alpha will ensure all Lycans follow the Book of the Law and conduct themselves in such a manner so as to not endanger, or bring undue attention to, the Lycans who reside there.*' But you forgot subsection two. "*...provided that the Lycan in question does not have an Alpha in another territory. Transient Lycans may use a letter of exemption from an Alpha so they are not bound by the dictates of another pack.*'"

"You can quote the Book of the Law?" His response momentarily distracted her.

"I'm a rogue. Not an idiot. And yes, I've picked things up here and there." He sent the punching bag back in her direction and she neatly caught it.

"I'd argue that you aren't transient. You're living here." He was silent and she pushed her advantage. "Plus, you don't have a letter of exemption. So, tell me, what are you up to?"

He clamped his mouth tightly shut. She had a feeling he had a valid rebuttal, but some reason was reluctant to use it. Instead, he glowered at her.

She returned the look full force. "I asked you a question and you *will* answer."

"I don't have to put up with this crap." He moved to leave and she stepped in front of him not in the least fazed by the cold look on his face.

"You're not leaving until you tell me what you're up to." When he tried to step around her, she grabbed his arm and yanked him back. She could see him clenching his jaw, knew his temper was rising. Her wolf urged her to press him further, to engage in a fight to prove she was the dominant one here.

"You don't want to do that." There was a definite warning in his voice. "If we fight, I'll win and you really don't want to lose to me."

"As if."

"I mean it, Sam. You're good, but I could have taken you in the alley if we'd been fighting for keeps."

"How?" She jutted her chin.

"You move your left foot before you throw a punch. You drop your arm too much when you do a roundhouse kick and you don't get it up fast enough afterwards. It leaves your chin exposed."

She frowned. Years ago, her instructor had often told her about projecting her punches through her stance, but she'd thought she'd fixed that problem. And no one had ever mentioned her arm. "Show me."

"No. I'm not in the mood." He took a step towards the door, but she grabbed his arm again.

"We're not having sex. You don't have to be in a 'mood'." She rolled her eyes. "Cancel that. Actually, you look in the perfect 'mood' for a fight."

Damien sighed heavily. "Fine." He moved towards the middle of the matted floor space, but she wasn't waiting. Her wolf was pushing her, eager to confront the male before them. Swinging out her leg, she caught Damien in the back of the thigh.

"Why you—!" He staggered but caught himself and spun around to face her.

"Never turn your back on your opponent," she jeered, nimbly hopping out of reach.

"If that's the way you want to play it." He launched himself at her and she barely sidestepped in time. As it was his shoulder brushed hers. It was enough to knock her off balance and, when she leapt to the side to avoid his kick, she landed awkwardly.

Damien moved in, landing a hit to her ribs then one to her thigh before she regained her footing. He attacked with a calm, focused intensity, each kick and punch delivered in rapid succession. Sam blocked him over and over, barely having time to deliver any strikes of her own. When she did, they counted as evidenced by his grunts of pain.

Left, right. Spin and kick. Keep her arm up. Dodge to the side. Duck under his blow and come up inside.

Adrenaline surged through her, heightening her senses. His scent, the sound of his breathing, the tang of sweat in the air. All her attention was on the man before her. The purpose of the fight, the reason she'd confronted him to begin with, faded into the background.

Sweat dripped down her face; she shook her head to clear her vision and then moved to deliver a roundhouse kick forgetting his comment about her dropping her arm too much. That was when he made his move.

Damien knocked her backwards, the force of his blow reverberating through her so that she staggered and fell against the wall. Before she could react, he moved in, his hand gripping her throat, his body pressed fully against hers.

For a moment they froze in place. Damien's lips were drawn back in a snarl, the silvery blue of his eyes seeming harder and colder than usual. Sam swallowed with difficulty, her neck stretched so that her chin tilted upward, the vulnerable arteries exposed. She was vividly aware of how her damp t-shirt stuck to her skin, the way every breath he took caused his chest to rub against her breasts. His thigh was tucked between hers, his fingers pressed into her flesh. He could easily crush her windpipe, yet she wasn't scared. Exhilarated, breathless, horny...

Damien took a deep breath and slowly released her throat. As he moved to step back, her wolf howled in protest and, before she could even think, she reached up, grabbed his head and kissed him hard.

His body stiffened, but she didn't care. Here was a male she could meet on her own terms. Rising to her toes, she assaulted his mouth and, when he began to relax she pulled him closer, dragging her fingers through his hair, pulling at the silky black strands.

Sam felt him hesitantly wrap his arms around her. For some reason he was fighting his desire for her, but his resolve was crumbling. Yes! She wanted him, needed him. Whimpers escaped her as she urged him onward and then, as if released from a tight rein, he crushed her to him, kissing her as if he'd been celibate for years. He grabbed her hair, holding her head still as his tongue plunged into her mouth. She met him, stroke for stroke, challenging him, teasing him, revelling in this new battle they waged.

Desire raged out of control and she straddled his thigh, desperate to be closer, to feel more of him. He wanted her. The evidence nudged against her through their clothing. She clawed his shoulders, arched her back as he squeezed her breast. His hand cupped her rear, lifting her, and she wrapped her legs around his waist.

Betrayed: Book Two – The Road To Redemption

Damien rocked against her and she moaned at the building inferno within her. Licking his jaw, she made her way down his neck. Her tongue encountered a slight mark on his skin, what felt like an old scar and just as she kissed it, he jerked as if ice water had been dumped on him.

Before she could even process what was happening, he was pushing her away, barely giving her enough time to get her feet under her before stepping back.

He was breathing heavily, his eyes reflecting his confusion.

"Damien?" She took one step towards him, but he backed farther away.

"No. I... Sorry." He dragged his hand through his hair and shook his head. "This was a mistake."

"The kiss? Or the fight?" Sam frowned, trying to understand.

"The kiss. Maybe both." He looked away. "I'm mated, Sam."

A cold feeling washed over her at those words. Had he lied? She hated liars. "I thought you said she was dead."

Damien blinked. "Yes. Beth is...dead." He swallowed hard and began to back away from her. "Uh... Listen, we'll talk later...about fighting techniques. I have to go." He turned and walked quickly towards the stairs.

Sam debated about pushing the issue. After all, she still hadn't found out what he was up to when he went out on his own, but this wasn't the time. Besides, she wanted to mull over their encounter. His mate was dead; she should feel guilty that she was relieved by that fact. Wishing someone dead wasn't...nice. Her mouth twisted at the bland word, but how else did you put it?

"Tonight on patrol. We'll talk then." She called the words after him. He didn't reply.

As the sound of his footsteps faded, she leaned back against the wall and slowly ran her tongue over her lips. The taste of him lingered there and the animal inside her hummed its approval. Strange. Her wolf had never reacted this way before. Human males were, quite frankly, boring. And Lycan males… Well, being a female Alpha had certain disadvantages in that area. Her grandfather had warned her numerous times to be wary. *'You're attractive enough to get a mate on your own merit, but your position in the pack will require extra caution. You'll never know if a male is simply trying to find a fast track to power. If anyone shows an interest in you, double check his motives first.'*

She'd heeded his advice, turned away a few losers who thought to fuck their way into power, but that shouldn't be a problem with Damien. He was a rogue who picked up odd jobs here and there, not the type to want to take over the pack. Of course, rogues didn't settle down, but was that what she was looking for?

He is a male worthy of us. The others were not. Her wolf cleared up the confusion. *This is the one we should keep as our mate.*

"Really? You know this already?" Sam chuckled at the animal's quick decision, but then narrowed her eyes as she caught sight of her own reflection in the mirror. Puffy lips, flushed cheeks, her hair askew. She ran her hand down her body, recalling how it had felt to have Damien's hands on her, to feel his body rocking against her aching core. Even now she still felt the need for him.

Damn. She wasn't looking for a mate, she had enough to do right now. But Damien had potential. He was a good fighter, sexy, plus he made her laugh. And her wolf approved. Indecisiveness wasn't typical of her. Weighing all the factors, she gave a quick nod and set her course of action.

Damien stood in front of the bathroom mirror staring at the faint scar on his neck, the physical reminder of his blood bond with Beth. He touched it with his fingertip, tracing the slight roughness, trying to recall how it had felt to have Beth kiss him there. Instead of the usual flood of old memories, he could only think of Sam, the roughness of her tongue on his skin, the feel of her lean, muscled body against his, the way her scent lingered on him.

When she'd pulled his head down and kissed him, he'd been shocked. That was the last thing on his mind today. He'd been too angry over his failure to find Dante to even think of sex. But when Sam's hot mouth had teased his, desire had slammed into him. Feelings long denied had clamoured for release, and he'd allowed himself to get caught up in the moment.

Even now, his body ached uncomfortably. A quick glance down showed his arousal would still be obvious even to the most casual observer. Giving a snort of disgust, he stepped into the shower, turned on the cold water and gritted his teeth.

The icy drops stung against his still sensitive skin, but he welcomed the discomfort. It was a small enough punishment for the sin he'd almost committed. He'd pledged his life to Beth using the old, traditional human vows of sickness and health, good times and bad, 'til death…

"I'm mated, Sam."

"I thought you said she was dead."

"Yes…"

That snippet of conversation played over and over in his head. Why had he agreed? Yes, Beth was dead, but her spirit lived on in his heart. Her dying words had asked him to never forget, and he'd kept the vow since that day. Now guilt twisted inside him.

His wolf paced restlessly, too. It was disturbed by the encounter, not angry with him like in the past, but for once unsure of what the correct course of action might be.

"Ha, I have the upper hand this time, old boy." Damien shut off the water and grabbed a towel. "What we need to do is focus on our job and forget about Sam Harper. And that should be pretty easy. After all, she's nothing like Beth."

He concentrated on bringing an image of Beth to mind. Her dove grey eyes, her gentle smile, her long hair he loved to wrap his hands in. For once, the picture waivered, refusing to come into focus. Shocked, he froze in place, the towel clenched in his hand. His breathing quickened, a nervous fluttering began in his stomach. What was going on?

Furrowing his brow, he tried harder, imagining her light laughter, her soft touch. Like a will-o-the-wisp her memory drifted by, escaping as he attempted to latch on to it. How had she tasted when he kissed her? And her scent had been…

When he could finally see her, he exhaled, the feeling of panic that had been threatening easing off.

Beth was still with him.

Chapter 11

Sam sighed and wished she'd ignored the summons to her grandfather's room. Over the past several months she'd been going through some of the boxes in the attic, sorting out old ledgers and journals based on which Alpha they had belonged to; making digital copies of the most important historical data, and purging what didn't need to be kept. She'd been periodically giving him some of the items to read, thinking it would keep him busy. However, this latest batch, his own private journals, had sent him into a querulous mood for some reason and now she was taking the brunt of it. For the past half hour, he'd been grilling her about how she was managing the pack, with pointed references to how things had been done back in his day.

"And why haven't I met this rogue you hired yet?" Sam's grandfather growled at her from his chair near the window.

"You've been sick the past few days. And you know that your medication makes you sleepy. You wouldn't want to meet him when you weren't at your best."

He clamped his mouth tightly shut, obviously not pleased that she'd pointed out his weakness. However, it was the truth and Sam tried to stick to plain speaking when it came to her grandfather, despite his age and health.

Rather than concede that she was right, he came at the topic from another angle. "I saw him come in earlier today. I want you to bring him to me now."

"Now?" Hell. She wasn't sure what had gone wrong with Damien in the exercise room and had no idea what type of a mood he might be in.

"That's right. Otherwise you'll come up with another damned excuse."

"It wasn't a '*damned* excuse', it was a perfectly good one. But, I'll bring him here if that's what it takes to make you happy."

"Good." Her grandfather folded his arms and glared at her. "Get moving. I haven't got all day."

She bit her tongue to hold back a rude reply. There was no point in provoking a slanging match. Reluctantly, she headed upstairs to find Damien.

He responded slowly to her knock and she wondered what he'd been up to. The look on his face was less than welcoming and he made no effort to invite her in. Surely he couldn't be brooding over their kiss. It had been a simple lip lock, not an orgy for heaven sake!

Having put up with her grandfather's mood for the last half hour, she wasn't going to give Damien an opportunity to start in on her. Her plan was to forget the small talk and get straight the point. "I need you to come with me."

"Why?" He leaned against the doorjamb, his expression cool.

"Command performance. My grandfather wants to meet you."

Damien raised his brows but pushed off from the wall and followed her. "I'm surprised he hasn't asked to see me before this. Alphas usually meet new members as soon as they arrive."

"He hasn't been feeling up to having visitors. Besides, as acting Alpha, I carry out all the required duties and," she paused on the landing to look at him, "you aren't technically a member of the pack. This is a temporary position."

A shadow passed over his eyes, but it was gone so swiftly she might have been wrong. Yet when he spoke, the typically sarcastic manner she'd come to expect from him seemed forced.

"Any words of warning before I face him? Hiram was telling me your grandfather had quite a reputation in his day."

Sam shook her head, imagining the tales that had been told. Hiram was a storyteller at heart and could weave fact and fiction into the most plausible plots. She kept encouraging him to write them down, but as far as she knew he'd yet to act on her suggestion. "In his younger days he did, though Hiram might have exaggerated a bit."

Damien gave a soft huff of laughter. "One of the tricks of command is to have the reputation as a hard nose precede you."

"True. But Grandfather's bark and bite are pretty similar. Watch what you say." Having reached their destination, she tapped on the door to the older man's room.

"No need to knock. I know you're there. I'm not deaf, just laid up with my back and a damned cold." The older man growled the words and, despite their differences, she gave Damien a look of sympathy before ushering him in.

Damien glanced about the room Sam had led him to noting that, like the rest of the house, it had been renovated at one time, the original dimensions having been changed perhaps to convert several single rooms into a suite. This particular space had a small sitting area with a fireplace, two chairs and table. A door, ajar on the far side, gave glimpses of a bedroom and bathroom beyond that. It was relatively neat, except for the large stack of old books and files that sat on a table and spilled over onto the floor. He took it all in before focusing on the elderly man who was eyeing him up and down with a look of distrust. So this was the elusive Samuel Harper, Senior.

"Grandfather, this is Damien, the rogue I've been telling you about."

The older man shifted his gaze to Sam. "And who else would it be? I assume you wouldn't ask in a stranger off the street."

Sam sighed. "I was trying to make a polite introduction. And stop acting like some constipated old man."

Damien bit the inside of his cheeks to keep from smiling. Sam seemed to have a comeback for every occasion.

"Hrmph." The man glared at her before switching his attention back to Damien. "You look impressive enough. What's your background?"

He shrugged. "I'm a rogue. I've worked my way back and forth across the country doing odd jobs."

"And on what side of the law were those jobs?"

"Whatever side they needed to be." Damien hooked his thumbs in his belt loops, his posture not quite slouching, but not at the stiff attention he was sure the old Alpha usually expected.

For perhaps the count of a minute, he stared at Damien, tapping his fingers on the arm of his chair. Damien waited, casually looking about the room. The stack of books interested him. They appeared to be old journals. Was that how Harper spent his time now? Reminiscing about his glory days?

Finally, the old man nodded. "Honest. I like that. I've never known a rogue that didn't cross the line a time or two. So…" He jerked his head towards Sam. "What do you think of my granddaughter?"

Sam stiffened at his side. Damien flicked a glance at her and then looked back at old man Harper.

"She's doing a good job. I've no complaints from what I've seen."

"As it should be. I've trained her for the position almost since she was old enough to walk. My son never had an aptitude for the job, but Sam here, she took to it like a natural. Smart, quick, a good fighter. Everything an Alpha could want in a successor."

"And a female." Damien murmured the words. Beside him, he heard Sam's swift intake of breath. He'd struck a nerve, but that was too bad. It was the grandfather's reaction that mattered.

"Yes. Well…" The old man cleared his throat and twisted his mouth. "I know what you're thinking, and I'll admit I had my doubts at first. However, her father died before giving me another heir, which left Sam as the only successor. It took me a few years to come to terms with the situation, but once I did, I worked her hard and she met every challenge."

"I'm still in the room, you know." Sam interrupted, narrowing her eyes.

Damien ignored her comment and kept his eyes on her grandfather. "So you feel that lineage is more important than suitability for the position?"

Sam turned on him, waves of outrage emanating from her. "If you've got a problem with me, you tell me to my face!"

At the same time, her grandfather raised his voice. "Chicago has belonged to my family for over a hundred and fifty years. Every generation has produced an Alpha and this one is no different. Sam is the best qualified member of the pack."

Damien put up his hands as if to hold off the verbal attack. "Just playing devil's advocate since you're worried about being taken over."

The old man leaned back in his chair, the colour that had briefly graced his face now fading leaving him looking grey and tired. "You're smart, boy. That's how Sinclair will be thinking, but it won't do him any good. I'm still hanging on to my title." Abruptly, he ended the audience with a flick of his hand. "You can leave now, but I'll be keeping an eye on you. Sam, you stay."

"I'll see you for patrols." Sam shot Damien a meaningful look.

He could only begin to imagine how patrols would go tonight. A thorough grilling, that's what he had to look forward to and as to his comment about females… Maybe a set of earplugs would be useful.

As he returned to his room, he mulled over the meeting he'd had. Sam's grandfather was a cantankerous old man who seemed to enjoy watching others squirm; rather like a geriatric version of his old boss, Captain Fielding.

Sam had stood up to the aged Alpha, though. Of course, she would have had to learn that skill at an early age given that she'd been 'in training' for most of her life. It was surprising that the man had spent the time on her. He seemed very old school and a female Alpha was unusual among their people. How long had it taken old man Harper to come to terms with the idea? And what had happened to the son, Sam's father? That might warrant some investigation.

He sat on the edge of his bed and pulled out his phone. The old man's insistence on keeping the pack in the family might be a point Kane could use. The successor to the position should always be the most capable wolf in the area. Packs weren't meant to be run like a royal family. Years ago that had been the case, but revisions to the law in the last half century had put an end to the practice.

And the old man's health was definitely in question. In the few days he'd been there, Damien had seen no evidence that the man ever left his room. His hands were thin, blue veins and gnarled knuckles showing, and his colouring was poor. There was a faint quaver in his voice, too, despite the growls and bluster. And the abrupt end to the meeting had likely been to hide the fact that the old Alpha had used up his energy.

Yes, definitely time to make a report to Kane.

He turned the phone over and over in his hands. Should he mention Dante? No. Kane had enough on his plate. This was his own problem. Dante and he had had run-ins before despite the fact that they were both supposedly working for the same side.

It galled him that, despite his warning, the bastard was still in the area and his attempts to track him down had fallen short. If he could devote all his time to the hunt, it might be a different story, but trying to do it on the sly was less than ideal. And Sam was already suspicious.

A smile tugged at the corner of his mouth. She kept him on his toes and, in different circumstances, he might have actually enjoyed the barbed banter they usually fell in to. Too bad he was here to bring about her downfall.

Elise curled up beside Kane, her hand idly tracing a path across his chest, their legs intertwined. He was stroking her hair, the gentle tug soothing as the afterglow of mating faded. Sex between them had always been amazing and this time had been no different. Her mate was a skilled lover and over the years they'd come to know each other's likes and dislikes as well as they knew their own.

Too bad it couldn't always be like this. No work, no pack members, no pressure from outside. The children napping so it was just the two of them in a warm cocoon where cuddling and making love was all they had to do. She smiled at the thought, knowing it was impossible but still wishing.

Kane's cell phone rang and his hand stilled on her hair then he gave a disgruntled groan. With a sigh, she detached herself from him and stared at the ceiling as he reached over to answer the call.

"Sinclair." It was some small consolation that his tone was gruff; he wasn't pleased at being interrupted either.

She stared at the ceiling, cursing the caller and wishing Kane had shut his phone off. Of course, that wasn't possible. He was the Alpha and, if an emergency arose, he had to be available; she'd heard that explanation over and over. The topic of conversation began to catch her attention and she cocked her head to hear more clearly.

"What do you have to report, Damien?...Really?...That's very interesting. I can probably use that to help build my case. Good work....Keep me posted."

Kane hung up and Elise rolled over to face him.

"Damien had some good news?"

"Yeah. Samuel Harper is treating his pack as if it were a dynasty. His granddaughter's been prepped to take over, regardless of whether or not she's the most suitable candidate."

"Is she? Suitable that is?"

Kane shrugged. "I've no idea. But that particular pack has been in the Harper family since its inception. It makes the process they use for choosing a successor highly suspect." He folded his arms behind his head, a pleased expression on his face. "I'd say there's a high degree of certainty that the Harper pack is about to lose control of Chicago."

"Hmm…"

Kane looked her way. "You don't sound happy. This is what we've been waiting for."

"I know…" She idly ran her hand over his chest.

He turned on his side to face her. "Don't you want us to gain control of Chicago? It will mean I can split the pack, have more free time, plus it's a strategically impressive move which should look good when they consider me for a position on High Council."

"I'm wondering how the Chicago pack is feeling, how I'd feel if the shoe was on the other foot. It must be sad to see your home being taken away."

"Everything changes," Kane countered. "They had their chance to run that territory but now it's time to move on."

"I suppose." She studied her mate, noting the faint lines on his face. He'd changed since they'd first met. The idealistic young Alpha she'd mated had matured. He was still amazingly good looking, the lines adding rather than detracting from his appearance. Some were from age, most were from stress and overwork. Of course, she'd changed too. Birthing two children had added weight and stretch marks. Kane was right, everything changed. The way it was changing was what had her concerned. "Are you sure this is a good move? That it will mean less work? Ever since you've set your sights on Chicago, you're busier than ever."

He shrugged and pulled her close. "Everything worth having requires work and I've got to look my best if I want that High Council position."

"But you'll be managing two territories, in two separate states, thousands of miles apart, and then if you get on High Council…"

"Elise, quit worrying. I can juggle three balls at once."

Leah chose that moment to wake up and begin to cry. Elise disentangled herself and pulled on a robe. "Real life is calling."

"She's been crying a lot lately."

"Teething. I've been up with her every night. I'm so tired in the mornings my eyes won't focus."

"I'll get up with her tonight."

"Thanks, I could really use an undisturbed night." She looked up from the knot she was tying in the sash of her robe but Kane wasn't watching. He already had his phone in his hand again. She stared at him for a moment, waiting for him to look her way, but he'd already tuned her out.

When they'd first mated, he'd always watched her dress and undress, his attention making her feel as if she were the most precious thing in the world. Now the phone and work held most of his attention. She felt the knot in her stomach twist again. Yeah, everything changed.

Chapter 12

"What sector are we patrolling tonight?" Damien had been waiting outside the pack house for about ten minutes before Sam made an appearance. She was late and he wondered what the holdup was. Chris trying to sneak out of the house again? Or maybe Jonah getting territorial in the kitchen? He didn't ask. Becoming interested in the pack members was pointless. He'd made his report to Kane and the Chicago pack's days were numbered. Besides, as Sam had pointed out earlier, he wasn't really a member, anyway.

"There are several forest preserves beyond O'Hare. They'd be a good place for a wolf to hide and, since Hiram is still picking up trace scents of an intruder..." She ran down the steps, tossing a couple of bottles of water his way. "We'll take the bikes and then shift when we get there."

He drew up a mental map of the area and nodded. Some time on the highway might be just what he needed to rid himself of the mood he was in. "So you still think Hiram is right? That there's another Lycan in the area?"

"Yep. I'm sure it has to be Sinclair's spy. And since none of my patrols have managed to track him down, he must be using the masking technology I've heard rumours of."

Damien didn't comment, keeping himself busy storing the water bottles in one of the saddlebags. Lycan Link's so-called 'secret defence' wasn't that much of a secret any more. Rumours about the scent mask were flying around the Lycan underworld, and some enterprising souls were producing synthetic street versions.

Sam kept talking. "If he's using a scent mask then he could be anywhere, watching us, taking notes. I've told everyone to look sharp, to go about their duties with no slacking off. I'm not letting Sinclair build a case against us for shoddy work."

"Why's Sinclair focusing on you?" He knew the answer but was curious as to Sam's perspective.

"Because he's a power hungry ass. I had some dealings with him a while back. Someone he had an issue with was in my territory and he wanted me to deal with the guy."

"And did you?"

"Yeah. Just not as fast as Sinclair wanted. He got it into his head that he could do a better job." Sam slung her leg over her motorcycle and turned on the engine. Damien did the same. Over the roar of the motors, she shouted. "Then his ass of a brother used the old Finding clause to claim a wolf that was in the area. We needed her, but did he care? No! The bastard took her right from under my nose. Well, not again. Sinclair isn't stealing anything else from me. This pack is mine." And with that, she took off.

Damien followed considering what she'd said. Yeah, from her point of view, Kane was a bastard. But from Kane's perspective, Chicago was a sizeable territory. It could easily sustain more Lycans. Too bad Sam felt as passionate as she did about her position as Alpha.

He leaned into a curve and concentrated on the joy of the ride. He sucked at moral dilemmas. Best to just do the job he'd been given.

But which job? His wolf asked. *Helping Kane save his family life? Or helping Sam save her home?*

They rode in silence, the noise of the engines preventing conversation. Damien followed Sam's lead as they wove through the streets and onto the open highway. The wind tugged at his clothing and pulled at his hair. He leaned lower, the engine throbbing beneath him. Scenery whipped past, mere blurs of green and grey and brown. Speed had always seemed freeing to him, blowing away his concerns, and that's what he needed right now. He gunned his engine and shot past Sam. A moment later, she was beside him, shooting a look his way, before inching ahead. For a while they battled against each other before settling for riding tandem. As they neared their destination, they slowed and then, as one, swung into the first nature preserve on their list for the night.

Sam brushed her hair back from her face and grinned at him. "Good ride."

He nodded, taking in the picture of her. For some reason, he found the sight of such a tiny woman astride a big motorcycle sexy as hell. Her eyes sparkled, a light flush of excitement stained her cheeks. It was good to see her like this. Sam was usually all business, which was odd for someone so young. She needed more fun in her life, he decided, thinking of his own youth. Did she ever cut loose and do something crazy for the hell of it?

She swung off her Harley and hung her helmet on the handles, her features assuming their usual 'all business' expression. "You go left, I'll head right. Meet back here in an hour."

"Sounds like a plan." He watched her shift and disappear from sight among the trees. His own wolf urged him to follow her. "She doesn't need our protection, boy." It was a hard fact to swallow. For most of his adult life he'd been in the role of protector, saviour even. But Sam was more of an equal. He wasn't quite sure how he felt about that.

Giving his head a shake, he changed forms and padded off into the wooded area. For all that the nature preserve was considered part of Chicago, it was easy to forget that a bustling city lay beyond its borders. The trees where thick, undergrowth abounded and evidence of wildlife was everywhere. Squirrels chattered in annoyance at his appearance and the faint rustling of grass let him know that rabbits had sensed his presence. Not many predators were in the area, though a fox had passed through recently. Most definitely no signs of a wolf nor was the telltale scent of lilacs to be found either.

No, Dante loved his creature comforts too much to spend his time holed up in a den. Of course, he couldn't tell Sam that. Instead, he spent his time exploring, allowing his wolf some freedom before eventually circling back to the appointed meeting spot.

He arrived early and took out a water bottle, chugging the contents. The moon was rising, no longer full as it had been a week ago, but still large enough to illuminate the small clearing and reflect on the tiny lake they'd parked beside. It was a hot evening, the air humid and sticky and he eyed the water longingly. Deciding he had enough time, he stripped down.

The dry fall grass pricked at his bare feet only to be replaced by the damp soil of the shore as he made his way to the water's edge. Frogs and insects chirped from the reeds while an owl hooted in a distant tree. He savoured the moment, allowing it to seep into him and ease the tension from his body. Slowly, he waded in, the water lapping about his legs, cool and refreshing. Taking a deep breath, he sank beneath the surface.

Sam returned to the clearing and was immediately drawn by the sound of splashing coming from the water. She approached the edge, noted Damien's pile of clothing on the ground and grinned. Her temporary Beta was skinny-dipping.

The surface of the water broke and Damien appeared. Moisture glistened on his broad chest and dripped down his belly, darkening the arrow of body hair that disappeared intriguingly into the water's surface. He raised his hands to sluice the water from his face.

"Naked Lycan in the moonlight." She called out the words and he turned to look at her.

"What?"

"Naked Lycan in the moonlight. That's what I'd call a picture of you right now."

"Are you insane?" He brushed the hair from his eyes.

"No more than usual. Enjoying yourself?"

"Yep. You should give it a try." He leaned back and floated in place, a glint in his eye.

She cocked her head considering his suggestion. They should continue on with the patrol but the implicit dare he'd issued stirred something within her.

Betrayed: Book Two – The Road To Redemption

He's challenging our courage, her wolf declared, pacing back and forth as it eyed the male who stood a few feet away. *Backing down is unacceptable.*

Sam grabbed the lower edge of her shirt and pulled it over her head. Next she sat down and tugged off her high-heeled boots before standing to shimmy out of her jeans. Only when she moved her hands to the front fastening of her bra, did she pause. It was black with a lace edge. She loved sexy underwear and wondered if it surprised him or not. A glance at his face showed his eyes were fixed on it. The fact that she had his attention pleased her. She bit back her smile and raised a brow instead. "You gonna watch?"

"You want me to?"

Did she? Her inner wolf said yes. She shrugged and undid the front fastening keeping her eyes locked on his face. As her breasts were revealed to him, his eyes appeared to darken and she was sure the rise and fall of his chest quickened.

She stepped close to the shore, all too aware of the gentle sway of her breasts, the way the humid night air caressed her naked skin. Knowing he was looking at her caused her own breathing to quicken and her nipples pebbled with excitement.

Without warning, Damien dove beneath the water.

For a split second, she was startled by his move and then laughed. His dare had left her feeling uncharacteristically light-hearted. Skimming off her panties, she ran into the water and was decently covered by the time he resurfaced near her.

"Didn't think I'd do it?" She taunted him while pushing her wet hair back from her face.

"I guess I should have known better."

"Uh huh."

His gaze swept over her and she resisted the instinctive move to cover herself with her hands. She knew he couldn't see anything important. Without her boots, the difference in their heights was emphasized. While the water lapped at his ribcage, it covered all but the upper slopes of her chest. Still, it gave her a curious thrill to think they were both naked and mere feet away from each other.

He cocked his head to the side. "Do you accept every challenge that comes your way?"

"Most. Unless they're crack-head stupid."

"And stripping in front of me isn't?"

"No. Not really." She looked away, took a deep breath and then stared directly into his eyes. "I like you, Damien."

The smile left his face, but she continued on.

"You're a lot like me. You don't take crap. You're tough and a good fighter. I can match wits with you, make a wisecrack and you have a comeback for it. Plus…" She flicked a glance over his chest and gave a crooked smile, "you're hot."

He huffed a laugh. "Thanks."

"Any time." She paused and wet her lips before broaching the next hurdle. "I know you were mated and that she's dead. It must be difficult."

"Yeah." He looked away. A closed look had come over his face, but she didn't let that deter her.

"But you have to move on. Life doesn't stop."

She watched as his muscles tightened and his jaw jutted. "And what do you know about that?"

Staring down at the water's surface, she moved her hand gently, causing a ripple to extend out in ever-growing rings. "My father never got along with my grandfather. They were two very different people. He left the pack as soon as he was old enough, moved west and married my mother. When I was four, we returned here." She made a wry face. "I was quite a shock to my grandfather."

"He didn't know he had a grandchild?" Damien glanced her way.

"He knew about me. Just not about my background." She made another ripple and watched how it lapped and curved about Damien's lower ribcage.

"What do you mean?"

"My eyes. They're violet."

"And…?"

"It's usually a sign of having Fae or witch in your background." She sighed. "Somewhere in my mother's pedigree, there was the proverbial 'black sheep' and it showed up in me."

"My mate was part Fae."

"Really?" Sam looked at him with interest. "Cool. I don't have enough tainted blood in my system to qualify me for any extra abilities."

"It's not tainted blood. Don't let anyone ever tell you that!" Anger laced his voice and he stepped closer, brushing his hand over her cheek in a comforting gesture, before resting it on her shoulder.

"I know. It's just an expression I've heard."

"A filthy one."

"Probably." She paused to gather her thoughts. Damien's thumb was stroking her shoulder ever so lightly, the heat from his palm emphasized by the coolness of the water lapping against her arm. She doubted he even realized what he was doing, but it felt good so she made no comment on his actions in the hope he'd continue. Clearing her throat, she spoke. "Soon after we got here my father died. He slipped and fell in front of the train."

"I'm sorry."

She nodded and stared off into the distance. "I was with him and saw the whole thing. One minute we were standing there and the next…someone brushed past us and he fell into the path of the train just as it was arriving. There was no time for the engineer to stop."

"What about your mother? Was she there?"

"No, but she moved away soon after. I don't think my grandfather made her feel very welcome given that she'd contaminated the blood line. I visit her every few years, but we've not much in common. There's too much of my grandfather in me, I guess."

She placed her hand on his chest. "So, you see? I know about loss and pain and moving on."

"Sam, I…"

"It's okay. I just want you to know where I stand. I'm interested in you, Damien." She reached up and kissed him briefly on the cheek. "And I might not let you forget it." Unexpectedly she reached low and pinched his hip before jumping back.

She laughed at his expression and then returned to her Alpha mode.

"We've wasted enough time. Five minutes to swim then we're back on patrol."

Damien watched her turn and strike out along the shore. Their conversation had been unexpected to say the least and had revealed a new side to Sam Harper. She was interested in him. Not shocking news given the way she'd kissed him in the cellar. And her life hadn't been an easy one. He frowned, thinking they had more in common than he'd expected.

Chapter 13

Kane watched Jacob pedal around the patio on his tricycle, his little legs pumping as fast as they could go. There was such a look of determination on the boy's face that he couldn't help but smile with pride.

"He'll make a fine Alpha one day."

"Does being an Alpha have to be his goal?" Elise frowned at him from the other side of the table. They were seated on the patio outside the kitchen supposedly enjoying a 'family' breakfast, but Elise was in a mood for some reason.

"What's wrong with wanting him to be an Alpha?"

"Well, he could be a doctor or an accountant. Something that would allow him some time with his family."

That again. "I'm spending time with the family. We're eating together." Kane gestured at the table between them. It was laden with waffles, bacon and orange juice. A pot of hot coffee was within arm's reach and bowls of cereal for the children were ready.

"Right. You've had two phone calls and answered four text messages since we sat down."

"I tried to keep them brief."

She ignored him and continued on with her theme. "And last night, you promised me you'd get up with Leah if she was teething."

"She didn't cry once all night." He glanced at his daughter who was seated in her highchair. Her cheeks were a telltale pink and she drooled as she chewed on a hard biscuit, but he hadn't heard her once during the night. Reaching over, he tapped her nose and she giggled giving him a still toothless smile.

"Ha! That's because you didn't come to bed until after three in the morning. She was screaming for hours before I finally got her settled."

He winced. With the office door shut and a set of ear buds in, he hadn't heard a thing. "Sorry. I got caught up researching legal precedents and didn't realize how late it was."

"And they were more important than your promise to me and your daughter?"

He clamped his mouth shut and counted to ten. "Elise, I said I was sorry. I know you're tired." His own eyes were gritty from lack of sleep, but he wasn't harping away.

"Damn…er…darned right." Elise shot a glance at Jacob who had an annoying habit of picking up every inappropriate word he heard. She continued in a low voice. "She's been up almost every night since we got back from Stump River. I'm exhausted, Kane. I'm at work all day. The restaurant's a disaster with half of it under construction and plaster dust everywhere. Then, when I get home, the children want all my time and—"

"Why not ask Helen?"

"It's not her responsibility to raise *our* children. Sure, she doesn't mind helping out, but she's getting older, you know. Plus she takes care of the house and does the cooking. That's more than enough for someone her age."

He sighed knowing the conversation was going nowhere. They'd rehashed the problem too many times in the past. "I'm doing the best I can, Elise. I'm trying to build a strong case against Chicago. Once that's done and some of the pack moves there my work load should lessen and I'll have more time for you and the children."

Elise looked away, her jaw jutted. She was still angry, but there was nothing else he could do. He leaned back and drank his coffee, brooding over the fact that if they weren't having sex, all they did was argue. It hadn't always been like this between them, but over the past year their relationship had slowly changed. There wasn't a specific event he could recall that had caused things to sour. Frowning, he wondered if this happened to every couple. Certainly his own parents hadn't lived in harmony… The idea that he was following that same path was depressing and he took another sip of coffee to muffle his sigh.

Eventually, Elise must have calmed down for when she spoke her voice sounded even, though she still didn't look at him. "How's Damien doing?"

As far as olive branches went, it wasn't much, but he accepted it anyway. "Fine. He's given me some good information. Most of the Lycans in the Chicago pack are older, working well past the age that they should. Old man Harper himself is basically crippled and he has his granddaughter running the show. And the man is putting lineage over suitability when selecting the next Alpha."

Finally, she looked at him. "You mentioned that last night. I was wondering about Damien himself."

"He's fine, I guess. I think the girl, Sam, is giving him a run for his money."

"That's what he needs." Elise gave him a hint of a smile—she'd always had a soft spot for Damien—and, for a moment, the tension between them eased. She poured herself a cup of tea. Jacob climbed on his lap, demanding some bites of waffle and Kane helped him spear a piece with his fork. Leah cooed and babbled at a butterfly causing them both to laugh.

He wondered why it couldn't always be like this. It wasn't as if he enjoyed working such long hours. It was what the job demanded. And now that High Council was considering adding younger Alphas to the mix, he had to look sharp if he wanted to gain one of the coveted positions. He frowned, thinking of the extra travel the job would involve. It meant more time away which was a negative, but the title was very prestigious.

His phone rang and he picked it up, leaning to the side to avoid a sticky bit of waffle that Jacob was now waving about.

"Sinclair here ... Yes, I have it. It's in my office. Just a second..." He stood and tucked Jacob under his arm, but the boy began to whimper.

"Daddy, no! Waffles! I want mo' waffles!"

The sticky fork landed against his cheek. Kane tried to juggle the phone and his son while keeping from having his eye poked out. His voice came out harsher than he'd planned. "Jacob, be careful! Elise, take him before he blinds me."

Elise stood up, a tight look about her mouth, and took the boy.

"Go. Take care of your *third* phone call. I'll watch the children by myself. *Again*."

He bit back a retort that it wasn't his choice and headed to the office. The position on High Council was looking more appealing by the minute. At least if he were away from home more, he wouldn't be constantly criticized for doing his job!

Elise fixed Jacob his own plate of food and then sat back down in her chair. She blinked back tears and took a sip of tea, trying to swallow past the lump in her throat. A simple family breakfast. Was that really too much to ask? She'd planned it all last night, right down to Kane's favourite waffles and he hadn't even mentioned them. He'd been too busy checking his messages!

"Momma mad?" Jacob was looking at her with a worried expression.

She tried to school her features into some semblance of a smile. "No. I'm not mad."

"You yelled."

"I..." She tried to be honest with Jacob, but how to explain? "I was mad, but not any more. And not at you. Don't worry."

"Okay."

Elise bit her lip. Yelling at Kane wasn't the solution. He had his work to do, and it was important. She was just overtired...

"Kane's gone already?" Helen stepped onto the patio and looked at the still laden table.

"He had to take a phone call."

"Ah!" She paused. "Are you okay?"

Elise debated about giving the usual 'fine', but she wasn't fine and she needed to know if she was being a shrew or not. "Helen, can I talk to you?"

"Sure. I'm good at talking, and listening. Which do you need?" The other woman sat down and poured herself a cup of coffee.

"Both, I guess." Elise carefully lined up the cutlery as she spoke. "Kane is always working. He never has any time for me or the children. Even when we were in Stump River, supposedly on a vacation, he was taking calls and emails." She left off moving the spoons about and looked directly at Helen. "Am I expecting too much to want some of his time for us?"

Helen shook her head. "No. But I do know exactly what you're talking about. Something similar happened to me and my Zack." She stirred her tea, a far off look in her eye. "I'd get so irritated because I expected him to be there for birthdays, or even a family supper, and he'd be called away. And then, when he finally did show up, I'd have to bite my tongue even though my feelings were hurt that the needs of others came before our family. I'd feel I was being selfish, yet at the same time angry because he wasn't here building memories with the children. It was time we could never get back."

"That's it, exactly!" Elise wiped Jacob's face and sent him back to play on his tricycle. "You must have come to terms with it, though."

"As a couple, we had to, or it would have torn us apart. Being an Alpha is a demanding job. Lots of people are counting on you, all wanting a piece of your time. And being the mate of one isn't a life-style everyone is cut out for."

A cold knot twisted in Elise's stomach once more and she stared at the table, unconsciously straightening the cutlery yet again. "I'm beginning to wonder if I'm cut out for it."

"Elise?" Helen slowly set down her cup and sat up straighter.

"We fight a lot these days." She whispered the words, ashamed to admit her weakness and fearful Jacob would overhear. "I'm tired, and I get irritated with him. Sometimes it's his fault and sometimes…I don't know. It's as if I want to hurt his feelings, just like he's hurt mine. I know he doesn't mean to, but I want to scream 'don't you notice me?'" Tears were threatening as she finally looked up at Helen, fully expecting a well-deserved condemnation. "I must be a dreadful person. I know he's the Alpha, but inside I'm so full of resentment."

"Oh, honey." Helen reached over and squeezed her hand. "Every couple goes through a rough patch now and then."

"I know, only this keeps getting worse and worse. I've thought about selling my half share of the Grey Goose but…" She exhaled and tried to explain. "All my life I've done what I was told. When I wanted to go to college, my father said no. When I wanted Bryan as my mate, I was told it would be Kane. Everyone expects an Alpha's mate to take charge and jump into the role, but I never wanted that! I love Kane, but I want my own life, too. Even if it's only for a little while…" Her voice trailed off and she felt guilty, unable to believe what she'd admitted.

"You know, not everyone is meant to stay at home, just like everyone isn't meant to have a career. Personally, I love my life. Some of the younger ones might look at me and think I'm a household drudge with no mind of my own or no ambition, but running a big house like this is hard work. Yet, I'd never wanted to do anything else. It's almost reverse discrimination that people devalue the work I do because it's confined to the home."

"Helen, I don't think—"

"I know. But just because I love my job within the pack, doesn't mean it's for everyone. Maybe you're going to blaze a new trail for the role of the Alpha's mate. Maybe she doesn't have to be defined by her mate's position."

"Me? A trailblazer? I don't think so." She shook her head and gave a rueful smile.

"Don't sell yourself short. You're one of the quiet ones, but that doesn't mean you aren't effective. Some people are in your face and shoving their will down your throat. It can turn people off." Helen nodded as if she had personal experience with those personality types. "But you come at it a different way. Soft like, making suggestions, getting people to think and before they know it, they're doing what you want and believing it was their own idea. You handle being the Alpha female just fine. You've grown into the job, making it your own rather than a carbon copy of what all the other packs are doing."

"Maybe." She felt her face flush at the praise while, at the same time, wondering when Kane had last told her she was doing a good job. "I think the real problem is that Kane works too much. He hates to delegate, even though I'm sure John could handle a lot more than he already does."

"Carrie has mentioned that John's been chomping at the bit lately. As Beta, he has leadership quality and wants to use it."

She nodded. "I know. And now that High Council is looking at Kane, he's working even harder trying to be some 'Super Alpha'."

"Kane's already an exemplary Alpha."

"Try and tell him that."

"Hmph. I guess I don't have any words of wisdom for you. All I can say is talk to him. Each couple has to find the balance that works for them."

"I guess." She made a face, not holding out much hope that would work.

Leah started to fuss and Elise picked her up, joggling her on her knee. Jacob had abandoned his tricycle and was on all fours trying to stalk a squirrel as if he were a wolf. It was adorable and she sighed, wishing Kane was there to share the moment.

~~~

Damien realized he was being followed barely two blocks from the pack house. The sixth sense he'd relied on so many times in the past had been working overtime lately. More than once this past week, he'd been sure someone had him under surveillance, yet he'd never been able to determine the source. It had to be Dante, but the bastard's use of the scent mask made it damned near impossible to locate him. Maybe today would be his lucky day.

Using the side-view mirrors of the parked cars, he managed to catch a glimpse of someone in a ball cap and jacket some distance behind him. Down wind. Clever, but not good enough.

On the off chance that it was simply a case of two people travelling in the same direction, he slowed his speed. The other person did the same. Yep, he was being followed, but without tipping off the tail by staring, he wasn't sure who it might be. His gut told him it was a Lycan; not Dante as he'd first suspected. Too short for that. Sam? The size was about right. He growled in frustration.

Yesterday, she hadn't questioned him about his trips out by himself and he'd hoped their heart to heart in the pond had driven the topic from her mind. Yeah, right. Somehow he knew Sam had the tenacity of duct tape. It was more likely she'd decided he wouldn't talk and was trying to ferret out his secrets on her own.

He'd been searching for Dante these past three days, and this morning had received a mocking text from the man as well as a demand to meet at the local pool hall. How Dante had managed to discover his number, he didn't know. The man had sources everywhere.

Well, Sam couldn't see him with the bastard again; she'd start asking questions he wasn't prepared to answer. He'd have to shake her off his tail and fast if he was to get to the meet on time. But would she give up that easily? Not likely. It was more probable that she'd keep looking and stumble upon him just as he had Dante by the throat.

On to plan B. Confrontation followed by redirection.

Damien turned the corner, ducked in a doorway and, when Sam appeared, stepped out in front of her and grabbed her arm. Except it wasn't Sam.

"Chris?" He released the firm grip he had on the boy's arm. "Why are you following me?"

"Oh! Er... Hi, Damien." Chris quickly transformed his shocked expression into a cocky grin.

Damien didn't return the greeting. Instead he folded his arms and widened his stance.

The smile faded from Chris' face.

"I'm...er...not following you. Really. Just going the same way."

Damien raised one brow and waited for the boy to incriminate himself even further.

The boy shuffled his feet and looked at the ground. "Okay. I was following you."

"Did Sam put you up to this?" He couldn't believe she'd use the boy that way, but with so few pack members she might have felt pushed into doing so.

"No. She never gives me any fun assignments to do." Chris shook his head. "I was only practising. I heard Sam talking to my folks about me maybe going to the Academy in a few years, and I thought I'd start to get ready."

"Huh." Damien considered the boy's story and relaxed his pose. "Okay, I believe you. But you made some pretty basic mistakes. You were downwind which was good, but way too close."

"Really?" Chris's shoulders slumped. "I've never tried to follow anyone before. I guess it's harder than it looks."

"Yeah. It is." Damien turned back towards the pack house and Chris fell in beside him. "I can give you some pointers, if you'd like."

"That'd be great. What about right now?" The boy grinned and began to walk with a bit of a swagger.

"No, not today. I have to meet someone." They turned the corner. The pack house was right ahead. He'd ditch Chris and might still have enough time to get to the pool hall before Dante. "No more following me. If you ever did manage to catch me unaware I could hurt you before I realized who you were."

Chris' step faltered and he rubbed the spot on his arm where Damien had grabbed him. "My dad said you're a rogue and rogues can be really dangerous."

"He's right." Damien slid a sideways look at Chris wondering how he felt about that fact. From the look on the boy's face, it wasn't a negative in his young mind.

"That must be way cool. Everyone would be intimidated by you. You can roam all over the country doing whatever you want." There was a definite look of hero worship in his eyes.

"Having no family. No friends. No pack. Never knowing where you'll sleep or get your next meal. People always suspicious of your motives. Struggling to keep control of the animal inside you." Damien tried to counter the picture the boy was painting, but doubted it worked.

They stopped in front of the pack house and Damien checked his watch. Damn. It was later than he'd thought. He reiterated his warning. "Chris, I meant what I said. Don't follow me."

"Sure, Damien. As long as you give me those lessons you promised." Chris gave him a cheeky grin before heading inside.

Damien waited until the front door closed behind the boy and then walked quickly towards his meet with Dante. He'd intended to be there before the man, but that wasn't going to be possible now.

"Chris, come in here!" Sam called out to the young Lycan as he entered the pack house. Through her office window, she'd seen him talking to Damien. No problem with that except, she glanced at the clock, the boy should have still been in school.

"Hey, Sam!" Chris entered, his hands in his back pockets and a self-satisfied smirk on his face.

"Where've you been?"

"Out with Damien."

"At this time of the day? Shouldn't you be in school?"

"Nope. We have the afternoon off. The teachers have a workshop or something."

"Hmmm." Sam tapped a few keys on her computer and pulled up the school calendar. Okay, the kid was telling the truth. "So what were you and Damien doing?"

"I was practising following him, but he caught me."

Sam raised her brows. "Following Damien. And how did he feel about that?"

Chris shrugged. "I dunno. He said I was pretty lousy at it, but he'd teach me some tricks. Not today, though. I think he was in a hurry to meet someone."

"I see." She drummed her fingers on her desk then nodded. "Okay. Head to your room and start studying for that test you have on Friday."

"But they gave us the afternoon off!"

"Too bad. You're still grounded and your marks suck."

Chris scowled but did as he was told. Sam sighed wondering if she'd been as bad at that age. Probably.

With Chris out of the way, she slipped out of the house. Damien was meeting someone. On the off chance that she could pick up his trail, she'd try to track him down.

Chapter 14

The pool hall wasn't crowded; a few of the tables were occupied, some patrons were seated at the bar watching a game on TV. Damien stood in the entry letting his eyes adjust to the darker lighting while his nose detected Dante's scent…or at least the lilac scent the dirt ball was using to hide behind.

He was at the far end of the bar. Clever of him. Private enough for a conversation, but public enough that the bastard would feel relatively protected.

Damien strolled across the room garnering a few glances from the locals. The bartender raised an eyebrow and he shook his head to the silent inquiry for a drink.

Sliding onto a stool beside Dante, Damien fixed his eyes on the TV screen. The game was loud enough to cover their voices from human hearing.

"Why the hell are you still in the area?"

"Is that any way to greet an old friend?" Dante feigned a hurt tone.

"We were never friends."

"Partner, then."

"No." He'd only ever had one partner, Reno, and the idea that Dante would even consider himself to be in the same category caused his blood to boil. "We were never partners. Circumstances might have forced us to work towards the same goal, but that was as far as it went."

"Tsk. Tsk." Dante took a drink, his eyes fixed on the TV screen. "You never were a team player. Deirdre often commented about that."

"Cut the crap, Dante. I'm here because I have a job to do. Why are you still stinking up the city with your presence?" He made no mention of what he'd overheard at Marcello's; it could provide him with some leverage if need be.

Dante eyed him speculatively, likely trying to decide how much he'd overheard. Damien carefully schooled his features to reveal nothing.

Finally Dante answered. "Chicago's such a lovely place. And since I found myself temporarily unemployed and without funds..."

"You resorted to robbing old men? I gave you enough money to drag your carcass somewhere else."

"Perhaps. But I've since found several new sources of income and they require me to stay close by." A slow smile spread over his face as he flicked a glance at Damien. "Very close as a matter of fact."

A sinking feeling settled in Damien's stomach. His experience with Dante had taught him to never underestimate the man. If he claimed to have a winning hand, he usually did.

"Okay, I'll bite. What are you up to?"

Dante didn't speak for a moment, no doubt savouring the moment before he sprung his news. In the background, the faint thud of a pool cue could be heard followed by the clatter of balls as they careened together before dropping into a pocket. The sportscaster on TV was droning out statistics, and patrons were exchanging good-natured gibes with the bartender.

"How are you coping with Sam Harper?" The non-sequitur had Damien turning his head to look at the man.

"What does she have to do with this?"

Dante shrugged. "I heard she's quite a tough little bitch."

Damien gritted his teeth at the term but outwardly didn't react. The scuzzball was up to something. "She's an Alpha, what do you expect?"

"Ah! I've heard rumours about her, that she's not completely Lycan. There's some witch or Fae in her background, I believe."

"Your point?"

"Nothing. It's just that I'd imagine she'd hold a certain appeal to you. You were always trying to champion the mixed blooded ones."

He made a non-committal noise. It wasn't a fact he could deny, but it wasn't an issue in his dealings with Sam, either.

"Not going to bite on that, are you?" Dante sighed. "Oh well, it doesn't matter to my little venture anyway. I have enough leverage as it is."

"Leverage?"

"You wouldn't want her to know that you're not the rogue she was looking for, would you?" A self-satisfied smile started to spread over Dante's face. "I know a lot about you, Damien. What you used to be, what you're doing now, spying for Sinclair. It would be a shame if Harper found out."

Damien stiffened in his seat. "Are you trying to blackmail me?"

"Yes." Dante looked him straight in the eye. "I need money and I'll get it any way I can. Friendship doesn't stand in my way when it comes to getting what I want."

"Like I said before, we were never friends."

"Exactly."

"And what if I said I didn't care?" Damien stalled for time, his mind racing. Dante seemed to be going on a blackmailing spree. First Marcello, now him. Who was next on the list?

"Really? You're going to disappoint Sinclair and his little family? Aren't they counting on you?"

"Kane doesn't need me here. He can build a case against the Chicago pack on his own."

"But if Lycan Link were to find out that he'd sent you in as a spy, they wouldn't look kindly on him. And he was harbouring you before the pardon went through. I don't know how that would affect his chances for a seat on High Council. Lycan Link can be so stuffy about things like that." Dante made a moue and shook his head. "Such a shame. He was a promising candidate, too."

Damien clamped his mouth shut, trying to control the anger building inside him. He couldn't be the cause of Kane's downfall. Kane had been trying to help him, to give him a sense of purpose, when he'd sent him here. And Sam…he was operating under false pretences with her, but for some reason, he'd prefer she never found out and certainly not from the likes of Dante.

"What? No questions as to who my source is? No threats?" Dante gave up staring at the screen and looked directly at Damien.

"Leave. Now." Damien spoke between clenched teeth. He could feel his muscles bunching, a haze beginning to shimmer before his eyes as his wolf struggled to escape.

"I will. For the moment." Dante chugged the last of his drink. "But you'll be hearing from me."

"I should have killed you in that alley." A growl rumbled up from his chest.

"Probably. Mercy always was your downfall." Dante nodded towards the front window. Through the layer of filth that coated the glass, Sam could be seen walking towards the establishment. "Your 'boss' is looking for you, so I'll be on my way." He stood, a wince of pain crossing his features.

Damien curled his lip, pleased that the man's knee hadn't recuperated yet from their fight. No doubt his dissipated lifestyle was ruining his Lycan metabolism. "Watch your back, Dante. I'm going to hunt you down."

"If you can find me. I've played this game longer and harder than you have, Damien. And I've always won. Next time we meet, I'll be expecting payment for keeping my mouth shut. A couple of hundred will do...for now." Dante limped away, and Damien wondered what the chances were that he'd be able to kill the man in broad daylight without anyone noticing.

The bastard had the nerve to hold the door open for Sam as she walked in. His inner wolf growled when the man eyed her like a piece of meat. If Dante ever touched her, there wouldn't be enough pieces left to identify. The idea was extremely satisfying.

Sam stood in the doorway, her stance was confident, as if seedy pool halls were her everyday environment. For some reason, he tried to picture Beth here and knew his little mate would have been out of her element. She would have looked about with wide-eyed fascination, and stuck to his side in case trouble should break out. Beth wasn't a fighter. Sam, on the other hand, would probably grab a pool cue if a fight broke out and ram it into the stomach of any troublemaker who dared come near her. Yeah, the two women were like night and day.

Sam nodded to the bartender as she crossed the room. He immediately poured her a drink and was sliding it down the bar by the time she reached the far side of the room. Sitting in the seat Dante had vacated, she flicked a glance at the empty space on the counter in front of him and then at the TV screen.

"No drink, so you're not here to tie one on. Must be that you had a burning need to watch the game, right?" She blinked at him innocently and gave him a sweet smile before belting back her whiskey. It was so incongruous that he laughed.

"Uh huh. That's it." He twined two fingers together and held them up for her to see. "Me and baseball are like this. Don't try to keep us apart."

She snorted. "Yeah, right. And I like to make tea cosies in my spare time."

"Really?" He tried to keep a straight face but failed miserably.

The corners of Sam's mouth twitched despite the fact she was glaring at him. "So what's the real story? You've been sneaking off on your own every day now."

"No, I haven't." He countered. "If I was really trying to sneak off, you wouldn't have caught me."

"Okay. Sneaking was the wrong word, but the question is still the same. What gives, Damien?"

He thought quickly, wondering how much to say. "I was meeting someone. He had information to give me."

"Lilac Man?" She sniffed the air and made a face. "The same guy you were talking to at Club Mystique the other night?"

"Yep." She made no mention of the supposed robbery at Marcello's, and Damien gave a silent sigh of relief. She still hadn't realized Dante and the thief were one and the same.

When he offered no more, she huffed and prompted further. "Does this information have to do with your current job? With me and my pack?"

Damien hesitated. "Yes, but I need to verify a few facts. 'Lilac Man' isn't always reliable."

"And that's all you have to say?"

"Actually, no." He winked at her. "Wanna play some pool?"

Sam hit him in the arm. Hard.

"What was that for?" He rubbed his bicep.

"You're trying to distract me from asking more about Lilac Man."

"Yep, that's my plan, but I really don't know much about shooting pool and thought you could give me some pointers while we talk."

"How do you even know I play?"

"The bartender knows you."

"Maybe I just come here to drink."

"Do you?"

"No."

"There you go." He stood up and tugged her towards an open table.

Sam gave a sigh and followed. "Okay. But if I win, you have to share the information Lilac Man was giving you."

"Fair enough." He'd played enough games with Reno that he felt confident he could win. And if he didn't, he'd come up with some tidbit of information to attribute to Dante.

"You agreed too quickly." She narrowed her eyes. "How do I know you're not some pool shark?"

"You don't." He gave her a crooked grin. The look she returned would have sent most normal men running. Luckily he was a Lycan and a rogue at that. She grabbed two cues while he racked up the balls.

"Eight ball—that's the black one—goes in the middle of the rack." Sam called the instruction over her shoulder while she chalked her cue.

"I know."

"Just checking. After all, you said you weren't a pool shark."

"I'm not an idiot, either."

She smiled and didn't reply.

Damien shook his head. God, she was fun to banter with. When was the last time he'd actually had fun? When Beth was alive? Most likely. She'd loved to tease him as well. A warm feeling of familiarity filled him as he realized the similarity between the two women.

"Heads or tails?" Sam had taken out a quarter and was about to toss it.

"Don't bother. I'll let you go first so you can show me how it's done."

He leaned back against the wall, his hands lightly resting on the cue stick, and watched Sam take aim. A quick movement of her arm was followed by a cracking sound as the cue ball struck the others and they broke formation.

"One solid, one stripe in. I call stripes." She spoke without looking at him, circling the table and assessing the possible shots.

Damien watched silently as ball after ball rolled into the pockets. With only two striped balls left, she missed.

"Your turn." Her face was set, her attention focused on the table. Definitely the competitive sort.

Pushing off from the wall, Damien considered his first move.

"Red ball, far corner pocket is your best bet."

He flicked a glance at Sam. "Thanks." Following her suggestion, he took his shot and sunk the ball.

"Green ball, middle left."

He turned and looked at her. "Who's playing? You or me?"

She widened her eyes. "You said you wanted some pointers."

"Right." He turned to examine the table. She was right. The green ball *was* the best shot. As he bent over, quite unexpectedly he felt Sam beside him. He looked over his shoulder at her. "Yes?"

"If you aim for the blue ball and catch the left edge of it, it will ricochet to the right and hit the yellow ball, knocking it into the pocket. The cue ball will bounce off the cushion, hit the orange which will then take the green one with it into the middle left."

Damien straightened and looked at her, one brow raised.

"Or you could just sink the green." She shrugged and leaned on her pool cue.

"I asked for help." He turned to study the table. "Explain the shot to me again."

"It's geometry." She explained, once more pointing out the angles and trajectory of each ball.

Damien nodded in understanding. "I get it, now. Thanks."

"Move a little bit to the right, like this."

Sam pressed against him, moving him slightly, adjusting his hold on the cue. Her scent wrapped around him just as her arms did. Leather and spice. It stirred his blood and his wolf raised its head, a low rumble of approval rising in its throat. When she'd kissed him the other day, his reaction had been intense, but this was even more so, as if the long dormant feelings inside him were now awake and demanding to be fed after years of fasting.

His arm brushed against her as he moved to take his shot. His skin registered every inch of her that he touched, fogging his thinking.

He gave his head a slight shake and narrowed his eyes. Pool. That's what he needed to concentrate on.

"That's right. Don't rush it. Long, slow strokes as you build up momentum. Then one hard, firm thrust." Sam cooed her instructions at him. Out of the corner of his eye, he could see her caressing her cue, trailing her fingers up and down its length. The image that her action brought to mind had his breathing accelerating. Dragging his gaze back to the table, he took a deep, steadying breath, exhaled slowly and then made his move. Unfortunately, the shot was off. The cue ball barely brushed the blue one which half-heartedly rolled across the felt surface and came to a stop near the eight ball.

"Oh. That's too bad. Better luck next time." Sam cast him what was likely supposed to be a sympathetic look, only the twitching of her lips gave her away.

"Purposely rattling your opponent isn't fair, you know."

"I know." She hip checked him out of the way.

"Two can play at that game." Damien leaned his cue against the wall.

"You can't rattle me." Sam didn't even glance his way. She was circling the table looking for the best shot.

Damien waited until she stopped and then moved to stand behind her. "I hope I'm not bothering you."

"Nope. Not at all." She leaned forward.

"Great view when you do that."

She wiggled her ass at him but didn't look up, all her attention on the purple ball she was hoping to sink.

He chuckled, waited until she was going to take her shot and then cracked his knuckles. Her ball rolled true, but the complicated shot she'd been attempting didn't quite work. While one ball found its mark, the other stopped right on the rim of the pocket. For a moment it seemed to waiver as if considering falling into the opening but then changed its mind and settled into place.

"Damn."

Sam stepped back and Damien took his turn. His next shots went in as planned until he was tied with her. They each had one ball remaining and it was still his turn. Plus, the shot he had left was easy.

"Not a pool shark?" Sam gave him a look of disbelief.

"Would you believe your lesson was amazing and I'm a fast learner?"

"No."

"I didn't think so." He waggled his brows and gave her his best leer. "What will you give me when *I* win?"

She flicked her eyes up and down the length of him before looking him right in the eye and slowly wetting her lips. "Are you sure you want to know?"

The teasing atmosphere between them noticeably changed. With their gazes locked, tendrils of awareness seemed to stretch between them. He watched as she bit her lower lip, felt his own heart rate quicken. Sam wanted him, but did he want her?

Yes.

Physically, at least.

He was attracted to her. She was fun and smart. His body clamoured to experience release again, but... He'd made a vow to Beth. It shouldn't matter that she was dead. They'd been as one, and still were.

He took a deep breath. Sam's scent filled his nostril and teased his mind. He tightened his grip on his pool cue as body, mind and heart battled.

"I—" He didn't finish the statement. A cracking sound beside him drew his attention. He'd snapped his pool cue in half. One half tipped and fell on the table, the slight movement enough to knock Sam's purple ball into the pocket.

The faint clunk of the ball hovered between them for a second before Sam pumped the air in victory. "I win!"

Damien shook his head, thankful for the distraction. "No, you didn't. It was accidentally knocked in. Besides, it's my turn."

"Too bad. I say it counts."

"And I say it doesn't."

They stared at each other for a moment and then Sam threw her hands up.

"Fine. We can't finish the game anyway since you broke your cue. But I know *I* won." She reached out and grabbed the broken stick from his hand and looked at it in disgust. "How are we going to explain this?" She jerked her chin toward the bartender who was glaring in their direction.

"Complain that the cues are inferior quality and demand your money back." Damien suggested in jest.

Sam appeared to think about it, then gave a shrug. "It's worth a try."

Damien watched as she crossed the room. While he didn't know for certain, he had the feeling that he'd rattled her by not taking her blatantly sexual offer. He'd been caught in his inner battle and hadn't noticed if his hesitancy was affecting her or not, but his gut was saying yes. She'd switched gears too quickly, dropping her suggestive demeanour and focusing on the false win. Could it be that Sam Harper wasn't always as cool and confident as she presented herself to be?

Chapter 15

Damien stirred the pot of chili he was making while studying the recipe on the counter beside him. Sam had left him in charge of kitchen duty while she went to check on Mr. Marcello and he figured this was a safe and easy recipe to follow. All the ingredients had been added and now it just had to simmer. Strangely enough, he was anxious that the meal would turn out well and meet with the pack's approval. It made no sense, of course. Since when did he care what other Lycans thought?

A Lycan should want to please its pack, his wolf suggested.

But they aren't our pack, he reminded the beast.

Really? His wolf twitched its ears at him and he frowned in response.

This is a temporary arrangement he reminded the animal. Don't go getting too comfortable.

As he turned the burner to a lower setting, the back door slammed shut and Hiram came hurrying into the kitchen.

"Damien! I'm glad you're here."

"What can I do for you?" He and Hiram had fallen into an easy friendship despite the difference in their ages. Most days, the older man sought him out mid-morning with a cup of coffee in hand, and then proceeded to talk his ear off as he 'helped' with the various repairs Damien was undertaking. Some might have found it annoying, but Damien enjoyed the man's stories and hearing his perspective on the world. The wisdom of the elders wasn't something to be ignored.

"My nose might be acting up on me, but I'm sure I scented another Lycan in the area."

"Where?" Damien stiffened, his wolf's territorial instincts immediately kicking in, even if this was only temporarily his home.

"In the alley behind us. I'm wondering if it's that spy of Sinclair's."

Or Dante, he thought to himself. "Show me where you noticed the scent."

"I tracked it from the bus stop and down the alley, just hints of scent, nothing definite. Then it faded away. All I can smell now is flowers." Hiram explained as he led the way. "Like I said, it could be my nose acting up again. Getting old has its drawbacks."

"With age comes wisdom, Hiram. Never think you don't have something to give the world, no matter how many years you've accumulated."

"Thanks, Damien. Too bad the rest of the world doesn't see it that way." Hiram tugged at his ear. "Seems if you're not at your peak, you're looked down on."

"Yeah, well the thinking of a lot of the world is screwed up." Damien put his hands on his hips and began to survey the area wondering where their quarry had gone. From the faint trace of a scent that remained, he was sure it was Dante. "He's using a scent mask."

"A scent mask? I didn't think such a thing was possible."

"Lycan Link technology," he replied distractedly. "They've been working on perfecting it for the past few years."

"So the spy is from Lycan Link?"

"Not necessarily. The prototype of the formula was leaked during the early days of its development. There are several black market versions available that I'm aware of, however none are as effective as the one Lycan Link perfected." Damien spoke as he prowled the area, hoping to find a lead. "Even so, it's against Lycan law to use it without a permit."

"Sinclair likely bought some illegally and gave it to his spy." Hiram nodded emphatically.

Kane was the least likely Lycan to break a law, but Sam's pack would never believe that, so he settled on making a noncommittal sound. Crouching, he studied the ground. "No evidence of tracks. I wonder which way the bastard went."

"He could be trying to get inside to snoop around. Maybe even using the old passageways to gain entrance to the house."

"Passageways?" Damien looked up at the man in surprise.

Betrayed: Book Two – The Road To Redemption

"Back in the days of prohibition, members of the pack worked for smugglers. Liquor came from Windsor, Ontario across the border into Detroit. The Purple Gang—"

"The Purple Gang?" Rising to his feet, Damien wondered if this was one of Hiram's tall tales.

"Weird name, I know, but that's what the Detroit gang called themselves. Anyway, the Lycans brought the liquor into Chicago and hid it under the house until it was delivered to the blind pigs."

"Blind pigs?" He had to be joking. "Hiram—"

"I'm not kidding. Blind pigs, speakeasies; that's what the humans called the places that served illegal liquor."

"Okay, I believe you. Thanks for the history lesson, but what does this has to do with…er…the spy?"

"There's a passageway from the cellar—the workout room Sam fixed up—that leads into the house. It's narrow, barely two feet wide and runs between the walls." Hiram paused in his explanation and frowned. "I've never checked it out myself, mind you. Alpha's privilege. And I doubt it's been used in ages. Or maybe I'm letting my imagination get carried away again."

If the passageway existed, Damien had no doubt that Dante could have found out about it somehow. Had the man been sneaking around the house right under their noses?

"I'd better look, just to be sure. Any idea where the door to this passageway might be?"

"Not really. I don't recall Sam mentioning it when she renovated the cellar. It could even be sealed up I suppose."

Damien couldn't imagine Sam not being aware of a secret entrance, but she might have kept the information to herself like the proverbial ace up her sleeve.

"You know, you did well to pick up that trace of a scent, Hiram. It could be that you actually scared him off."

"You think so?" Hiram stood a bit straighter.

"Yep." He glanced around the area once more. "Listen, your shift is over. Go take a break and I'll check the cellar then report what I find to Sam when she gets back."

"Well… If you're sure."

Damien clapped him on the back. "I am."

Hiram nodded and went on his way, much to Damien's relief. While it was doubtful Dante was still around, he didn't want to chance his confrontation with the man being observed.

He entered the cellar, all senses on alert. The room appeared normal, no hint of lilacs, no prickling of that mysterious sixth sense he'd come to rely on over the years. Relaxing, he began to patrol the perimeter looking for evidence of the secret passageway Hiram had spoken of.

Eyeing the walls, he looked for obvious cracks in the stone work and minute gaps in the wooden framing. Nothing was immediately evident, but he'd have expected nothing less of Sam. If the pack house had a hidden entrance, she'd have kept it under wraps, an Alpha's privileged information. The mirrored walls, however, presented a distinct possibility and he soon found what he was looking for. One was hinged and, when it swung outward, it became evident there was a false wall along that end of the cellar.

A small knothole proved to be a makeshift door handle and he soon found himself in a narrow room. Conveniently, a small flashlight hung on a nail near the entrance, giving evidence that someone used the space on a regular basis. He shone the light around the cramped space. Old, dusty crates were stacked at one end as well as a few empty liquor bottles, remnants of the illegal alcohol Hiram had spoken about. Childish scrawl on the wall, boldly signed with a flourished 'S', hinted at the fact that Sam likely had discovered the room years ago.

He imagined her as a child, playing imaginative games in the small room, perhaps hiding from her grandfather when she was in trouble, or keeping a secret stash of candy for emergencies. A smile curved his lips at the mental image of wide violet eyes in a small face, perhaps her dark hair held back in pigtails. Would her pups share her unique eye colour? His heart gave a quiver at the idea and he frowned, forcing himself to recall his purpose. Now where was the entrance to the passageway?

He tested the walls then studied the ceiling. Cobwebs festooned most of the area except one corner and closer examination showed a well-hidden hatch. Using one of the old crates as a step stool, he peered into the space. It was narrow, about eighteen inches across, barely wide enough for a grown man to squeeze through. From what he could see, the passage extended about ten feet and then a simple wooden ladder led upwards. Well, that explained the discrepancies he'd noticed in the rooms of the house on his first day. Some enterprising Alpha had constructed a series of false walls throughout the place. Damien nodded at the ingenuity before stepping back down and returning the hatch to its proper location. Sometime when he knew Sam would be gone for a few hours, he'd have to explore this further. Right now, he'd better get back to the kitchen. Somehow, he knew she wouldn't be pleased that he'd discovered her secret.

As he left the cellar and headed towards the kitchen, a bit of movement near his motorcycle attracted his attention. A scrap of string was dangling from the handles. Some garbage that was blowing in the wind or…?

It was a piece of yarn with a piece of paper attached. He was sure he could hear Dante's taunting tones as he read the message: *Damien, I congratulate you. You're doing an excellent job as Beta. I'm sure the remuneration is sufficient that you won't mind sharing it with me, given that it was supposed to be my job to begin with. Unless you want me to have a chat with Sam Harper, that is. I'll be expecting payment tonight."*

Damien crushed the paper in his hand and did a slow turn, looking for any signs of the man. The bastard had been here, right under his nose, dammit, and he'd missed him. Was he still in the area, watching and even now laughing?

Glancing at the paper once again, he noted the location and time. Crap. Sam would be expecting him to be on patrol with her. A frustrated growl escaped him. He'd have to think of an excuse and fast.

Sam was approaching the pack house when she noticed someone exiting the driveway. Nothing unusual, really. People did stop by from time to time. However, something about how this individual was moving caught her attention. There was a furtiveness in the way they looked around and then quickly walked away. The size and build were correct for it to be Damien's friend, Lilac Man.

If it was, it would be like pulling teeth trying to get information out of Damien. Deciding she'd find out for herself, she began following him.

After turning the corner, the man visibly relaxed. Sam sneered at his self-assurance. His pace was moderate, giving no indication he'd noticed she was following him. As they wove in and out of the other pedestrians, she sniffed the air, trying to pick up his scent, but it was indiscernible from that of the other humans around them. The lilac smell she'd come to associate with him was there, though it seemed to dissipate at a strangely fast rate.

The pedestrian traffic thinned and she had to slow down, increasing the space between them in order to avoid being noticed. The neighbourhood changed from residential, to business and eventually to warehouses. It was an older area, a number of the buildings were empty and sprayed with graffiti. Most people would hesitate to walk by themselves through this part of town but Lilac Man didn't slow his pace. She was trying to speculate where he might be heading, when he suddenly turned down a side street.

Giving a curse, she hurried to catch up, anxious to keep him in sight. There were plenty of places for someone to disappear into if they didn't want to be found. Rounding the corner, she looked for the man, but just as she'd feared he was nowhere to be seen.

"Hell." She cursed but wasn't ready to admit defeat quite yet. Cocking her head to the side, she moved forward listening carefully, scanning the area for movement. Bits of garbage slowly scuttled down the street in the gentle breeze. Sun glinted off broken shards of glass. Behind her, she could hear the distant sounds of traffic, but this particular street was devoid of vehicles of any kind.

A noise to her right had her turning sharply. It sounded like someone kicking a tin can. Had Lilac Man forgotten to watch his footing?

Sam licked her lips and glanced around her. It could be a set up. Some gang luring her behind a building only to jump her once she left the supposed safety of the street. Or it could actually be her quarry.

Well, faint hearts never won and all that other crap, she muttered to herself deciding to follow the source of the noise.

Her wolf nodded in agreement, on its feet and ready to react if called upon.

Step by step she approached the rear of the building. Another sound had her tensing her muscles prepared to react, then the scent of several humans began to tickle her nose. No hint of lilacs, but that didn't mean he wasn't in the area. Voices became audible next and, as she rounded the corner, she shook her head and relaxed.

"Hey, Wes." She called out the name of a local thug. Small time, no threat to her or her family. She'd kicked his butt more than once for messing with people in the neighbourhood, though.

"Sam." He nodded, looking less than pleased to see her. The kid beside him—he was all of eighteen from the look of him—wasn't someone she knew, but the tough guy stance he took made her want to laugh.

"I haven't seen you around for a while." She hooked one thumb in a belt loop and casually rested her weight on one leg.

"Guess we don't move in the same social circles." Wes replied mockingly.

"True." She didn't rise to his bait. "I'm looking for a friend. I thought I saw him head this way."

"No one here but us."

"Hmm...okay." She nodded then flicked a glance to the male who was slowly inching his way towards her. "Wes, tell your friend to back off, or he'll be very sorry." Her tone was conversational, matter of fact. She could handle the situation, she'd just prefer not to.

"Back off, Mick."

"She yours?" Mick looked between the two of them.

Sam gave an inelegant snort and Wes scowled at her.

"Nah. She's an ice queen, don't bother. Your dick would freeze."

Mick shrugged and stepped away.

Sam didn't react to his comment. He wasn't worth it. Instead, she gestured towards the purse Wes was holding. "Making a fashion statement or stealing from little old ladies again?"

Wes shifted uneasily, likely recalling how she'd broken his nose last time she'd caught him picking on the seniors in the neighbourhood. What humans did to each other wasn't her concern, but sometimes she felt the need to step in when the battle was decidedly unbalanced.

"No. I...er...Mick found it. Somebody lost it and we were looking to see who owned it."

"Right." She didn't bother to hide her disbelief. "Hand it over and I'll make sure it gets back to its owner."

Wes hesitated, rubbed his crooked nose and then tossed the purse on the ground at her feet.

"Hey—" Mick started to protest, but a look from Wes had him closing his mouth.

"Believe me, Mick, it ain't worth it. Best leave before she goes psycho bitch on you."

Mick gave her a disbelieving look, but another warning glare from Wes had him giving a shrug and walking away.

"You're protégé is a real tough guy." Sam mocked.

Wes' face flushed. "Don't mess with me, Sam. I'm moving up in the world. Been hired by some guy with international connections."

"I'm so impressed." She rolled her eyes.

Wes glared at her. "You should be. He's got a big score going down tonight and I'm helping him."

Betrayed: Book Two – The Road To Redemption

"Is it as big as your mouth is?" What kind of idiot bragged about an illegal job? It was a miracle Wes wasn't already in jail.

"One of these days…"

She raised a brow and he immediately shut up.

Loser, she thought to herself as he walked away.

Her hormones were out of whack, she decided. Wes had declared she was an ice queen and it irritated the hell out of her. Not that Wes would know; she'd never even considered his lame pickup lines. But following on the heels of Damien's rejection at the pool hall, the comment had definitely soured her mood. It wasn't often she made a blatantly sexual play for a male. Damien's hesitation had stung.

Hell, twice in one day males had made her question her femininity. Watch out men, she said to herself, the next guy to piss me off is going to regret it.

She bent down and grabbed the purse and checked the ID inside. Yep, a little old lady. Wes was going to get it next time she saw him. Elders deserved respect.

Stuffing the wallet back inside the bag, she headed towards the nearest mailbox trusting the post office to ensure it was returned. Trying to hand it over to the cops would result in too many questions.

As she left the area, a distinctive twitch formed between her shoulder blades. Someone was watching her. Lilac Man? She resisted the urge to spin around and look. Let the bastard think she was unaware for the moment. It would make him bolder, less cautious and then, next time, she'd get him.

Chapter 16

Damien glanced around the table. Dinner was unusually silent. Perhaps it was his excellent chili or, his gaze strayed to where Sam sat, more likely it was the fact that she'd returned in a mood and everyone was picking up the vibes she was giving off. Whatever the case, Damien watched her surreptitiously as he went through a mental list of excuses to get out of going on patrol. If need be, he'd pull the rogue card and just disappear. It wasn't ideal, however he couldn't chance Dante showing up here and blowing his cover.

Hiram spoke, breaking the silence. "Damien and I think Sinclair's spy was in the area today."

Sam looked up from her meal and shot a look at him. "And you didn't think to tell me until now?"

"No chance." Damien calmly took a bite of chili before elaborating. "You were late getting home. I was busy in the kitchen."

She set down her spoon with exaggerated care. "I have time now. Elaborate."

"I was heading home when I picked up the scent," Hiram began.

"We checked the area but couldn't find him." Damien continued, hoping to prevent Hiram from mentioning their discussion of the hidden passageway. "He was likely testing your defences, but since Hiram noticed him right away, I'd say he has nothing to report back to Sinclair."

"Good work, Hiram." She gave the older man an approving smile.

"And Damien, he helped too." Hiram added seeming eager to share the praise.

"Of course." Sam nodded, but it was distinctly cool.

The group fell quiet again. A few members shot sympathetic glances his way, apparently having decided he was the one who would end up taking the brunt of Sam's temper. He gave a brief smile appreciating their support. It was a nice feeling, knowing they were on his side.

Time ticked by, only the faint clinking of utensils against the dishes breaking the silence. Damien was about to broach missing patrol when Sam pushed back her chair and stood up.

"I'll go on patrol by myself tonight."

Damien opened his mouth to reply but she beat him to the punch. "You can't go, you're on kitchen duty, remember?"

"Right. Perhaps Keith...?" Damien cast a look at the man in question.

Sam didn't give Keith time to answer. "He was on last night. I've done patrols by myself for years. I don't need someone to hold my hand."

"I wasn't implying that you did," Damien countered.

"Are you two going to have a fight?" Christopher glanced between the two of them, his eyes wide in anticipation of a show.

"No. We're not." Sam answered sharply.

Damien said nothing. While this worked in perfectly with his own plans, the idea of Sam heading out on her own seemed wrong. Why, he wasn't sure. Perhaps it was the routine they'd fallen into, but being by her side during patrols seemed natural, like having a partner again.

His wolf nodded its agreement. *We should be there to watch her back.*

Nothing much ever happened on patrols, he countered. The vague worry that plagued him was uncalled for. Sam could handle herself in most situations. Besides, her welfare really wasn't his concern. He had to deal with Dante. There was no way he was letting that scum blackmail him.

The traffic light turned green and the sea of humanity surged across the street. Sam moved with the crowd, jostling to hold her own. Someone pushed her from behind and she bit back a curse. It wasn't any more crowded than usual, but her patience was thin. She should have picked a less populated area to patrol tonight.

She ducked into a doorway and let the crowd pass. The theatre district was bustling tonight, art patrons leaving the various shows, seeking out quaint bistros where they could have a late meal and discuss the entertainment they'd just viewed. Too bad she wasn't in the mood for culture.

Her hope had been that patrolling on her own would clear her mind. That's how it used to work. Sure, she was a devoted Alpha and checking her territory was part of the job, but in the past it had also been a way for her to wind down, to mull things over without being interrupted.

Now, she kept opening her mouth to make a comment to Damien. Except he wasn't there. Illogical as it was, she was irritated that he hadn't pushed harder to accompany her. She'd asked to be alone. He was just following orders. Stupid man.

Something twinged in the region of her heart. Was it because he'd been relieved not to go with her?

Don't be ridiculous, her wolf chastised her. *Of course, he wanted to go. He was even concerned that you'd be by yourself.*

Sam made a face. Yeah, right.

Shoving her hands in her pockets, she stepped back into the crowd and continued her patrol, peering into the shadows, lightly testing the air for any hint of other shifters. She studied the people around her. Young couples, old couples, middle-aged couples; she was surrounded by them. Being an Alpha sucked sometimes. You had to be strong, resilient, self-sufficient. Sometimes, doing your duty made you seem hard and it could push people away. Sometimes, it was…lonely.

She took a deep breath and shook off the self-pity. There was work to be done. She'd covered most of this district. Before heading home, she'd swing along part of the Kennedy Expressway area. It passed by the old warehouse district where she'd encountered Wes earlier. If he was there, she could vent some of her bad mood on him. After all, he was partly to blame.

The rusted metal door screeched as Damien pulled it open, acting as an alarm and announcing his presence. That was likely one of the reasons Dante had chosen the abandoned warehouse for a meeting spot; he didn't like being taken by surprise.

Damien paused inside, head cocked to the side as he listened for any hint of the other Lycan's whereabouts. Except for the occasional rustling of rodents, the building was quiet.

"Dante?" His voice rang out, echoing off the walls.

No one answered.

Walking deeper into the building, his footsteps echoed hollowly in the cavernous space. High stacks of metal barrels ran down the middle of the building, and the perimeter was lined with piles of wooden pallets and boxes. A few streaks of moonlight managed to penetrate the filthy windows that edged the top of the walls near the roof, creating pools of weak light and deepening the shadows. Damien peered into the darkness, his senses on high alert.

Our quarry is here. His wolf quivered in excitement.

Damien tested the air. The animal was correct; the scent of lilacs was there, barely discernable over the chemical smells emanating from the barrels. A faint sound behind him had him spinning around. The glimmer of a light could be seen in an office on the far side of the building. It was just like Dante to make himself at home.

Shaking his head, Damien strode across the room, intent on getting the meeting over as quickly as possible. If Dante had thought this setting would intimidate, he could fuck that idea. It was actually a perfect location. He could grab Dante's scrawny neck and shake him like the rat he was.

The barest of whistling noises was the only warning he had before he caught a glimpse of a two by four being swung at his head.

"Hey!"

He fell to his knees, his head throbbing, his vision blurred. Someone kicked him in the back and his face smashed into the concrete floor. The taste of his own blood filled his mouth and the world began to grow dark.

"Not so tough, after all." A voice, one he couldn't place, came from somewhere above. A foot was pressed firmly between his shoulder blades.

Damien managed to lift his head, blinking, trying to clear his vision. Stupid rookie mistake on his part. "Who are you and what do you want?"

"I'm the welcome wagon. Your friend, Dante, hired me to greet you."

A string of expletives escaped him. Typical. Dante always did like to get others to do his dirty work for him. When Damien would have risen to his feet, the man behind him pressed down harder on his back.

"Not so fast. Dante isn't ready for you yet."

His arm was grabbed roughly and cold metal was clamped around one wrist. A growl rumbled in his chest. There was no effing way he was going to let this human cuff him! He gathered his strength, preparing to surge upwards and deal with the annoying twit, when a loud metallic screech filled the room followed by a reverberating bang as steel hit steel. Someone had entered the warehouse making no attempt to conceal their presence.

"At it again, Wes?" The sound of Sam's voice had both men freezing in place.

"Shit!" The man, Wes, cursed.

For a split second, Damien wondered what the hell Sam was doing here, then used the distraction she'd provided to twist over and grab the douche bag's leg. Wes gave a yelp of surprise and then a grunt of pain as he landed on the cement floor. Damien scrambled to his feet, the world spinning wildly as his head protested the movement. He swayed and braced himself with his hand on a barrel.

"Damien?" Sam called his name as she crossed the floor. There was no doubt that she hadn't expected to find him there.

He flicked a glance her way, blinking rapidly to clear his vision, then swung his attention towards the back of the building, wondering whether or not Dante was still in the building or if the sound of Sam's voice had scared him off. His stomach lurched, apparently in cahoots with his head about the inadvisability of moving too quickly. He took a deep breath, willing the contents of his stomach to stay in place.

"Damien?" Sam said his name again. "What's going on here?"

At the same time, somewhere near his feet, he could hear Wes cursing, scrambling to get to his feet. Hell, there was no time to explain, he was sure he'd caught sight of a wolf skulking in the shadows. "Watch the dickwad. I'll be back in a minute."

Dante was not getting away from him this time.

Damien approached the piles of pallets and boxes with caution. They formed a maze of short corridors and Dante could be hiding in any one of them. He sniffed the air but there was no scent of wolf, not even lilacs. Damn, the hit to his head had really messed him up. His vision was clearing but now his nose wasn't working.

Behind him, he could hear Sam chewing out his attacker, Wes. A glance over his shoulder showed them facing off, but it wasn't anything Sam couldn't handle. Wes was a skinny little runt and, from the look on her face, Sam had a bone to pick with the man.

Now where was Dante hiding?

A grunt, a scuffling sound then a crash sounded behind him. He turned to see what Sam was doing and a wave of icy fear washed over him. Sam and Wes had careened into the barrels, which were now teetering precariously over the grappling couple.

"Sam!" Even as he shouted out the warning, the topmost containers began to give way to gravity. Without thinking, he raced towards her, envisioning her being crushed under the heavy weight.

Everything seemed to happen at half speed. Each step he took was impossibly slow. He stretched out his arms to grab her. The first barrel came closer and closer to where she stood, her eyes widening in shock as she looked up and realized the danger she was in…

Betrayed: Book Two – The Road To Redemption

And then time returned to normal. Grabbing her by the waist, he jumped to the side, wrapping his arms around her in an attempt to shelter her. His momentum had them hitting the ground and sliding along the concrete floor. The metal containers crashed to the ground, the cacophony of sound drowning out all else. Damien winced as a barrel bounced off his shoulder, then another landed inches from his head. He could feel Sam clutching his leather jacket, her face buried in his chest. Ducking his head, he pressed his face to hers, the scent of her calming him despite the hell that seemed to be breaking loose all around them.

It was likely only seconds, but seemed longer before the cascade of barrels finally stopped and the warehouse grew quiet except for the pounding of his heart. Damien exhaled and loosened his grip on Sam before lifting his head and looking around. Barrels were strewn over the warehouse floor, a domino effect seeming to have taken place. He sat up and pushed away a barrel that rested against them. Sam got to her feet and he did likewise.

"Thanks." She brushed the dirt off her pants and jacket, her face pale, her voice not quite steady.

"No problem." He rolled his shoulder wincing as it protested the movement. A barrel landing on him, skidding along the ground, or being hit by a two-by-four; who knew what was the cause of the injury. At least nothing seemed broken.

"Your face is covered in blood." Sam reached up and smudged her thumb across his cheek. Her touch made his skin tingle and his breath catch. He leaned into the warmth of her palm for a moment before catching himself and stepping away.

"A face plant on concrete will do that." He touched his nose experimentally. It seemed to be intact as well. "Any sign of that guy, Wes?"

Sam stared at his blood on her fingers before wiping them off on her jeans. Without comment, she began wading through the barrels, finally calling out when she found his assailant. "He's here. Alive, but out cold." She fished through the man's pockets and pulled out his cell phone. "911? Yeah, we need an ambulance." After giving the address, she dropped the phone at his side.

"We should get out of here." Damien gestured towards the door.

"Yeah. Cops mean questions. Speaking of which," Sam gave him a sideways look. "Why were you here letting Wes use you as a punching bag?"

He thought quickly. "I was trying to track down Sinclair's spy. I thought this might be a good place for him to hide."

"And you were so busy, you let a two bit thug jump you?"

"I thought I saw someone near the back of the building." He shrugged. "Everyone makes mistakes."

"Likely you saw one of Wes' flunkies rather than Sinclair's spy." She snorted and Damien gave a silent sigh of relief that she mustn't have noticed the scent of lilacs.

As they left the building, Damien took one last look back. His sixth sense was telling him someone was still there, that being watched feeling was back again. It had been too much to hope that the bastard had been crushed by one of the falling barrels.

"You into kinky games?"

Her non-sequitur had him turning to her in surprise. "What?"

"The cuffs." She gestured towards his arm. "You and Wes role playing or something?"

He glanced at the handcuff that was still attached to one of his wrists then gave her a filthy look. "Not even remotely funny, Harper."

"Sorry, nearly being crushed by a gazillion barrels messes with my sense of humour."

Giving the cuff an experimental tug, he scowled. "I need to go back and see if Wes has the key on him."

Sam shook her head and urged him to keep walking. "Too late, I can hear the sirens already."

"I hope I can pick this with my left hand then," he muttered, studying the mechanism.

"Don't worry." She gave him a friendly shoulder nudge. "I've picked my share of locks."

"Why doesn't that surprise me?" He grinned at her, liking how she was bouncing back from her near death experience so quickly. No crying or going into shock for Sam Harper.

He gave her a ride back to the pack house. She sat behind him, lightly holding his waist. The feel of her body, so close to his, played havoc with his concentration. When he took a corner too sharply, she asked if he was concussed.

"No, my head's harder than that." He didn't add that the problem was his pants were too tight. Their brush with danger had excited him; a natural response, or so he tried to convince himself.

As Sam prepared for bed that night, she paused in front of the mirror and experimentally, prodded the bruises that adorned her body. None were serious and would likely fade by morning, but they were still tender to the touch. She could have been hurt a lot worse if Damien hadn't pulled her out of the way of the greatest danger.

She relived how it had felt to be held tightly in his arms, her head pressed to his chest. Being protected, sheltered, was an unusual experience for her. It had felt…good. Not that she wanted to be treated with kid gloves, she assured herself, but once in a while, with the right person, it was a nice change.

Unbidden an image of Damien appeared. She envisioned him standing behind her, his hands lightly holding her shoulders as he pressed tender kisses to her bruised flesh. What would it be like to feel his hands stroking her body? She narrowed her eyes and tried to imagine him removing her hot pink bra, replacing the cups with his palms. His hands would be work-roughened, manly, and he'd demand a response from her. The idea made her shiver in anticipation.

The right person. Was it Damien? Her wolf seemed to think so. And the pack liked him. He was good with the older members and patient with Chris. He'd risked himself to save her tonight, and she'd actually missed him while on patrol. A smile widened her mouth and stayed there as she climbed into bed and shut off the light.

Chapter 17

"We have to what?" Damien looked at Sam, sure he'd misheard.

"Pick apples. Jonah is going to make us apple pie for dessert tonight."

"That's what I thought you said." He looked back at the newel post he was tightening. The banister for the staircase to the second floor was too loose for safety so he'd toenailed a few screws into it. "Why can't you buy them from the store?"

"I could, but we have that old apple tree in the backyard and it's loaded with fruit. Plus, they're free. And it's fun."

"Fun?" Damien wasn't in the mood for fun. Dante had eluded him last night and, as a result, he'd spent much of today waiting and watching for the bastard to appear.

He gave the post a final tug before turning to give Sam his full attention. That she was obviously anticipating the chore with glee surprised him. Apple picking didn't fall under any Alpha duties that he was aware of, yet her eyes were definitely sparkling, the unusual violet shade seeming lighter than normal.

"Of course picking apples is fun!" She gave him a look as if he'd said he didn't know Harleys were the best ride. "Picking apples is a fall tradition. And even in the middle of the city, it does you good to 'get back to nature' for a while."

"If you say so." He didn't try to hide the doubt in his voice and she cocked her head to the side.

"You've never picked apples?"

"Nope. I've led a deprived life." He began to pack away the tools he'd been using.

"Deprived or depraved?"

Damien straightened as he heard the teasing tone in her voice. So they were back to where they'd been. Apparently sleep had mellowed her mood. Good. Tension between the

Alpha and Beta wasn't healthy for the pack. The fact that he found bantering with her enjoyable was merely a side benefit.

A smile twitched the corner of his mouth. "Which do you think?"

Sam shook her head. "I'm not touching that one. Come on." She headed to the backdoor and Damien followed, her happy mood causing his own to lighten.

A large apple tree stood near the back of the property. It was gnarled with age and leaned precariously towards the fence, almost half the branches hung over the alley that ran behind the pack house. He'd noticed the tree before, only vaguely registering that it was an apple tree. As he examined it, sure enough, he could spot apples festooning the branches and the ground below.

With his foot, he nudged one of the apples that lay neglected on the ground. It was decidedly squishy and a small swarm of fruit flies arose from it, protesting his disturbance of their home. They swirled around his foot for a moment before returning to feed on the fruit. This was going to be dessert? "A lot of these are rotten."

Sam was placing a ladder against the fence. She glanced at the ground and shrugged. "We don't spray for bugs so yeah, we lose some, but there are plenty of good ones still on the tree."

Damien didn't argue the point. It was her tree so she must know what she was doing. "Do you want me to go up?" He gestured towards the ladder.

"No. I'll go. The higher branches are pretty thin. They'd never support your weight." She rested one foot on the lower rung of the ladder. "You steady the ladder for me, and hand me the baskets."

He wanted to protest, but as he studied the tree from the ground, he recognized the truth of her statement. While he was stronger and taller, this was one case when that wasn't an advantage. The upper branches *were* skinny things. Resigning himself to the role of assistant, he positioned himself at the base of the ladder holding it steady while she ascended. Once she was seated on a branch, he climbed a couple of rungs and stretched to hand her a basket.

"You must have some monkey in you," he commented, watching her as she nimbly moved from branch to branch.

"I love heights." She grinned down at him before continuing to pluck the fruit.

In no time, the first basket was filled and she handed it down to him and accepted a new one. She began edging out farther and farther on the branches trying to reach the fruit.

"Be careful." He felt the urge to caution her. The branches were beginning to bend even under her slight weight.

"I'm fine. I've been climbing this tree my entire life. It's like walking through my bedroom; I can do it with my eyes closed." As she spoke, she leaned out, one apple mere inches from her fingertips.

"Sam…" Damien issued a warning.

She chuckled at his caution. The tree was old but sturdy. Glancing down, she noticed the concern in his face. It created a warm bubble of happiness inside her. Just like last night, he was concerned for her; it was a nice feeling.

See? He cares. Her wolf prompted her once again.

She looked down again. Only a faint bit of bruising remained on his face from where he'd been hit. Even with a Lycan's enhanced healing, injuries were still possible. For a while, she'd even wondered if he'd had a concussion.

"Sam…" Damien began what was likely another warning, but he didn't get to finish his statement.

There was cracking sound, she shouted in surprise, and the entire branch broke under her weight.

"Damn!" In the nick of time, she grabbed a branch over her head and swung her legs around it, keeping herself from falling. Unfortunately, the branch she'd been on hadn't fared as well and was now on the ground, surrounded by several baskets worth of apples. She hoped they weren't too bruised to be used in Jonah's pie. And Damien…

He was down! Last night he'd been hit pretty hard on the head and now... Hell! This apple picking adventure had seemed a good way to make amends with him, not get him killed!

As quick as she could, she scrambled down the tree, jumping the last few feet since the ladder was now on the ground. As soon as she landed, she froze in place, completely shocked by the sight before her.

Damien was slowly getting to his feet, not seriously injured as she'd first feared. He stood, rubbing his arm, surrounded by apples. His dark brows were lowered in a deadly scowl that would have had most wolves cowering in fear.

"I... I'm..." Sam tried to speak, but a fit of laughter overtook her. Damien, her Beta, the oh-so-tough rogue, was standing there with the remains of a smashed apple on top of his head and juice dripping down his face.

"What's so funny?" He wiped apple juice from his cheek, and kicked at the apples that surrounded his feet. "Being pelted with dozens of apples hurts, you know."

"Apple... Head..." She pointed at the top of his head, unable to get any other words out.

Frowning, Damien reached up and when his hand encountered the apple pulp, a look of understanding passed over his face. Compressing his lips, he snatched the remains of the offending fruit off his head and stared at it as if he couldn't believe an apple would have had the audacity to hit him and then stick around to gloat. "It's not that funny," he growled.

"Yes, it is." She leaned back against the trunk, holding her sides.

"Really? Then let's see how you like it." He stalked over, the apple mush in his hand.

Trying to control herself, she eyed him warily. "Damien, what are you thinking?"

"Guess." He was only a foot away, but Sam tried to dodge past him.

Damien shot out his arm and stopped her. When she would have moved in the other direction, he stepped sideways, fencing her in so she was trapped between his body and the tree trunk.

"Damien, mashing an apple on your Alpha's head is *not* a good idea." She tried to look stern, however the bit of apple pulp still caught in his stubble had the corners of her mouth twitching.

"He who laughs last…" Damien leered and raised the crushed apple towards her head. Sam squirmed and grabbed his wrist. He fought against her restraining hand, oh so slowly winning the battle. The mushy apple came closer and closer. In desperation to distract him from the dastardly deed, Sam reached up and licked his face.

"Hey!" Shocked, Damien stopped.

"Mmm…fresh squeezed apple juice." Sam gave his cheek another lick.

"Sam! That's…" He paused seemingly at a loss for words.

"Kind of hot?" Sam suggested. Holding his gaze with her own, she slowly flicked his lower lip with the tip of her tongue.

A growl rumbled in his throat and she repeated the performance, only this time she didn't withdraw. Grabbing the front of his shirt in her hands to steady herself, she teased his mouth, placing her teeth over his lower lip and tugging gently before replacing her teeth with her lips.

"Sam," he groaned, shutting his eyes. A battle seemed to wage within him until desire finally won. Gathering her close, he settled his mouth on hers, brushing back and forth slowly until her lips were so sensitive even the whisper of his breath over them sent shivers through her. Then he leaned in, kissing her fully, the tip of his tongue teasing hers before sliding into her wet, welcoming warmth.

The taste of him, the heat of him… At some point, he'd started to lean against her, and she was now pressed between him and the tree. Sam was lost in the moment, wrapping her arms around him, caressing his back. She rubbed her body against his, urging him on as shivers of delight swept over her.

Her wolf hummed with approval and when Damien dragged his mouth along her jaw, she arched her neck to give him better access. His teeth raked her flesh and she gave a whimper of need.

"Damien… Please, I—"

He jerked away at the sound of her voice, panting; the all too familiar look of guilt dawning on his face.

"Sam, I…can't…"

Need drove her onward. She grabbed his face, forcing him to look her in the eye. "Yes, you can! There's no reason…"

"I'm mated."

"She's dead and has been for three years. You said so yourself."

"No! I mean, yes. I mean…." He pulled away and dragged his hand through his hair. "I made a vow to her, Sam. I can't forget her."

"But that doesn't mean you can't still live. You aren't dead, Damien."

"You don't understand. Her last words to me were…" He paused and almost choked as he tried to speak. "She said 'never forget, love'. It was her dying wish, Sam." He shook his head. "I can't turn my back on that."

"And you won't forget her. She'll live on here, in your heart." Stepping closer, she pressed her hand to his chest. "And here, in your memories." She brushed her hand over his temple, her fingers lingering over the feel of his silky hair. "But you need to live in the present. You deserve to be happy."

His mouth twisted, a haunted look passing over his face. "I don't deserve anything."

"I think you do."

"No." He reached out and brushed his thumb over her lips. "Nice of you to say so, but, no."

"Everyone has skeletons in their closet." She pulled back from his touch.

"Well, I've got a whole graveyard."

"Yeah, right." Sam planted her hands on her hips. Soft and tender obviously wasn't going to work. "You're wallowing, Damien. Scared of me. Scared to take a chance at being happy."

"Nice try. I've heard all the 'scared' crap before." He looked away, his jaw tense.

"Maybe it's crap, maybe it isn't. Maybe your mate really was so selfish that her last wish was for you to spend your life alone with only a ghost to keep you company. Or maybe you're thinking is just so fucked up that it isn't worth my time trying to make you see reason!" Sam pushed him out of the way and stormed across the yard.

Damn the man, why did she keep coming back to him time and time again? He'd kicked her in the teeth more than once, throwing her advances back in her face. You'd think she'd have gotten the message. It wasn't as if she was a slow learner.

Stomping up the steps of the house, she slammed the back door behind her.

"Hey, Sam!" Jonah called out from the kitchen. "Do you have those apples for me?"

She didn't pause, merely calling over her shoulder. "They're in the backyard. Get Damien to bring them in. Unless he'd too afraid to commit to them, too!"

Chapter 18

Sam stared at the spreadsheet that outlined the month's expenses and income. The numbers blurred in front of her eyes, her mind otherwise occupied with Damien. Two days in a row now, he'd rebuffed her. The scent of his arousal had been obvious both at the pool hall and under the apple tree, so the question was why is he so reluctant to admit that he's attracted to her. It was damned confusing and neither she nor her wolf could come to a definitive conclusion as to whether or not the man wanted them. He responded only to pull away. She knew he found her attractive, had felt the physical response of his body, so what was the problem? Yes, he'd mentioned his mate, her dying words, but that had happened three years ago. No one was that devoted. Were they?

Or maybe he was. Maybe he really was still madly in love with his dead mate. In a way, it was admirable, something every female probably dreamed of; having a man so besotted with you that nothing could cause him to stray, not even death. Such a male was one in a million and it made Damien all the more appealing. That was, if she could get him to transfer that loyalty to her.

A twinge of guilt pricked her. Did she have the right to go after him? She hesitated on that point and then shook her head. If his mate had really loved him, she wouldn't want him to be alone and unhappy for the rest of his life. Real love wasn't that selfish. Reassured, Sam considered the problem from another point of view.

Perhaps it was her approach. Perhaps he liked to do the chasing, wanted her to be timid and shy. She made a face. There was no way she could pull that off for very long. If that was what he wanted they had no future together.

Her wolf twitched its ears angrily. *We are not giving up.*

"I didn't say we were."

You were thinking it. The creature pointed out. *But that's not the answer. I can sense both him and his wolf. They are confused but interested, so we must continue the pursuit.*

"It's not like we're chasing him through the wilderness, you know."

Of course not. We'll chase him through the back alleys. Her wolf looked smug as it settled down, for the moment content to dream of pursuing Damien through the city before cornering him in a dead-end alley. The ensuing fight would be exhilarating and, of course, could only end one way.

Sam had serious doubts about the plan even if the mental image appealed. Giving her head a shake, she once again tried to concentrate on more pressing matters, such as the pack's finances. She was just settling in to the task when a knock on the door interrupted her train of thought. Biting back a sigh of frustration, she gave permission to enter.

"How are the books looking this month?" Jonah wandered in and sat down opposite her.

It wasn't a secret from any of the members that they were in financial straits. Everyone pooled their resources from their 'human' jobs and she felt it only fair to let them know the state of things.

"We're in the black…barely. The bookcase I sold allowed me to pay our bills."

"Have you mentioned the sale to your grandfather yet?"

"You'd have heard him yelling if I had." She leaned back in her chair and folded her hands behind her head. "He hasn't been out of his room in ages and with how I've rearranged the furniture, I don't think he'd notice even if he did come out…or at least, not right away. And with any luck, I'd have time to take cover!"

"Would he really be that upset?" Jonah mimicked her pose; there was no strict formality between her and her packmates, unlike the protocols some of the older Alphas imposed.

"My grandmother loved those antiques, so yeah, he'd have a fit." She grimaced, imagining the fallout, but sentimentality didn't pay the bills. For the most part, she played things straight with her grandfather, but there were a few topics that were best avoided. Their financial status was one of them.

Samuel Harper had had a…unique…book keeping system, and she'd been hard pressed to figure out where their money had gone when she'd finally taken over that part of the job. It was puzzling given that he was so meticulous in most other areas. And when she'd asked him, he'd merely grumbled that research into infertility had taken a lot of it. She'd finally decided he simply wasn't a numbers man. After all, it didn't really matter; the facts remained the same. They'd owed a ton of money in back taxes and their utilities were on the verge of being shut off. She'd done what was needed to keep a roof over their heads and was now trying to build some financial security for the future.

She looked at the man sitting across from her. Jonah was in his mid-thirties, both he and his mate, Laurie, were lifelong members of the pack. What would happen to them and the others if there was no money to support them in their old age? And even now, it cut her to the core to have to deny them. They'd yet to produce any pups; another couple falling victim to the genetic flaw most seemed to carry. While they'd talked of adopting, parentless Lycan pups were rare and there wasn't money to pay for more fertility testing.

Feeling guilty, she gave him an extra warm smile. "What can I do for you?"

"I wanted to let you know that I switched patrols with Hiram. He and Damien are working on rewiring the kitchen and, since I'm a hazard when it comes to repairs, I said I'd do an extra shift."

"It's fine with me. Thanks for keeping me in the loop." Sam shuffled a few files, found the duty roster and made a notation of the change. "Was there something else?"

Jonah hesitated before speaking. "I made no secret regarding my reservations about taking on a rogue, but Damien seems like a decent guy. I've seen him talking with Hiram, asking him his opinion on how to fix a few things around the house. Makes Hiram feel good, you know?"

"I know." Sam nodded. She'd seen the same thing. For a rogue, Damien had a soft spot for the older members and went out of his way to talk to them.

Her wolf gave her a nudge. *See? This is why we need to continue our efforts. Damien is what we need and what the pack needs as well.*

"Anyway, I wanted you to know that I've changed my mind about him." Jonah stood up. "I have to get to work now."

"Evening shift this month, isn't it?" She flicked a glance at the chart she kept with everyone's schedule. Given that most of the members had jobs, she had to make sure their pack duties didn't conflict with their employment.

"Yep. I have to shower before I head over to the restaurant." He pushed out of the chair and left with a casual wave. Jonah worked as a chef at a local restaurant. Too bad he shared his culinary expertise with his packmates only once every two weeks. She was on kitchen duty tonight and knew the wieners and beans she'd planned were pathetic.

Her computer chimed indicating she'd received a message and Sam shifted her chair bringing it closer to the screen in order to check her email. It was from Lycan Link. Probably nothing important, but reading a dry newsletter was much more appealing than tackling the budget or working on dinner. Clicking on the message, she started to lean back only to freeze in place as she realized it was from OPATA, a division of Lycan Link. The word 'urgent' followed by her grandfather's name had her pulse beginning to race. This wasn't some general news release.

Leaning forward, she began to read.

"The Office of Pack Administration and Territory Allotment wishes to inform you that Kane Sinclair, current Alpha of Smythston, Oregon, has officially filed a request to take over the Chicago pack."

Her chest tightened and a cold feeling washed over her before settling in the pit of her stomach. She'd been expecting this, dreading it, hoping against hope, but to actually see it on the screen before her…

Swallowing the sick feeling that rose in her throat, she tried to read more but her vision blurred with fear…and anger. Fear had no place in her life so she grabbed onto the anger, dragging it to the foreground and whipping it into a fury.

"Hell and damnation!" She shoved her chair back and began to pace the small room. "Kane Sinclair, if you were here, I'd grab you by the neck and…" She clamped her mouth shut, allowing her imagination to run wild with the unspeakable things she'd like to do to the bastard.

Running her hands through her hair, she kicked the chair before exhaling. Calm down. This isn't the end. It's just the beginning of the fight. She had a few tricks up her sleeve and the Harpers weren't going down without one hell of a fight. What she needed to do was to see what he was building his case on.

Returning to her desk, she read the remainder of the message.

Sinclair claimed there were too few members to carry out the required duties for a territory of this size. Patrols, safety, resource management, economic development… Was the man crazy? Chicago was a city, not some backwoods territory that needed economic development!

There was a tap on the door and she glanced up to see Damien there, a look of concern on his face.

"Can I come in?" He'd heard her cursing—louder than usual, that is—and both he and his wolf had felt the need to seek her out. He'd been reluctant to give in to the instinctive pull. It smacked too much of having an emotional connection to her and that wasn't possible; his heart and soul already belonged to someone else. Hadn't he reminded her, and himself, of that yesterday? Yet at the same time, the antsy feeling had demanded action, and now, almost against his will, he found himself outside her office door.

She waved him in distractedly, no hint that she was still upset with him. That was one good thing about Sam Harper; she blew up but then it was over. No holding a grudge.

"Something wrong?" It couldn't be young Chris; the kid wasn't even home from school yet.

"Hmm? Yeah." Her eyes were still focused on the computer screen.

"Anything I can do?" He perched on the edge of her desk, forcing his hand to remain loosely at his side despite the fact that he wanted to give her a comforting touch.

"No. Yes. I don't know." She dragged her hands through her hair, finally looking at him. "That ass, Sinclair, has issued an official takeover request."

"Really?" Damien stood up and went to look out the window, guilt making him feel caged in. He shouldn't be surprised to learn that Kane had finally made his move. "On what grounds?"

"Too few members to handle the responsibilities."

He made a non-committal sound. It was a legitimate point, one he'd confirmed for Kane.

"It's complete crap, of course. My pack and I take excellent care of the area. We never slack off on patrols, we keep an eye on any shifters in the area and—"

Damien interrupted. He knew how hard she worked and didn't need her to point it out to him. "So, what are you going to do?" Turning to face her, he kept his expression bland as she sifted through the papers on her desk before pulling out a page. It was a copy of the month's duty roster.

"Prove he has no grounds for his claim." She tapped some keys on her computer and files appeared on the screen. "I have it all here and just have to update this past week; a list of duties, the pack members who carried them out, dates... Crap."

"What's wrong?" He stepped closer and peered over her shoulder.

"You aren't listed as an official pack member. That's the sort of thing Sinclair will pounce on."

Betrayed: Book Two – The Road To Redemption

He silently agreed. Kane was an expert at finding minute inconsistencies in reports. It was how the man had managed to get the Black Devils out of trouble on several occasions when youthful antics had put them at odds with the Academy's version of campus police.

"At least it's an easy fix. I can edit this report, add your name to the membership..." She paused and glanced his way. "When I hired you, you were Dante Esparza, but now....?"

"Damien Masterson will do." There'd been no point in making up a new identity for such a short period of time. Kane would take over the pack in a matter of weeks and he'd be on his way.

She typed in his name then scrunched her face. "Masterson? That suddenly sounds familiar. Like I've seen it come across my desk before."

He shrugged. No doubt his name had passed over her screen in one of Lycan Link's newsletters. There wouldn't have been a lot of information, though. Rogue Enforcers tended to be kept hush-hush so the general Lycan population didn't panic. Details would only have been given out on a need to know basis. And if Dante had been telling the truth, he'd been pardoned, so the record would have been purged. "Just a name I pulled out of a hat."

"Hmm..." Thankfully, she seemed more concerned about her report than double checking his story. She continued to enter data into her computer and then leaned back, a satisfied smile on her face. "There. We're now up one member. It'll even give the impression that the pack is growing."

"Why isn't it? Growing that is?"

"I told you. Infertility." Sam didn't even look his way, tapping a pen on her chin as she studied her duty roster.

"I know, but what about recruiting new members? It seems to me that would be an easy fix to the number problem. And new members would add to your gene pool which would dilute the genetic flaw."

Sam stilled the pen tapping before beginning again. Something about that small pause had him narrowing his eyes and trying to read her body language. She was hesitating, seeming to choose her words carefully. "Grandfather is very selective in who he wants joining the pack."

"Selective? How so?"

She shrugged. "You've met my grandfather. Not many measure up to his standards. He's very demanding and set in his ways. It doesn't make attracting new members easy." Grimacing, she stood up. "I have to tell him about the message from OPATA. Wish me luck."

Kane climbed the stairs to his bedroom suite, humming under his breath. He'd finally made his move against Chicago. It could have happened sooner, but he'd wanted to make sure he had a sound case. Now that he'd played his cards, all he had to do was wait and see what response Sam Harper—Senior or Junior—came up with. It wouldn't be much. They didn't have a leg to stand on and he had plenty of ammunition to back his initial offensive, thanks to his own research and the additional information Damien had given him.

Speaking of which, he hadn't heard from Damien in a few days though his silence wasn't a huge concern. The Chicago job was a safe assignment compared to some of the others the man had taken on over the years. Maybe he was actually relaxing a bit or, more likely, bickering with Sam Harper's granddaughter. He chuckled picturing the two together. It would be good for Damien to have someone challenge him.

"Elise!" He called out his mate's name as he entered the bedroom, eager to share his news with her.

She was crouched on the floor, Jacob seated on their bed in front of her. "Kane? Showing up in time for dinner? I thought you'd be holed up in your office for at least another three or four hours." Her smile was tight and there was an edge to her voice.

His step faltered. "I said I was sorry for missing dinner last night."

"And the night before."

"Yes, that, too."

"It was Helen's birthday, you know."

"I realized that later on and I apologized to her. Can you give it a rest?" He took a deep breath and then moved to stand behind her. "Hey there, buddy, what are you doing?" Reaching out over top of Elise's head, he ruffled Jacob's hair.

Jacob looked up at him with solemn eyes, his bottom lip pouted outward.

"Jacob? What's wrong?" Kane frowned, noting the tinge of pink on his son's nose and the faint tracks of dried tears staining his cheeks.

"He's in trouble and pouting about it, so don't encourage him." Elise pushed to her feet and Kane finally had a clear view of Jacob's knees. Both sported large bandages.

"What happened?"

Elise gathered a bloody washcloth and headed into the bathroom, calling out her explanation. "He was running in the house again, despite being told not to and took a tumble down the stairs. Thankfully, he only ended up with scraped knees. He could have broken an arm or hit his head."

"Jacob, you know better than to run in the house." He lightly scolded the boy. Instead of looking repentant, Jacob tried to lower his little brows into a scowl before averting his gaze and folding his arms. Kane did his best to hide his surprise while murmuring to Elise. "I think he's going to take after his Uncle Ryne."

Elise ignored his comment, instead brushing past and taking Jacob by the hand. She led him towards his room. "You'll stay in your room until you're ready to apologize for your bad behaviour.

"Elise, I don't think—"

She cast him a deadly look and Kane stopped speaking.

Once Jacob was in his room and the door was shut, she turned to him, speaking in hushed tones. "You don't think what?"

"Putting him in his room until he's ready to apologize – it isn't a good idea. He's stubborn and might not cave in."

"Then I'll wait him out." She folded her arms and jutted her chin, glaring at him.

"Elise—"

"And don't criticize how I discipline the children. You can't come waltzing in here—"

"I didn't *waltz* in—"

"And expect to take over—"

"I wasn't trying to take over—"

"When you're never around!"

"I am not 'never around'. I'm here at least as much as you are."

"I mean here with me and the children, not locked up in your office."

"It's not like I'm hiding or having a good time, you know. I'm working."

"And, of course, that's the most important thing."

"Well, the Chicago deal certainly is important. It's what's going to stop this." He waved his hand between them. They'd both acknowledged the bickering between them was getting out of hand and that his plans for expansion would solve the problem.

"But will it really?"

"What do you mean?"

"Will splitting the pack really mean you'll have more time? Or is it just another way to look impressive for High Council?"

"Impressive?"

"That's right. Impressive. You started talking about the Chicago takeover right after rumours began that High Council was mentioning your name." Elise straightened the bedspread, her movements brisk. "Ever since then Chicago and High Council are all you talk about, all you think about…"

"That's not so."

"Yes it is. Don't forget, I'm privy to your thoughts and feelings, Kane Sinclair. Work figures a lot more prominently than the children or I ever do."

"That's only because things are busy right now."

"And, of course, having two packs to watch over will push the children and me to the top of your priority list."

"Elise—"

"Kane, it will be twice the work. Two sets of books, two pack meetings, you'll have to fly out there several times a year."

"It won't be like that. I'll appoint someone—"

"Who? Who do you trust enough to handle all that authority? Certainly not John. You hardly let the man do anything around here."

"I trust John."

"Then you need to show it. He spends half his time twiddling his thumbs."

"That has nothing to do with Chicago."

"No, but it's something you need to consider. If you don't start using him, you're going to lose a good man."

"All right. Fine. I'll talk to him." He rubbed his neck wondering how the conversation had become so off topic. "The point is, we both agreed that Chicago—"

"No, we didn't. *I* never agreed. I said *maybe* Chicago was an option we could look at, and you jumped on that as an excuse to do what you wanted." She stopped straightening the covers and looked him in the eye. "I've gone along with it, but there's this sinking feeling in my stomach that it's wrong. The wrong move, the wrong time. Just…wrong."

"It's not the wrong move. You're worrying over nothing." He stepped forward and placed his hands on her shoulders. "I've contacted OPATA and they've forwarded my official bid to take over the Chicago pack."

Elise twisted away and moved to stare out the window. He tried to read her mind but was surprised to find she'd locked him out.

"Elise, what's this really about?"

"It's about us. Or the lack of 'us'. There's you and there's me, but we're separate from each other."

"No we're not." He scoffed at the idea. "We're blood bonded—"

"But that seems to be all we have. And it's not even doing us much good." She turned to face him. "Do you know how long I've been blocking you?"

"Well, right now and—"

"Two days, Kane. And you didn't even notice, did you?"

"I don't keep constant tabs on you. That's not what a blood bond is for."

"I realize that, but you should have noticed, at least once, that it was missing."

"I was busy—"

"Exactly. You're busy. You have no idea what's going on in my life."

He folded his arms. "You're renovating the Grey Goose."

She arched her brow. "And what else?"

Kane searched his memory, trying to recall anything else she'd said, but came up blank.

"See?"

He rubbed his forehead. "Elise, I'm tired. I came up here hoping to tell you about Chicago and grab a nap before the pack meeting tonight."

"Fine. Go take a nap. Don't let me and my petty concerns about our relationship get in your way."

"Elise—"

The sound of crying interrupted him.

"Leah's awake." Elise brushed past him and shut the door firmly behind her.

Kane stared at the closed panel and cursed softly. Why did Elise have to pick now to be so difficult. He was trying his best, dammit.

Chapter 19

Sam stared at her grandfather, wondering why he didn't speak. She'd told him about the message from OPATA and had expected him to rant and bluster about Sinclair. Instead, he'd gone silent, his eyes focused on something only he could see. The clenching and unclenching of his hands on the arms of his chair were the only indication as to how he was feeling.

"Grandfather? Is there something else you think I should have done?"

"What?" He looked at her, appearing almost surprised that she was there. "No. No, you did what you could. Now we need to see what his next move will be. Sinclair's a sly one. He'll have more complaints against us."

"Like what?" Sam shoved her hands in her pocket and widened her stance. "I've done everything by the book, just as you trained me."

"That won't matter. He'll twist and turn facts, use the Book of the Law against us. Dig up the past..." He shook his head.

"What do you mean, 'dig up the past'? If you mean the bootleggers, that was over half a century ago and—"

He waved his hand as if to brush her words away. "I need to think. Be on your way."

"I—"

"On your way, girl!" He growled the order and Sam snapped her mouth shut in surprise.

It had been years since he'd used quite that tone with her and she was taken aback by it. Part of her wanted to snap at him in return, but she could see he was agitated. She left the room without a word and pulled the door shut behind her.

Standing outside his room, she frowned. He'd been frail, physically, for some time, but mentally he'd always seemed sharp. Was that mental acuity fading? Were his moods more extreme than before and she hadn't noticed until now? Her stomach clenched at the idea that her grandfather's mind could be failing as well. For all that it irked to be an acting Alpha, it had also been comforting knowing he was there to bounce ideas off of, to turn to for confirmation now and then.

There was a rustling sound coming from her grandfather's room and she cocked her head trying to hear better. He was moving some papers about, perhaps opening a book. The old journals she'd given him?

He cursed softly and she wondered what he was reading and if it had something to do with his concern that Sinclair would 'dig up the past'.

Perhaps she should have demanded that her grandfather explain…and perhaps it was nothing. Perhaps he was merely an old man confusing events. She hated being indecisive, but she wasn't sure if pushing was the right move. Her wolf was puzzled, too, sensing the concern of the aging beast that dwelled within her grandfather.

Giving her head a shake, she headed towards the cellar. Exercise often helped her clarify her thoughts, and it might also help with the knot of tension that was growing between her shoulder blades.

Damien sat on the edge of his bed, staring at the phone in his hand. He hadn't checked in with Kane for a few days but knew his friend would be expecting a call. Kane had made his move and would be wondering what the reaction was at this end.

He pressed the required sequence of numbers and brought the device to his ear. Stalling was for cowards and he'd always tried to face his problems head on.

"Damien? About time you checked in."

"And hello to you, too." Damien leaned back against the headboard. "Your phone manners are almost as good as Ryne's."

"Insults? Is that why you called?"

Betrayed: Book Two – The Road To Redemption

"No." He laughed softly remembering how the three of them had enjoyed taking jibes at each other. "I wanted to let you know that OPATA delivered your message to Sam Harper."

"And?" The teasing quality immediately left Kane's voice.

"She was royally pissed off. Sent in a duty roster outlining how all required jobs are being covered."

Kane snorted.

"And…yours truly is now officially on the pack membership list."

"You are? What name did you give?"

"My own. No point in hiding." He got up and moved to stare out the window. "I heard that I've been pardoned. Lycan Link isn't about to throw me in detention anymore."

There was beat before Kane replied. "I only received that news two days ago and was waiting for confirmation before forwarding it to you. Who's your informant?"

"No one you know." There was no need for Kane to know about Dante. Smythston was a quiet, quaint corner of the world; slime balls like Dante had no place there. Damien intended to keep it that way.

"He must have some inside connections."

Kane was pressing for information, but Damien didn't bite. How Dante got his information had always been a mystery, but his abilities in that area had been one of the reasons Deirdre had kept the man in her stable.

After a moment, Kane cleared his throat, wisely realizing he was at a dead end. "Well, it's still good news. You won't have to be looking over your shoulder all the time."

"At least not for Lycan Link's Trackers."

"Right." Another pause and Damien could sense Kane's curiosity. Too bad. There were parts of his life he shared with no one, not even his closest friends. "So, you said Harper countered my claim."

"Yep. What's your next move?"

"I'm submitting that the pack is operating under false pretences. Old man Harper isn't really the Alpha anymore.

You said yourself that he hasn't left his room since you've been there and the granddaughter does all the work." There was a faint creaking noise as if Kane were leaning back in his chair. "'*All packs that are members of the Lycan Link affiliation must maintain honest and up to date records of pack administration. This is not only for the benefit of Lycan Link but so that there is a clear line of accountability should problems arise.*' That's a direct quote from the Book of the Law."

"It might work." Damien watched out his window as Chris walked across the yard, returning home after his day at school. How would the boy do under Kane's administration? There'd be more pack members for the kid to interact with, but Kane was strict…

"You still there, Damien?"

"Yeah, sorry. What did you say?"

"Nothing important. Keep me posted as to what's going on at your end. Between the two of us, we should have the Chicago pack transferred over to me before month's end."

Damien signed off. By the end of the month Kane would be in charge, and Sam… What would she do? Would Kane allow her to stay on, perhaps as a Beta? And would she accept the position if it were offered?

She could come with us. His wolf suggested.

The idea appealed. When he was around Sam, the flat dead feeling he carried inside faded away. But in the end, he had nothing to offer her. Sam was a pack animal through and through while he had no home and no plans beyond this job for Kane. There was a physical attraction between them, but his heart and soul were dead. No, he'd be leaving by himself when this job was done.

"Hey, Damien!" He could hear Chris' footsteps thundering up the stairs. In a moment, the pup would be knocking on his door, eager to work on the motorcycle again. His mouth twisted as he contemplated how Chris would react if his deception was ever revealed; the kid had developed a case of hero worship. He felt like a bastard just thinking of how crestfallen the boy would be.

Betrayed: Book Two – The Road To Redemption

Damien rubbed his thumb over the phone and shook his head wondering how it could be that, once again, he found himself caught in a situation of divided loyalties and blurred lines of right and wrong. Did he have an effing sign over his head or something?

Patrol that night was tense. Sam didn't feel like talking and neither, apparently, did Damien, which was actually a good thing. If she opened her mouth, she'd vent her bad humour on whoever was nearest and somehow she knew Damien wouldn't stand there and take it.

Instead, she grumbled to herself over what she saw as her personal failures. She hadn't been able to pick up the trail of Sinclair's spy. She hadn't heard back from OPATA, yet. Hell, she hadn't even figured out what Damien's dubious friend had told him, despite the fact that her gut was telling her it was something worth knowing. Add to that her grandfather seeming preoccupied when she'd stopped by before leaving...

She grimaced. Too many unknowns made her grumpy. Being in control was important to her, and right now she had the feeling that everything was slipping through her fingers.

God, what if she lost the territory? After a clear line of succession for over a century and a half, the Harper name was synonymous with Chicago. The shame of losing ownership could very well do her grandfather in. And what would happen to her packmates? Would Sinclair assimilate them, or kick them out? It would be his right, if he won. She gnawed her lip wondering who would take in Hiram. Perhaps, his daughter's new pack might consider him, but he was old, a drain on a pack's resources...

Her grandfather had gone against tradition by training her and putting her in charge. She couldn't let him or her packmates down. If worse came to worse she'd issue an old fashion challenge, a fight to the death if need be. Excitement and fear filled her at the thought.

She could take Sinclair, couldn't she? Sam recalled the last time she'd met the man. It had been when they'd been arguing over the fate of Cassandra Greyson. The man was definitely fit. She flicked a glance at Damien; he was of a similar build. Perhaps...

"Are we going in here tonight?" Damien drew her attention to the fact that they were outside Club Mystique.

"Is your friend, Lilac Man, waiting for you?"

He shrugged. "Maybe. I never know when he'll turn up. And for the record, he isn't a friend."

"Whatever. We might as well check the place out since we're here." She pushed her way through the crowd and, as usual, the bouncer ushered her in. He didn't try to stop Damien this time either. Her Beta did tend to leave an impression.

"I'll wait at the bar while you look around." She shouted the words in order to be heard over the music. It appeared to be a Woodstock theme tonight and the sounds of Joplin were blaring over the speakers.

"Drinking again?" He quirked his brow at her and she felt the mood between them lighten. There was something about the man's teasing that was immensely appealing to her.

"Only around you."

"You're not the first to say that." He chuckled and slipped into the crowd.

Sam watched him disappear from sight and then made her way to the corner of the bar, catching Tina's attention as she approached. Tonight, the bartender was dressed in iridescent blues and had butterflies painted near the corner of each eye.

"Back so soon." Tina set a drink in front her and leaned against the bar, twirling a strand of hair around one finger, a distant dreamy aura surrounding her.

"Are you buzzed?" Sam gave the woman a suspicious look.

"No. Just trying to look the part. Tonight's theme is the summer of free love, drugs, and rock and roll."

Sam snorted. "Well, float down off your cloud for a minute. I need some information and I don't have long." The music was loud enough that she didn't have to worry about lowering her voice.

Tina's eyes lost their unfocused look. "What's up?"

"Another Alpha wants to take over my pack. What do you sense? Does he have a chance?"

"Perhaps." Tina stared off into the distance, her eyes unfocused.

Sam nursed her drink and waited. Exactly how 'Others' did whatever it was that they did, she had no idea.

Eventually, Tina gave a shiver and shook her head as if to rid it of something unpleasant. "A battle will be fought; the lovers' hearts will be like a phoenix, dying as the masks are torn off. The winner will be the loser and the loser will win."

"Say what?" Sam blinked.

"I know. It's weird, but that's what I felt." Tina made an apologetic face.

Sam compressed her lips. "I get the battle part, but 'lovers like a phoenix'?"

"Have you taken a lover recently?" Tina gave her a speculative look.

"Let's say I'm considering it." Sam took a sip of her drink while watching Tina's expression. Delighted was too calm a word to describe it; the woman was a romantic at heart.

"Really? Who? Not someone from the neighbourhood."

"No." She looked over her shoulder to make sure Damien wasn't nearby. "The rogue I hired; he's…interesting. Hot."

"Wow. First time I've heard you say that." Tina glanced about the room. "I take it he's here."

Sam nodded. "Tall, dark hair. Watch when I leave and you'll see him."

"Not going to introduce us?"

"No." She sighed. "And nothing might happen. He's hung up on his dead mate."

"That's too bad." Tina made a face and then brightened. "Hey! Remember what I said a while back, when you asked if there was a Lycan in the area? I sensed he had two faces.

Maybe it meant your rogue. His past and his future could be what the two was referring to."

"Maybe," Sam said doubtfully. "But I think you're stretching things."

Tina pouted and then sighed when she noticed the other bartender glaring her way. "I'd better get back to work. Gwyneth is glowering at me."

"Since she's the owner, I guess you better."

"Yeah." Tina picked up Sam's empty glass and wandered off, her 'Woodstock' expression in place once more. Sam turned around to survey the room.

The place was more packed than usual. Rather than fighting the crowd, she decided to stay in her usual spot at the bar and study the patrons from there. She'd let Damien do the leg work. Besides, she wanted to consider the information Tina had passed on—if it could be called information. A poetic prophecy was a more apt term, but it was better than nothing.

'The winner would be the loser and the loser the winner.' Now what the hell could that mean? Winning a battle against Sinclair would in no way make her a loser; it would secure the territory. That was her prime concern. And if Sinclair lost, how could he become a winner?

Maybe her grandfather was right and she was a fool to put any stock in the vague mutterings of an Other. She grimaced and shook her head, not wanting to be as narrow minded as he was. After all, Tina was the closest thing to a female friend that she'd ever had and the woman *had* been useful in the past. Hadn't Tina's vision helped locate young Chris last time he'd broken curfew?

Spying Damien making his way through the throng, she slid off her stool and met him half way. "Did you find him?"

"Lilac Man?" Damien gave a ghost of a smile. "No."

"The information he had for you—would it help me stave off Sinclair's bid?"

"Not really."

As usual, Damien wasn't being a font of information, but this wasn't the time or place to argue the matter and she wasn't sure it was a battle she'd win anyway. Sam sighed in irritation and brushed past him, making her way out of the club. Dealing with a rogue was damned annoying. She'd tackle the problem of Lilac Man eventually, right now a more pressing matter needed to be addressed.

Once they were in a relatively quieter location—if you could call a busy street corner quieter—she turned to present him with an idea she'd been mulling over.

"I want you to train me."

Damien had been staring across the street, seeming to search the shadows. He gave her a surprised look, almost as if he'd forgotten she was there. "What was that? Train you? Why?"

"So I can fight with Kane Sinclair."

"Fight?"

"You heard me. Hopefully, it won't come to that, but I need to be prepared. I'm good, but, as you pointed out the other day, there are areas that I could improve." She looked him up and down. "Plus, you seem to be about Sinclair's size from what I can recall. It would be good practice for me to have a larger opponent."

He didn't respond right away and she gave an impatient growl. "You can agree on your own or, as your Alpha, I can order you to do it."

"Order me?" Damien raised his brows. "I'm a rogue. Orders and I don't get along."

"Then I suggest you agree voluntarily." She placed her hands on her hips and lifted her chin, her gaze steady.

"Damn, Sugar. You are a spitfire, aren't you?" He cocked his head, a hint of admiration showing in his expression.

She growled at the despised nickname he'd given her. "Well?"

He hesitated, then shrugged. "Sure. I'll give you a few pointers."

"Pointers?"

"You're good. You said so yourself. It won't take much to bring you up to speed."

His praise created a warm feeling inside her. She didn't lack self-esteem, but it was still nice to hear that someone respected your skills. Of course, she couldn't let it show.

"Good. We'll start tomorrow." She nodded across the street. "What were you looking at?"

He stared across the street and rubbed the back of his neck. "Probably nothing. I think I'm getting paranoid."

"With Sinclair breathing down our necks, we all are." Shoving her hands in her pockets, she took off down that street at a brisk pace. They needed to complete their patrol.

Chapter 20

Damien lay on his bed at the pack house, staring at the ceiling. It was two in the morning, they'd returned from patrol around midnight, but he wasn't sleepy and hadn't bothered to get undressed. Instead, he mulled over his conversation with Sam.

She'd asked him to help train her. Surely, she wasn't thinking of issuing a challenge; an old fashioned fight to the death.

It would be suicide on her part, his wolf fretted. *She's good, but Kane is twice her weight. Size alone gives him a distinct advantage.*

The animal was right. It had to be nerves, desperation even, that had her thinking along those lines. His stomach twisted at the thought of Sam and Kane locked in a battle to the death and he quickly pushed the image aside. In the end, she'd come to see reason. OPATA would issue its decision based on clear cut facts and legal precedents; a challenge wasn't even remotely in the cards.

We could play along, help her train, his wolf suggested, *but at the same time, make sure she knows the folly of her idea.*

He nodded in agreement. Kane taking over the pack was the only logical outcome. She just had to face facts, no matter how unpalatable they might be.

What will she say when she learns the truth about us? The beast had grown fond of Sam and had been nudging him about the issue all day.

"Nothing," he replied. "She won't say anything because she'll never know. Once Kane takes over, we'll slip away. Our job here—both the one she 'hired' us for and the one Kane sent us on—will be done."

His conscience pricked as he considered how he'd deceived both Sam and the pack members. It was nothing new; he'd done it many times during his days working for Deirdre, and even a few times as an Enforcer when he'd gone undercover.

But this seemed different somehow. It shouldn't; it was just another job. Or so he kept telling himself.

He rolled over and plumped his pillow, his gaze falling on the bedside table and his wallet that sat there. Reaching out, he flipped to Beth's picture and studied it. How would she feel about what he was doing? She'd never approved of Deirdre; her spirit had always gently chided him during those dark days.

"What do you think, Beth? Is Sam being unreasonable? Am I doing the right thing, informing on her to help Kane?"

No voice echoed in his mind. Beth's image didn't change. Her eyes stared out at him from the photograph, focused on some distant point, her smile soft but vague. There was no approval, no reproachful look. For once it seemed to be only a picture, an image printed on paper using various shades of ink.

It was...unsettling.

Damien frowned and slowly closed the wallet.

Beth? He sent out the mental message, but beyond the faintest wave of warmth brushing over him there was no other response.

He pushed himself upright, a restlessness invading him not unlike what he'd felt during his days as a complete rogue. The room suddenly seemed too confining and he moved to the window, pushing it open and then leaning out. Arms braced on the frame, he breathed in the air that spelled freedom, but did he want it?

The need to do something, anything, was building inside him like a pressure cooker waiting to explode. He could go hunting for Dante. Since the incident in the warehouse, he'd not heard from the man. Maybe the bastard had been injured by the barrels...or maybe he was tormenting some other victim. Like the after effects of a greasy pizza, the man would be back again. It was only a matter of time and there wasn't a damned thing he could do about it.

Moist night air touched his skin, the slight breeze ruffling his hair. The moon had started to wane but was still bright enough to illuminate the small yard below. His gaze fell on his motorcycle and without thinking, he swung himself out the window and shimmied down the drain pipe.

A ride with nothing but speed and open highway was what he needed right now. The wind in his face, tugging at his clothing, wiping all thought from his mind.

Lightly, he dropped to the ground, then padded silently across the dew drenched grass. The house was in darkness, the windows like blind eyes not noticing his passing. There was no point in waking everyone, so he planned to push his motorcycle to the street. Mere yards from where he'd parked, he froze at the sound of a voice coming from the shadows.

"Going somewhere?"

He turned to see Sam a few feet away. She was astride her own bike.

"Yeah. I need to take a ride, blow the cobwebs out of my brain." His answer was terse; he didn't feel like talking.

"Really?"

He could sense her watching him and soon realized why. He'd been showing Chris how to clean the carburetor and his ride was still in pieces. "Damn."

She cocked her head, amusement in her eyes, a dare evident in her voice. "Wanna share?"

He eyed her and her bike, the need to get away warring with his need to be alone. Finally, he gave a shrug. Once they were out of the city, he could always shift and go for a run. With a nod he walked over and climbed on behind her.

His thighs cradled her hips, her back brushing his front. It was an intimate position, but he did his best to ignore it, his hands lightly resting on her hips to steady himself. She was short enough, that he could almost rest his chin on the top of her head, but of course he didn't. Instead, he studied her back; her straight spine, the muscles playing under the thin tank top she wore. He could see the nape of her neck and frowned, realizing she had a tattoo there. Two words in a swirling script. Before he could make them out, she moved and the edges of her hair hid them from view.

Sam started the engine, apparently not caring that most of the neighbourhood was sleeping, and steered the bike out on to the street.

"Where you headed?"

"A little place about ten miles from here."

"Another bar?"

"An all-night ice cream parlor."

"Ice cream?" He wasn't sure he'd heard right over the roar of the engine. "You've got to be kidding."

"Nope. I need ice cream. The good stuff, not frozen yogurt or ice-milk. I need the kind made with real cream and smothered in hot fudge."

Despite his mood, Damien found himself chuckling softly. Sam Harper, the bad-ass, leather-clad, motorcycle-riding Alpha, needed a sugar fix.

"You want some?"

"Can't I steal some of yours?"

"You do and I'll break your arm."

Through the rearview mirror, he was able to catch a glimpse of her expression. She was smiling, her eyes crinkling in the corners, as the wind whipped her hair away from her face. It wasn't a look he often saw on her; she was usually serious, caught up in taking care of the pack. He smiled, pleased that she was able to find a way to relax, even if it was only for an hour or two.

When they arrived at their destination, Damien looked around with interest, noting the number of people sitting on benches near the shop. Who'd have thought eating ice cream in the middle of the night was so popular.

"They're only open until Halloween," Sam explained as she dismounted. "After that, they close up shop and head to Florida where they have a similar place."

"Seems like they do a good business."

"Quality product and good service." She approached the takeout window and placed her order, then glanced his way. "What'll you have?"

"You choose." He wasn't an aficionado and figured whatever she ordered he could handle.

In a matter of minutes she was leading him towards an empty bench, a bowl of ice cream in each hand.

"Here." Sam sat down and handed him his bowl. He stared at it. The concoction was blue with colourful chunks of some candy-like substance showing here and there.

"What is it?" He sniffed the ice cream suspiciously and poked it with his spoon.

"Bubble gum."

"Bubble gum ice cream?"

"Yep. See those coloured chunks?" She pointed with her spoon. "Real bubble gum. When you've finished the ice cream you can chew it."

Damien made a face but gamely took a bite and then nodded in approval. "Not bad. What do you do with the pieces of bubble-gum?"

"Tuck them between your gum and your cheek. Or you can spit them out into your hand until you're done eating the ice cream, then chew them."

Damien considered his options while watching Sam enjoy her own treat. She scooped up a bit of ice cream onto her spoon and then dipped it in a pool of hot fudge, swirling it around before popping it into her mouth. Her eyes closed as her lips curved upwards, a blissful expression settling on her face. As she drew the now empty utensil from her mouth, a low moan of pleasure escaped her. Opening her eyes, she beamed at him.

"Heavenly."

"Really?"

"Definitely." She kept her gaze fixed on his as she licked a trace of fudge off her spoon, a mischievous glint in her eyes. His body hardened in response and he shifted in his seat.

"Uncomfortable?" She blinked innocently and he growled at her.

"You're playing with fire, Sugar."

"I like the heat," she countered.

He was tempted, so tempted, to reach across the table, cup the back of her head and kiss her until she was aching as much he was. Instead, he took another bite of his ice cream, willing the cold food to cool his ardour as well as his mouth. A change of topic seemed in order.

"Tell me about your tattoos."

"My tats?"

He nodded. "I saw you had one on your nape but didn't have a chance to get a good look."

She turned and bent her neck so he could see the two words. Duty. Strength. Each was written in an elegant script that somehow contrasted with the meaning of the words and yet also fit. He traced each with his fingertip and Sam shivered at his touch. She turned to face him, her cheeks lightly flushed.

"Nice." He didn't comment on the fact that his touch appeared to have affected her. "Why'd you choose those particular words?"

For once she didn't meet his eye, instead idly watched a group at a nearby table. "They represent the qualities of an Alpha. Grandfather said there were three, but I had to discover them for myself. Each time I figured one out, I had it tattooed on."

"Which came first?"

"Duty. That one was obvious." She flicked a glance at him. "An Alpha has to put the needs of the pack above his, or her, own wants. No matter how tired or pissed off you might be, you do your duty and make sure everyone is safe, has food and shelter. A pack has to work together like a well-oiled machine; that can only happen if the Alpha sets the example."

"And strength?"

Sam ate another spoon of ice cream, swallowing before she answered. "That one took a bit longer to figure out, but I eventually realized it. Strength is important. Not just physical strength, though you need that in order to keep the wolves in line, but strength of mind and character." She spoke with such conviction that Damien felt strangely proud of her. He cleared his throat.

"Makes sense. And the third one...?"

She scowled. "I don't know. Every time I think I have it figured out, Grandfather says no."

"Maybe he's stringing you along?"

"No. My grandfather doesn't joke. There's a third quality and he says when I finally figure it out, I'll automatically know it's the missing piece." She thoughtfully scraped the last drops of ice cream from the bowl. "Every quality I've come up with has been good, but I never get that 'this is it' feeling."

Without meaning to, he found himself reaching out to gently squeeze her hand. "I hope you find it one day." He meant the words. Being Alpha was her life. And it made him feel like crap.

"Thanks. For a rogue, you can be pretty nice, you know."

He looked away and didn't answer.

Chapter 21

Damien dreamed of Beth. Not of the fire or the pain of losing her and his unborn child. Instead, pleasant memories invaded his sleep. Small snippets of daily life that brought a smile to his face and left him relaxed and refreshed upon waking. He showered and dressed, humming under his breath and then went about some of the chores he'd set for himself, the first of which was putting his bike back together.

Luckily the task was easily accomplished. He chuckled thinking how much faster it went without having to explain each step to Christopher. It wasn't that he minded the boy hanging around him; it just slowed things down a bit.

Wiping the grease from his hands with a rag, he studied the pack house. It had been solidly built and the basic structure was still sound, but wouldn't remain that way much longer unless repairs were made. Today, he'd decided to caulk the windows to keep water from seeping in. If it wasn't dealt with soon, there'd be plaster damage. With any luck, he could have the bottom floor windows done before it was time for his sparring session with Sam.

They'd arranged to meet in the cellar and, while he worked, he mentally prepared a list of moves to practise. It was strange being on the instructing end and made him think of the Enforcer sessions he'd had with Reno. The man had been tough and had expected the men working under him to be equally so. An unexpected urge to talk to Reno came over him and he actually paused, wondering if he dared. How did you start a conversation after so long and what would the other man say?

Damien scowled. He sucked at social niceties. Should he act as if nothing happened or should he apologize? And what exactly would he be apologizing for? Yeah, he'd made some crappy decisions, but at the time, they'd seemed the right thing to do.

Hell. He set down the tools he was using and pulled out his phone. Dithering made him edgy. Might as well just do it.

He punched in the numbers, then leaned back against the house, and began to mentally count the rings. Thankfully it wasn't too hot yet because making this call was causing him to sweat. Wiping one hand on his pants, he exhaled loudly, then shifted from one foot to the other.

"Smith." Reno's voice rumbled in his ears.

At the sound of his old friend's voice, Damien felt tongue tied. He glanced about wildly, randomly noting facts. The old picket fence was weathered and needed painting. A nearby tree had only a few coloured leaves despite the fact that it was now autumn. White puffy clouds were marring the bright blue sky. Damn, he was an idiot.

He cleared his throat and spoke. "Hey, Reno. What are you up to?"

Now the silence came from the other end of the line. Damien held his breath, his heartbeat pounding in his ears. Would Reno reply or hang up? A second ticked by, then another. Finally, an answer.

"I'm doing damned paperwork. What about you?"

Damien closed his eyes and exhaled in relief. The hardest part was over; the first words had been spoken. "I'm caulking windows."

"Windows?"

"Yeah. Windows."

Reno chuckled. "That's not the kind of 'cocking' you used to do."

And with that, they fell into their old banter. No mention was made of Beth or Purists or any of the things that had driven them apart. It was a short, banal conversation about the weather and the state of the world. Damien asked about Brandi, Reno's mate. Reno asked how he was feeling.

"I'm good. Eating every day, a roof over my head." Damien answered lightly.

"Glad to hear it." There was a pause. Damien could sense Reno wanted to ask more, but didn't dare.

Damien exhaled knowing the conversation had run its course and was teetering on the edge of getting awkward. "Listen, I've got to go."

"Yeah." Reno cleared his voice. "Those windows are waiting for you, I'm sure."

He laughed lightly, as he was meant to. "And your paperwork."

"Right." Another pause. "It was good to hear from you, kid."

Kid. Reno had called him that when they'd first become partners. It sort of choked him up to hear it again.

"Same here, old man."

"Call again?"

"I will. Soon." Damien hung up and clenched the phone in his hand. The ice had been broken and it felt good. Sure, they needed to have a serious talk, but for starters… He gave a nod and shoved the phone in his pocket. Two more windows to do and then it would be time to meet Sam.

"Damn, that hurt." Sam rubbed her jaw and checked her teeth with her tongue. All there and none were loose; a miracle given the blow she'd just received. She scowled at Damien. "Did you even try to pull that punch?"

He shrugged. "Not much. If you want to fight an Alpha like Kane, then you have to be prepared to take the pain."

"And what's with the effing rhymes? You sound like that boxer, what's-his-name." She worked her jaw back and forth, decided it was still functional and then resumed her fighting stance.

"I thought women loved poetry."

"Not when you're beating the crap out of them."

"You asked me to."

"Yeah, I know. I'm an idiot." She shook her head. "Come at me again."

Damien gave a devilish grin and Sam felt her heart lurch. The overhead lights emphasized his dark good looks, the shadow of stubble, his silvery eyes. How could one man— She didn't get to finish the thought before he launched himself at her again and she was forced to concentrate on defence.

Protect your chin, protect your chin. She chanted the mantra to herself as she blocked his blows while trying to find openings to strike back. Damien came at her like some automated fighting machine, no expression on his face, just hit after hit after hit. When she did manage to take a shot at him, he barely grunted.

Irritation grew within her. She'd been in more fights than she could recall. Her opponents had always shown at least some reaction to her assault. Doubt began to creep in and—

"Argh!" She flew backward and hit the wall. Not even trying to catch herself, she slid down and landed on the floor, jarring her spine. Sweat dripped in her eyes and her hair stuck to her forehead and neck. A towel hit her in the face and she caught it just before it fell to the ground. "Thanks." She glared up at him.

He stood over her, hands braced on his hip, breathing heavily. Sweat stained his shirt and he pulled the garment off, using it as a rag to dry himself. "You dropped your guard again."

"I know. You don't have to tell me." She twisted her lips, totally disgusted with herself.

"Yeah. I do. I'm training you and I need to know why your fighting form fell apart so we can fix it."

"Why I fell apart? I..." She shrugged. "I don't know."

"What were you thinking?" He squatted in front of her so their eyes were almost level.

Sam made a face, hating having to confess her own sense of failure. It made her feel...exposed. Rather than look at him, she studied the towel she was bunching in her hands. "I was thinking that I wasn't having any effect on you. All my other opponents would have been giving some sign that I'd hurt them..." She let her voice trail off and flicked a look at him.

"And by doing that, they would have fed into your sense of power, let you know you had a chance against them. Your wolf would see their weakness and attack with even more ferocity."

She reflected on what she'd felt during previous fights and nodded. "That's true. And when you didn't react just now, it made me have doubts."

"Which, in turn, gave me the advantage." He shifted to sit against the wall beside her. "Every animal looks for weakness in another and when they see it, they instinctively attack. If you're fighting another Lycan you can't show any vulnerability because it gives your opponent power."

"So I did hurt you?"

"Sadistic little thing, aren't you?" Damien gave a soft huff of laughter. "Yeah, Sugar, I've got aches and pains yelling at me, but I try not to let it show. Being a rogue helps of course. My wolf is more ornery than most."

Sam mulled over what he'd said. "So basically, it comes down to blocking out physical discomfort, staying focused and believing you can win."

"That, and protecting yourself." He reached out and tapped her chin. "Especially here."

She rolled her eyes and got to her feet. "Right. Ready for another round?"

Damien nodded and went to get up, wincing slightly as he straightened his leg.

"You okay?"

He brushed off her concern. "Old wound. It stiffens up sometimes."

"I've noticed you have a bit of a limp. It must have been pretty bad not to heal."

"It was." A shadow crossed over his face, the teasing quality disappearing. "I didn't give it sufficient time to repair fully. That ornery rogue in me again." He brushed his hair back from his face and braced himself. "I'm ready. Do your worst."

"Or my best." She quipped before tackling him once again.

Half an hour later, Damien declared they were done. "Good enough. You're getting tired and sloppy."

As much as it galled to admit it, Sam knew he was right. Still, it had been a good session and she'd picked up some pointers. Fine tuning, that's all it really was. An Alpha had to be open to new learning. She paused, water bottle halfway to her mouth trying to decide if that could be the missing third quality.

Openness.

Nah, it didn't feel right.

"What are you thinking now?" Damien was watching her and she shrugged.

"About being an Alpha."

"Is that all you ever think about?" He was wiping off his chest and she followed the movement of his hands, visually tracing his sculpted pecs and rock hard abs. When he dropped the towel he'd been using and bent to grab his own water bottle, she couldn't help but notice how the lightweight track pants clung to his tight butt. What would it be like to cup her hands around those curves and press him close? Or, better yet, to trace the intriguing V that the low riding pants revealed.

"Earth to Sam." He waved his hand in front of her face and she blinked. A knowing grin spread across his face. "I guess there's at least one other thing you think about."

Sam could feel her face flushing and groaned inwardly. God, she was no better than some giggling schoolgirl. She tried to brazen her way through the moment. "Well, I *am* a female. Of course any half decent looking male is going to catch my attention now and then."

"Half decent?" His hurt expression was obviously feigned.

"Well... Let me take another look." She walked around him slowly as if she were considering buying a car, taking a drink of water now and then, looking him up and down. Finally, she stopped, head cocked to the side. "Okay. I stand corrected. Half decent wasn't the right term." She turned to walk away, struggling to keep a straight face. Teasing Damien filled her with an evil delight. "Only a quarter decent would have been more appropriate."

"A quarter?" He let out a hyperbolic growl and grabbed her from behind, his arms around her waist.

She gave a yelp, half surprised, half laughing, and immediately dropped her weight while lunging forward, sending Damien off balance. They crashed to the floor in a tangle of arms and legs, Damien tickling her while she tried to push him away.

"Apologize." Damien's voice rumbled in her ear.

"Never!" She responded through fits of laughter. Her stomach and underarm were exceptionally vulnerable to tickling and he'd quickly honed in on the fact.

"Then you'll have to suffer the consequences." He renewed his assault while Sam pushed against his chest, squirming beneath him until her thigh suddenly came in contact with something hot and hard.

She froze, the evidence of his arousal burning against her inner leg.

"Do you surrend—" Damien stopped mid-sentence, registering her stillness. His breathing was as heavy as hers from laughing, his chest brushing against her chest with each breath he took.

"I..." Sam wet her lower lip as she stared up into his eyes. The teasing light in them shifted, growing darker. Hotter. Slowly, she moved her leg, purposely brushing against his erection, letting him know she was well aware of how he felt.

His hips flexed in response and he slowly lowered his head, still keeping his eyes fixed on hers. She levered herself up on her elbows, raising her head from the mat they lay upon, closing the distance between them. Tentatively, questioningly, their lips touched. Once. Twice. And then with a groan, Damien pressed his mouth to hers in a hot, needy kiss that went straight to her core. As he bore her down, she gripped his shoulders, making no pretence of denying what she felt.

Heat raced through her at a temperature that made Papa Tony's hot peppers seem mild in comparison. She was burning, aching, needing the man that pressed against her in a way she'd never experienced before. Sam ran her hands over his back, tracing the indent of his spine reaching lower to cup the buttocks she'd ogled earlier. His flesh was hot and hard and powerful causing her wolf to whimper with excitement.

She wrapped one leg around his hip, eager to pull him closer, to feel him against her needy body. When he nibbled at her neck and rocked against her, she shivered with excitement. Her heart was pounding so hard that she could barely make out the words he was whispering.

"…beautiful. You smell so good." Damien was rubbing his nose along her throat, his hand cupping one of her breasts. Usually, she scoffed at such words, but coming from him they made her glow with pride, pleased that he approved of her.

Sam arched her back and buried her fingers in his hair, pulling his head closer, wanting to feel his lips on her breast. He complied, the wet heat of his mouth seeping through the fabric of her tank. So good, so good…

Something was clawing at her insides, demanding release, making her limbs tremble. She began to pull at his clothing and hers all at the same time. Her hands worked awkwardly, her brain too overwhelmed with sensation to allow her to apply the usual cool efficiency she brought to most tasks.

She needed him. Needed him now. Needed his bare flesh on hers. Needed his flesh *in* her…

"Damien." She panted his name. "Damien, please…"

"I know, I know." He fumbled between them, pushing his clothing down while she did the same to her own.

One leg free. The other was somehow caught. Frustration had her gritting her teeth. Damned, stupid pant— She kicked it free just as Damien slid his hand between her thighs. He probed her carefully, teasing her tender flesh, murmuring words she couldn't begin to hear over the pounding of her heart.

Gently, he nipped and licked his way down her body, all the while pleasuring her with his fingers. She tried to return the favour, marvelling at the hot length of him in her hand. So firm and yet so silken. When the need in her had shudders shaking her frame, he finally grasped her thighs and drew them up to cradle his hips. Then his hot flesh was grazing hers, sliding through her wetness, entering...

Sam gasped and bit her lip as he slid in. Stretching. Filling. Going deeper and deeper. When his balls finally touched her body and he could go no further he paused, his forehead resting on hers. His eyes were closed, his breathing sounding harsh in her ear. She could feel his body trembling as if he was struggling for control. Wrapping her arms around him, she absorbed the feeling of being so close, his weight holding her down, their bodies joined as one. His body *inside* hers...

A soft sound of need escaped her and that was all it took. Damien began to move, sliding in and out, long and deep, short and shallow.

She urged him on, revelling in the feel of his flesh sliding over hers, grasping his butt and pulling him closer. His rhythm was relentless, racing them both towards the release they craved as if demons were chasing them. When that perfect moment came, she bucked under him, shudders wracking her body as she spiralled to the heavens and then floated back to earth.

The coolness of the cellar finally registered as the euphoric haze slid away. She was aware of Damien beside her, the delicious ache of her body, the way their scents had combined to create something uniquely theirs. A happy, relaxed smile spread over her face and she exhaled, rolling onto her side to view her lover.

Reaching out, she trailed her fingers down his chest, her hand sliding easily on the thin sheen of sweat that bathed the muscled surface. So strong, so male. Darting her tongue out, she tasted the saltiness of his skin. Mmm... She could get used to this. Sure, Damien was a pain in the ass, but when the danger of a takeover was past, she'd seriously consider keeping him around. Purely for entertainment purposes of course, she added.

A part of her winced at the thought. Her inner wolf had a limited tolerance for lies, even to herself.

Okay, perhaps Damien might be slightly more than entertainment, but she wasn't yet ready to examine exactly what else he might be either. That was a road best left explored another day. If there was one thing she'd learned in her years as acting Alpha, it was not to count too heavily on the future. And anything involving Damien was definitely for the future. Right now she had enough to deal with.

Damien inhaled deeply and sighed it out. She propped herself on her elbow to better see him.

"Hey. You were pretty good." She gave him a crooked smile and brushed a lock of hair from his forehead.

He stared at her for a moment, the expression in his half hooded eyes unfathomable before he shifted his gaze to stare at the ceiling. "Thanks." Abruptly, he sat up and turned away, leaving her with a fine view of his back. He ran his hand through his hair and looked about distractedly.

Sam waited a beat before prompting him. "I think this is when you're supposed to say I was good, too. Maybe even fantastic." She traced an imaginary line between the two tiny dimples above his butt. His demeanour puzzled her, but she tried not to show it.

"Yeah. It was fine." He tossed the comment over his shoulder while leaning forward and snagging his pants. Rising to his feet, he pulled them on, never once looking her way.

Sam sat up, uncaring that she was naked, exposed to his glance should he care to look. "Damned by faint praise, am I?" She replied lightly, giving no hint of the hurt that was growing inside her. This wasn't how the script was supposed to go.

"Sorry." He cleared his throat but kept his back to her. When he spoke his voice sounded tight, strained. "I've got a few things I have to do. I'll talk to you later." Without looking back, he exited the cellar, sliding the door quietly shut behind him, leaving Sam frowning at the wooden panel.

She blinked and raised her chin, unwilling to acknowledge the tears that stung her eyes. Just as she'd suspected, all those stupid romances were wrong. In her heart she'd known it, but hadn't expected them to be quite this far from the truth.

Betrayed: Book Two – The Road To Redemption

Slowly, she stood up and gathered her discarded clothes. She could see her reflection in the mirrors that lined the one side of the room. Hair tousled, the beginnings of a pink rash on her skin from his whiskers, faint smears of blood on her inner thighs.

Grabbing her discarded water bottle, she dampened the towel she'd used earlier and wiped away the evidence of her folly before getting dressed. Staring at the stained material she let a bitter laugh escape her. In the olden days, it would have been displayed proudly as proof that the Alpha had mated. But not in present day Chicago. Here, the sign of her 'sacrifice'—or was that stupidity—was going to be bundled up and thrown in the garbage. Thankfully, the cellar had a secret passageway that would take her to her room. She'd hate to have to explain to her packmates why she was carrying a blood stained towel through the house.

Chapter 22

Self-loathing tore at his gut.

He was a bastard.

A fucking bastard who'd just betrayed the only woman who'd ever loved him. Beth had accepted him, believed in him, loved him no matter what. And what had he done with her faith? He'd tossed it aside, let lust take over and cloud his judgement.

Could he possibly sink any lower than to have sex with Sam Harper?

Damien paused outside the cellar, pinching the bridge of his nose and fighting to keep from throwing up. Damn, what had he done?

He took a deep breath and willed the contents of his stomach back down. He had to get out of here. Should he take his Harley…? No, he was in no condition to drive. Forcing his legs to move, he headed inside, seeking the sanctuary of his room.

"Damien? Have you seen Sam?" Florence's voice drifted to him from somewhere near the front of the house. He didn't respond. He couldn't talk to anyone right now, especially not about Sam.

He quickened his pace. It wouldn't surprise him if Sam came looking for him any minute and, when she found him, she'd probably rip him a new one. While he might deserve it, he couldn't handle it right now.

A dark, sardonic laugh escaped him as he imagined the fire spitting from her eyes. What were the chances that any of her previous lovers had ever walked away from her? But then again, her previous lovers most likely weren't dying inside from guilt.

"*Ours?*" His wolf pronounced the word half questioning, half as a claim, puzzled over how to deal with what had happened. They'd had a mate before and had now claimed this female...

Damien jerked his head in denial. No. They hadn't claimed her. Sam was just... He scrubbed his hand over his face, not knowing the answer.

Hell, what a mess.

He stepped into his room and shut the door, relieved he hadn't encountered anyone. The relief was short lived. His gaze immediately went to the night stand where his wallet lay, and the heavy weight of guilt crashed down upon him once again, removing the strength from his legs.

Slumping back against the door, he buried his head in his hands and cursed himself. He always had Beth's picture with him, but for some reason this morning he hadn't taken his wallet along. And now he'd betrayed her.

For three years his libido had been dead. It had died, along with his heart and his will to live, in the fiery blaze that had claimed his Beth. He'd lost everything that day and now... Now he'd lost something else. He'd vowed to always be faithful to her, to never forget her...

Shit! Couldn't he even do this one thing right? He turned and buried his fist into the wall, welcoming the physical pain of bruised knuckles and aching wrist. Plaster dust floated in the air and he stared disinterestedly at the cracks that appeared around the hole he'd created.

The corner of his lip curled in a sneer at the sight. A hole, with cracked and jagged edges. How poetic; it was just like his heart. An empty, broken place in his chest.

Pressing his forehead against the damaged surface, he closed his eyes and slowly rocked his head from side to side while whispering his confession.

"I'm sorry, Beth. I didn't mean to. Sam was there. We were joking around. She was teasing me and I...I wasn't thinking, I just reacted..." He twisted his lips. "You remember how I'd do that, don't you? You were always telling me to stop and think first."

Betrayed: Book Two – The Road To Redemption

He didn't even try to hold back the tears that stung his eyes. "I miss you so much, Beth. I miss having you by my side, having someone to hold at night, someone I can connect with. Sometimes, I…I'm so damned lonely." His voice broke as emotion overwhelmed him. The years stretched ahead, years spent without companionship, bleak and barren. His inner wolf threw back its head and howled in despair.

A black pit was opening before him. Three years ago, he'd wallowed in it, but lately it had seemed to grow smaller, less noticeable. Now it loomed in front of him again, beckoning, urging him to step forward and lose himself in the darkness once more.

Pushing off from the wall, he headed for the bedside table and yanked open the drawer. A bottle of whiskey sat inside; the strong stuff, not the watered down crap humans drank. He hadn't had a drop since his first night at the pack house, having felt the need to keep his wits about him when Sam was around. Now, he only wanted to escape.

Throwing himself down on the bed, he propped himself up on the headboard and twisted off the cap. The scent of alcohol hit him and he hesitated for a moment before raising the bottle to his lips. What did it matter if he got roaring drunk or not?

As the liquid burnt its way to his stomach, he closed his eyes and tried to bring Beth's image to mind. She was there, just beyond his reach, looking at him with her dove grey eyes. Her fingers would brush his hair from his forehead and then she'd kiss his lips softly.

'Never forget…love… Never forget to love…'

Sam slammed her glass down on the bar at Club Mystique and signalled for another. She sat alone at the polished wooden surface; a popular song was now playing and almost everyone was on the dance floor enjoying the throbbing music. It was just as well that they kept their distance; given the mood she was in, it wouldn't take much for someone to set her off.

Gwyneth, the tall, redheaded owner, poured Sam another drink and served it with a look of disapproval. "Don't be thinking of getting drunk here, Lycan. I run a respectable establishment."

"Stuff the holier-than-thou act, witch."

"Better a witch than a bitch."

Sam started to snarl but stopped when she caught the look on Gwyneth's face. The damned woman might just put some sort of hex on her and that was all she needed right now.

Taking a gulp of her drink, Sam nodded. "I'm not here to cause trouble. Just waiting for Tina."

"I figured as much. Her shift starts in five; behave until then."

Sam watched the woman as she walked away. The owner was a no nonsense person who was equally acerbic to Lycans, Fae and Witches alike. Gwyneth had established the club years ago as a place where shifters and others could meet individuals of their own kind while in the city. The only requirement was that everyone kept their unique abilities safely tucked away. If a DC officer had to be called in, you were banned for life. The human patrons couldn't have any idea that they were rubbing elbows with the magical realm.

Well, she had no plans to cause problems at the club. Her day was crappy enough as it was. Drawing idle patterns in the condensation on the bar, Sam mulled over how Damien had walked away from her after having sex. What had gone wrong? She wasn't the kind to mope and cry, she was more the beating-somebody's-ass kind, but before she did that, she needed a voice of reason.

Ha! Tina, a voice of reason? Now there was an oxymoron, but she really didn't have anyone else to turn to. Telling any of the pack members about having sex with Damien would only stir up speculation and trouble. And, of course, it would get back to her grandfather, and there was no way she wanted to deal with the crap he'd give her.

"Hey, Sam! What's up? Gwyneth says you're in a funk and drinking yourself into a stupor."

Sam looked up to see her friend adorned in skin-tight silver lame topped with shocking pink hair. Tina's appearance caused a momentary smile. "I'm in a funk, but not even close to a stupor; not on this watered down crap she serves."

"Yeah, well at least half the people here are human, so watered down crap is all they can handle."

Sam made a non-committal sound, the smile fading from her lips. She took another sip from her glass.

"So, what can I do for you?" Tina settled down beside her. "I've got a few minutes before my shift starts."

"I need advice…on men." Sam winced, unable to believe she'd actually managed to get the words out.

Tina began to grin. "Advice on men? Is it that rogue you hired? I caught a glimpse of him when you guys left the other night. He's a hottie."

"Yeah. That's the guy. I had sex with him."

"You had—" Tina looked at her, speechless.

Sam flicked a glance at Tina, taking in her shocked expression. "Shut your mouth, you look stupid." She scowled down at her drink, feeling inexplicably embarrassed by the whole conversation. In a rush, she delivered all the important details. "We had sex. He was my first, but I doubt he knows it. Afterwards, he got up and left without a word." She twisted her lips. "No, wait. That's not quite true. He said it was 'fine', that he had things to do and would talk to me later."

"Bastard!" Tina spit out the word. "Want me to hex him or—"

"I thought you said you'd sworn off all that hexing stuff." Sam looked up from her drink.

"I did…temporarily. But I'd be willing to dig out my old books for you."

"Thanks. Unfortunately, I still need him, for a while at least."

"So…what are you going to do?"

Sam shrugged. "I don't know and that's what's driving me crazy. I'm the Alpha. I'm supposed to know these things." She turned in her seat to face her friend. "That's why I came to see you. What would you do?"

"If I didn't hex him?" Tina tapped her neon pink fingernail against her lips. "I suppose I'd put the whole thing behind me, try to avoid him if possible."

"I can't do that. I have to work with him."

"Bummer. Act like nothing happened?" She gave a one shouldered shrug. "Sorry, this is beyond my experience."

Sam sighed. "It figures that my first lover would be a dud. I'm so not good with the whole 'girly-girl' thing."

"A guy that hot was a dud? You mean he didn't even get you off?"

"No. He got me off. And from what I've read it ranked in the superb range."

"Well, at least that's something." Tina gave her a friendly shoulder nudge. "My first was that football jock I had a crush on back in high school. Remember? He had no technique, finished before I started and then dumped me a week later."

"You wanted me to beat him up." Sam smiled at the memory.

"And you wouldn't. You said it wouldn't be fair and that it might break your Keeping rule."

"I did sabotage his car for you, though."

"I know."

They exchanged looks and laughed as they recalled the boy's reaction to finding he had four flat tires and no gas left in the tank.

Gwyneth walked by, tossing a towel at Tina as she passed. "Your shift started two minutes ago."

"I'll be right there." Tina slid off the stool. "So, what are you going to do?"

"Nothing, I guess." Sam swirled the liquid in her glass. "Act like nothing happened. Business as usual."

"Sorry I wasn't more help."

Sam gave her a smile. "That's okay. I really just needed to talk to someone."

"Any time."

Tina left, and Sam nursed her drink a bit longer. If she was honest, she was…hurt. Something about Damien had grabbed her attention from the very beginning. Not only was he good looking, he was strong and physically fit. Plus he was smart, had a sense of humour, and seemed to care about the members of her pack. Sure he could be sullen and closed mouthed, but she understood that since he obviously carried a hurt deep inside.

Damien made her heart flutter. She found herself looking for ways to make him smile, waiting for him to tease her. When she was with him, it was like she was with her other half. Hell, he even rode a Harley! He was the male image of herself. In all respects they seemed a perfect match. Naturally, when the opportunity presented itself, she'd gambled hoping he felt a similar attraction to her. The odds had seemed in her favour, and her instincts were usually pretty good.

She shook her head and downed the remainder of her drink. Life and love; they were both a crap shoot.

There was a break in the dance music and the patrons were starting to gather at the bar, thirsty from their exertions. Sam was preparing to vacate her seat when a tingling at the back of her neck had her pausing. She looked into the mirror that backed the bar and scanned the crowd gathering behind her. One person stood out. Older than most of the group, he had greying hair and a lined face. Something about him seemed familiar. She didn't let her gaze linger despite the fact she was sure he was staring at her.

Where did she know him from? As she pondered the point, someone bumped into her, spilling part of their drink on her arm. Ignoring the half drunken apologies of the man—had the fool really thought that was a good pick-up line—she looked in the mirror again. Damn. He was gone.

She spun around, searching the crowds, hoping for a glimpse of him even though she knew it would be futile. Who was he and why had he been watching her? Probably some dirty old man looking for some sweet young thing. Well she might be young, but tonight she certainly wasn't feeling sweet!

Grumbling under her breath, she finished drying her arm on her shirt. Men. Nothing but a pain in the ass.

Chapter 23

Sam pounded on Damien's bedroom door. The scent of alcohol oozed from beneath the wooden panel and added fuel to the rage already smouldering inside her. He hadn't shown up for dinner last night, patrol duty or breakfast this morning. Coward. She'd expected better of him.

Thud, thud, thud.

She knocked again and then jiggled the door handle. It wasn't locked. Taking that fact as an invitation to enter, she stepped inside wrinkling her nose at the smell of sweat and booze. The room was dark, the blinds drawn. As she flicked on the lights, she noticed a hole in the plaster and snarled. He'd damned well better fix that before he left!

Stalking across the room, she opened the drapes and pushed up the window panes to let the stench out.

A low groan came from the bed as a beam of light fell across it.

Damien was sprawled there, bare chested and still dressed in the same grey track pants from yesterday. One arm was slung over his eyes, the other hung limply off the bed. A whiskey bottle lay open and empty on the floor where it had fallen from his hand.

Walking over to the bed, Sam stared down at the unconscious Lycan. His chest rose and fell with each deep breath. He was sound asleep.

For a moment, she admired the pure beauty of his form. Broad chest, narrow hips, the hint of a treasure trail disappearing into his pants. His jaw was heavily shadowed with stubble, his lips barely parted. Thick, dark hair showed above where his arm shielded the rest of his face. God, he was gorgeous. Too bad he was also a douche.

Her toe nudged the bottle on the floor and she bent to pick it up. The faintest trace of golden liquid still remained. Giving a shrug, she downed it, enjoying the burn. It was the good stuff.

Sam wiped her mouth with the back of her hand. "Time to wake, sleeping beauty."

She went to the bathroom, filled the bottle with cold water and returned to his bed side. Holding the container over his lower abdomen, she tipped it and let the icy liquid serve as an alarm clock.

"What the hell!" Damien shot up, a look of bewildered outrage on his face.

"Time to get up." She dropped the bottle on him. It landed exactly where she'd planned and she watched with grim satisfaction as he gave a yelp of pain and automatically grabbed the offended area.

"Watch what you're doing." Growling in displeasure, he swung his legs off the bed.

"I was." Sam gave an evil smile and stepped back.

"Damn, woman. Have some compassion." He ran his hands through his hair, wincing as if the very roots were protesting in pain.

"I told you no drinking except on your own time."

"It was my own time."

"The drinking might have been, but the hangover is on my time, so suck it up."

Damien got to his feet, swaying slightly and peered at her with bleary eyes. "Okay, I'm up. What'd you need?"

Sam looked him up and down, shaking her head and curling her lip. "Was the sex between us so bad, you had to get drunk?" She clamped her mouth shut, not having intended to ask the question.

He blinked at her, and slowly straightened. Her comment seemed to have sobered him better than the cold water she'd dumped on his crotch. "Uh, no. Not at all."

"Good." She pulled back her arm and slugged him, a feeling of satisfaction filling her even as her fist protested in pain.

Damien staggered backward and hit the wall, shocked surprise on his face. Then he started to laugh.

"What's so funny?" She scowled at him, hands on her hips.

He shook his head. "You wouldn't understand, Sugar."

She huffed in disgust at the annoying name he kept using. "When you're done laughing like a hyena, get cleaned up. There's a pack meeting in an hour."

Damien slid into his seat on Sam's right and scanned those gathered around the table. Jonah, Laurie, Andrea, Keith, Hiram, Florence… Only the pup, the grandfather and three others were missing. A pathetically small showing for what had once, purportedly, been an impressive pack. Their demeanour in no way indicated they were hanging on by the tips of their claws, however. Each appeared confident, relaxed, well-balanced. Sam did a good job leading them, instilling in them a sense of security.

They nodded or gave him a friendly greeting, before resuming their casual conversations. There was no sign given that they were aware he'd bedded their Alpha. Not that he expected Sam to be the kind to kiss and tell; it was his own self guilt over his betrayal that was making him edgy. He took a deep breath and buried the feeling; if he dwelled on it, the others would sense his unease. It was best to put the incident behind them.

Sam cleared her throat and drew the attention of those gathered. "I've called this impromptu meeting to bring you up to speed with what's happening regarding the possible takeover of our pack by Sinclair."

She stood with her fingertips resting lightly on the back of her chair, her voice steady as was her gaze while she looked over those assembled. Such a statement should have disquieted those gathered, but her demeanour calmed the others, just as it should. The pack always followed the Alpha's example. Damien was sure he was the only one present who could see how her thumbnail was digging into the wood on the back of the chair. Inside, she was likely a churning mass of seething anger and worry; if it had been him in the same position, that's how he'd feel.

"As you know, Sinclair is trying to build a case against us. He claims we have too few members to carry out our duties." She began to walk around the table. "It's completely untrue, of course. I've sent Lycan Link a copy of our duty roster showing how we manage. I even added Damien's name to the list so our ranks are showing growth, albeit by one."

Her statement was followed by soft chuckles from the pack and a few shot appreciative looks toward their new Beta. Damien merely nodded, his blank expression hiding the squirming of his conscience.

"Sinclair's latest bit of 'ammunition' against us is to claim that Grandfather is no longer the Alpha and we've been operating under false pretences."

"Of course, he's our Alpha!" Florence interrupted, her cheeks flushed. "It's utter nonsense to say otherwise."

"I agree." Sam placed her hand on the woman's shoulder and gave it a comforting squeeze before continuing to circle the table. "As most of you know, all packs that are members of the Lycan Link affiliation must maintain honest and up to date records of pack administration." She turned to face Damien. "Would you care to explain to the pack why this is required?"

Surprised by her request and not sure of her motivation, he nodded. "According to the Book of the Law, accurate records must be maintained not only for the benefit of Lycan Link, but also to make sure there is a clear line of accountability should problems arise." He raised his brows and gave Sam an inquiring look to see if she wanted him to say more.

"Thank you." Turning her back on him, she continued.

Inwardly, Damien frowned. Had she hoped to catch him off guard and embarrass him in front of the pack? Or had she been trying to include him, to make him seem part of the pack leadership? She wasn't spiteful, so it was likely the latter. A united Alpha and Beta was what the pack members needed when someone began questioning the validity of the leadership, and Sam was all about caring for her pack.

Betrayed: Book Two – The Road To Redemption

He shifted in his seat and focused on what she was saying once again.

"As you know, I am the acting-Alpha. The Book of the Law clearly states that if an Alpha is temporarily unable to fulfill his duties, the Beta will step into the role for that period of time until the Alpha is able to resume his normal place."

"So, what is Sinclair's problem?" Jonah growled.

"He claims my position isn't temporary since I've been acting-Alpha for over four years, and since no one has seen or heard from Samuel Harper, Senior, in ages, his position, even his existence, is in question."

"That's outrageous," Andrea stated, rising to her feet. "Sinclair is basically stating your grandfather is dead and we just 'forgot' to tell anyone!"

Her mate, Keith, laid a calming hand on her arm and she slowly sank back into her seat.

"While I agree it is utterly ridiculous, the fact remains that we have to counter his claim. That's where you come in." She swept a look over everyone there. "I've had Christopher busy pulling all the records from the attic and bringing them down to the living room. Each of you will be given one box to go through and I want you to find every piece of paper that my grandfather has signed or initialled over the past four years."

The pack members murmured in approval, obviously pleased to be able to do something to help out their cause. Damien clenched his jaw, feeling more and more like a traitor.

"I can help Chris carry the boxes down." He rose to his feet and moved to leave.

"No, I have another job for you." The sound of Sam's voice stopped him and he turned to face her. She nodded towards her office and he followed her there.

"Yes?"

"Are you recovered from your hangover?" Her expression held a look of mild interest, no hint of accusation. Still, he answered cautiously, not sure where the conversation was headed.

"I'm fine."

"Good." She paused and he wondered if she'd bring up their...encounter...in the cellar. She opened her mouth as if to speak, only to close it and begin again. "I want you to check on Mr. Marcello. I've tried to stop by each day since the break in but won't have time today. Could you take care of it, please?"

"Sure." He wondered why this required them speaking in private. "I'll do it right away. Anything else?"

"No. Yes." She took a deep breath and looked directly into his eyes. "Our fucking in the cellar was obviously a mistake, but it can't get in the way of our jobs, especially now. Understood?"

Her use of the coarse word shocked him. Not because it seemed strange to hear her use it—Sam's vocabulary was anything but dainty—but because a part of him didn't want what they'd done to be reduced to something so base. His wolf was in total agreement.

"It won't be a problem." His answer reflected none of his inner turmoil.

"Good. I'll go help with the boxes. Report in when you get back." She opened the door and waited with her hand on the knob.

As he passed by, her scent hit him in the gut, stirring the animal inside, urging him to reach out and touch her. He could barely force himself to keep walking. Hell, this was going to be harder to deal with than any of the casual encounters he'd had in his misspent youth.

Damien walked out of the office and out of the pack house, giving no visible sign of his struggle. Down the sidewalk, around the corner and now... Out of the sight of prying eyes, he braced himself against a fence and took deep cleansing breaths. Sam's unique scent of leather and spice continued to linger, taunting him with memories of holding her close, of being buried in her...

Why did he keep thinking about Sam in that way? Yes, he'd slept with her, but it was a mistake. One he couldn't repeat. He gave his head a shake. Hopefully, the walk to Marcello's would help clear his mind.

Chapter 24

From his vantage point across the street, Damien studied Marcello's business. A faded green awning extended over the front, protecting the interior from the damaging effects of the sun. The scalloped fringe waved gently in the breeze, the shadows it created dancing over the aged brick in random waves. When the fringe moved just right, rays of light hit the gold lettering on the door that proclaimed the name of the business, Marcello's Antiques and Collectibles. The letters were chipped and scratched, showing their years as did the wood of the door.

Damien noted that the pedestrian traffic in front of the shop was moderate; no one was stopping to admire the old vases, furniture and bits of jewellery that were carefully displayed in the front window. It wasn't an affluent area and he wondered how Marcello managed to make a living. It seemed unlikely that the man would be able to pay Dante's demands for any length of time.

He was curious as to the conversation he'd overheard between the old man and Dante and wanted to know more. While he doubted it was significant to the takeover of the Chicago pack, Dante was scum and any opportunity to bring the man down couldn't be overlooked.

Since no one had entered the business in the past half hour, he decided Marcello must be alone which made this the perfect time for his visit. Damien pushed away from wall he'd been leaning against and crossed the street to enter the shop.

The wind chimes softly announced his entrance and while he waited for Marcello to appear, he began to wander the room.

There were some nice pieces, enough to attract the attention of casual customers but nothing worthy of commanding an exorbitant price. No doubt those items, when they came in, were quickly whisked off to professional collectors.

He ran his hand over a side table then turned at the sound of footsteps behind him. It was the shopkeeper.

"May I help you?"

"Mr. Marcello, I'm a—"

"A friend of Miss Samantha's!" The look of polite inquiry on the man's face was replaced with a welcoming smile. "Yes, yes! I recall you from the other night." He reached out and shook Damien's hand. "Are you here to shop or…?"

"Sam…Samantha…sent me to see how you're doing today."

"Such a conscientious girl. She's been keeping an eye on me ever since that nasty incident the other night. I told her, I'm fine. It was an unfortunate experience that I have put behind me."

The man's words were at odds with his body language. The clues were subtle; a slight tremor in his voice, the way his eyes scanned the room, the nervous way his fingers played with the buttons on his vest.

Damien decided he wouldn't call him on it quite yet. "You have an interesting array of items in your store."

Marcello beamed as he looked over the room. "Yes. I have some fine pieces here. I go to the flea markets—you never know what you might find there—and people bring items in for me, as well."

"And your customer base? Not many of the local residents would be looking for antiques, would they?" Damien studied what, to him, was an exceptionally ugly lamp.

"A few from the neighbourhood come to buy…" His voice trailed off and he gave a speculative look. "But you are not really interested in who my customers are, are you?"

Turning from the lamp, Damien tilted his head, his expression bland. "And what makes you say that?"

"Because you are a friend of Miss Samantha's and too much like her. She has been asking questions, too. Trying to decide who would try to rob an old man of his hard earned cash."

Damien gave a small, crooked smile. "You're partially right. But I'm not interested in who robbed you."

"No?"

"I want to know about who is blackmailing you."

Marcello's face paled beneath his olive toned skin. "Blackmail? I've no idea—"

"Yes, you do." Damien gave him a steady look. "I was in the building long before Samantha and overheard most of the conversation."

Tightening his mouth, Marcello shook his head. "It is none of your business."

"Perhaps not," Damien agreed and then allowed the deadly coldness in his eyes to show. "But the bastard who's squeezing you—Dante—is an old acquaintance who I'd love to find."

"This person is a friend of yours?" Marcello drew himself up as tall as he could, his face clouding with indignation.

"Not a friend. Never."

Marcello brought his brows together. "Then what?"

"I can't give you details. Suffice to say, I might be able to help you deal with him if I know what hold he has over you." He watched as the old man pursed his lips obviously debating how much trust there was between them.

"I cannot afford what he is expecting me to pay, but Miss Samantha shouldn't be burdened with this either."

"With what?"

Marcello looked Damien up and down then walked to the front of the store and turned over the 'open' sign that hung in the window. Returning to where Damien stood, he jerked his head towards the back of the store. "Come with me."

Damien followed him, ducking past the curtain that separated the store from the back room which served as Marcello's office. He looked around, noting the small table and chairs, a shelf with a tea kettle and several mugs, a paper strewn desk and several stacks of books. It appeared much as it had the other night.

"Sit." Marcello gestured towards the table and chairs. "Tea? Or something stronger?"

Damien declined, but Marcello drew out a bottle and poured himself a glass of liquor—cognac by the smell of it.

"Miss Samantha's grandfather and I shared many a glass of this." Marcello declared, taking a sip of the liquid. "We have been friends for years. You know what that means, yes?" He quirked a brow.

"Enlighten me." Damien leaned back in his seat, rocking on the back legs.

"Friends share secrets. Know about each other's lives. The secrets they do not want the rest of the world to know." Marcello gave him a meaningful look and took another sip of Cognac.

Damien's mind raced. Was Marcello telling him he knew about the pack? Had Samuel Harper broke the Keeping? He couldn't judge without knowing the circumstances, but the way Marcello was talking, it would seem the fellow knew the seriousness of the situation.

Marcello sighed and stared into his glass. "Samuel and I shared many secrets. Secrets kept from the world. Secrets from his family. From Miss Samantha." His mouth turned down. "I always told him it wasn't a good idea, that someday the truth would come out and Miss Samantha would be hurt, but he was a stubborn one."

"What truth?"

"You won't tell her?"

Damien gave a one shouldered shrug. "I'm not here for that long. And this secret—whatever it is—isn't mine to share."

"No. It isn't, and I'll tell you only because I want you to know how important it is to keep this Dante person from speaking to her."

"Dante's downfall is my main concern. I've no desire to hurt Sam."

"Good." Marcello finished his drink and set the glass down. Taking a book from the stack on his desk, he set it on the table near Damien. "This is one of my personal journals. I've been keeping them ever since I came to this country over fifty years ago."

"And?"

"This one contains my entries from the year—the day in fact—that Samantha's father died."

Damien eyed the book, wondering what it said.

"I was at the train station the day it happened. By chance, on the same platform." Marcello opened the book and flipped the pages. "Samantha and her father were a few yards ahead of me. They hadn't been back in Chicago long—a few months perhaps—but I'd come to recognize her by the little purple coat she wore; it matched her eyes." He smiled at the memory. "I'd just called out their names when the train roared into the station. Samantha turned and saw me, letting go of her father's hand. He turned to grab her, I suppose not knowing why she was leaving his side, when someone came rushing up behind him and pushed him onto the tracks."

Marcello shook his head. "It all happened so fast. There was no time to try to save him. He fell a mere second before the train arrived. The timing couldn't have been worse. He was killed instantly."

"And the person who pushed him?"

"Was never found...officially." Marcello had reached a spot in the book where there were torn edges; evidence that pages had been removed.

"But you know who it was?" Damien slowly leaned his chair forward until the front legs were touching the floor again.

Marcello nodded. "Samuel's friend, Gary. His second in command."

The Beta? Damien stiffened in his chair. "Why?"

"I've no idea. At the time, I was shocked. Sure I'd been mistaken. I didn't know the man well; he kept to himself, however, it *was* him. I caught a glimpse of him standing some distance away when the ambulance arrived." He traced the seam of the book with his finger. "I wrote it down here, but told no one. What happened within the...family...was not the concern of the rest of the world. Samuel had told me that often. And so when the police asked questions…I said nothing."

"And the journal entry?" Damien nodded towards the book.

"I tore the pages out and put them in the safe, thinking they would be my protection against Gary. I could hold it over his head; my silence in exchange for my life."

Damien frowned. Something didn't add up. "Why didn't you approach the old man? Tell him what you saw?"

"I don't pretend to understand the way of your people; I know they can be ruthless. For a while I wondered if Samuel had ordered the 'hit'. He'd expressed his doubts as to his son taking over leadership of the family." Marcello shrugged and closed the journal. "I wasn't sure if he was capable of such an act. There is a dark side to the man that I do not understand." His voice trailed off. "We didn't speak for some time after the accident. I lived in fear, not knowing who to trust."

"So what changed? You and Samantha seem quite friendly; she says you're an old friend of her grandfather's."

"It was quite some time before Samuel came to visit again. If he noticed I was cool towards him, he didn't mention it. By then he had custody of Samantha and spoke mostly of the challenges of raising her." Marcello gave a reminiscent smile. "She was a lovely girl, so curious and full of life. Always asking questions about my collections, dressing up in the jewels, skipping about the store and playing pranks."

Damien said nothing. Sam had certainly changed over the years. He'd seen glimpses of her mischievous side, but mostly she was all about business. Strange how life could affect a person. It made him think of himself in his younger years, always joking, not a care in the world. That, of course, had all changed since Beth…

"We eventually fell back into our old friendship, and I tried to put what I'd seen that day out of my mind. It worked for the most part until Samuel began talking about his decision to have Samantha take over the family. She was still so young, but he said she needed to start training for the job." Marcello sat down in the chair opposite Damien. "I began to worry. It came to me that Gary was hoping to take over, perhaps that was why he'd killed her father. Would he do the same again? Try to eliminate Miss Samantha? I knew I had to speak then, tell Samuel what I had seen."

Marcello pulled out an old fashioned handkerchief and mopped his brow. "Samuel was enraged, at me for assuming he'd kill his own flesh, for not speaking sooner, and at Gary for the murder. At himself, as well. He seemed to feel it was his fault somehow. Gary left the family and a week later his body was found in a wooded area. The police report said he'd been attacked by a wild dog while camping."

Silence hung between them, the truth unspoken. Damien knew how such a betrayal of pack loyalty might have been dealt with. Marcello obviously knew, too, but had chosen to not delve too deeply into the truth. Funny how humans managed to arrange their memories so conveniently.

Clearing his throat, Marcello continued, seeming relieved to have made it through the tale. "After that, Samuel changed. He'd injured his back somehow and moved more slowly. He still led the family, but I could see the difference in him. He was less prone to laughter, quieter, harder. He made me swear to never tell Miss Samantha, and I did. There was no point in telling a child about such a messy business, was there?" Marcello shrugged. "To this day, she doesn't know. She focused on being what Samuel wanted her to be. It was difficult for her at times, but she never complained, only wanted to please him."

Damien nodded in understanding. Living up to the Alpha's expectations was central to being part of a pack. It was one of the reasons he'd never truly fit in; he didn't give a rat's ass what any Alpha wanted. He was his own boss.

Picking up the journal, Damien turned it over in his hands. "What you've said explains the background, but how did Dante find out? Did he gain access to the pages you had locked up? Did you tell someone?"

"No and no." Marcello shook his head. "I destroyed the pages after Gary's death—protection from him was my only reason for keeping them. And I never spoke of this to anyone except Samuel."

Rubbing his neck, Damien considered the situation. "I guess the 'how' doesn't really matter; the fact is he knows and is threatening to tell Sam."

"Correct, and I can't let that happen. Samuel was adamant about it."

There had to be more to the story than Marcello knew; something between Sam Harper, senior, and the Beta. "Your loyalty is commendable, Mr. Marcello."

"Samuel saved my life once, many years ago. This is the least I could do."

"Has Dante been around since?"

"Just once. I gave him his payment and he said he'd be back for more next week." The man got to his feet and walked to the corner, picking up a baseball bat. "When he returns, I am ready for him this time. I've worked too hard all my life to give it away to the likes of that man."

"With any luck, I'll have this taken care of by then." Damien rose to his feet. "If you hear from Dante before then, contact me right away." He scribbled his number down on a scrap of paper and pushed it across the table.

Marcello pocketed the paper. "Thank you. I care for Miss Samantha and don't want to see her hurt."

"Neither do I, Mr. Marcello. Neither do I."

Chapter 25

Sam sat in her office surrounded by boxes of paper. The pack's records were extensive, but in the attic, they hadn't seemed to be quite this numerous. At least the pack members had managed to get through most of the files during the afternoon. They'd found bits and pieces that would help her create a paper trail to establish her grandfather's role as Alpha back several years.

She checked the piles of paper she had arranged on her desk, one for each year. Unfortunately, the most recent three were the smallest, only the monthly reports to Lycan Link bore his initials. It would be enough, wouldn't it?

Damn Sinclair, the greedy ass! Why couldn't he be satisfied with his own territory? She muttered under her breath as she counted the reports in the pile designated for the current year. For some reason, there were only seven reports and there should be nine…

Her office door opened and she looked up to find Damien.

"Decided to finally return, did you?" She scowled. He'd been gone much longer than the simple errand required, and being surrounded by paperwork had put her in a bad mood.

"It's nice to see you, too, Sugar." He leaned against the doorjamb, his thumbs hooked in his belt loops.

She bit back her retort over his use of the name 'Sugar'. He wanted to get a rise out of her and she wasn't going to give him the satisfaction. "How was Mr. Marcello?"

"Fine." Damien straightened and stepped into the room, glancing over the stacks of boxes. "Did you get through all of these?"

"Yeah. I'm sure I have enough evidence to convince Lycan Link that Sinclair's claim is as insane as he is." She counted the slips once more and frowned, then checked the neighbouring pile.

"What's wrong?"

"I'm missing copies of the last two reports to Lycan Link. I always have Grandfather initial them—it makes him feel like he's still involved—and they're part of my 'proof' that he's still our Alpha."

"Did you wait while he signed them or did you leave them with him? Maybe you forgot to pick them up?"

"I might have." She stood up. "I'll check his room. He has quite a few files in there right now—going through old records and journals keeps him busy—so they might have become mixed up."

"I can help you look." Damien fell in beside her as she made her way upstairs.

"You'll have to be quiet," she warned. "He always has a nap at this time of the day."

Sam eased open the door and peered inside. The room was in semi-darkness, the curtains pulled. From the bedroom, the faint sound of snoring could be heard. Years ago she'd never have been able to sneak into his quarters, but age and medication had made him less alert.

As quietly as possible, they gathered up as many files as they could and then left the room.

Sam chuckled softly. "That reminded me of how I'd try to sneak into his room to get my allowance money when he confiscated it."

Damien gave a crooked smile. "Sounds like a stunt I would have tried. Did you ever manage to pull it off?"

"Only once and he noticed right away. I was on latrine duty for a month after that."

Back in her office, Sam took the evidence she'd already collected and slid it into a folder, clearing a spot for them to work.

Damien set the files down and they began to read the headings.

"Some of these are really old," he commented looking at the dates. "The pages are even discoloured."

"Hmm... A lot of these are my grandfather's old records. Flip through them and see if you notice any newer looking pages. We don't have time to be reading them."

They worked companionably, side by side, for some time. Sam found one of the missing reports but not the other.

The clock in the hall chimed and she sighed. "I've got to go fix dinner."

"Wieners and beans again?"

"No. Frozen lasagna—and don't you dare say anything." She glared at him when he would have commented. "I know I'm a pathetic cook."

"I wasn't going to say a word about it." He blinked at her innocently. "I was only going to ask if you wanted me to keep looking through the papers."

"You're a liar, Masterson, but yeah, keep looking through the papers."

Sam headed to the kitchen pleased that she and Damien seemed to have fallen back into their usual banter. They still had to work together, regardless of the fact that they'd had sex. And while she still hadn't given up all hope of having some kind of relationship with him, for the moment saving the pack had to take priority.

Dinner came and went. The lasagna had been a bit cool in the middle and crunchy on the edges–who knew that cranking the oven up an extra seventy-five degrees wouldn't compensate for shortening the baking time? At least the garlic bread and salad had been good, and ice cream for dessert was a no brainer.

Damien hadn't had any luck finding the missing report so as soon as the dishes were done, she planned on returning the files to her grandfather's room and taking another look around. With any luck he wouldn't have too big a fit over her sneaking into his room earlier. The needs of the pack overrode personal privacy...or at least that's what her defence was going to be! She rinsed the last pan, dried her hands then went back to her office.

The door was ajar and she could see a pair of booted feet resting on her desk. Damien was settled in her chair reading.

"Make yourself at home." She folded her arms and gave him a hard stare.

"I did, thanks." He gave her a cheeky grin before gesturing with the file in his hand. "This makes for some interesting reading."

"I've been going through some really old ones, trying to familiarize myself with the pack's history. Grandfather was always pretty tight-lipped about it." She shoved his feet off her desk.

"Hey! I just got comfortable."

"Your feet on the floor or my foot on your ass; make your decision."

"Fine." Damien set down the file and moved from her desk. "You're a cruel woman, Sugar."

She curled her lip and gave him a territorial growl before laughing. Glancing at the date on the file he'd been reading, she frowned. "That was a bad year. My grandfather and the Beta had a falling out over something. Grandfather never replaced him."

"Do you know what they disagreed about?"

"No. I wasn't that old. I remember them arguing loudly. It scared me, and Florence took me to see a movie. When we came back, the Beta had left."

"Hmm…" Damien seemed about to ask another question then changed his mind. "Are you going to return these files to your grandfather or put them in storage?"

"I'd better give them back. I don't know how many he's read over."

"Okay, I'll carry them." Damien scooped up the files and gestured for her to lead the way.

"Good. He's going to be pissed when he realizes we were in his room. If you're carrying the files, you can take most of the blame." The look on Damien's face made her chuckle. It was one of the things she liked about him; he made her laugh. There hadn't been a lot of laughter in her life, mostly only training and work. Being an Alpha was no walk in the park.

Betrayed: Book Two – The Road To Redemption

Her grandfather's door was ajar when they arrived and she gave the obligatory tap before pushing it open. "Grandfather, we… What are you doing?"

A wave of heat hit them as soon as they stepped into the room. Despite it being summer, he had the fireplace lit and was sitting in front of it, feeding papers into the blaze.

"Purging my old notes." He didn't look up from his task, but Sam gasped and hurried towards him.

"Don't do that!" She snatched the papers from his hand.

"Give me those back. Those are my personal files!" He tried to grab them back, but she moved them out of reach.

"No. I'm missing one of the monthly reports and it might have become mixed up in your papers."

"Samantha!" He shouted her name and tried to stand but lost his balance and tipped sideways. Sam dropped the papers and caught him, struggling to support his weight and keep him from crashing to the floor.

Damien rushed over to help ease him into his chair just as Florence appeared at the door, a tray of food in her hands.

"What's going on here?"

Everyone started to talk at once until Damien finally put his fingers to his mouth and let out a loud whistle that caused everyone to stop and look his way.

He rubbed the back of his neck and sighed loudly. "Can everyone calm down, please."

Sam scowled but knew he was right. "Yeah. Everyone calm down." She turned to look at her grandfather. "First of all, you know better than to stand up without your cane or something to hang on to. If you fall and break a hip, you'll really be in trouble." When he would have spoken, she raised her hand and continued. "And yes, you can burn all the papers you want, as long as they're yours and not recent pack files. Once I've checked that the missing report isn't in there, you can do whatever you want with them."

"You are *not* going through my papers. I'll look myself!"

"Grandfather, I don't have time—"

"And why the hell not?" He glared at her.

"Because of fucking Sinclair!" She ran her hands through her hair, exasperated and overtired from too many hours of sorting through papers. God, she needed to go for a run or a ride on her Harley. Taking a deep breath, she explained. "Sinclair says you're no longer Alpha because you've been absent too long and we're operating under false pretences. I'm trying to build a paper trail of things you've signed to prove you're still in charge."

"Of all the idiotic—" Her grandfather began to bluster, his face flushing with temper.

"I know, but Lycan Link is listening to him and somehow I've misplaced that report and we need it."

Her grandfather flattened his lips then jerked his head towards Damien. "Let him look for the paper. The rest of you, get out."

"You want Damien to...?" She threw her hands up in exasperation. "Fine."

"Samuel, you haven't eaten." Florence held up the tray of food.

"Set it on the table. I'm not hungry."

Florence looked as if she'd argue, but a growl emitted from the old man's throat and she gave in. Setting the tray down, she left the room with Sam.

They walked to the bottom of the stairs and then paused to talk.

"Any idea what's going on with him?" Sam leaned against the newel post, rubbing her forehead as it throbbed dully. If anyone knew what was going on with her grandfather, it would be Florence. The woman had taken care of him for as long as Sam could remember.

"He's been in a stir all evening." She hesitated, seeming to be weighing how much to say. "Someone called just before dinner. Samuel asked me to leave the room while they talked." Her lips pursed in disapproval. "Whoever it was on the phone upset him. When I came back, he wasn't himself at all."

"Any idea who it was?"

"No. The person has called before—I recognized the voice—but Samuel's never used a name."

Sam nodded. "Okay. Thanks for the information."

Florence turned to go and then paused. "Oh, and Sam? Whoever it is that calls, I don't believe it's a friend. Your grandfather is always in a mood afterwards, but never as bad as this."

Chapter 26

Damien stood in Samuel Harper's room waiting until the door closed and the sound of Sam and Flo's footsteps faded. He then cocked an inquiring brow at Harper.

"Why me?"

"You're a rogue. You've seen the grimmer side of life, know we all do things we aren't proud of but have to do anyway."

"And that's what's in your papers? Things you aren't proud of?"

Harper snorted. "Perhaps. But would I do them again? In a heartbeat."

Damien nodded, understanding where the man was coming from. He'd been in those positions himself more than a time or two. He gestured towards the papers. "May I?"

"Go ahead. I'll tell you part of the story while you pick them up. Save you trying to snoop." The old man chuckled darkly and Damien quirked his lips in a surreptitious smile. It was easy to tell that Sam and the old man were related. "Don't tell my granddaughter any of this. She doesn't need to know and it would only upset her."

"Understood." That made two people now trying to shield Sam from the truth. Damien didn't see her as being that delicate, but said nothing as he continued to sift through the pages looking for the elusive missing report.

"My Beta killed Sam's father and I killed my Beta. That's the crux of it."

Damien froze and turned his head to look at Harper. At least the abruptness of the old man's statement helped him to give the appearance of being shocked. It wouldn't do to let on that Marcello had basically told him the whole tale earlier on in the day.

Harper nodded, studying his reaction. "I don't believe in beating around the bush. Those are the facts."

"I'm sure you had your reasons." The heat from the fireplace was searing his skin and he concentrated on the papers he was gathering, eager to move away from the crackling flames.

"Damned right. Gary was my Beta for almost ten years. I knew he was ambitious, but I trusted him. When my son came home from out West with his family in tow, I expected Gary to be pleased that the heir to the Chicago dynasty had finally seen the light and was ready to take his rightful place."

"But he wasn't."

"Hell no, though Gary was careful not to show it. Thing is, my son never wanted to be Alpha; too much like his mother, rest her soul. We had words over it more than once." Samuel grew silent for a moment then cleared his throat. "Apparently Gary had it in his head to take over once I stepped down. But with my son home, he saw me urging the boy to fill the position. He must have felt his chance was slipping away so he took matters into his own hands. Pushed the boy into the path of a train."

"Clumsy of the Beta to let you see this happen." Damien was curious as to Harper's take on what had occurred.

"I didn't realize at first. In fact, it was a few years before I discovered the truth. Once I did, I dealt with it the only way I could."

Damien rose to his feet, the papers in his hand. "It's a tragic story, but not one that would shock Sam." There had to be more, Damien reasoned. Something else happened that Harper wanted to keep from Sam, something he didn't want found in his private papers.

Harper pressed his lips together and shook his head. "That's the gist of it; all you need to know anyway."

Damien didn't contradict him, but in his gut he knew the man was lying.

"Did you find what you're looking for?" Harper held out his hand expectantly and Damien handed over the pages that he'd flipped through. Thankfully, during the initial confusion, the old man hadn't noticed the files they were returning.

"No. Perhaps the pile over there?" He gestured towards a stack on the table near the window.

Harper shook his head "I'll check those myself in the morning. And before you start whining that Sam wants that report now, you can tell her she'll just have to wait. I'm still the Alpha here, and it won't make a hill of beans worth of a difference if Sinclair has to cool his heels for a day or two."

Whining? Damien bit back the smile on his lips. He couldn't ever remember being accused of that. "I'll pass the message along to Sam."

"You do that." Harper began feeding pages into the fire again. "And send Flo back. That dinner will be cold by now."

Damien hesitated. There was definitely something significant in the papers that the old man wanted to keep buried. It wasn't any of his business, but Dante was and somehow Dante knew about the whole debacle. "The room's warm with the fireplace burning. Why don't I let some of the evening air in to help cool things down?" He moved to the window and fiddled with the latch. Harper didn't turn, seeming to be lost in thought as he stared at the crackling flames.

The files were less than a foot away.

"I'm surprised the house doesn't have central air." The distant sounds of traffic spilled into the room as he pushed the window open. Damien used the noise to cover his movements, quickly sliding random pages out of various files, hoping they'd give him a general idea of what was inside of each. If anything proved to be of interest, he'd find a way to sneak back in and get the rest of them.

"Air conditioning? Don't need it. Bunch of wimps who can't stand a bit of hot weather, that's what people are nowadays. Too damned expensive to run, too." The old man grumbled.

"True." Damien quietly folded the pages, and tucked them into his waistband before pulling the edge of his shirt over top. He walked to the door. "I'll give Sam your message."

"And send for Florence."

"Of course." Damien pulled the door shut, wondering at the relationship between the two. Not mates, but more than patient and caregiver. Flo had a look about her when she was with the old man.

Intent on heading to his room to read over the papers he'd purloined, a sound from below had him pausing on the landing. From his vantage point he could see the front door. Sam was holding her leather jacket, seeming to test the weight in her hand, her face a study of indecision.

"Not sure if it's yours?" He couldn't resist the teasing comment.

"Hmm?" She looked up at him. "No. I was going to go for a ride, but I'm having second thoughts. My head's pounding." She shrugged. I think I'll sit on the porch instead."

"Good idea." He paused. The weary set of her shoulders tugged at him. "I'll join you in a minute, if you don't mind. I just need to send Florence to see your grandfather."

She gave a barely perceptible nod and opened the front door, disappearing into the darkness.

Damien headed to his room and tossed the papers on his bed. Why he'd said he'd join her, he had no idea. He should be reading through these papers, not sitting on a porch wasting his time. Yet, even as he pointed out the folly of his choice, his feet were taking him downstairs. A quick stop to deliver the message to Florence and then he made his way outside.

The porch was in darkness, the sun having set some time ago. Damien's eyesight quickly adjusted to the change in lighting, locating Sam sitting on the porch swing. Her head was propped up by her hand, purplish smudges showing under her closed eyes. He hadn't taken much notice of how she looked earlier, but with her guard down, it was easy to see her weariness. Was it the strain of being Alpha, or worrying about the takeover that was taking its toll on her?

Or, his wolf whispered, *our relationship?*

We don't have a relationship, he silently countered.

His wolf sniffed and raised a brow. *Liar. There's something between us. We just haven't figured out what it is.*

Damien scowled, not wanting to be reminded of the conflict that raged inside him.

He walked across the porch, his steps sounding on the wooden planks. "Mind if I sit down?"

"Would it matter if I did?" She opened one eye and peered at him.

A smile tugged at the corner of his mouth. She always had a comeback.

"Maybe." He sat down anyway, the swing creaking a bit under his added weight.

She didn't reply.

Using his foot, he set the swing into a gentle rhythm, the newly repaired chains and moorings silently doing their job. It was peaceful, just sitting there, the occasional passing vehicle or the sound of distant voices punctuating the chirring of night insects. Damien inhaled deeply and sighed, relaxing into the seat.

The scents of the city intermingled with hints of the approaching autumn; drying grass, the mustiness of leaves beginning to decay, the sweet smell of ripe fruit from the apple tree out back. He chuckled softly thinking of how their apple picking had gone the other day.

"What?" Sam turned her head to look at him.

"Nothing. Just thinking about apples." He slid his eyes sideways to look at her.

A grin slowly spreading across her face. "You looked damn funny with that apple on your head."

"Glad I could amuse you."

They shared a brief smile, neither spoiling the moment by bringing up the fight they'd had afterwards.

Sam let out a gentle sigh. In contrast to the heat of the day, the night air was cooler and damp. A cold front was predicted to be moving in, bringing a storm that would finally break the unseasonably hot spell. Already the beginnings of a breeze were stirring the leaves and causing goose bumps to rise on her skin. The heat generating off Damien's body made the chill of her own that much more noticeable. She shivered and rubbed her arms wishing she'd worn her coat rather than leaving it on the newel post.

Much to her surprise, Damien shifted closer and moved his arm so it rested across the back of the swing near her shoulders. Despite his behaviour in the cellar, he must have at least one chivalrous bone in his body. His warmth wrapped around her, comforting and secure. Briefly she thought of moving away, denying what might be seen as a weakness, but then went with the moment. She relaxed her muscles, surprised that she'd been holding herself that tense.

Neither spoke. He continued to rock the swing gently. Eventually, his fingers began to play with the hair at her nape, occasionally brushing over her skin. The fleeting contact sent frissons of awareness through her and she twitched her shoulders.

"Still cold?"

"No. My…er…shoulder muscles are tight."

Damien gave a grunt and pushed on her shoulder, turning her so her back was to him. "I'm pretty good at this." He dug his thumbs into her muscles, probing and pressing on the knots.

"Hmm…" Sam gave a moan of relief as the tight muscles began to relax. "You *are* good."

"Thanks. I used to do this all the time for my—"

"Don't say it." She reached back and laid her hand on his thigh. He was going to mention his mate again and she really didn't want to spoil the harmony between them.

Damien paused his ministrations. In the window, she could just make out his reflection. His mouth had tightened. Sam was sure she could see him swallow hard as he closed his eyes briefly before giving a sigh and continuing to work the kinks out of her muscles.

"Sorry." She whispered the apology, feeling mean-spirited and selfish. The man had obviously adored his mate. What right did she have to want to intrude, to force him to abandon his cherished memories? Love and devotion should be celebrated, even encouraged. And yet, she was drawn to him, wanted him to choose her.

"Sam..." He stilled the movement of his hands. They rested on her shoulders, the heat generating from them soaking into her flesh.

"Yes?" She kept her eyes fixed straight ahead, ignoring his reflection in favour of studying the peeling paint on the window frame.

"I... I like you." The words seemed to be forced from his throat, harsh, as if spoken against his will.

"Thanks." She wet her lips and then dared to ask. "Is that you or your wolf talking?"

"The wolf...and me." He gave a rueful laugh. "We both find you...interesting."

She nodded. "My wolf...and I...feel the same way about you."

He squeezed her shoulders gently and then she felt the faintest brush of warm moisture on the back of her neck as if he'd run his lips over her nape. Her heart started to pound faster, warmth washing over her as she recalled his kisses from the previous day and where they had led.

"Duty...strength..." She felt him trace over the words and her stomach fluttered as she wondered where this would lead. Should she push for more? Last time she had they'd ended up having sex, yet it hadn't brought them any closer together. "Your grandfather was a wise man when he said these were important qualities for an Alpha."

Sam forced herself not to twist her fingers into fists. Don't give anything away she told herself. Keep it light. Clearing her throat, she asked, "Did you find the missing report in grandfather's papers?"

"No." His breath teased her ear and she could feel him inhaling deeply, taking in her scent. "He had a few more files that he said he'd go through."

"It's okay. I was getting worked up over nothing. Even without that one report, I have enough evidence to convince Lycan Link that Sinclair is talking out of his ass."

"Probably."

He'd been brushing his thumbs over her shoulders, but he abruptly stopped and removed his hands. She could sense him pulling back, both emotionally and physically. What had caused the sudden change? She quickly reviewed her last statement yet found nothing about it to warrant his retreat.

The cool night air filled the space between their bodies, emphasizing the distance between them. Hell and damnation, how had she let herself fall under his spell again? Damien liked her, but he'd spoken of nothing deeper. It was wishful thinking on her part that he was hinting at anything more.

Suck it up, she told herself. You don't always get what you want in life. She'd learned that at a young age.

Sam stood up and rolled her shoulders, forcing her tone to be light and detached. "Thanks. That feels better."

"Headache gone?"

"Pretty much."

"Good." Damien stood as well, the movement bringing him into close proximity again. She took half a step back denying the awareness that sparked between them.

"I'd...er...better get inside. There are a few things I need to finish in the office."

"Yeah. I have some things I need to do, too." He flicked a glance at her, then looked away, shoving his hands in his pockets.

To keep from touching her? The idea was intriguing, but she didn't allow herself to explore it. She was trying to be noble, after all. "See you in the morning."

"Night, Sam."

"Night." She went inside and pulled the door shut behind her. Through the window, she could see him standing on the steps staring up at the sky. Was he looking for inspiration? Talking to his dead mate? Or simply admiring the constellations? It didn't matter. Damien was her Beta and, unless he did an about face, that was likely all he'd ever be.

Chapter 27

Damien lay awake for hours staring at the ceiling. His mind, heart, body, and soul were at war with each other and he couldn't see any way of resolving the situation. He'd like to be able to blame Sam, but truth was she'd done nothing that night to encourage him. Unlike previous encounters when she'd been the instigator, tonight it had all been his fault.

He'd been the one to move closer when she'd shivered. He'd started massaging her shoulders. He'd pressed the light kiss to the nape of her neck. Thank heaven she'd mentioned Kane. It had knocked some sense into him before he'd made a monumental mistake.

Betraying Beth once, he could almost forgive. To do it again… He shook his head. His body might respond to Sam's physical attractiveness, but that didn't mean he should act on it. His heart and soul belonged to his blood bonded mate.

She's been dead three years, his logical half stated, but you're still alive…

Round and round the arguments raged until he flung the covers off and sat up, dragging his hands through his hair in frustration.

His wolf was strangely silent, and so was Beth. He'd tried to summon her earlier on, but only a fleeting image had wavered in his mind's eye. She'd seemed distant, smiling softly, her attention fixed on some distant place he couldn't see. A part of him feared she was angry with him, but Beth wasn't like that; she'd always forgiven him, no matter what.

Rubbing his face, he spied the papers he'd taken from Harper sitting on the bedside table. Since he wasn't sleeping he might as well do some reading. Switching on the bedside lamp, he hitched up the pillows behind his back and grabbed the first page, peering at the faded scrawl.

'The woman my son mated has destroyed our blood line. I don't know why he can't see it. Every time I look at the child's eyes, I know the truth.'

A sneer curled Damien's lip as he read the words and then recalled what Sam had told him that night in the pond. 'Tainted blood', wasn't that what she'd said? He shook his head and flipped to another page.

'My son is dead. My heir, my future. I've no idea what to do. Gary says not to worry, he'll do his duty by the pack. I know I can depend on him. He's a good man, but I'm loath to see the territory pass out of the family. It's been our heritage for years. There is the child, of course. A female, but at least flesh of my flesh. If only her eyes didn't give her shame away...'

"The bastard." Damien spat out the word, imagining how Sam must have felt growing up, believing her very existence had brought shame to the pack. Resisting the urge to crumple the paper and toss it out like the garbage it was, he set it aside and read the next one.

'Gary's fighting me on this. He doesn't think the girl can one day lead the pack. In a way I can't believe I've come to this decision either. For years, our pack has supported The Cause and yet what other choice do I have?'

Well, this seemed to confirm what Marcello had said. The Beta had wanted to take over and Samantha would have been in his way. Old man Harper mustn't have been aware of the fact though. There was no hint that he didn't trust the Beta implicitly.

After skimming the rest of the page, Damien went back to look at the other two, searching for other entries that had to do with Sam or the Beta. There was a lot of information about what had been served for lunch, the arrival of the latest electricity bill, boring stuff and not what he was looking for. It seemed Harper was the kind who kept notes on everything, thorough to the point of being obsessive.

The distant sound of the hallway clock chiming reminded Damien it was three in the morning. He yawned, his eyes feeling gritty, and set the papers down. It would seem that he'd have to pilfer a few more papers from Harper's personal collection if he wanted to learn more about what happened with the Beta. True, it wasn't really any of his business, but he could justify it by saying he was trying to determine how Dante had learned of the situation. Sliding down in bed, he adjusted the pillows and began to plot how he'd get his hands on Harper's files.

Sam let out a muffled scream and grabbed a nearby mug, ready to chuck it across the room, only the realization that it was one of her favourites kept her from completing the action. She set it down and grabbed the newspaper, proceeding to rip it to shreds.

"I take it you didn't like your horoscope?" Damien wandered into the room carrying two cups of coffee and eyeing the shredded bits of paper on the floor around her.

"Don't mess with me today, Masterson. I'm not in the mood." She tossed down the last bit of paper on the floor and then kicked it out of her way so she could pace the room.

He raised his brows and held out one of the cups. "I brought you a coffee. Looks like you might need it."

"Thanks." She accepted the cup and took a gulp not caring that it was still hot.

Wisely, he said nothing and after a few minutes she calmed down enough to speak. "I had another communiqué from OPATA."

"And?"

"Sinclair has *another* complaint against us."

"Really?" He sat down, legs casually extended and took a sip of his coffee.

"Yes. He says that since I was never listed as Beta on the books, I had no right to step into the position of acting Alpha. If anything, *you* should be in control since your name is on the official roster as the most recent Beta in the pack."

"What?" Damien sat up straight and set his mug down with a definite thud. "Let me see that."

Sam spun her laptop around and allowed him to study the screen while she stalked to the window taking angry sips of the drink she cradled in her hands. A storm was definitely brewing, grey clouds rolled across the sky while the wind whipped leaves and bits of garbage across the road. It seemed fitting; there was a lot of garbage being whipped around inside as well. Where the hell did Sinclair get off—

"The fucking hell, I'll—" She turned at the sound of Damien's expletive. He'd clamped his mouth shut on whatever else he'd been intending to say.

"I take it you're not chomping at the bit wanting to take over?"

"What sort of shit is he pulling?" Damien was on his feet now, looking as incensed as she was feeling. Sam decided it was nice to be able to share this with someone; for a rogue, Damien was a pretty decent guy.

See? Her wolf whispered. *I knew there was a reason we should keep him.*

"It's like he's trying to chip away at us, one little piece at a time." She shook her head, admiring Sinclair's strategy even though she hated his guts. "He didn't present his whole case to Lycan Link at once. They would have looked it over, cross-checked the facts with me and then dismissed him. This way, he keeps drawing their attention to us over and over, making them dig deeper, causing them to question minor details."

"Risky," Damien murmured. "Some might view it as harassment."

"From some small time Alpha, it might be seen that way. But Sinclair has a solid reputation." Sam walked back to her desk and stared at the computer screen. "Hell, a few years back when I was first taking over I even admired him. He was young, progressive, interested in moving with the times."

"And now?"

"He's a power hungry bastard." She flopped down in her chair.

Damien sat as well and picked up his mug, staring at the contents. "So what's your next step?"

Betrayed: Book Two – The Road To Redemption

"I really don't know. I'll have to confer with Grandfather first." She checked her watch. "I have enough time to talk to him before he leaves."

"Leaves?" Damien looked at her with interest.

"He has a doctor's appointment this morning. We don't have our own in-pack physician anymore, but there's a human doctor with pack member status that we use when we have to."

"So you'll be taking him?"

"No. Florence gets the joy of that job." Sam gave a dry laugh. "He'll grumble and complain the whole way there and tell the doctor he's fine. Then Flo will give the real story. She's a godsend when it comes to dealing with him."

"Your grandfather and Florence are…close."

"I don't pretend to understand their relationship. They're more than friends, but…" Sam shrugged. "It's between them. My grandmother's been gone for decades."

Damien made a non-committal sound, seeming lost in thought.

She sighed and hitched her chair closer to the desk. "I'd better print a copy of this and go read it to Grandfather. He can mull it over while on his way to the doctor's office."

"It might cause his blood pressure to spike." Damien warned. "I know mine did."

"Mine, too." Sam smiled at him, pleased he cared so much given that this was a temporary job for him. Maybe when all the takeover crap was done, she'd be able to convince him to stay. For all that last night she'd resolved to back off, in the light of morning she was filled with a new resolve. She and her wolf hadn't totally given up on the darkly handsome rogue. The game wasn't over yet.

Damien left the room cursing Kane under his breath. What kind of a friend shoved you into an awkward situation like this? Suggesting he, as Beta, should be in charge of the Chicago pack! Kane knew he didn't want any part of belonging to a pack, let alone being in charge of one. Sure, Kane had sound reasons for wanting control of the territory, but Damien didn't want to be in the middle of the fight. His only job was to give a report now and then.

Guilt twisted his stomach as he considered the fact that without his reports Kane's case might not be as strong. Of course, nothing he was reporting was a secret. A little digging would reveal that the pack was underpopulated, the Alpha old and sick; he was simply making it happen faster.

Walking into the kitchen, he set his now empty cup in the sink and stared at the worn and chipped counter-top. The Chicago pack was in serious trouble, even without Kane's threatened takeover. They didn't have the finances to fix up the pack house, or have enough members to keep going beyond this current generation. The influx of money and bodies that Kane could provide would actually revive the pack, right?

He rubbed the back of his neck wishing he'd never let Kane talk him into coming to Chicago. Riding his bike, a loner, a rogue, that was how he wanted to live his life. No emotional involvement, and certainly not being in charge of a pack. While other Lycan pups might dream of being an Alpha one day, it had never been his goal. All those people depending on you was not his style.

"Reno depended on us. And Beth," his wolf reminded him.

"Yeah, and look at how I screwed that up." He muttered. Guilt still ate away at his soul, no matter how anyone might try to convince him otherwise. And there was no way he wanted to be in charge of the Chicago pack. Time to set Kane straight on that one.

He headed upstairs to make his call.

~~~

"Quit? As in sell my half ownership? But I just started!" Elise stared at Kane, unable to believe what he'd said.

"You say you're overtired. Then let something go. You can't do everything. It's not realistic." He folded his arms and stared at her from the other side of the bed. Water from his recent shower glistened on his skin, dripping down his broad chest before disappearing into the towel he had casually wrapped around his waist. A year ago, the sight of his nearly naked body would have had her knees weakening, but lately she was too tired and too angry with him to care.

"*I* can't do everything! What about you? You're so caught up with impressing High Council—"

"Elise, be reasonable."

"And, of course, reasonable is doing what you want me to do."

"It's the logical solution. You said you were so tired you didn't want to get up this morning." He walked to the dresser, pulled open a drawer and took out socks and a pair of briefs.

"Why do I always have to be the one to give up what I want to do? Maybe I don't want you on High Council." She walked to the closet and began sorting through her clothes, her movements brisk to give vent to her mood.

"High Council is an important job."

"More important than the children and me?"

"I didn't say that." His tones were clipped, and when she turned to look at him she could easily see the muscle in his jaw flexing. He was angry, but for some reason she couldn't resist prodding him even more.

"What if you had to choose? Our family or High Council?"

He ran a hand through his hair. "Elise, you're being ridiculous."

"Oh, so now I'm ridiculous for wanting to be first in your life. Well, thank you very much. I guess I know exactly where the children and I stand."

"Elise! You knew I was Alpha when we mated."

"Like I had a choice in that." She tossed her blouse and skirt on the bed.

"What do you mean?" He went dead still.

"Being an Alpha's mate was never in my plans." She stalked to the dresser and pulled out a bra and panties. Kane was standing a few feet away and when she looked up their gazes locked in the mirror.

"I see." He stared at her, his face unreadable. "I'm sorry you find it such a burden to be my mate. I'll make sure I keep my distance."

"Kane, that's not what I meant!" She turned to face him, a sinking feeling in her stomach.

"I think it was." He roughly pulled on the rest of his clothes. "I won't be home tonight. If you or the children need something, John will help you." And with that he left the room.

"Kane!" She called his name, but he didn't return.

A horrible, sick feeling swept over her, her bitter words playing over and over in her head. She'd never meant to say them out loud. How would she feel if Kane had said something similar to her? Tears welled in her eyes. Hurting him, really hurting him, hadn't been her intention.

She tried to use her blood bond to connect with him but it was firmly shut. Was this it? Was this the end of them as a couple?

Chapter 28

Sam watched the muscles work in her Grandfather's jaw. He wasn't saying a word, his face white. Her grandfather grumbled and roared and complained, but this… This went beyond anything she'd seen before into pure unadulterated rage. She resisted the urge to back away like Florence had done, instead standing her ground and waiting for him to speak.

When he did, his tones were so low and cold she could hardly hear him at first. "Sinclair would dare to suggest I abdicate and let a rogue lead my pack? That the blood of a Harper might not be *suitable*?" His voice rose on the last word and his hand slowly crushed the paper until it was a mere ball. He threw it on the floor where it rolled across the carpeting, coming to rest at Florence's feet.

The older woman bent and picked it up. She cast a glance at the other two before smoothing the sheet out. With a trembling voice, she read the words. "It says '*Samantha Harper becoming Alpha of the Chicago pack is an unacceptable solution to the problem of an aged and chronically ill Alpha. The position must be filled based on suitability, not blood lines.*'" Florence looked up, aghast. "The man is crazy. He wants you to abdicate? And to suggest Samantha isn't qualified is ludicrous. Of course she's qualified! She's been in training for years!"

"Lycan Link doesn't know that, nor does Sinclair." Sam couldn't believe she was actually defending the man. She wasn't. She was merely stating the facts.

Samuel Harper thumped the arm of his chair with his fist. "Whether they know or not isn't the point. They have no business poking their nose into our affairs. This is what I fought against for years—"

"Samuel!" Florence cut him off with a sharp word and look of warning that had Sam wondering what was going on.

Her grandfather huffed, his fingers clenching on the arm of his chair. "We're not giving up the pack and certainly not to someone Sinclair has picked out. This pack belongs to the Harper family and no one else."

"I agree, Grandfather, but they don't."

"Suggestions?" Her grandfather looked at her.

Sam's heart began to beat harder and her mouth was suddenly dry. She had a suggestion, one she'd considered before, even started to train for, but somewhere deep inside she'd never believed it would actually come to this. Yet, her pack depended on her. Duty came before all else, regardless of any personal fears or concerns. She took a deep breath. "The only solution I see is…a challenge issued to Sinclair."

"No!" Florence immediately protested and swung a shocked look at the old Alpha.

Her grandfather didn't speak at first. Instead, he locked his eyes on hers; bushy grey brows topping faded blue, steadily staring into clear violet as if testing her measure. "Are you sure?"

She widened her stance and hooked her thumbs in her belt loops. Shoulders back, she lifted her chin denying the faint quivering inside. "I am. I've been training. I can take him."

The old Alpha nodded slowly. "Then so be it."

Damien finished his call to Kane, feeling his friend now understood his position. Terms like 'no fucking way' and 'I'd rather swim in shit' had helped clarify his feelings.

"All you have to do is take over for a month, tops," Kane had tried to persuade him. "Then abdicate and hand the pack over to me."

"Even a month is too long, Kane." He'd replied.

"And what else do you have to do with your time?"

"Not much, but I won't be part of this."

Kane's voice had hardened. "You're already part of it."

"But they don't know it, and I'd prefer to leave without a knife between my shoulder blades, which is what will happen once they find out."

Betrayed: Book Two – The Road To Redemption

"A knife?" Kane had laughed. "From my encounters with her I'd have thought Sam Harper was more the kind to rip out your jugular."

"She might do both," he'd agreed, thinking of his little spitfire. Realizing he'd used the term 'his', he frowned. Sam wasn't his and if he was thinking that way, it was all the more reason for him to cut out as soon as possible. "I need to get out of here, Kane. Itchy feet are a known failing of rogues like me."

"Are you sure it isn't another kind of itch? One named Sam?"

He'd snorted and denied the claim, ignoring the reproachful look of his inner wolf.

There'd been doubt in Kane's voice, but he'd finally agreed to look at other means of wrenching control of the Chicago pack from the Harper family.

Damien tucked his phone in his pocket and hoped Kane worked fast because, no matter what happened, he wanted out before the week was over. He was starting to feel closed in. The pack members were starting to depend on him, coming to him with their problems, making him part of their lives. They were like the vines that were growing on the outside of the house, working their roots into the mortar, slowly covering the house until you couldn't see the bricks anymore. Nope, he wasn't sticking around to be smothered like that.

He walked to the window and opened it, feeling the need for fresh air. It was a dull day, the clouds a deep purplish grey, warning of heavy rains soon to come. His leg ached as if confirming the change in the weather and he absentmindedly shifted his weight off the weaker limb. Below, he could see Florence and Sam helping the old Alpha into a car.

Ah, the doctor's appointment, which reminded him....

Leaving his room, he silently made his way down the stairs to the second floor. With the key players occupied, now was his chance to get his hands on the rest of Samuel Harper's files and find out the whole story behind the power hungry Beta and, hopefully, how Dante fit into the whole scenario.

Just to be on the safe side, he knocked softly first then cautiously pushed the door open. The room was silent. After checking over his shoulder to make sure no one was watching, Damien slipped inside. It didn't take long to scan the dates on the files and pull out the ones he wanted. Within a minute, he was done and headed back towards his room.

"Damien!" Sam entered the house, calling out his name, just as he began to climb the stairs to his room.

He was careful to keep the papers shielded by his body. "Yeah?"

"Meet me in the cellar. I want to practise." She kept on walking through the house, not even looking his way and he gave an inaudible sigh of relief.

"Sure. I'll be there in five."

The back door slammed and he wasn't even sure if she'd heard his reply. Giving a shrug he lightly ran up the stairs to deposit the papers. More bedtime reading he thought to himself as he stuffed them out of sight.

Sam was waiting in the cellar when Damien arrived. Energy surged through her and she was bouncing on her toes, ready to get started. Last time she'd trained with him she'd been trying, but the idea of a challenge had only been a vague possibility. Now that it was real, she couldn't afford to hold back.

She was nervous. Hell, scared was more like it, but fear was good. It made you work harder, think smarter. Only an idiot wasn't scared. Real bravery came from being afraid, but doing your job anyway. That's what an Alpha did and she *was* an Alpha, the Chicago pack Alpha, dammit, and Sinclair was going to learn it once and for all!

"You seem raring to go." Damien gave her a crooked smile.

She didn't smile back, merely nodding and taking up a stance. "I'm ready."

He raised one brow but made no comment, stripping off his shirt and tossing it aside. Any other day, she might have taken time to notice his ripped body, but not today. Today she had a job to do.

As soon as he gave a nod, she attacked. Not waiting for him like she did the last time, she went on the offensive, the idea of saving her pack foremost in her mind.

Rapid quick jabs. Keep your guard tight and your fist up. Push from the waist and shoulder. Each hit to his body jarred her own, but she ignored the pain. Repeating the basics of each move in her head, she noted with grim satisfaction that she'd forced him to step back. Time to celebrate her successful technique later, though. Right now she was training for what could be a life and death fight.

A front kick to force him back, then into a side kick.

Damn.

Her speed was off and he avoided it.

Return to her guard position. Chin protected. Block his blows. Face neutral so he had no idea how his hits reverberated through her frame. Look for an opening. Swing the arm out and around for a hook. Aim a kick to his groin…

"What the fuck!" He avoided her kick, catching her foot and almost flipping her onto her back. Barely, she maintained her balance.

"What?" She paused, shaking her hair from her eyes. Half crouched, she was ready to attack again.

"Kicking me in the balls during practice is *not* part of the deal." Damien glared at her, sweat dripping down his face, his breathing rapid from exertion.

Sam pulled her lips back in a satisfied grin, pleased her opponent was showing signs that her attack was taking its toll. "Fine." She wiped the sweat from her eyes, talking between heaving breaths. "I'm ready. Come at me again."

He lowered his fists. "What's with you today? Hard practice is one thing but—"

"You're training me to fight Sinclair." She took a jab at him, but he nimbly stepped aside and shook his head.

"Yeah, only we don't need to permanently injure each other." He flexed one of his legs. Part of her remembered how he'd said that one had been injured years before and had never properly healed. Always know the weaknesses of your opponent, her grandfather had told her. She tucked the information into the back of her head.

"There's no mercy in a real challenge fight. When I take on Sinclair, I'll need to—"

"When? You mean *if* you take him on."

Sam shook head. "No. It's *when*. I'm issuing a challenge." She took up her fighting stance again, but Damien didn't respond.

"Are you insane?"

"No. I'm fighting for my pack." She straightened, glowering and not appreciating the incredulous look on his face.

"You can't challenge Kane Sinclair. He's twice your size."

"Size doesn't matter. I'm faster. I can get under his guard—"

"You can get yourself killed." Damien put his hands on his hips. "No way are you fighting him."

"Yes, I am. I've sent the notice in to Lycan Link."

He shook his head. "Your grandfather—"

"He knows and agrees it's the only way."

"It's fucking archaic and—"

"And the Book of the Law still allows it." She narrowed her eyes. "Now are you going to help me or not."

He reached out and grabbed her by the arm, pulling her so close their bodies touched. "Sugar, you are *not* fighting Kane."

Sam struggled against his grip. "My name isn't Sugar and I am fighting him. This is *my* territory, *my* pack, *my* wolves. It's my duty to do what's best for them."

"And you think getting yourself killed is what's best for them?" His black brows were lowered over his piercing silvery blue eyes; the look he gave her was seething with anger.

"I won't get killed. I'm—"

"Sam!" He interrupted with a growl and then kissed her hard, his mouth crushing hers, enveloping her in heat, causing her head to spin. And then, before she could react, he pushed her away. "I'm talking to your grandfather about this."

Betrayed: Book Two – The Road To Redemption

"I've already said he knows and agrees."
"We'll see about that." Damien stalked from the cellar. Sam cursed and took out her ire on the punching bag.

Chapter 29

Damien's feet pounded on the stairs as he made his way to Samuel Harper's door.

"What the hell is he thinking, letting Sam issue a challenge." He growled the words as he rapped on the door only to realize the man wasn't back from the doctor's yet.

"Hey, Damien. What are you doing?" Chris came bounding up the stairs, a look of excitement about him.

"Nothing." Damien compressed his lips, trying to rein in his temper.

"Did you hear the news?" Without giving him a chance to respond, Chris continued. "Sam's issued a challenge against Sinclair. Isn't that way cool?"

"Cool?" He raised his brows.

"Yeah. Challenges hardly ever happen anymore."

"For good reason. They're dangerous."

Chris shrugged. "Sam's tough. She's the toughest Alpha ever. She'll kick Sinclair's ass so hard—"

"But what if she doesn't? What if she's hurt? Left permanently disabled?" He doubted Kane would take it that far, but in the heat of a fight things happened.

"Well…" Uncertainty washed over the boy's face.

"Fighting isn't fun or exciting. It should only be used as a last resort."

"But you've been in fights, haven't you? I'm mean, you're a rogue."

"Yeah. I've been in fights." He paused, recalling how the rush of victory was always followed by a sick feeling, images of the dead still burned into his brain. "A lot of them I regret."

"But not all?"

Sharp of the kid to pick up on that. He sighed heavily. "Sometimes you have to fight. When the enemy is evil and won't listen to reason. When the lives of the innocent are at stake."

"Sinclair is evil. He's a power hungry bastard who wants to take over our pack." Chris regained a little of his confidence as he quoted the phrase Sam so often used.

"There are degrees of evil, kid."

"But Sam—"

"Sam might die." His tone was harsh and Chris' face whitened.

"I..."

"Think about it, Chris. Is Sam's life really worth it?" He walked away, not waiting for the boy's response.

Once in his room, Damien paced restlessly. God, what a mess. He'd never anticipated Sam would actually issue a challenge. Sure, she'd talked about it, but he'd never really believed she'd follow through. When he'd started this job, he'd seen it as a fact-finding mission, assuming Kane would go about his takeover through legal wrangling.

Sam might die.

The words he'd spoken to Chris played over and over in his head. He couldn't stand to lose another person he...cared...about.

Cared? His mind stuttered on the word. Other, more suitable ones hovered, but he didn't want to—dare to—use them.

Care.

It was a lukewarm term.

Bland. Nondescript. Very unlike Sam. An image of her moments ago came to mind. Her dark hair wet with sweat, her eyes blazing. The determined set of her chin as she faced him, muscles tight and fists clenched. The way her thin grey tank had clung to her body. Her mouth, hot and sweet. Yep, that was his spitfire.

Damn her grandfather for ever agreeing to a challenge. He could have stopped it; he was still listed as the official Alpha. The Book of the Law allowed challenges, but if there was an existing Alpha he could have issued a protest, bogged down the process until Sam could think of another solution.

Clenching his fists, he wished he had a way to vent his anger. The hole in the plaster still existed from last time he'd punched the wall. No point in having two to fix. Calm down and clear your head. Wasn't that what Beth would have told him?

His thinking skidded to a halt.

Beth.

Why was he so fired up over Sam when... He dragged his hands through his hair and looked around the room, unable to make sense of what was going on inside his head.

He spied the papers he'd pilfered from Harper earlier on and latched on to them like a lifeline. Focus on finding out Dante's connection to this pack; there was no emotional ambiguity in that. He knew exactly how he felt about the slimeball. From the first moment of meeting, he'd instinctively hated the man. Finding a way to bring Dante down should keep him occupied while he waited for old man Harper to return.

Grabbing the papers, he dropped down on the bed and began to read.

'For years I've supported The Cause, selected my pack members carefully, given financial aid, but now I'm beginning to doubt my beliefs. The child looks at me with her violet eyes and I know the truth, but she's my son's daughter. I'm torn between family and party loyalty...'

The 'Cause'? Damien frowned. Harper had used those words before... He skipped to an entry written a week later.

'My decision has been made. The girl will begin her training to one day lead the pack. It will take time to mould her, but it can be done. The Harper blood will show through in the end. Gary isn't happy about my decision and I'm beginning to suspect his loyalty. More than once he's ended a phone conversation when I've entered the room. Is he reporting me? I'm sure I can scent deceit in the air. The question is which way does the rest of the pack lean?'

The pack must have stuck by Harper...or was that part of the reason for the low numbers? Had some left when they realized Samantha would one day take over? Was that part of the reason for the small membership?

'My Beta's betrayal runs deep. He coveted my position, killed my son, scorns my chosen heir. And now he threatens the wrath of The Cause against me. I've confined him in the cellar and tomorrow, we will hold a judgement...'

Judgement. A pack's version of a legal hearing. From what Marcello and Harper had told him, Damien knew the outcome but read on, curious as to how everything had unfolded. He flipped through several pages, but there was a definite gap in the dates and still no mention of Dante. It seemed he'd need more recent files if he wanted to know how the story ended.

A look outside revealed the car was still gone. Odds were there'd be enough time to sneak into Harper's quarters again. With most pack members working it was easy enough to move about undetected. Once inside Harper's quarters, he'd have to be selective about the files he took. He couldn't remove all of them, their absence was sure to be noticed.

It took less than two minutes to leave his room and make his way to the old man's. The room was silent, not even the ticking of a clock disturbing the stillness. Flicking through the dates on each file, he found those that were most likely to contain the information he was interested in. Just to be sure, he opened one and began to skim for Dante's name.

Household bills, quarrels between pack members, the purchase of a new freezer... Harper had documented almost everything. Boring except... Damien paused and studied a ledger page showing income and expenses. Large quantities of money had begun to be paid out. They would seem to be going to a medical research facility. The fertility issue Sam had mentioned? He began to read more carefully.

'The experts claim our declining numbers are the fault of a limited gene pool. Is this how I am to be paid back? Years of supporting The Cause—ensuring the finest blood runs through our veins—and now it has come to this. There has to be a better solution. I'll not be encouraging my members to go out and mate with just anyone.'

Betrayed: Book Two – The Road To Redemption

A cold chill settled over Damien as he read, the niggling of a suspicion beginning to grow into an evil entity.

'Salazar came to visit me today, the bastard. Luckily he used the passages so no one knows he was here...'

Bingo. There was the connection he'd been looking for. Salazar was one of the aliases Dante used. So Dante was known to Harper. But, Damien frowned, if that was the case, then why had Dante planned on being hired on as the pack Beta. Harper would have recognized him right away. Unless that had been Dante's plan. To stay in the pack house, thumbing his nose at the old man knowing Samuel Harper wanted to keep their relationship a secret. Yeah, that would be Dante's style.

'Severing ties with The Cause isn't a simple act. There can be...repercussions. Or so Salazar is telling me. Punishment for daring to turn my back on the organization. He says he'll use his position within the organization to wipe our records from The Cause's files, but it will cost me. I'm not a fool; I know blackmail when I see it. One payment won't be enough, yet what else is there to do? I've never healed properly from my injuries; if I was still fit, I'd kill him just as I did Gary. Salazar knows my weakness, knows where to twist the knife.'

So the old man was being blackmailed. That's why the pack was so poor. All the money that had supposedly been channelled into fertility research had likely gone into the pockets of Dante Esparza. And the pack's fertility problems stemmed from selective breeding.

Damien rose to his feet, suddenly feeling dirty. 'The Cause.' Hell, it was another name for Purists and he was living in the middle of them.

A sound from the hallway had him cursing. He'd been so busy reading, he'd forgotten his intention had been to slip in and out quickly. There was nothing outside the window to climb on and a two storey drop would likely guarantee a broken ankle. The passageways?

Turning, Damien tried to determine the most likely location for a false wall with a hidden entrance. Not the outside walls. As quickly as possible he encircled the room, testing the walls. The fireplace? He examined the structure and…there. A tiny crack where the brick met the wainscoting. Most would take it to be the result of the house settling with old age but… Damien crouched and pressed his fingers along the panel. It snicked open just as the door to the room opened. He slipped inside and slid the panel back into place, then stood very still controlling his breathing.

There was a chance they'd detect his scent in the room but he was laying odds on the fact they'd ignore it. He'd been in the house long enough that his scent had become part of the background, like the ticking of a clock no one noticed, but drove newcomers crazy.

"Quit fussing, Flo. Doc said I'm fit as a fiddle."

"No. He said given your age you weren't doing too bad, but your nerves are strung too tight."

Harper blustered ignoring the comment and Florence could be heard moving about the room, helping him get settled. Damien began to cautiously inch his way along the tiny passage deciding their conversation would cover his movements. He had no idea where he'd end up, but anywhere other than Harper's room had to be preferable. Not that he really cared what a bunch of Purists thought about him, but he'd like to live long enough to share the news with Kane. This was exactly the leverage needed to oust the Harper family from Chicago for good.

The passageway ended in a linen closet near the end of the hall. Slipping out, he didn't bother to brush the dust and cobwebs from his clothes. His only concern was to get out of the house as fast as he could. Breathing the same air as effing Purists made him sick.

He gathered his things from his room, throwing them into his bag as fast as he could. There wasn't much; he'd learned to travel light over the years. Hitching his old knapsack over his shoulder, he grabbed his leather jacket and made his way downstairs.

"Damien? Where are you off to?" Sam stood in the doorway of her office.

"I'm leaving." His answer was curt. He couldn't even bear to look at her and kept his face averted.

"Leaving? Why?"

He compressed his lips, wanting to shout at her that he knew the truth, knew her pack belonged to the Purists, that they were no better than the bastards that had killed hundreds of half-breed Lycans over the years. Killed his Beth.

His throat tightened. Beth. He'd kissed Sam, held her body while his Beth lay cold in a grave. Guilt tore at his gut. How could he have betrayed his mate? Betrayed her with a Purist, the very cause of her death!

"I'm a rogue. I come and go as I wish."

She stepped forward and laid a hand on his arm. "But—"

He shook her hand off, unable to bare her touch. Turning, he didn't bother to hide the hatred in his eyes as he spat out his reply. "Keep your filthy Purist hands off me."

"Filthy Purist?" She gaped at him for a moment before anger took over. Eyes narrowed, hands on hips, she snapped back at him. "Fine. Go then. See if I care."

He didn't reply. Rage blurred his vision making it difficult to see, to even think. His whole body shook from the extreme control he was exercising. The need for revenge was once again beginning to burn within him, blackening his soul, clouding his judgement. He had to get out, get away... Without another word, he headed towards the back of the house where he'd parked.

"Damien, I thought we should tackle the grout on these tiles." Hiram was in the kitchen, his tool box open on the table.

The look of pleasure on the old man's face almost had him pausing, but the knowledge that Hiram was one of them overrode everything else. "Sorry, you're on your own for that one." He didn't wait for a reply.

Allowing the door to slam shut behind him, he stepped outside. The wind was whipping the trees, leaves blowing across the yard. Splots of rain were beginning to fall as well and he hunched his shoulders against the weather. After the heat of the last few weeks, the cool dampness of the air was shock.

His Harley was parked near the fence sharing a tarp with Sam's. There was an intimacy to that fact that soured his stomach and he tore the tarp off, leaving it flapping in the wind. He roughly stored his gear in the saddlebags, swung his leg over the seat and started the engine.

For a moment, he stared at the old pack house. In the gloom of the storm the decrepit exterior was hard to see. Instead, light and the impression of warmth spilled from the windows. His throat tightened as images of the past few weeks flashed before him. But it had all been a lie—a Purist lie—and that was unforgiveable.

Gunning the engine, he roared out of the yard and drove away.

Inside the house, Sam kicked the door of her office shut. Fucking asshole. She should have known better than to depend on a rogue! How dare he just up and leave? And where did he get off calling her names?

Throwing herself into her chair, she scowled at the computer screen. Damien Masterson, Beta, Chicago pack. Only minutes before she'd finished designing a new letterhead that included him as second in command.

Dickwad.

Stretching out her hand, she jabbed the delete key.

Chapter 30

Kane negotiated a turn on auto-pilot as he talked on his hands-free phone to Damien. Good thing he'd driven the road for years because what he'd just heard was taking all his attention. "The Chicago pack is full of Purists?"

"Yep. Old man Harper's notes confirmed it. He never said 'Purist' in so many words—called it 'The Cause'—but there could be no other meaning."

"Damn. Never expected to uncover that."

"Me, either." The bitterness was evident in Damien's voice.

"Sorry to have put you in that position. Considering what you went through with Beth—"

"No need to apologize." Damien cut him off, which wasn't unusual. The man seldom wanted to talk about this dead mate. "I'm just glad we found out and are in the position to do something about it."

"Being a Purist isn't illegal." He hated pointing that out, but freedom of expression and belief were outlined in the Charter of Rights and Freedoms.

"I know, but if we take over the pack—"

"We?" Kane was surprised at Damien's word choice.

"I'm with you in this, at least until we root the Purists out, then I'll hand the territory over to you."

"I'm not following you." Kane frowned.

"Harper's issued a challenge. Haven't you heard yet?"

Kane swore. "I've been out of touch all day, up in the mountains. Lots of dead zones." He checked his rearview mirror and then moved to pass the slow moving vehicle he'd been following for the past few miles. "A challenge from old man Harper, you say?"

"Not him. Sam. The granddaughter."

"That bit of girl?" He let a chuckle slip out. "I'd have to fly to Chicago—"

Damien interrupted again, his tone hard, determined, almost eager. "I could act as your proxy."

Something about Damien's response caught his attention. He answered slowly, trying to gauge his friend. "A proxy is allowed under the Law, but rarely used."

"It's still legal."

Yeah, something was definitely up. "What gives, Damien? It sounds like you're spoiling for a fight."

A bitter laugh came over the phone. "Let's just say I don't like games. Harper's pack is pretending to be something it's not. And you know how I feel about Purists."

"That I do." Kane paused, weighing the facts. He wanted Chicago, but Harper had been wiggling like the proverbial worm on a hook trying to get away. A challenge would solve things once and for all. Damien wanted to fight. Fighting against Purists was right up his friend's alley. And Samantha Harper wouldn't be much of an opponent. "All right. I'll send a message to Lycan Link as soon as I get home. Is tomorrow soon enough for you?"

"Yeah. It's good."

"We pick the time, they pick the place. That's what the rules state."

"I'm fine with that. I know the area."

Kane nodded. "All right then. I'll call you with the confirmation."

The doorbell rang, but Sam didn't look up from the computer screen. She was researching Sinclair, trying to find out everything she knew about the man. Know your enemy, wasn't that what they always told you to do? With Damien walking out on them, she was feeling the need for every extra edge she could find. If Lycan Link found out she'd lost another member...

"Excuse me, Sam."

Betrayed: Book Two – The Road To Redemption

She growled in acknowledgement of the words that followed a faint tap on her door. "What do you need, Andrea?"

"Someone's here to see you. Says he's a friend of Damien's. I didn't know if you'd want to talk to him or not." Andrea's voice was hesitant and at another time Sam might have smiled. They all knew to tiptoe around her when she was in a mood, and that's definitely what she was in right now. Several members had commented on Damien's absence at dinner and her reply had been abrupt in the extreme, ending the usual round the table chatter.

"A friend of Damien's?" Her first instinct was to tell whoever it was to get the hell out of her house. Curiosity got the better of her. Maybe this 'friend' could shed some light on her Beta's sudden departure.

"Send him in." Sam leaned back in her chair wondering who would come through the door. It was an older man with a limp, vaguely familiar. Ah, the man she'd seen at Club Mystique!

"Good evening, Ms. Harper." His tones were smooth and cultured, clearly at odds with his appearance. Greying hair, lined face. Good quality clothes that were showing some wear and didn't quite fit his frame. "My name is Dante. Dante Esparza."

Slowly, she sat up straight. "Excuse me?" That was Damien's name! Or at least the name he'd used when applying for the position of Beta.

He laughed, a raspy sound that made her skin crawl. "Your reaction does not surprise me."

Sam compressed her lips. She didn't like being taken for a fool. "Explain."

"May I? I recently re-injured my leg." He gestured towards a chair and then sat without waiting for her to agree. "It's come to my attention that a...friend...has been playing a rather nasty trick on you."

"So it would seem." She studied the man. There was something about him she didn't like, but her curiosity was piqued enough that she'd suffer his presence.

"*I* was the rogue you'd been in contact with and were planning to hire. Unfortunately, I was delayed and asked Damien to give you my regrets. I've recently learned that he took it upon himself to assume my identity." Dante shook his head, his mouth forming a moue. "He's always been opportunistic in that way."

"Yet it took you all this time to realize what he was up to?" Something didn't ring true.

Dante shook his head. "I knew within a few days, but it seemed harmless enough so I let it slide. I'm not one to cause trouble."

Yes he is, her wolf growled, having also taken an automatic dislike to the man.

"What changed your mind?"

"I've come into some disturbing information about Damien, information I think you need to know." He steepled his fingers and looked at her over top them.

"Really."

"Yes. Normally, I'd ask for payment for such information—I'm a poor man and have to eat after all…." He looked at her expectantly. "But as a gesture of goodwill, because my name was used to deceive you, I'll provide it gratis."

She inclined her head, not taking the bait he was dangling. No way would she offer him money.

"Damien works for Kane Sinclair." A grin slowly spread over his face as he delivered the news, obviously pleased at the reaction she hadn't quite been able to control. "You're shocked, and well you should be. It isn't a secret within the Lycan world that Sinclair hopes to take over your territory. Damien has been feeding him information, aiding in your downfall for financial gain."

Pure white hot rage filled Sam, causing her vision to blur at the edges. She clenched the arms of her chair, a growl emitting from her throat.

"I met with Damien on several occasions, trying to tell him what he was doing wasn't fair, but he wouldn't listen. Money always has ruled his head."

Betrayed: Book Two – The Road To Redemption

Sam forced her temper under control. "How…interesting."

"Is Damien about?" He raised a brow and looked around. "If you need assistance to remove him, I'd be only too happy to help."

"No. He actually left earlier today."

"Really? Now that's interesting." The look of polite inquiry left Dante's face, replaced by narrowed eyes. "He didn't say why? Didn't mention the name Deirdre or Stone?"

"No." Sam shook her head, not really interested in Dante's questions. Damien had been working for Sinclair the whole time. When they'd shared a meal, swam in the pond, kissed, had sex… He must have been laughing the entire time! The bastard! What had Tina said once? That the wolf had two faces. Well that prophecy had certainly been right. She shot a look at Dante. "You say you're a friend of his?"

"A friend? No, neither of us would call the other friend. We've moved in the same circles out of necessity, nothing else."

Sam nodded and got to her feet. "Thank you for the information, Mr. Esparza."

Dante rose slowly. "I'm happy to have been of service. Er…now that Damien has left, if you're still in need of a Beta…?"

"I'll keep you in mind."

"Thank you." He gave what was likely supposed to be an ingratiating smile. "Oh, and your grandfather, is he still well?"

"My grandfather? You know him?"

"Acquaintances from long ago. I haven't heard from him in a while and had originally thought to surprise him by showing up here as Beta. Since that didn't work out, tell him I'm looking forward to hearing from him again. Use the name Salazar. He'll know who you mean."

"I will." Sam ushered the man out, feeling she needed to disinfect the house to rid it of any remnant of his presence. He knew her grandfather? Hmm…

Sam headed upstairs to her grandfather's room. She hadn't broken the news of Damien's departure to him yet. No time like the present.

"Grandfather?" She knocked before pushing the door open, then shook her head at the sight before her. "You're still sorting through your old records?"

He had papers spread about him and looked up with a scowl. "Have you been looking at these?"

"No. You said they were your personal papers. I'm only going through the official pack files." She stepped into the room and moved closer.

"Someone has been. I can tell. Some of the pages are dog-eared. I never do that."

Sam shook her head. "Maybe you forgot—"

"I don't forget important details like that." He growled the words and Sam rolled her eyes, praying for patience.

Changing the subject seemed a good idea, even if it was to deliver bad news. She pulled up a chair. "I have something to tell you."

"What's wrong?" Something in her tone must have given her away for her grandfather looked at her sharply.

"Damien has left."

He nodded. "It's to be expected. Rogues can't be counted on."

"And..." She paused. There was no easy way to say this. "Damien was working for Sinclair."

"Sinclair?"

"Yes. It's all my fault." She sat up straight willing to take the blame. "I'd checked his background as best as I could before hiring him. He seemed suitable, but I've just learned he was using an assumed name."

"Sinclair planted a mole!" He seemed to be stuck on that point. "How did you find out?"

"The real rogue—the one I'd been corresponding with—showed up and told me."

"And this rogue would be...?"

"Dante Esparza. He said you knew him by the name of Salazar."

Her grandfather stilled. "Salazar? He was here?"

"A few minutes ago. He said you were acquaintances from long ago and he'd love to hear from you again. Apparently, he knows Damien—"

"He wants to hear from me?"

"Yes. He'd hoped to surprise you by taking on the Beta role—"

"Sneaky bastard. How dare he come around here!"

Sam frowned wondering why her grandfather seemed more concerned with Dante than he did with the fact that Damien had been spying for Sinclair.

"He was warning me about Damien—"

"Did he ask for money?" He interrupted once again.

She gave a huff of laughter. "You have him pegged. He hinted as much, but I didn't offer."

"Sneaky, thieving cur."

"I can see why you wouldn't keep close contact with him."

Her grandfather made a noncommittal sound, rubbing his jaw thoughtfully.

"Grandfather? What's between you and Esparza...er...Salazar?"

"Old business. Not your concern."

Sam raised her brows but let it pass. She had more immediate concerns. "So, what do you think about Damien being a spy for Sinclair?"

"I was gone today and my papers were disturbed. Right after that your rogue leaves." He shifted his gaze to her. "I'd say he's run tattling to Sinclair."

"Tattling?" That meant there was something to tell. "What did he find out?"

He shook his head and Sam surged to her feet, throwing her hands up in exasperation.

"Listen, you won't tell me about you and Esparza. You won't tell me what's so damned important in your personal files. Do you really want me finding out the truth from someone else? Because if Damien found damning information he's sure as hell told Sinclair, and it will only be a matter of time before Lycan Link is breathing down our necks about it!"

A growl erupted from her grandfather and he glared at her. At one time, his growl would have had her backing down, but not now. There was too much at stake.

"You can't intimidate me like that." She planted her hands on her hips and raised her chin.

Their eyes locked in a silent battle until her grandfather finally shook his head. "I trained you well."

"Yes, you did. Now spit it out."

He sighed heavily, looking older and more tired than usual. "I'd hoped to keep this from you. Hoped you'd never discover the truth." He gave a bitter laugh. "I should have died sooner and then you'd never have found out."

"Cut the dramatics."

"It's true. These papers would have been destroyed upon my death – it's in my will. Hell, I've even started to do it on my own, but I wanted to read them one more time. I shouldn't have. Reliving the past does no one any good."

"Neither does regret. Now what's so bad that you have to hide it from me?"

"Our past isn't as illustrious as you might believe."

"The liquor smuggling? Ancient history and no one cares anymore."

"No. Not that." He hesitated before speaking. "Your father's death. It wasn't an accident. It was my fault."

"Yours?" She looked at him, stunned.

He nodded. "I made some bad decisions. Put too much emphasis on blood purity. Drove my son away when he wouldn't follow my beliefs. Chose a Beta that wasn't trustworthy—

"You drove my father away?"

"When he was about your age, we argued. He left and went west. Met your mother, had you." He gave a sad smile. "He came back at my insistence. It's my fault."

"I don't follow you."

"If your father had stayed away, Gary wouldn't have known you weren't pure blooded. He wouldn't have tried to kill my heirs because they were no longer suitable."

"Gary? Your Beta? He killed my father?" Sam sank down onto the edge of the bed, her legs feeling wobbly.

"He planned to kill you, too, but, I've been told, at the last minute you let go of your father's hand. That's all that saved you from being pushed onto the tracks with him."

"I...see." Sam didn't know what to say, her brain was trying to process what she'd learned. It had all happened so long ago that it didn't actually seem real, but to know that someone actually murdered your parent… "I can recall bits and pieces of that day. I let go of his hand for some reason. He turned and called my name and then…" She shivered, the screams, the sight of her father being struck barely dimmed by the passage of the years.

"I didn't find out Gary's part until several years later. It was when I decided to train you to take over that it came to light."

"He wasn't happy with your choice."

"He wanted the job. You were a female and…not purebred."

"My eyes." She twisted her mouth in disgust. While some might marvel at the colour, she'd always hated them, knowing they were a visible reminder that she was different from the others in the pack.

"There's no denying it." He gave a quick nod. "You were a shock to all of us when we first saw you, I won't lie."

Sam gave a one shouldered shrug. It was old news.

He cleared his throat. "For years I'd embraced the belief that keeping the Lycan bloodline clean was of utmost importance. When I was presented with the problem in my own family, I didn't react well at first. I didn't welcome you or your mother with open arms."

As a child she'd always known on some level she was a source of disappointment to him. Because she was female. Because she didn't train hard enough. Because of her eyes.

"All my life I've worked hard to please you, to be what you wanted me to be."

"And you've done well."

"As well as a female, non-purebred can do." She qualified.

"As well as anyone could have done." A muscle twitched in his jaw. "I'm...er...proud of you, Sam." Their eyes met briefly and then both looked away.

"Uh...thanks." It seemed awkward to hear him say that and she didn't know quite how to respond. She coughed to fill the silence that fell between them. "So that's what you didn't want me to know?"

"I killed Gary when I found out what he'd done." He lifted his chin and faced her straight on, no cowering in shame for him. "And I take my share of the blame as well. I was the one that brought Gary into the pack. I knew his leanings, that he valued the purity of our race. I never suspected he was that extreme, but as Alpha it was my responsibility to control the members of the pack, and to discipline them as needed."

She wasn't totally shocked by his admission, having always sensed the ruthlessness within him. Her grandfather had followed many of the old ways. "Do I have to worry about a cold-case file at the local precinct? Will the cops be knocking on the door one day?"

"No. They wrote Gary's death off as a wild dog attack."

She raised her brows but said nothing, waiting for the other shoe to drop. It did.

"Years ago, I was young and idealistic." He steepled his fingers and stared at them. "I thought I knew what was wrong with the Lycan way of life, that if we returned to the old ways and closed out the rest of the world, we could return to the days of former glory."

"Former glory? What the hell does that mean?"

He shook his head, a sad smile on his face. "I don't even recall. When you're young, you have dreams." He sighed and looked up at her. "I joined The Cause."

"The Cause?"

"Some call them the Purists."

"Shit." She jumped to her feet. So that's what Damien had meant when he left. It wasn't a random slur. "Shit." She repeated the phrase as she ran her hands through her hair while looking blindly about the room. He'd kept mentioning the purity of Lycan blood yet for some reason she hadn't made the connection. The way he'd always been so selective about who joined the pack… The evidence had been right in front of her and yet… Stupid, stupid, stupid. Was this how the family of a serial killer felt when they finally learned what he did on the weekends? If the news got out they had a Purist background, who knew how much trouble it could spell for them?

"I broke off my formal association with them when I became an Alpha, though I never completely severed my ties, or my belief in some of their ideology. At the time, it didn't seem to matter. It was only when I came to accept you as my heir that the break became official."

"That was good of you." She shot a bitter look at her grandfather. "Might have been awkward otherwise, given that you were harbouring a mixed-blooded Lycan like me."

He narrowed his eyes. "Don't judge me too harshly, Sam. It was a different age, a different way of living. I supported some of their ideals, but not all. The important thing is that I saw the error of my ways."

"And?" There was more; somehow she knew it.

He shifted in his seat. "Salazar…Dante Esparza…had some connection to the group. He started to blackmail me, threatening harm to you if I didn't pay him."

"Me?"

"The Cause…the Purists…don't look kindly on those who leave the group. They would have punished me by harming you. Salazar purged the records…for a price.

"And you've been paying him ever since? How? There's no spare money."

"The money for the fertility research. Most of it went to him."

The shoe finally dropped. The lack of money, her grandfather's incomprehensible bookkeeping system. He'd been covering the fact that he'd siphoned off money to pay Dante. "You've been lying to the pack all these years?"

"For you. To keep you safe."

She looked at him, stunned.

"And it didn't all go to blackmail. Research has been done. Unfortunately, there's no cure except widening the gene pool."

Sam was silent, thinking of all the years of scrimping and saving, of doing without. Of the despair in the pack members' eyes when year after year there were no pups born.

"I can't believe this."

"I did what I thought was right at the time." He lifted his chin, remnants of the Alpha he once was still showing. "The Harper line had to continue through you."

She paced the room, hardly registering what he was saying. "Sinclair will have a field day with the news that we're Purists."

"Were. Not any longer. Those that wouldn't change their views left after Gary's death."

"So everyone in the pack knew except me?"

"Hiram, Florence…the older ones. Andrea and Keith, Laurie and Jonah, those nearer your age won't recall. We vowed not to mention it again. The stain of guilt will die with my generation. Our sins shouldn't be visited on you."

She paused by the window, not wanting to look at her grandfather. All these years, he'd been tough on her, hard to please, miserly with his praise, yet she'd always looked up to him. Had placed him on some sort of pedestal. Now, she didn't know what to think.

Rain spattered the window pane, blurring her vision of the yard below, but she could still make out where her Harley was parked. It was alone, the space where Damien's ride had been was empty, the tarp they'd shared blowing forlornly in the wind.

"Sam?" Her grandfather's voice sounded hesitant.

She cleared her throat. "Today sucks big time, doesn't it?"

Chapter 31

Damien sat at a table near the back of Club Mystique. With the challenge happening in a few hours he was confident Sam wouldn't be stopping by the place. She'd be strategizing, prepping for the fight, all the things any sane person would do. He, however, was sorely in need of a drink—the good stuff, not the mouthwash the humans drank—and this club was about the only place he could get it.

Already on his third drink, there was no sign of a numbing buzz invading his brain yet. Maybe he was too worked up for alcohol to even take effect. Downing the contents of his glass, he signalled for another.

His emotions churned with a violence that matched the storm that still raged outside. It had rained all last night and all day; the remnants of some tropical storm venting its fury on them.

He understood fury, just couldn't decide who he hated more. Himself or Sam Harper. She'd lured him in, played him for a fool, caused him to betray his blood bond with Beth. And he'd fallen for it hook, line and sinker. Why hadn't he picked up on the clues? The fertility problems, the fact the old man was selective about who joined the pack, the way she'd spoken of contaminated blood... Fucking Purists, the whole lot of them.

"Here's your...oops!"

Ice water suddenly descended on him and he jerked back in surprise only to have the legs of his chair tip out from under him. He landed on the floor in an ungainly heap.

"What the bloody hell!" He shoved his wet hair from his eyes and glared up at the waitress. If he didn't know better, he'd swear she'd kicked his chair out from under him. From a few tables over he could hear the barely suppressed sound of someone chuckling. If he didn't already have a fight scheduled, he'd go over there and—

"I'm so sorry, sir. Let me help you up." The waitress righted his chair as he clambered to his feet, her neon orange hair appearing to glow in the overhead lights.

Ignoring her outstretched hand, he warily took his seat, not taking his eyes off her. She had another pitcher of ice water balanced on her tray. Wasn't she the barmaid he'd seen Sam talking to? The hair was different but... "Are you a friend of Sam's?"

"Sam? Er...." Her hesitation gave her away.

He scowled. "Any problems Sam and I have are between us."

The girl glowered at him. "Sam and I go way back. We stick together. You disrespected her—"

"*I* disrespected her?" He wondered what the girl was talking about.

"So you admit it!" She almost pounced on his words.

"No, I—"

"Yes you did! You talked her into having sex with you and then walked away once you got off!"

"What? How do—"

"As if that's any way to treat a woman when it's her first time. You should have—"

"Wait a minute. Hold on." Damien held up his hand and shook his head, not believing what he'd just heard. "Did you say her *first* time?"

"Well, yeah." She let off her verbal attack and cocked her head to the side, staring at him. "You didn't know?"

"No!" He scowled, stunned at the news.

"Well... " She paused and cracked her gum. "You're still an asshole. First time, tenth time, you don't walk away the minute you're done." She took a cloth she had draped over her arm and threw it at him. "Here. Dry yourself, dickhead."

He caught the cloth just before it smacked him in the face. After slamming his drink down in front of him, she stalked away. Orange hair, purple mini dress, neon green stilettos with little lights in the soles that flashed with every step she took. Hard to imagine Sam was friends with someone like that.

Sam.

He'd been her first? Damien still couldn't believe it. Shouldn't he have noticed? If not during, then at least afterwards? Of course, he'd been kicking himself too hard after the fact to really notice anything.

He really felt like a piece of shit now. No one deserved to be treated that way. Not even if she was a Purist.

Noticing he still held the towel the server had thrown at him he wiped off his face and set it aside. His clothes were wet too, not that he could do anything about that. He plucked at his t-shirt, making a face as the cold material immediately returned to cling to his skin. Evil-minded witch...

Witch? Yeah, the server likely was one, definitely not a shifter or he'd have noticed the scent.

He leaned back in his chair and rubbed his chin. So what was Sam doing befriending a witch? Purists didn't befriend humans or Others. He took a sip of his drink and frowned. Sam was friends with a witch. She had violet eyes. She'd admitted to him that she had tainted blood. That didn't gel with the pack being Purist.

Yet, the old man's notes had said... He rubbed his face trying to recall the exact wording.

Elise stared out her bedroom window, arms wrapped tightly around herself for comfort. Kane still wasn't home. They hadn't spoken since their fight the previous day. He hadn't come home to eat or sleep and she'd spent a restless night constantly waking to check if he'd returned. The other side of the bed had been empty and cold, and the night had seemed to go on forever.

Leah's tooth had finally come in during the day. With the pain gone, the baby had slept soundly, not providing any distraction from the slow ticking of the bedside clock. She'd arisen several times to check on the children. Looking down at Jacob, she smiled at how he protectively clutched his teddy bear in his chubby arms, then moved to the crib to brush the soft brown curls from Leah's face.

So sweet and innocent. It would be easy to spend hours staring at the marvellous little beings she and Kane had created. Indeed, hadn't they done that after Jacob's birth? She recalled standing in the doorway, her back pressed against Kane's chest, his arms wrapped around her as they watched their sleeping son. They'd promised to always be there for him, to put his needs first, to make sure he always knew he was loved and cared for.

A tear crept down her cheek. Both she and Kane seemed to have forgotten that promise. She wanted to have her own life, her own career; Kane was just as bad, with visions of grandeur guiding his decisions. Maybe she should cut back her hours at the Grey Goose. Not sell out—someday the children would be older and she'd want an outlet—but a few less hours each week. Mr. Mancini had run the place for years and the staff were more than capable.

It might help if Kane was willing do his part, too. Would she be able to convince him?

She wandered into the sitting room and found herself drawn to a statue they'd received as a bonding gift. Sitting on the floor in front of the table, she studied it. It was an intricate carving of a wolf guarding his mate. The artist had somehow managed to make the wolf appear both fierce and loving at the same time.

Gently, she ran her fingers over the polished surface. As always she was mesmerized by the fine details, the fluidity and passion the piece managed to evoke. She gave a small smile as she recalled how things used to be between them. Kane had been so loving and protective, strong yet vulnerable as he'd shared his hopes for their future, his desire for a family... "Beautiful, strong, loving." She whispered to the inanimate creature. "You're the Kane I fell in love with."

"Really? And all along I thought it was me."

"Kane!" Elise looked up surprised to see her mate leaning against the doorjamb. His face was drawn but otherwise expressionless. There were dark shadows under his eyes and stubble covered his chin. "I...I wasn't sure if...when...to expect you."

Kane pushed off from the door and walked into the room. Sitting on the sofa, he nodded towards the statue. "Do you talk to it often?"

She felt her face flush. "No. I mean, sometimes. I guess it used to remind me of you."

He picked it up, studied it, then looked over at her. "Used to? But not any longer?"

She shrugged and looked away.

Carefully he set the carving back down and rubbed his hands over his face before studying her with weary eyes. "Are you going to leave me?"

"I..." Her throat tightened, pain stabbed through her chest straight to her heart. She didn't know what to say. Did he want her to go? Had her petty complaining driven an insurmountable wedge between them? A panicked feeling filled her and she blinked to hold back the tears that welled in her eyes. A future without him was unthinkable. She clenched her hands tightly in her lap to stop them from shaking.

Kane stared across the room. A muscle worked in his jaw and when he finally spoke his words were measured, determined. "I know the noble thing would be to let you go without a fight, but I won't do it." He swung his gaze towards her; the intense expression in his amber eyes made her gasp. "I love you, Elise. I love you and our children and I want to make this work for us."

"Kane..." She rose to her knees and stretched out her hand towards him, but he kept speaking.

"I know our mating wasn't of your choosing." He stared down at his clasped hands, his voice low. "You were forced into it but I think, despite that fact, something special has happened between us. That first night I vowed to myself that I'd make you happy." He turned his head and looked at her, a definite sheen in his eyes. "Somewhere along the way, I've forgotten that. Grown complacent. It's all my fault." His mouth twisted bitterly.

She placed her hand on his leg, looked up into his tired yet beloved face. "Kane, I'm sorry..."

He paled and she felt the muscles of his thigh tense beneath her palm. "That's it? You can't forgive me?" The devastation in his face nearly broke her heart and the tears she'd been holding back spilled down her cheeks.

"No!" She rose to kneel before him. "That's not what I meant. I'm sorry for the way I've been acting. You're the Alpha, I have to accept that—"

Kane pressed a finger to her mouth. "No. You should never have to settle for being second best. My mate should be my first priority." He cupped her face, his thumbs wiping away the tears. "I'm sorry. I never wanted to hurt you, to make you cry." Drawing her closer, he pressed a tender kiss to her forehead. "We need to work this out together, to sit down and plan as a team. If both of us compromise for the good of the family, then both of us will win as well."

"I'd already decided to cut back on my hours at the Grey Goose." She sat beside him on the sofa, leaning against the solid warmth of his body and he wrapped his arm around her shoulders.

"And I'm telling High Council to take my name off the list of possible candidates."

"But Kane, that's such an important position!"

"If it's meant to be, the job will be offered to me at some point in the future. The prestige of being the youngest Alpha ever appointed isn't worth risking our happiness." Kane stroked her cheek, his touch tender.

She turned her face and pressed a kiss to his hand, a feeling of peace filling her heart. This was the man she'd fallen in love with. "What about the Chicago takeover?"

"What do you think?"

"You're actually asking my opinion?" She raised her brows.

He chuckled. "Yes, I really want to hear what you think, not just what I want to hear."

"Well, I'll tell you..." She wrinkled her nose "after you've had a shower. Did you sleep in those clothes?"

"Yeah. I spent the night in the car." He sniffed his shirt. "A bit gamey, am I?"

"More than a bit."

He stood and pulled her up. "Do you want to help me?"

She laughed. "As I recall shower sex was one of your favourite things when we were first mated."

"It still is." He scooped her into his arms and then stared down at her, seeming to drink in her features. "I really do love you, Elise."

Her heart felt as if it were swelling with happiness as she looked up at him. "And I really do love you, Kane Sinclair."

Chapter 32

The rain had finally let up by the time Sam arrived at the clearing she'd chosen. It was a nature preserve on the outskirts of the city, seldom visited by humans. Long grass covered most of the makeshift roadway that led into the area, overgrown trees and shrubs flanked either side, their branches stretching out, making passage difficult. It was a location her pack frequently used for their monthly runs and, over the years, she'd become well acquainted with the terrain. Home turf advantage was always a plus during a fight. She knew where the land swelled, where slight dips in the soil were hidden by foliage. Her chances of being taken unawares by a sudden change in footing were a lot less than her opponent's.

Was the choice of location unfair? Nothing in the rules prohibited it, but her wolf's sense of fair play was kicking in. She shook her head. This was a fight for survival; ethics be damned.

Shoving her hands in her pockets, she began to circle the area. The ground squished underfoot, soggy from the intense rain of the past twenty-four hours. Sam shivered as the cool breeze rattled the overhead branches and drops of water rained down leaving damp spots on her shirt.

The storm front that had moved through had caused the temperature to drop dramatically from the unseasonable highs of the previous weeks, and thick clouds still blocked the sun. It was a dreary sort of day, the kind that reminded you that summer was gone and the cold bleakness of winter was just around the corner.

Perfect for my mood, Sam thought dourly.

She swung her arms back and forth, then bounced on her toes. Nervous energy filled her. Maybe she shouldn't have arrived so early, yet she hadn't been able to handle staying at the pack house any longer. Tension had been running high with everyone wanting to come and her insisting they didn't.

"It's my right to see who will be the successor," her grandfather had insisted. "And it damned well better be you!" She hadn't voiced an opinion, still too angry over his revelations to speak to him.

"This big of an outing could do him in." Florence had protested.

"And why the hell would it matter if I lived or died?" He'd retorted. "According to Lycan Link, my existence is already in question!"

Hiram had walked up to her and given her a hug. "We know you'll do your best. But no matter what the outcome, we'll still love you."

She'd given a quick nod, emotion choking her throat. Hiram, Flo, her grandfather…at one time they'd all belonged to an organization that hated her, would have killed her simply because her eyes were the wrong colour. Yet when she looked at Hiram's greying hair and lined face she didn't see the hatred. Just an old man that she'd loved all her life. Maybe he hadn't known. Maybe he truly regretted the past.

Chris had stood quietly in the background and seemed about ready to cry, yet had manfully held back his tears. He'd been so excited when he'd first learned of the challenge, but had grown progressively quieter as the time drew nearer. Most likely realizing it wasn't all glory, she thought, eyeing him from across the room.

Her pack. The young, the old, the good, the bad. They were her family and she loved them, flaws and all. I've got to win, she said to herself. They're depending on me.

The arguing about who should go to watch the challenge had continued to swirl around her until she'd thrown up her hands in despair and left them to decide on their own.

Now she stood in the clearing wishing for a distraction so she wouldn't keep seeing the faces of her packmates in her mind. The weight of responsibility weighed heavier on her than ever before. She rubbed the back of her neck, thinking of the words tattooed there. Duty and strength; she knew she had those; hopefully the elusive third quality was a part of her already and would carry her through even if she didn't know what it was.

Her cell phone rang and she thankfully answered.

"Sam? It's Tina."

"Hey, Tina." She smiled, relaxing at the sound of her friend's voice. Conversations with Tina were always good for a laugh and that's what she needed right now.

"The douchebag—your Beta—was in here a few minutes ago."

"Damien?" Sam stiffened as thoughts of his betrayal came flooding back once more.

"Yeah. I doused him with a pitcher of ice water."

Sam snorted, enjoying the mental image that came to mind. "Thanks."

"You're welcome. Next time he'd better treat you right."

"There won't be a next time. He's left the pack."

"Really? Oh. Well it's likely for the best. Once a prick, always a prick."

"In more ways than you know." She scowled thinking of how Damien had been spying on her pack all along.

"So, what are you up to?"

Sam looked around the clearing. "Nothing. Waiting for a fight."

"A fight?"

"It's a long story. The leadership of the pack is up for grabs and I'm hoping to hang on."

"Holy shit! Where are you? I'll be there as soon as I can!"

"No. There's nothing you can do."

"I've been practising my hexes again and I can try them out on your opponent."

"Tina, I really don't—"

"Don't worry, I've picked up your location with my cell phone's tracking app. Hold off the fight until I get there."

Tina disconnected before Sam could issue another protest.

Great, she thought as she put her phone back in her pocket. Just what she needed, another observer. And the few times Tina had tried a hex, they'd gone horribly wrong.

The sound of an approaching vehicle caught her attention. Her pack or had Sinclair arrived? She widened her stance and squared her shoulders, watching as a jeep pulled into place at the edge of the clearing.

A man got out, not someone she recognized though. The observer, perhaps? Lycan Link sent a neutral observer to challenges to ensure the rules of fair play were followed. Flaring her nostrils she caught his scent; strong, self-assured. He stood by his vehicle surveying the area slowly before finally looking at her and giving a nod.

She returned it and they began to walk towards each other.

"Samantha Harper?" His voice was deep, his face ruggedly handsome. In other circumstances she might have admired his impressive physique. Not today though.

"I'm Sam Harper. And you are…?"

"Reno Smith. Lycan Link has appointed me as the observer."

"Reno Smith?" She frowned. "I don't recall your name from the OPATA website." She'd spent considerable time going over every drop down menu and page the site had, learning all she could about the department.

"The tropical storm has caused several flight delays and the official designate won't be able to make it. Since I was in the area on personal business, they asked if I would mind stepping in. Provided that's suitable to you, of course. Otherwise, we'll have to reschedule."

"I've no complaints and I doubt Sinclair will either."

"Good." He turned to scan the area again. "This appears to be an excellent location. Remote." He quirked a brow her way. "No chance of humans wandering in?"

"No. There are two entrances to this area," she pointed them both out, "but neither are maintained or used anymore. This place is officially closed. Government funding cutbacks occasionally have their advantages."

Betrayed: Book Two – The Road To Redemption

Sam spent the next few minutes walking the circumference of the clearing with him, explaining their relative position with respect to the human population. It calmed her nerves considerably and she wondered if he'd done it on purpose or not.

Reno checked his watch. Half an hour to spare before the fight. He slid a sideways look at the slip of a girl beside him and mentally rolled his eyes. What the hell she was thinking, taking on a challenge, he had no idea. From what little he'd been able to find out on such short notice, she was well-trained and tough, but that only went so far. He'd said as much to his mate, Brandi, last night and she'd hit him for what she termed his chauvinistic attitude.

"I'm not being a chauvinist," he'd protested. "Just realistic. At some point, size does matter, you know." He'd given her a suggestive leer that had resulted in an actual demonstration of his point. Afterwards, she'd conceded that in some areas, size was an advantage.

"If she was taking on some lumbering lout, I'd not be concerned," he'd explained further. "Sinclair, however, isn't."

"She deserves her chance," Brandi had insisted.

He'd looked at his mate lying on the bed beside him. Her face was still flushed from their recent activity, her lips plump and moist. Wrapping one of her red curls around his finger, he watched it unwind. Her hair was like bits of living flame against the white of the pillowcase, as fiery as her personality. Tucking her close to his side, he rested his chin on top of her head. "I know. And I'll make sure she gets it. I just don't want her permanently disabled."

"Always the over-protective Alpha," Brandi had murmured, her hand straying over his chest and then sliding lower. He felt his body begin to harden again under her teasing touch. "If she's been running a pack, she's smart. She'll stand down if she has to."

"I hope you're right," he'd groaned against her mouth as she'd shifted her position to lie on top of him.

Their conversation had ended then, but it was haunting him now. Was Sam the type to back down? Some Alphas would rather die than concede.

Reno sighed wondering why he'd accepted the assignment. He and Brandi had been returning to Kolding's Pass, after doing a month-long stint of consulting for Lycan Link, when the plane had been rerouted due to the storm. Upon landing in Chicago, he'd checked in with Lycan Link hoping they'd be able to pull some strings and get him on a flight home. Instead, he'd been handed this job to 'help fill his time'.

Yeah, right. No other sucker in the area was likely stupid enough to agree, he muttered under his breath. Even his protest that he wasn't impartial—his former partner had once been friends with Sinclair—had fallen on deaf ears. He didn't know Sinclair personally so that was good enough for OPATA. More than likely the staff at OPATA were desperate. Challenges weren't that common anymore, and they were probably running around like a bunch of headless chickens.

Reno shook his head. He might still work for Lycan Link on a part time basis, but he hated all the bureaucracy involved. Too many rules, too much paperwork and all run by idiots who hadn't left the confines of their offices since they'd been appointed to their jobs.

Beside him, Sam made some comment and he responded automatically, keeping his face professionally neutral. He might have his issues with the organization he worked for, but it did serve a purpose for the Lycan population in general and he had to present himself as a trustworthy professional. At least that's what Brandi always told him.

"Do you have any questions or concerns about the challenge process?" He clasped his hands behind his back and looked down at her.

"No." She shook her head. "I've done my research."

"Good." Silence fell between them and Reno searched his mind for something to say. He sucked at small talk and hated waiting. Apparently Sam Harper did, too.

Thankfully the rumble of approaching vehicles broke the silence.

"Sinclair is early." Reno checked his watch.

"Or it could be members of my pack. My grandfather, the exiting Alpha, indicated he might come to watch. Some of the others might be with him."

"That could be viewed as intimidation by Sinclair, unless he has backup with him."

"If it bothers him, I can send them away." Sam's eyes were fixed on the direction of the approaching vehicles.

The energy coming off her was palpable; an appropriate dose of anticipation and nerves. Reno gave a small nod of approval. Confident but cautious; that was the best way to approach a fight.

He turned his gaze towards the roadway as well, idly wondering if Sinclair would have any news about Damien. Except for that brief phone call the other day, it had been well over a year since he'd last had contact with his former partner. As far as conversations went, it hadn't been stellar, but at least it had served as an ice-breaker and that was something given that they hadn't parted on the best of terms.

Initially, anger and disappointment had kept him from searching for Damien, but time did heal all wounds. Well, that and several tongue lashings from your mate about being a sanctimonious prick. Reno grinned as he recalled some of Brandi's choicer phrases.

After some soul searching, he realized he might have made the same choices Damien had, given the same circumstances. Now, he'd just like to see him again. Hopefully Sinclair would—

"Shit!"

The curse escaped from the little female beside him and he looked at her in surprise. Two cars were pulling into the small clearing that served as a parking lot, but her attention was now focused towards the other entrance she'd pointed out. It sounded like a motorcycle was headed towards them.

"Not a friend of yours, I take it?"

"No." She spat out the word. "One of Sinclair's."

Reno nodded. "Well, that evens the odds. You have your friends," he gestured towards the cars, "and he has his."

Sam's face tightened and she clamped her mouth shut, quite likely holding back a contradictory comment. Smart girl, Reno thought. Don't piss off the observer if you hope for a fair judgement.

He watched as she walked over and greeted her pack members. An elderly man—the old Alpha, perhaps—a middle aged woman, another older man and a girl about Sam's age with bright orange hair. Something about her gave him the idea she might be a witch. A strange collection to be sure, but certainly no one who appeared to be a threat to Sinclair.

"Tina, you shouldn't be here." Sam clasped her friend close.

"Remember my prophecy? A battle will be fought; the lovers' hearts will be like a phoenix, dying as the masks are torn off. The winner will be the loser and the loser will win."

"Yeah. It still doesn't make any sense."

"I think it means win or lose, you're going to be unhappy."

"Gee, thanks, Tina. That's exactly what I needed to hear right now." Sam made a face.

Tina took Sam's hands in hers and gave them a gentle squeeze. "That's why I came. I'm here to support you no matter what." She leaned closer and spoke in a conspiratorial whisper. "Plus I have my book of hexes."

"Don't you dare! There's an observer, Reno Smith, here from Lycan Link. Any hint of foul play and he could rule in Sinclair's favour."

A pout formed on Tina's mouth and she scowled in the direction of Smith. "Fine. Spoil sport."

Sam rolled her eyes and turned to look at the others. The trip had already left her grandfather tired. Despite her ambivalent feelings towards him, she moved around to the trunk to get a folding chair out for him. As the trunk lid swung up, a noise from within drew her attention.

"Christopher, what the hell do you think you are doing in there!" She reached in and hauled the pup out giving him a shake. "Riding in a trunk is dangerous. The exhaust fumes could kill you! And what if the car had been rear-ended?"

He swayed on his feet, his skin a sickly green colour. "They said I couldn't come."

"Damn right." Sam spoke through clenched teeth trying to keep her temper in check. "Hiram, take care of him. He looks more motion sick than anything else…thankfully." She handed the boy over and pulled out a chair for her grandfather. God, Chris was their last pup. If something happened to him… Her stomach clenched at the thought.

"Is there a problem?" Reno approached and Sam forced herself to calm down. Turning, she began to make introductions before standing back to listen as he fielded the questions her grandfather peppered at him.

Despite her back being turned, she could sense Damien coming closer, heard the crunch of his tires as he entered the clearing. Heard the silence as he shut off his engine. Schooling her face into a neutral expression and keeping her posture confident, she turned to face him.

Damien sat on his bike automatically noting the terrain and escape routes. In other situations, he might have looked for makeshift weapons or sources of cover, but in a challenge those weren't allowed. The Book of the Law stated it was hand to hand—or claw and tooth—combat. Any violations could result in a forfeit.

Only when he was satisfied that he had a good grasp of his surroundings did he take the time to look at the small cluster of Lycans on the far side of the clearing. Immediately, his eyes locked with Sam's. Across the distance, he could feel the pull between them, sense the heat—and the rage—that seemed to scorch the space separating them. She was as cocky as ever; her chin lifted slightly, a disdainful smirk twisting her lips. Her weight was resting on one leg, her thumbs hooked in her belt loops. The aura of a tough Alpha exuded from her. He doubted she realized what he could read in her eyes, though. A hint of fear and hurt, even betrayal. His fault. The knowledge cut him to the quick.

He recalled what her friend, the waitress, had told him just a short time ago. He'd been Sam's first. The idea caused a primitive possessiveness to rise within him as well as a fresh wave of guilt. If he'd known, he would have…

His thinking stuttered to a halt.

Hell, if he'd known, he never would have touched her. Correction. He never *should* have touched her, no matter what. Beth was his mate. Sam was a job. His mouth twisted. Job or not, he'd never wanted to hurt her. At least, he amended, not until he'd found out what she was. He looked behind her, identifying the members of Sam's pack; Hiram, Florence and old man Harper. Damned Purists, he thought whipping up his anger. His eyes fell on young Christopher and he cursed, wishing the boy wasn't there to see this.

An incongruous splash of colour moved about the gathering. The waitress with the neon orange hair—Sam's friend—was there as well. He frowned, wondering what a witch was doing at a Lycan challenge. For that matter what was a group of Purists doing hanging out with a witch?

He darted his gaze between them. The witch gave Sam a shoulder bump, drawing her attention from him. Old man Harper was looking at the two young women, stiff but not outright rude, and the others seemed to accept the orange-haired spell-caster without a qualm. The relationship made no sense to him.

Movement to the left of the group now caught his attention and he froze, instantly recognizing the man standing there. What the hell was Reno doing in Chicago?

Reno stared in shock at the sight of Damien. Meeting up with him here had been the last thing he'd have expected. Sure, Damien and Sinclair were friends, but Damien didn't do pack politics. It wasn't his thing; or at least it never had been. Even when they'd half-jokingly discussed starting a pack together, Damien had always been hesitant…

~~~

"Yeah, someday we'll tell Fielding to stuff it and head out on our own. You and me starting our own pack." Reno had lounged back in his chair sipping on a beer.

"You the Alpha and me the Beta? You'd kick me out after the first week." Damien had laughed and taken a swig of his own drink.

"Nah. I'd whip your butt and put you on night patrols for a month." He'd snorted as Damien deliberately rested his dirty boots on the table, using it as footstool.

"Story of my life. Me and packs don't get along."

"Ours would be different. You'd fit right in."

"It'd be nice but…" Damien had shook his head and taken another drink.

~~~

Reno frowned at the memory. Yeah, they'd start a pack together… That had gone nowhere. So why was Damien here and why was there no sign of Sinclair? It was almost the appointed time. Checking over his shoulder, he saw Sam was still talking to her pack. Good. Meeting up with Damien after all this time, and in these circumstances, could be awkward.

He covered the distance separating them. Damien had dismounted his Harley and was watching him approach.

"Damien."

"Reno. Good to see you." It was a casual greeting, as if they were mere acquaintances who often saw each other.

"You, too." Yep, same old Damien, keeping his feelings close to his chest, Reno thought. It was a game they both played, neither of them were good with the heart-to-heart stuff.

They studied each other, neither speaking. Despite seldom spilling their guts to each other, they'd developed a close relationship over their years of working together.

Shifting his weight, Damien looked away, glanced back then darted his eyes away once more. "Listen, Reno, about that last time…I…." His voice trailed off, a muscle working in his jaw.

"What last time?" Reno cocked his head to the side, hooking his thumbs into his belt loops.

Damien looked at him, his brows raised.

One corner of Reno's mouth curled upward.

Damien shook his head and rubbed the back of his neck, giving a brief huff of laughter. "Thanks."

"No problem."

With all the messy emotional crap out of the way, Reno checked over his shoulder to see what Sam was doing and then looked back at Damien. "You here with Sinclair?"

"Nope. I'm his proxy."

"His proxy?" Reno blinked. "How'd you get suckered into that?"

"I volunteered." Damien scowled in the direction of Sam's pack. "The Alpha is old, there's no Beta. The pack house is decrepit and they have no money. There are too few members to run the territory anymore. Kane needs the room to expand his pack. He can inject new life into the area and can run the place efficiently."

"A sound list of complaints, but why would you want to get involved?"

He curled his lip and spit out the words. "They're Purists."

"What?" Reno spun around to study the little group. He knew better than anyone that Purists came in all shapes and sizes, but a less likely group he'd never seen. "Are you sure? Have they been violating the Rights and Freedom Act in any way?"

"No, not that I'm aware. I found out when I came across some journals belonging to old man Harper. He was a Purist back in the day."

"Back in the day. But what about now?"

"Does it matter?" Damien shrugged, his eyes narrowed as he followed Sam's movements. She was walking their way. "Once a Purist, always a Purist," he muttered.

"Where's Sinclair?" Sam didn't look at Damien.

"Apparently there's been a slight change in plans." Reno compressed his lips not liking being in the middle of this. There was a definite conflict of interest on his part, yet he didn't want to hand this situation over to someone else.

While Damien had been pardoned, there was still an element within Lycan Link that was prejudiced against him and might not judge the challenge fairly. Plus, it seemed Damien had a bone to pick with the Chicago pack. Reno wanted to ensure his friend didn't lose control of his inner wolf and let revenge take over, like it had in the past. Purists were scum of the earth, but sometimes the past really was the past. People saw the error of their ways and changed. Watching Sam with her witch friend, he was hard pressed to believe she'd ever held a Purist view. She shouldn't be punished for the sins of her elders.

"What's the change? Was he too scared to show?" Sam curled her lip in disdain.

"No." Damien finally spoke. "I'm his proxy."

"Proxy!" She looked about to protest then snapped her mouth shut. Eyes narrowed, Reno could sense the venom behind her stare. "Fine. Can we get started then?"

Reno nodded. "Damien, do you have any issues with her pack members being here? It could be viewed as a form of intimidation."

Damien looked over at the group standing by the cars, a mix of emotions flitting over his face before he shook his head. "No."

"Then we'll begin."

Chapter 33

Sam stood on her mark six feet from Damien. Her stance was stable, weight balanced. The slight crouch she'd assumed was textbook perfect. Even her chin was protected.

Thanks, Damien. She mentally tipped her hat to him. Had he'd known it would come to this, the two of them facing off against each other? Likely not, or he wouldn't have helped her train. And he had helped her; it hadn't been a show and that was what puzzled her. If Damien was working for Sinclair then why give her pointers on her fighting technique? If anything, he should have refused to assist or perhaps tried to sabotage her by sharing incorrect information.

She eyed him noting he'd assumed a position much like her own. His face was impassive, his eyes trained on her, waiting for the signal to begin. He gave no hint as to what he was feeling. Hell, maybe he wasn't feeling anything. After all, what did he have to lose? Not like her; her pack, her home, everything she'd ever worked for, hoped for, could be won or lost today. Her throat tightened with emotion. She resisted the urge to flick a glance towards where her packmates were seated. Staying focused was the key right now.

"The first ten minutes will be fought in human form. Should the fight continue beyond that point, I'll give the signal and you may shift into wolves."

Sam nodded. It was part of the Book of the Law. Since the human half of a Lycan was considered the dominant member, they needed to prove their worth first. If the combatants made it beyond ten minutes then they were likely equally matched and the wolves would then be tested.

Reno continued to outline the rules. "The challenge will continue until one of you concedes, the challenge is revoked or I call a halt due to foul play. OPATA wishes it to be stated that, in principle, they disapprove of a challenge to the death.

Having said that, they also acknowledge that it is allowed under the Book of the Law. Do you understand and agree with the terms?"

"I do." Sam and Damien answered simultaneously and then both scowled at the other.

"Begin."

The word had hardly left Smith's mouth when she made her move. Nothing fancy or pretty, her purpose was to take control, to be the aggressor, to make her opponent defend himself.

Too bad he had the same idea.

They met in the middle, both trying for a vulnerable spot; the throat, the gut… Even in a challenge they both avoided going for the eyes. There was an understood code of honour they'd adhere to. A dirty fight was no way to choose an Alpha.

Damien managed to hook his foot around her ankle and they fell to the ground. Instantly, Sam rolled to her feet and charged at him, her shoulder hitting his chest as he got to his feet. The air left his lungs in a wheeze. He gasped for breath, but he hadn't trained as an Enforcer for nothing. Keep your guard up, especially when you're at your weakest. How many times had that been drilled into his head?

Damien sensed rather than saw her aiming a kick at him; it was the type of move he would have made. He dropped to the ground so her leg swung over him, then came up inside her guard and flipped her over his shoulder.

She landed face down but rapidly rolled to her feet while spitting out bits of dirt. A kick to the stomach was his next logical move—attacking before your opponent gets reoriented was basic strategy—yet he hesitated for a fraction of a second. Fighting, rather than training, with a female didn't sit well with him. That small delay was enough for her to scramble to her feet and lunge at him again, pushing him back against a tree.

"Ready to give in?" She had her forearm pressed against his throat.

Betrayed: Book Two – The Road To Redemption

A harsh laugh escaped him. "That's what I like about you, Sugar. You always have a smart comment, no matter how deep in shit you are."

"You're the one about to lose."

"Dream on." Scruples be damned. He shoved her back, and they ended up on the ground again, a tangle of arms and legs. Grunts filled the air as blows made contact with flesh, yet neither let up their assault. Two spirits, equally determined, battled for supremacy, oblivious to everything but the need to win.

Of one accord, they broke away, both panting, sweat and dirt staining their clothes. Sam swallowed with difficulty, her throat dry, her heart pounding. How long they'd been fighting, she had no idea. Were the ten minutes almost up? A sick feeling filled her at the thought. When Smith announced they could shift forms, she'd be at a disadvantage. Her human half had always been the better fighter. While her wolf was small and fast, Damien would have the advantage of power and weight, not to mention the ruthlessness of a rogue.

She cautiously began to circle to the left, searching for an opening in his guard. Damien mimicked her movement, studying her with equal intensity.

"So why are you helping Sinclair steal my territory?"

He took a jab at her, but she leapt backward. "You're Purists. You don't deserve to run a pack."

"I'm not a Purist, asshole."

His lip curled in a sneer. "Right. And the notes in your grandfather's journals are just stories he made up for the fun of it."

"Ancient history. He made some bad decisions. When he realized it, he severed his relationship with the group." She feinted right, then left, and then attempted to deliver a hit to his chin but he dodged out of her way. A successful uppercut would have ensured her victory. Damn him for eluding her!

"Leopards don't change their spots."

"Wrong species," she snorted. "And you have no right to point a finger. You lied your way into the pack, acted as if you were befriending Hiram and Christopher when all along you were using them."

A shadow passed over his face. Regret? Not likely.

"I did what was necessary."

"In order to help Sinclair. You never cared about m—" She caught herself in time and switched her wording. "Us." How he'd laugh if he ever learned she'd actually considered him as a potential mate.

"Kane's pack is too big. They need the space."

"And that justifies betraying our trust? Tearing my pack apart. Taking our home!" Unbidden tears sprang to her eyes and she blinked quickly to hide them.

He clamped his mouth tightly shut. She pressed her advantage. If she could distract him... "What will happen to Flo? And Hiram? No pack will take them in at their ages. And my grandfather—"

"Purists deserve no pity." His expression hardened.

"So everyone is punished for the sins of one? Haven't I suffered enough? My father was killed by a Purist, you know!"

Damien flicked a glance behind Sam to where her pack members stood and his resolve waivered. He could see young Christopher's scared face, the worry on the face of the witch with the neon coloured hair. Hiram's expression was grave and her grandfather... The old man was expressionless. Damned Purist had no feelings. He didn't care that his kind had caused Beth's death. Damien felt the rage building within him again and returned his gaze to where Sam stood.

In that moment, she charged into him, the force of her movement driving him back. He stumbled on a tree root, his weaker leg giving way under the unexpected strain of both their weights. He could feel himself twisting sideways, falling with Sam in his arms. She felt thin and delicate beneath his hands and a memory flashed before his eyes. He could see himself holding her as they'd made love... No! Not love, sex.

Betrayed: Book Two – The Road To Redemption

At the last instant, he instinctively turned, protecting her, taking the brunt of the fall.

"You're nothing but a liar!" She hissed the word as she landed on top of him.

Startled, he stared into her face wondering how she'd known what he was thinking, but her next words dispelled that thought.

"You lied your way into my pack. You lied about who you were." Her lips curled. "The real Dante paid us a visit."

"You let that scum into your pack house?" He rolled them over so he was on top.

"As if you have any right to judge. You're no better than him."

"Never," he growled down at her, "accuse me of being like him."

"How are you any different?" She bucked and flipped their positions.

"At least I'm trying to make the world better. Dante's only concern is saving his own skin and lining his pockets."

"Stealing my territory improves the world?" She swung her hand, intent on a karate chop to his throat but he caught her wrist before she connected.

He shook his head. "Stopping the Purists. They killed my mate and my child—" His fingers tightened around her wrist.

She struggled to free herself from his grip. Slowly, he was winning, pushing her hand away. "Just like my father was killed. Just like they wanted to kill me."

"You?" The pressure he was exerting let up and she began to gain ground again.

"My grandfather paid your friend, Dante, blackmail money for years in order to keep them from finding out about me."

A whistle pierced the air followed by Reno's voice. "Time. Opponents shift forms."

The two wolves circled each other, heads lowered, hackles raised. Snarls and growls filled the space between them, yet neither seemed inclined to make the first move.

Sam studied her opponent, noting his size; the solid black of his fur making him seem even more massive than he already was. She should attack, take the offensive, but her wolf was reluctant to do so. Not out of fear; her inner animal was quick and nimble. If they came in low they could go for his throat, his belly...

She should make her move—*had* to make her move; her pack was depending on her.

A few steps to the right. He moved as well. His weaker leg gave a bit as he side stepped. That's where she should attack. Snap his hind leg. It was strategically correct. Yet still she hesitated.

Another step and another. She recalled the time they'd spent together; riding their Harleys, eating ice cream, skinny-dipping in the lake. His kindness to Hiram, how he'd taken Chris under his wing. The way he'd teased her, the tenderness of his touch... A dull ache in the region of her heart made it hard to breathe. She... Her wolf... Both of them had thought they'd found the male they needed. Had it all been a lie?

He'd once said his mate had been part Fae. And now, knowing that his mate and child had been killed by Purists, his actions made some sense. He had every reason to hate, to want revenge. But was that even true or was he twisting the facts for his own purpose, to help Sinclair? And even if it was true, should her pack pay the price?

She was an Alpha. An Alpha put duty first. An Alpha had to be strong, had to do what must be done regardless of personal feelings.

With a snarl, she lunged forward.

~~~

Elise stared at her hand, noting how her fingers were laced with Kane's, how his thumb was idly stroking her skin. Her hands were always cold—cold hands, warm heart he'd often say—but right now she could feel his warmth seeping into her.

Betrayed: Book Two – The Road To Redemption

This was how it should be; male and female connected and supporting each other.

It had been a long time since they'd actually sat down and talked. Sure, they'd often commented on the weather or what present to buy Jacob for his birthday. But throw away phrases weren't enough. Today they'd really been trying to communicate and she felt it was finally working.

"So we're agreed?" Kane drew her attention away from their hands. They were sitting on the picnic table in the backyard, just the two of them. Kane had turned his phone off and Helen was watching the children.

"Yes. Agreed. The renovations at the Grey Goose can happen without me being there every day."

"And I'm overworked and the solution isn't taking on more responsibility. I need to trust John as my Beta and delegate more."

And the fact that our pack is getting too big...?"

"I'll have to...I mean *we'll* have to get creative."

Elise smiled at how he'd caught himself. It wouldn't be easy for Kane. Alpha males instinctively took charge, but he told her to kick him in the pants whenever he started to slip into the 'Super Alpha' zone again and she planned to hold him to it.

"I'll place that call to OPATA now...if it's okay to turn my phone on again, that is."

She gave him a mock scowl before agreeing and then listened as he talked to the officials. It had been hard for Kane to agree to back down, she'd seen the conflict in his eyes, but in the end she'd helped him realize their happiness couldn't be built on someone else's loss.

"I hope it isn't too late," she said as he ended the call.

Kane nodded. "If Damien's already won he'll be shocked as hell to realize he's now an Alpha."

"It might be good for him to have a pack depending on him. I sometimes wonder if his 'I don't give a damn' attitude is just a façade. Is he really become that much of a loner or does he just not want to get hurt again?"

"Maybe a bit of both. He has rogue tendencies—you can't change a wolf's basic nature—but it doesn't have to totally define them. In the right circumstances, with the right person, he might do just fine in a pack."

"Perhaps this Samantha Harper he's been dealing with is the one he needed." Elise leaned against Kane's shoulder. "Sometimes you find the right person when you least expect it."

"That might be stretching things. I doubt that after this challenge she'll even want to speak to him."

Chapter 34

"Stand down!"

The command rang out too late for her to stop. Damien turned his body, taking the brunt of her hit on his shoulder. Her teeth slashed his flesh, the metallic taste of blood stinging her tongue, his yelp of pain echoing in her ears. He staggered and went down. Somehow she knew it was due to his leg.

She scrambled to her feet, shifting form as she moved, torn between concern for Damien and wondering why the observer had called a halt.

Damien stood awkwardly, blood dripping down his arm, his face paler than normal. Concern for him had her taking a step towards him, but the observer was there first.

"You okay?" Smith asked, his voice laced with concern.

"Yeah. Twisted my leg. I've handled worse." He pressed a hand to his injured arm. Blood continued to seep between his fingers.

Sam looked away, her jaw clenched. Blood didn't bother her but her stomach was churning at the sight of Damien's. She blew out a long breath and tried to concentrate on what was important.

"Why did you tell us to stand down?" She looked at Smith. Had she committed some sort of foul? Was he going to rule against her?

He held up the cell phone he had in his hand. "Kane Sinclair called."

"And?" Her mind raced wondering what kind of a trick the bastard was pulling now.

"He's calling off his takeover bid."

"He's what?" She felt her eyes widen, stunned at the news.

"Why?" Damien took a hobbling step closer.

"I've no idea. OPATA didn't give details."

"So it's over? It's not some kind of a trick?"

Smith shook his head. "According to the Book of the Law, a Lycan can only issue a challenge once for a particular pack. He's had his chance. If he contacts you about this again, his butt will be in a sling."

Exultation mixed with relief and she turned towards Damien, even beginning to reach out to him before remembering they were on opposing sides. Letting her arms drop to her sides, she took a deep breath and looked at Smith, forcing herself to speak calmly. "Thank you for helping out with this. I know challenges are rare, so this probably wasn't part of your usual job description."

"No problem." Smith moved his gaze between her and Damien, a slight frown marring his brow. "Being an Enforcer has a pretty broad job description."

"An Enforcer? I thought…?" She let her voice trail off making no effort to hide her confusion.

"The storm delayed the official observer. I was asked to take over in his place."

She nodded in understanding then shifted her feet, feeling at a loss. After the intensity of the past few hours it was hard to suddenly return to 'normal'.

Smith seemed to understand. He jerked his chin towards her pack. "There are some Lycans over there who are likely wondering what the hell is going on. You should probably go tell them."

"What? Oh, yeah." Glancing towards her pack, she saw that they were all on their feet, worried expressions on everyone's faces. She started to walk towards them, stopped and turned towards Damien. It felt wrong to walk away from him. Her gaze took in his bleeding arm, the way he held his leg putting minimal weight on it. His face was expressionless. No hint of anger. No teasing. No…anything. "Damien, I…"

He raised one brow but she didn't continue. What did you say to someone who you'd thought had been a friend, a lover even, only to find they'd been deceiving you all along?

"Was it all a lie, Damien?" She surprised herself by voicing her thoughts.

Betrayed: Book Two – The Road To Redemption

A muscle twitched in his cheek and for a moment it looked as if he'd speak. Instead, he turned his head away.

So she had her answer. She gave a nod and walked towards her pack. It hurt. It hurt more than she'd ever thought possible, but an Alpha didn't cry, at least not in front of her pack. Calling on all her inner strength, she pinned a smile on her face. "Hey guys, guess what?"

Damien listened to the fading sound of her footsteps, willing himself not to watch her walk away.

Reno cleared his throat. "Want to tell me what that was about?"

"No."

"Fair enough. So…" Reno shoved his hands in his pockets. "What are you going to do now? I take it you've been spending some time with Sinclair. Are you going back there?"

He shook his head, sneaking a peek out the corner of his eye to where Sam was being hugged by her family. His throat felt tight and he had the oddest desire to join in the celebrations. They wouldn't want him there, though. Rogues were seldom welcome. Even if he hadn't betrayed their trust, the job had been temporary, only until the threat of the takeover had passed.

"Brandi would love it if you came to stay with us for a while."

He shifted his attention back to Reno. "Maybe later. I need some time to myself. I've been living with that pack for too long. We rogues need our space, you know." He forced his lips to curve in a mocking smile.

"At least that's what we've always thought."

"Come again?"

"I thought I needed my space, too. But now I find I kind of like being settled, being part of a pack." Reno slid a look his way. "You might want to try it someday."

The fake smile left Damien's face. "I've tried settling down. It didn't work."

"It worked. The problem was that it was taken from you." Reno actually looked him in the eye this time. "That doesn't mean it couldn't work again." He glanced over at Sam. "I've no idea what's going on here, but I'd hazard a guess that there's some unfinished business between the two of you."

Damien looked at Sam as well, but shook his head. "No. Beth is my mate. Her last words to me were to never forget."

"Are you sure?"

"Don't try and mess with me, Reno." He scowled. "I was there. I felt her pain. I heard her dying words to me." Anger started to rise in him. He didn't like talking about that day. It hurt too much to remember. He started to walk away only Reno grabbed his arm and pulled him back.

"I was there, too, Damien." His voice was low. Intense. "And I was there in the hospital when you were in and out of consciousness, so doped up on pain killers you didn't know what was going on. I heard you calling out for Beth, I heard you replaying your final conversation with her. You even told me over and over. She said 'never forget *to* love'. That one word makes a hell of a lot of difference."

Damien felt the blood drain from his face. "No. I don't believe you."

"Why would I make it up?" Reno folded his arms.

"I..." He ran his hand through his hair, not sure what to think. "I was doped up. You said it yourself. I was probably babbling."

"Maybe you were. Maybe you weren't. But you said it more than once."

Damien jutted his jaw not wanting to believe that what he'd held on to, what had kept him going these past three years, had all been a figment of his imagination.

"That doc you met when you were in Canada last year, Rafe McRae, he said sometimes our minds twist things around. That we remember what we want rather than what actually happened."

Betrayed: Book Two – The Road To Redemption

Damien remembered McRae all too well. They'd ended up working together out of necessity but... He shook his head. "No. It's so clear. I can still hear her voice."

Reno seemed about to speak then shrugged. "The ball's in your court." He cleared his throat. "Listen, my flight doesn't leave for a few more hours. You and Brandi and I could have dinner."

It sounded appealing yet at the same time he felt the need to get out of Chicago, to hit the open road with only the wind and the roar of the engine to keep him company. "Maybe another time." He checked his arm. The bleeding had almost stopped. "It was good to see you again, Reno."

Reno nodded. "Same here." He extended his hand and they shook. At the last minute he pulled closer for a quick one-armed hug. "I've missed you, bro."

Damien blinked, choked up by the unexpected show of emotion from his normally stoic friend. "I've missed you, too."

A muscle worked in Reno's jaw. "Whenever you're ready, you always have a place with me and Brandi."

"Thanks. I'll be in touch. I promise."

Reno's phone rang and while he answered it, Damien used the opportunity to get away. His leg throbbed as he walked to his bike but he kept his stride even. Never show that you're hurting, inside or out.

Damien got on his bike and started it up. He took one last look across the clearing. Sam was watching him, her face expressionless. There was a connection between them, a feeling he hadn't experienced in ages. Almost...almost, he was tempted to go to her, to try to explain. But there was too much between them, too many betrayals.

He gave her a nod, revved the engine and drove away. The road to redemption had been a dead end.

Sam's throat felt tight and she tried to deny the ache in her chest as she watched Damien. She loved him, even if she was only willing to admit it after the fact. He'd lied, betrayed her trust, spurned her, but she still loved him.

Spurned? Hell, how fucked up was she? She didn't talk like that. It must be those stupid romances Tina kept giving her to read. The damned things were nothing but a pack of lies.

She sniffed and wiped away the stray tear that was slowly dripping down her cheek. Well, Tina's prophecy had been right. A battle had been fought. Her heart felt like it was dying. She'd won but she'd lost, and the masks…well, Damien had certainly been wearing one. Her grandfather, too, for that matter.

Purists. They fucked up everyone's lives.

Her mouth twisted as she thought of Dante and his blackmail scheme. Hmm… Smith was an Enforcer. He probably knew something about dealing with dickwads like Dante.

"Hey, Smith? You got a minute? I think I have a job for you."

Damien pulled into a truck stop a few miles from the nature preserve and turned off the engine After the roar of the machine, the relative silence seemed to echo in his ears, the quiet allowing thoughts and feelings he'd been suppressing to push to the foreground. He'd seen Reno again, fought Sam, lost to Sam and then walked away from her. He closed his eyes and swallowed hard. It had been quite a day; the kind of day that made you want to give up. After all, what was the point of continuing? Once again he'd lost everything.

He sighed and opened his eyes, bleakly surveying the rows of transports and cars that filled the lot. They all had destinations, places they had to be, people expecting them to arrive. He had none. If he disappeared right now, no one would notice or even care.

A car horn sounded somewhere behind him, the noise reminding him that he should move. Ever so slowly he dismounted, clenching his jaw against the pain in his leg as it protested the movement. He'd messed it up bad, not that he'd let on to Sam or Reno but truth was he felt like being sick.

Betrayed: Book Two – The Road To Redemption

He eyed the distance from where he was parked to the doorway of the truck stop. It wasn't that far; he could make it. He'd handled worse. Yep, easy as slipping in shit.

Thankfully no one seemed to notice his slow, deliberate walk. The clerk at the desk barely even looked up from his magazine when he said he wanted a shower, merely giving him a pass and nodding his head in the direction of the shower stalls.

Once inside, he leaned against the wall and let out a shuddering breath. Keeping the proverbial stiff upper lip had drained his strength; now all he wanted to do was crash somewhere and sleep around the clock. He rolled his head to the side and looked in the mirror that was mounted over the sink. His face was pale and drawn, a sheen of sweat covering his brow. Dirt and dried blood were caked on his shirt. Yeah, he looked as bad as he felt.

He didn't really care how he looked but someone might question his appearance. Pushing off from the wall, he dropped his backpack on the floor and then shucked his clothes before stepping into the shower. The hot water stung on his various bruises and abrasions; Sam had done him proud with her fighting technique today. He gave a wry smile; it wasn't often you were proud of someone for beating the crap out of you.

There was a soap dispenser mounted on the wall and he squirted some into his hands and lathered up. What was Sam doing right now? Celebrating her win, of course, but was she okay? Despite his anger over her Purist connections, something inside him had forced him to use restraint during the fight.

We care for her, his wolf murmured.

Yeah, that we do, he admitted. In the end, he'd realized it wasn't fair to punish her for the sins of others. She'd suffered, too; he'd just been too caught up in his own grief to realize it at first.

Closing his eyes, he began to rinse. He could still see the look on her face when she'd asked him if it had all been a lie. He hadn't known how to answer. Where did the lies stop and the truth begin? It was all so tangled together he'd never be able to explain. From the look on her face, she'd assumed the worst from his silence.

It hadn't been his intention to hurt her, but in the end it was likely for the best that she wrote him off. He had no place in her life. And if he stayed, he'd only bring about her destruction. That was what always happened whenever he dared to get close to someone. For her own good he had to let her go.

Stepping out of the shower, he dried off and dug through his pack for clean clothing, stuffing the ruined shirt in the garbage. He'd get dressed, call Kane and see what was up with cancelling the challenge, and then crash in the lounge for a few hours. It was a simple plan but it gave him some direction. Once he woke up...well, he'd deal with that when the time came.

The truck stop was still relatively empty when he left the showers. A few truckers were seated in the cafeteria eating. One was in the lounge area reading a newspaper while another was watching the news on the TV. Damien was eyeing the couch in the corner when movement near the door caught his attention and caused him to go on alert.

Dante was just leaving the building.

Instinctively, Damien took a step to follow him but a jab of pain brought him to his senses. His leg wasn't strong enough to go after the scumbag right now. Tomorrow, once he was rested and healed he could try to track Dante down. He latched onto the idea. It gave him some small sense of purpose and that's what he needed right now.

Narrowing his eyes, he watched the man hurry across the pavement towards a small, grey car. Completely out of character, Dante was moving like he had the devil nipping at his heels. An arrogant swagger was more typical of the man. Frowning, Damien studied the area, looking for what had spooked the man. It was strange that he'd never followed through on his blackmail threat; Dante wasn't one to easily give up on a source of income.

Betrayed: Book Two – The Road To Redemption

There. On the far side of the parking lot. A man was standing near a pickup truck, his gaze intently fixed on Dante. Tall, muscular, perhaps with a scar on his cheek, though it could be the way the shadows fell across his face. Whoever he was, he climbed in his vehicle and drove after Dante. Curious but not completely surprising since Dante had a habit of pissing off everyone he met.

Damien gave the unknown man a mock salute. Why he was pursuing Dante didn't matter. Anyone who was against the bastard had his blessing.

From the looks of it, Dante was headed out of town. Damien gave a nod approval as he made his way to a couch and sank down onto the soft, leather surface. Sam didn't need the hassle of dealing with Dante; she had enough to do taking care of the pack. A shadow of regret passed over him that he was leaving her short-handed. Not that she'd want him around anymore, of course.

He wondered if they'd have a celebratory dinner tonight. Jonah would likely pull out all the stops in the kitchen and Hiram would entertain the pack with tall tales. Chris would try to get out of his homework and his mother, Andrea, would scold. A smile crossed his face as he imagined the warm, family atmosphere.

He leaned his head back against the cushions and closed his eyes. No one would care if he caught a few hours' rest in the lounge. It wasn't as comfortable as his bed at the pack house but he'd slept on worse.

Yeah, a few hours' sleep and then he'd move on. Just him and his Harley and miles of highway to explore. He tried to whip up some enthusiasm for the idea but failed. That's what happened when you stuck around one place too long. You grew attached and that wasn't a good thing especially if you were a rogue. Nope, not a good thing at all.

A rogue wasn't meant to settle down and rogue was all he was.

Chapter 35

After three months of officially being Alpha, her life hadn't changed much, Sam decided. She still had the same workload. More, in fact, with Damien gone.

Damien.

She shut the door firmly on that thought, just as she had every other time it had come into her head since the challenge. Thinking about Damien wasn't allowed. His betrayal still hurt and she still cursed herself for being duped. She'd trusted him, opened her heart to him, and that wasn't something she did easily. It was stupid of her to still think about him, to still care...and yet she did.

Some research into his background had given her a better understanding of where he'd been coming from. His life hadn't been easy. He'd lost everything to the Purists, and she could easily imagine how she would have reacted in a similar situation. It made sense that he'd work against a pack he thought had Purist leanings. Almost...almost...she could forgive him.

She wondered what he was doing now. Was he alone, aimlessly crisscrossing the country on his Harley? It hurt to think of him by himself like that with only the memory of his dead mate to keep him company. Sometimes, late at night, she had an overwhelming urge to hop on her bike and go searching for him. To ask him to return, to stay with her. It was a foolish idea, of course. Her life was here, caring for her pack and he was rogue with a rogue's restlessness.

No. Thoughts of Damien were counterproductive to getting her work done. Too bad memories of him seemed to pop up everywhere; on patrol, while working out, at the pool hall. Hell, even in the backyard by the damned apple tree!

There was no escape in sleep, either. How many times had she relived the challenge, seen the blood dripping down his arm, watched him limping away... And how often had she dreamed of his touch, recalled the ecstasy of being in his arms only to awaken aching for him? She even missed his sense of humour, annoying as it had been. On patrol she kept turning to look for him, hoping to see that glint in his eye, to hear him calling her 'Sugar' while a smirk twisted his mouth.

Sometimes she wondered if he'd return on his own; if he'd realize he missed her, needed her. He wouldn't, of course. Even if he hadn't been a rogue, her pack had a Purist background and that was something he'd never be able to forgive or forget.

The unfairness of the situation had her tightening her lips. Even though she'd personally done nothing wrong, she was paying for the sins of the past. Would the shame follow her and her pack forever? How long did you have to pay for the past before forgiveness was granted?

She didn't know the answer, but it was probably longer than she had.

It was a good thing she had her Alpha duties to deal with, otherwise she'd spend her time pining away for the impossible. Work kept her sane. If you were busy enough you didn't have time to think. Go on patrols, fill in reports, pay the bills, make some repairs around the house, help the pack members solve their problems.

In half an hour she had a conference call scheduled with Kane Sinclair and a negotiator from OPATA. This time, she'd been the one to make contact with the Smythston pack. Something Damien—make that *someone*—had once said about joining forces with Sinclair had given her an idea. She wasn't about to give up an inch of her land, but there were mutually beneficial alternatives.

A knock on the door interrupted her reverie. "Yes, Flo? What can I do for you?"

The older woman seldom stopped by the office and entered slowly, looking around with interest. Sam had made some changes since officially taking over, moving some shelves, hanging up a print of a biker riding into the sunset. The fact that it reminded her of Damien had been a mere coincidence.

"I'm sorry to bother you Sam, but... Do you have a moment?"

"Sure." She set down the pen she'd been using to sign the monthly reports. That was one change, she thought idly. Now that she was officially listed as Alpha there was no need to get her grandfather to initial the paperwork. "Is there something wrong with my grandfather?"

She'd avoided her grandfather as much as possible since the challenge, a short weekly visit was all she could handle right now. The knowledge that he'd once supported The Cause still didn't sit well with her.

Florence settled down on the edge of the chair and folded her hands neatly in her lap. "Your grandfather's well. He wishes you'd stop in and visit more often, though."

"Has he said that?"

"No, not in so many words."

"I didn't think so." Sam gave a bitter smile. "You know, I used to wonder why he never hugged me. I assumed he was just reserved. I never imagined it was because I didn't meet his standards of purity."

"Now, Sam, don't be like that." Florence shook her head. "He's the same man he was before you found out about him being part of The Cause. He really does miss you."

"Right." Sam got to her feet and made a show of filing some papers. "I'm quite sure he doesn't miss having my impure self around."

"That was years ago. He was young—"

"Did you know him back then?" Sam interrupted, partly to change the topic and partly out of curiosity. She'd never asked much about Flo's past, the woman had just always been there in the background, quietly doing her duty.

"I did. I've known him all my life. I even had a crush on him as a young teen but he chose your grandmother. She was a much more suitable candidate for an Alpha's mate than I was."

"That must have been hard, watching the two of them together."

Florence shrugged. "It was for the good of the pack, as your great-grandfather pointed out."

"My great-grandfather?"

She nodded. "He made sure the two of them met. For your grandmother, it was love at first sight; your grandfather was a handsome devil in his day." She smiled at the memory.

"And how did my grandfather feel about the match?"

"If he had his doubts he kept them to himself. Being Alpha was his calling and he did what he had to do."

"Duty. It's one of his favourite words." Sam thought of her tattoo; was she going to be like him as she grew older?

"It is." Florence picked at the material of her sweater before sliding a look up at her. "But duty doesn't keep you warm at night or hold your hand when you grow old."

"Come again?"

"Learn from his mistakes, Sam."

"You'd better not be hinting that he has a 'suitable' mate lined up for me!"

"No. He cares too much for you to do that."

"He cares whether or not I'm a good Alpha. He wouldn't want the family name to be tarnished."

"He paid to keep you safe from The Cause all these years."

"Safe? Or was it that I'm his only heir and he had to keep me alive so the family name didn't die out?" She shut the filing cabinet drawer with more force than necessary.

"Believe what you will." Flo got to her feet, likely realizing she was arguing a lost cause. "I can see you're as stubborn as he is."

"Flo?"

"Yes?"

"Has he ever told you he loves you?"

"No. He's not one to use the word; it's the way he was raised, I suppose." A shadow passed over the woman's face before she continued. "But I love him, and I've waited for him while he's done what he's had to do. He's never said the words, but words aren't always needed, Sam. Someday, when you find your mate, you'll understand." She paused in the doorway.

"Try to visit him. Please. I...I don't ask for much, but this... It would mean a lot. Don't make him pay for his sins forever."

Sam winced as her own thoughts from a moment ago were unknowingly thrown back at her. She nodded not knowing what to say and struck by the sadness in the woman's eyes, the tired lines on her face. Apparently her grandfather's happiness meant a lot to Florence.

When the other woman left, Sam stared at the door wondering how Flo had ever forgiven her grandfather for choosing another. Yet she must have or she wouldn't have stayed all these years. Maybe love was more about granting forgiveness than waiting for apologies. It was a hard concept for Sam to wrap her head around. Personally, if she loved someone, she'd fight for him, make him see that she was what he needed and wring an apology out of him.

Then why aren't we going after Damien? Her wolf twitched its ears.

Sam frowned. "It's completely different."

Really?

"Yes. He lied to us."

He was trying to help a friend. He agreed to the job before he met us.

"He also agreed to fight a challenge. He knew us by then. If he'd cared, he would have refused."

Do you think he was really trying during the fight? Might he have been holding back? Especially near the end. His leg giving out seemed almost too convenient, don't you think?

Had it been? She'd had enough bumps and bruises for it to feel like a 'real' fight. Was she really that good or had Damien had a change of heart and eased off his assault, tried to make it appear that he was faltering? There was no way of knowing.

Sam sighed. Maybe her wolf was right. Maybe he'd decided to throw the fight. Did it really matter? He was gone now.

He might still care but assumes you'd never forgive him.

All right. For the sake of argument, she'd concede that point, too. The question now was how much did he care? And did she stand a chance against his dead mate?

We'll never know if we don't try. You said you couldn't be like Florence, that you'd fight for your mate.

True. But she had absolutely no idea where he was.

The phone rang. Time for her conference call with Sinclair and OPATA.

Sinclair might know where Damien is.

That wasn't the purpose of the call. She was trying to negotiate for the future well-being of her pack. If Damien casually cropped up in the conversation maybe, just maybe, she'd try to slip in a question about his current location, but she wouldn't be the one to bring it up.

So Damien was headed to Canada. Sam mulled over that fact as she climbed the stairs an hour later. Her conversation with Sinclair had been productive and OPATA was impressed with the proposal she'd put for—

"Samantha Harper!"

The sound of her grandfather calling out her proper name had her stopping in her tracks. Being called 'Samantha' had always meant she was in deep trouble as a child and she automatically cringed in expectation of a browbeating.

The door to his room was open and she could see him glaring at her from his recliner. She pursed her lips. He never left his door open and she suspected Flo had done it on purpose in the hopes of forcing her to stop in to visit. For a moment, she considered continuing on her way but then sighed and gave in to his implicit command.

"Yes?" She stood just inside his room striving to keep her voice and expression neutral.

"I need to talk to you. Sit." His tone was as imperious as ever.

Reluctantly she complied, entering the room and taking a seat. She stretched her legs out in front of her and slouched in the chair. It was posture that she knew would annoy him. Childish on her part, but she didn't care.

"You're still angry with me."

She raised a brow and made no effort to deny the statement.

"That's fine. It's your choice. I've explained myself once. I won't do it again." He fixed his eyes on her. "What I want to know is what you're doing about the rogue?"

"You mean Damien?"

"Was there another rogue around here that I wasn't aware of?"

She made a face at his sarcasm. "No."

"Good. So what are you doing about him?"

"Doing? There's nothing to do. He's gone."

"And you're leaving it like that?"

She shrugged. "He deceived us but there's nothing to be gained by hunting him down."

"But you'd had your sights set on him as a mate."

She could feel her face warming. How had her grandfather picked up on that? Just when she thought his faculties weren't as sharp as they used to be, he came up with an astute observation like this! Well, like the rich and famous she wouldn't confirm or deny the report. "It doesn't matter. He's gone now."

"And you're willing to leave it at that?"

She clenched her hands in her lap. "I have the pack to take care of."

"What if you didn't have the pack? What would you do then?"

Sam stood. His questions were beginning to irritate. "Like I said, it doesn't matter. I'm the Alpha. It's my duty to stay here."

"Duty and strength. Have you determined the third quality yet?"

She blinked at his change of topic. "No. I'm still—"

"I never did." He looked away, his gnarled hands clutching the arms of his chair.

"I beg your pardon?"

"I said, I never found the third quality. At least not until it was too late. By then I was set in my ways and the damage was done."

Her interest was piqued and she sat down once again. "I don't understand."

He sighed. "I was ambitious. I wanted the pack to succeed, to be a name to be reckoned with."

"So...?"

"I chose your grandmother as my mate. She was strong, had an excellent background, her family was wealthy. A perfect Alpha's mate."

"And you eventually came to love her."

"No." He looked at her, his expression regretful. "She loved me, but I didn't love her. I wanted what she could bring to the pack. I thought it wouldn't matter as long as I tried to make her happy." He shook his head. "It didn't work."

"But..." Sam frowned. This didn't match the image she'd always had in her head. "Her antiques. You bought them for her. You're always so concerned that I take care of them because they were hers."

"Buying the furniture was my way of trying to ease my guilt. I gave her everything she wanted...except my heart." He cleared his throat. "I had it in my head strength and duty were enough. That anything else was a weakness."

Sam was silent, mulling over what she'd just learned and wondering why he'd felt the need to share the information now.

He seemed to be able to read her thoughts. "I made decisions based on duty and strength. I was a good Alpha, but I could have done better. Now that you're my successor, I expect you to exceed my accomplishments."

"Exceed?"

"Do better. Don't repeat my mistakes."

It gave her a strange feeling, to basically hear her grandfather admit he'd made mistakes. She wasn't quite sure how to respond. Luckily, he solved the problem for her.

"You can leave now. I need my nap. And Sam, I..." He paused, seeming to struggle with what he wanted to say.

Finally, he cleared his throat and gave his head what appeared to be a regretful shake. "Don't wait so long to visit next time." And with that, he closed his eyes and settled into his chair for his rest.

Sam nodded, her hand lingering on the door frame before she left the room. Something about the look on his face had caused a funny feeling in her heart. She twisted her lips ruefully. Yeah, he was set in his ways. Maybe Florence was right. Maybe words weren't always needed.

Chapter 36

Winter in northern Canada sucked.

Damien hunched his shoulders against the bitter wind and shoved his hands in his pockets. After leaving Chicago, he'd kicked his way around the country, made his way north and eventually stopped in to see his old friend, Ryne.

Ryne lived in a two-by-twice town called Stump River that was smack dab in the middle of nowhere. After spending the last hour hiking around the area in almost blizzard-like conditions, Damien was ready to swear an affidavit to the fact that Stump River was only the vacation destination of choice if you happened to be a polar bear.

He made his way down the street, bits of icy snow stinging his face, and pushed open the door to the Broken Antler, a local bar. The establishment wouldn't officially open for another hour, but he'd taken a room there so no one would complain that he was on the premises ahead of time. While there was plenty of room in Ryne's pack house, he'd opted against staying there. With a baby in the house and several Lycans in residence, it had felt too confining. Thankfully, the Broken Antler had a small room for rent; nothing special, but it was better than some of the caves he'd slept in during his days as a rogue.

A swirl of snowflakes accompanied him as he stepped inside, and he quickly pushed the door shut to block out the cold air that swept into the room. "Damn, it's cold today."

Armand, the owner, was arranging glasses on the shelves and barely glanced up when he walked in, a grunt his only acknowledgement. The man was a werebear and no doubt his inner beast was out of sorts, wishing it were hibernating. At least that was the reason Damien had attributed to the man's taciturn manner. Mel, Ryne's mate, insisted it was a broken heart that made Armand so bearish. Whatever the case,

Damien didn't really care. It suited his own frame of mind. Since leaving Chicago, he'd been out of sorts himself.

Across the room, a young girl was sweeping the floor. She was a member of Ryne's pack and, if Damien recalled correctly, her name was Tessa. She was a quiet thing who worked at the bar a few hours each week. Mel had insisted the girl take the job to help her 'get out of her shell'. Damien wasn't sure how effective the strategy was; in the time he'd been there, the girl had barely spoken to him.

Near the front, members of a local band were doing a sound check on their instruments. Thankfully, the discordant sounds coming from the makeshift stage wasn't an indication of their talent. Apparently, their folk rock music had gathered a good following and the Broken Antler was supposedly busier than ever on the nights they played.

Daniel, another member of Ryne's pack, was the drummer for the group, but at the moment he was spending more time watching Tessa than worrying about his drum kit. A bad case of puppy love afflicted him, or so Ryne had said, though Daniel was hardly a pup. Damien thought to tell the young man that love only led to heartache but doubted he'd listen. It was one of those lessons you had to learn for yourself.

The band members nodded as he passed by; Daniel finally joined in the practice, after a firm elbowing from one of the members, and the noise began to transform into actual music. Armand actually showed signs of smiling and Tessa started to sway back and forth as she swept. In years past, Damien might have felt inclined to linger but now he only wanted to be alone.

A steady drum beat accompanied his steps as he made his way up the stairs to his room. It was small and solitary and enough removed from the bar that he wasn't overwhelmed by the noise.

As soon as he entered, he pulled off his shirt; the heat from the kitchen below kept the space overly warm for a Lycan. A draft caused the curtains to sway, giving glimpses of the frosty world outside and he flopped down on the bed, letting the coolness bath over him.

Betrayed: Book Two – The Road To Redemption

He tried to rest. Surely, after the vigorous run he'd been on, his body would cooperate and let him drift into oblivion. After all, it had been months since he'd had a decent night's sleep. A few hours of rest wasn't too much to ask for, was it?

Apparently it was.

Instead of sleeping, he found himself staring at the faded wallpaper and the truly bad piece of artwork that hung on the wall. Armand had painted it, or so he'd been told. Someone really should get the man a new hobby, he thought idly, though in a place like this it was likely one of the few pastimes available.

In his opinion, there was really nothing to do in Stump River in the winter. Oh sure, you could go ice fishing, if you felt like freezing your butt off by sitting outside in minus temperatures. And his wolf enjoyed a romp in the snow, but by yourself it wasn't fun for long.

Cross country skiing, building a snowman, hockey, skating... Some of the locals had tried to entice him into the winter activities but he'd refused with varying degrees of politeness. Nothing interested him anymore. So far, beyond visiting with Ryne, the only thing he'd done was drink, play cards and watch TV at the Broken Antler.

Time to move on, he supposed, but to where?

"What do you think, Beth? Where should we go?" He tried to start a conversation with her but there was no answer. Since Chicago she'd been growing quieter, appearing to him less often. There was a distance about her, a sadness that worried him.

"What's wrong, Beth?" He concentrated hard on bringing her into focus.

In his mind's eye he could see her shaking her head.

"It's time, Damien."

"Time for what?"

"You know."

"No. I don't." He pulled away, something warning him he wasn't going to like where the conversation was going. His attempt at avoidance didn't work.

"I stayed because you needed me."

"I'll always need you, Beth." He imagined himself stroking her cheek, tucking a lock of her hair behind her ear. She looked up at him with her dove grey eyes. So young, so sweet. So serious.

"It's not the same. You know the truth now."

"I love you. That's the only truth."

"I love you, too, but there's more. I need to move on. You need to move on."

"No!"

"Damien…"

"Damn you, Damien!"

He jerked in surprise, realizing he must have drifted off. Beth didn't swear, so who…?

"Damien Masterson, open the effing door before I kick it down."

Sam? He stumbled out of bed still half asleep and jerked the door open.

"About time."

Sam Harper stood before him bundled up in a chunky sweater, jeans and high boots. Her cheeks were red from the cold and bits of her dark hair poked out from beneath the knit cap she had on her head. He blinked not believing she was really there, despite the fact that the scent of leather and spice was already twining its way around him.

"Are you going to let me in?" She didn't wait for an answer, pushing past him.

"Sure. Come on in." He shut the door and then leaned against it, arms folded across his chest.

She looked around the room. "I've seen worse…except for that painting."

A smile tugged the corner of his mouth. "I assume you're here to see me and not to critique the décor."

"Damned right. I wouldn't be caught dead here in the winter otherwise. Chicago's bad enough."

"Some people like the snow."

"And some people are stupid. It takes all kinds, right?" She pulled the cap off her head and tossed it onto the bed.

A huff of laughter escaped him and he pushed off from the door. "What do you need me for?'

"Dante is still at large."

Damien narrowed his eyes. "Is he bothering you?"

"No. I haven't heard from him since you left. Neither has my grandfather or Mr. Marcello."

"Marcello? You found out about that?"

"Yeah. The whole story came out, so Dante really doesn't have a hold over us anymore."

"That's good. So…" He let his voice trail off and quirked a brow at her.

"When you left, I told Reno Smith—that observer from OPATA—about Dante. Lycan Link will be on the lookout for him. He's a prime suspect in an information leak they've been having."

Damien nodded. That wasn't news to him, but it was good that Lycan Link would now be on Dante's case.

Silence fell between them. Damien waited for her to make the next move. He could apologize for deceiving her and her pack, but what was the point. She'd once said she hated liars and that was the story of his life. Sam shoved her hands in her back pockets and rocked on her heels, appearing uncharacteristically unsure of herself.

"Should we discuss the weather?" He finally suggested.

The look she gave him would have made lesser Lycans quake. As it was, he felt an amused smile twitch the corner of his mouth.

She gave an exasperated huff. "Look, I didn't come all this way to give you an update on Dante."

"I didn't figure you did. By the way, how did you find me?"

"Sinclair told me."

That caught his attention. "You've been in contact with Kane? Is he still trying to take over? It isn't allowed, you know. According to—"

Sam shook her head. "No. I contacted him. We've been talking. Trying to come to some sort of workable agreement."

She began to walk about the room, straightening the picture on the wall, glancing out the window. "He's going to sublet some of my territory. We're thinking of a twenty year lease. My pack can use the money. I'll help oversee his wolves. Any pups born in the area will have the option of becoming members of my pack."

"It sounds like it might work."

"There are still a few things we need to hash out, but it should be mutually beneficial to both of our packs."

"I'm glad you found a solution." He cocked his head to the side. "But I still don't understand why you're here."

"Because…" She paused and ran her hand through her hair before scowling at him. "Dammit, Damien, you screwed me and my pack over. You were trying to make us pay for the sins of the past and it wasn't fair. I can understand where you were coming from—Sinclair explained how you got involved and I guess I can forgive you for that—but we cared about you. *I* cared about you and as much as I hate to admit it, I miss you." She planted her hands on her hips and looked him up and down. "You're damned annoying. Your sense of humour makes me want to strangle you, but you're also sexy as hell and made a kick-ass Beta."

Damien froze, unsure of how to respond.

"Say something, dammit! I need to know if this is only on my side or not because I refuse to spend the rest of my life living with 'what ifs' running through my head." Her cheeks were flushed by the time she'd finished speaking.

"I…"

"I know you were mated. I know about Beth. I've researched the story." She pursed her lips and seemed to be choosing her words carefully. "What happened to you was horrible. You had your whole life torn apart. But I don't believe you were meant to live the rest of your life alone." She stepped closer to him. "You're a good man, Damien. You care about people. Yes, you have that rogue side, but that doesn't mean you can never be happy."

He looked away. Her words were so familiar. Hadn't Beth said similar things to him?

"When we had sex…were you just feeling horny?"

"I…" He wanted to say yes, that it had meant nothing. That, in the heat of the moment, he'd been overcome by lust. And while that was partly true, there'd been a part of him… Swallowing hard, he forced the words from his lips. "I really care about you, Sam. I…" He couldn't make himself say the feeling that was in his heart, but when he looked down into her eyes, he once again felt the pull between them.

He cupped her face, stroking his thumb over her cheek. She turned her head slightly, her lips grazed his palm. The light touch shot up his arm, to his heart and then his groin. A growl rumbled in his chest and she stepped closer, her body brushing against his.

"Things happen for a reason, Damien. Reasons we can't begin to understand. There's a reason for this…" She raised herself up and pressed a kiss to his mouth.

At first, he did nothing, feeling the softness of her lips moving against his, the warmth, the sweetness. When the tip of her tongue teased the seam of his mouth he couldn't resist and opened, allowing her to probe deeper, allowing himself to respond.

It was gentle and tender; exploring, testing, to see how deep the feeling went. He pulled her closer, slowly sliding his arms around her, running one hand up her spine to hold the back of her head.

Sam's hands rested lightly on his shoulders, caressing then clutching, sliding to grip his back. He groaned as she lightly raked his flesh then cupped his ass, kneading, pulling him closer.

They sank down onto the bed. Sam pushed his shoulders against the mattress, trailing kisses over his jaw, sucking on his earlobe, awakening a spark inside him. The feel of her hot, moist breath caused him to shudder in need. Her weight pressed down on his aching flesh, every move she made caused him to grow harder.

She nipped his chin then braced herself, hands on his shoulders and stared down at him. "This is how I feel, Damien. This is what I want, what I need from you. I fought against it these past three months, telling myself to let you go. I can't. We have so much in common, do you really believe we weren't meant to be together?"

He looked up at her, taking in her flushed face, the determined set of her chin, the intensity of her gaze. He slid his hands up her arms and cupped her face. Did he have the right to love her? Did he even dare? "Everything I've ever cared about—loved—has been taken from me. It's like I'm punished each time I dare to dream."

"Life is a risk, Damien. If you don't reach out and grab what you want, you might as well give up."

He looked away. "I've thought of that, tried it. Giving up, I mean. Beth wouldn't let me."

"Then I have to thank her for that." Sam brushed his hair from his forehead and then relaxed down on top of him, her head resting on his chest, encasing him in her warmth. "Never give up, Damien."

Slowly, tentatively, he wrapped his arms around her and held her close. She nestled in and he rested his chin on top of her head, listening to her steady breathing. It was comforting to have someone close like this, to feel their warmth seep into you... A sigh escaped him and he closed his eyes, intent on enjoying the moment.

At some point, he must have fallen asleep for when he awoke the room was in darkness. Sam was curled up at his side, the blanket pulled over the both of them. She felt small and delicate in his arms, but he knew she wasn't. There was a strong spirit inside her, a willingness to fight for what she wanted. Beth had been a lot like that; bravely reaching out to explore the Lycan side of her heritage despite the opposition of her family.

Beth.

Was she upset, seeing him holding Sam like this?

He carefully got up, tucked the blankets around Sam and walked to the window.

"Are you there, Beth?" He whispered the words as he stared outside.

The sky was the inky purple of night with an almost full moon gracing its expanse. Below, the ground was covered in white, the snow glistening in the chilly air. A yellow glow came from the windows of some of the houses, and beyond them the silhouettes of pine trees could be seen standing guard over the small town. It was a picturesque scene yet cold and lonely as if the world were frozen and waiting.

"Beth? Are you there, Beth?"

She didn't answer. His breath fogged the glass and he wiped it away with his hand, once more summoning her, using all his will to bring her back to him. Finally, faintly, he heard her voice.

"It's time, Damien."

"Time for what?"

"To move on."

She smiled at him, her love shining in her eyes. He was sure he could feel the whisper soft touch of her fingers stroking his face. His eyes drifted shut and he tried to lean into her hand, but there was nothing solid to connect with except the coldness of the windowpane.

"You aren't alone now. I never want you to be alone. I've stayed longer than I should—"

"Beth..." His heart began to hammer; fear, something akin to panic, taking over him. He knew what was coming. Knew it had to be, yet still he protested. "Beth, no! You can't. I want to go with you."

Her image shimmered before him, translucent and ethereal, the stars seeming to align to recreate her beautiful face in the night sky.

"No. It's not your destiny. You have another road to follow."

"But—"

"I have to go now. Your destiny is here, but mine isn't. I love you, Damien. I'll always love you. Never forget...to love..." The words

faded into a whisper, the image dimmed and then… there was nothing.

Emptiness swept over him, as if a vacuum had sucked every bit of life, warmth and hope from his soul, leaving him in a black void.

She was gone and he was alone.

He gripped the window frame, feeling the hard unyielding wood beneath his fingers, the cold draft seeping into his body, numbing his flesh. If it could only numb the unbearable pain that was growing in his heart.

In a movie, all would be silent, but life wasn't a movie. It didn't stop simply because one person felt as if they were dying inside, because a heart had shattered, or a soul had been ripped to shreds.

From the bar below, he could hear the thumping of a drum and the muffled voice of a singer. A car drove down the street, the tires hissing in the slush. The door to the bar opened and patrons spilled into the street talking and laughing, unaware of the devastated man above them.

"Beth?"

He tried one last time, a whispered plea, praying for mercy from the heartless gods that had forced this fate upon him.

There was no answer.

His Beth really was gone.

His body started to tremble as he fought for control, his eyes felt hot, his vision blurred. Fiercely, he blinked, firming his chin, staring straight ahead, unseeing. All the grief, all the tears he'd never let fall were now threatening to break free, and if he let even one escape…

Warm hands touched his arm, turned him around. Soft fingers brushed his cheek.

"Damien?" Sam was staring up at him, her eyes filled with worry. "What's wrong? Are you sick?"

He shook his head, unable to answer, his throat too tight with emotion.

Concern etched her face and she led him back to bed. He moved woodenly, forcing his legs to take each step. She made him lie down and wrapped her arms around him, pressing his head to her chest. Gently, she ran her fingers through his hair. "Tell me."

He tried to speak, struggled to make his mouth form the words. "Beth. My Beth… She's gone." Unable to hold on any longer, he sank into Sam's arms, sobs wracking his body as the pain he'd carried for so long was finally released.

Sam held him, rocked him, whispered platitudes and nonsense as she cried along with the man she loved. She cried for him and for herself, his sorrow giving her permission to vent her own pain.

She cried for the father she'd lost and the mother who'd left her behind, for the hurt she'd kept hidden over never living up to her grandfather's expectations. For the times she had to put the pack ahead of her own needs, for the doubts and fears, the weariness and loneliness that only an Alpha could know. And she cried over Damien's lies and deceit and her hopes for the future; hopes that might be dashed because of his love for a dead woman.

They held each other as they cried, each in their own personal hell yet inexplicably united through the shedding of tears.

When the emotional storm finally eased, they both took a deep, shuddering breath. Sam wiped her face on her sleeve and then shifted her position so they lay facing each other. Damien's lashes were spiky from his tears, his eyes haunted. She wiped his face with her fingers, the stubble on his jaw abrading her palm. "Can you tell me about it? Did you have a bad dream?"

"No." He shook his head. "Not a dream… Or maybe it was. Maybe it was a dream that lasted for years. All I know is that tonight…" He paused and seemed to gather himself. "Tonight Beth and I said goodbye."

"I don't understand."

"She's been with me all this time. In my thoughts, my dreams. Sometimes I was sure I could see her. But…" He blinked and swallowed hard. "She's not here, not anymore. She's gone. Gone...somewhere. Some place I can't ever follow. She said she wants me to stay here. To live my life, to...love."

"I'm glad you realize that."

He studied her face before rolling onto his back and staring at the ceiling. "I was always sure her dying wish was that I never forget her."

"I remember you saying that." She gave a sad smile, stroking one finger down his arm, idly noting the dips and swells of his muscular form.

"I was wrong." He turned his head to look at her. "She wanted me to never forget to love."

"She sounds like a very special person."

He nodded. "She was. Would you... Would you like to see her picture?"

"Okay." Sam wasn't sure she wanted to see the woman that had owned Damien's heart for so long, but you couldn't hide from facts.

Damien reached over and took his wallet off the nightstand. Pushing himself up into a sitting position he opened it up. Sam hitched herself up beside him and looked at the photograph of a young woman with long hair and a gentle smile. Pretty, but not stunning. Not until you looked into her eyes. They were like pools of wisdom and empathy that drew the viewer into their depth and touched the soul.

"She's beautiful."

Damien stared at the picture. "I loved her so much. A part of me will always love her."

Sam nodded, trying to be strong and supportive despite the fact that his words were like a knife to her heart. "That's how it should be. You were mates. She was an important part of your life."

"Yes." He stared at the photo for a long moment. "Yes, she was." His lips moved, some silent message Sam couldn't hear, and then slowly, almost reluctantly, he closed the wallet and set it back on the table.

Betrayed: Book Two – The Road To Redemption

Sam bit her lip, not sure what to say. She felt like a voyeur to some private intimate moment yet she couldn't leave. Her future was with Damien and she damned well had to make him see it.

Silence stretched between them as she considered and discarded a dozen ideas as to what to say. A band was playing in the bar below and she could almost make out the words of a song; a ballad about the futility of love. Hopefully it wasn't a prediction of how this meeting was going to end. She hadn't travelled all the way to Stump River to be rejected. Tina's prophecy had said something about the lovers' hearts being like a phoenix, dying as the masks are torn off. Well in mythology the phoenix always rose again, and she was going to do her damnedest to make sure it happened here as well.

"Sam?"

"Yes?"

Damien turned to face her. His expression was uncharacteristically solemn. There was no teasing quirk to his lips, no guardedness about his eyes. She felt she could see into his soul; see the loneliness, the pain, the vulnerability.

He, in turn, seemed to be searching her face, noting her features one by one. Ever so slowly, he reached out and brushed the back of his hand over her cheek.

"Make love with me? Please."

Her heart stilled, then began to beat heavily with hope…and fear. She didn't know why he was asking. If it was to fill the emptiness in his soul, or because he wanted her. She hesitated, but the need she heard in his voice had her ignoring her doubts. With a trembling hand, she stroked his face.

"Yes."

He turned and kissed her palm, then slowly eased her down onto the bed. Gently, he traced her features. She relaxed into the pillows, taking his weight, cradling him to her.

Their kiss began softly, lips barely touching, tentative, testing before slowly deepening. She caressed his back. His tongue stroked hers, lips sliding, teasing. His warm breath tickled her face as he moved along her jaw line to her ear, then the sweet spot on her neck.

She explored his shoulders, the dip of his spine, encountered the roughness of denim and made a mild sound of protest. Damien left off nibbling on her neck and sat up, popping the button of his pants and loosening his zipper. Staring into her eyes, he did the same with her jeans, a silent question in his look.

She nodded.

Leaning forward, he pushed her sweater up out of the way, exposing her stomach and then pressed a kiss to her belly button. She shivered at the feel of his warm, wet tongue, squirmed when he moved lower, easing her jeans down, increasing his access. When he slid his fingers under the waistband of her panties, she was sure her heart would pound out of her chest.

The sound of material rubbing against material seemed abnormally loud as he removed her jeans. Damien remained silent, but in the dim light she was sure she could see the approval in his gaze.

He caressed her calf and kissed her knee before moving higher. Stroking her thighs, he nibbled on her hipbone, then nuzzled the crease of her thigh. She combed her fingers through his hair, cradling his head, guiding him to where she needed him most.

When he touched her, she bit her lip, barely able to hold back the cry of pleasure that rose in her throat. Tenderly, skilfully he played with her, bringing her to the brink and then pushing her over.

As she floated back to reality, he stood and removed his clothing. In the dim light, she marvelled at the beauty of his form as each inch was revealed. Narrow hips, strong thighs dusted with hair. His need for her was evident, proud and erect. When he approached the bed, she had to sit up and touch him, to feel the hot silky skin that encased his hardness, to stroke and bring him pleasure as he'd done to her.

Betrayed: Book Two – The Road To Redemption

He closed his eyes as she caressed him, gently rocking against her palm, a low rumble of pleasure sounding in his chest. She swirled her tongue in his belly button, traced the intriguing 'V' of his abdomen. Pressed kisses, hot and wet to throbbing flesh. When he could stand it no longer he took control again, pressing her back onto the mattress.

Damien's hands were warm and rough as they kneaded her breasts, his mouth hot and avid on her nipples, tugging, nipping. The tiny pain shot to her core and she felt herself growing moister. Her body begging for his possession. She wriggled under him, pulling at his hips, urging him to take her.

He kneeled over her, and when he stared down into her eyes, it was as if the wolf in him was looming over her. Submitting did not come naturally, yet this was not the time to be concerned about dominance; tonight was for comforting, for sharing, for healing the pain they both had inside. She parted her thighs, inviting him to take her.

And he did. Settling into place, he probed, found her opening and began to slide inside. She trembled, holding her breath, focused on the sensation of him easing into her, sliding deeper, filling the ache within.

"I'm sorry about last time." He whispered the words as he penetrated her flesh.

She shook her head. "It was my idea."

"But—"

She pressed a silencing kiss to his lips.

He began to move, sliding in and out again and again. It was exquisite torture, the brushing of his hardness over her sensitive nub. Slowly at first, then faster as the tension began to grow.

Their kiss turned hard, his tongue possessing her mouth just as he possessed her body.

She clutched his back, holding on, her nails raking his flesh, her breath becoming pants. The exquisite feeling inside her grew, her muscles tightened unbearably until she was hovering in a place where only feeling existed. Her vision blurred, her lips parted in a silent shout of ecstasy and then, then she spiralled out of control.

Damien woke the next morning, his body spooning Sam's. His hand cupped her breast and he idly stroked the smooth slope feeling completely relaxed. He was awake but drifting, no particular thought in his head. Unusual. Instant alertness was the norm for him.

Sam sighed in her sleep, wriggled her body closer to his. Her short hair feathered across the back of her neck and he could see glimpses of her tattoo. Duty, strength... There was a new one there and he released her breast, sliding his hand up to move her hair out of the way, wondering what she'd decided the third quality of an Alpha was.

Love.

He traced over the word, frowning. Not what he would have expected.

Sam rolled over, her features relaxed with sleep. "Morning." Languidly, she reached up and brushed his hair from his forehead. "Mmm... I haven't slept that well in ages."

"Me, either." He smiled softly. She nestled her head against his chest, her fingers splayed on his chest, slowly stroking, circling his nipple.

Her attentions were rousing his body. It had been three years since he'd woken up with a woman in his arms. Three years since he'd held Beth. A twinge of guilt stabbed his conscience. He must have made a sound for Sam quit her teasing movements.

"What?"

"Nothing." He noticed the night stand with his wallet. Beth's picture was there. For the past three years, he'd greeted her each morning. Today, he hadn't.

Did she know? Was she hurt?

No.

Beth had told him it was time to move on. He compressed his lips, the memory still fresh enough to cause a small wave of grief.

Betrayed: Book Two – The Road To Redemption

"Damien?" Sam raised herself up on her elbow. "Is everything okay?"

"Yeah." He swallowed hard. Sam was watching him, concern in her eyes. "I see you added your third tattoo."

She nodded.

"Why love? Why not wisdom or integrity or…?"

"Well…" She sat up and hugged her knees, staring thoughtfully across the room. "Those are needed, but love is the most important. You can do your duty but if you don't love your pack you can become bitter and resentful. And you need love to temper the strength so you aren't too harsh or dictatorial."

"That makes sense." He sat up and pressed a kiss to her nape. "I'm glad you were able to figure it out."

"Thanks." She twisted to face him, a happy glow shining in her eyes. "I want you to come back to Chicago with me."

He blinked. He hadn't thought that far ahead. "Chicago?"

"Yes, Chicago. That's my home." She didn't add 'duh' but he could see it on her face.

Chicago. Did he want to go back there? To be part of a pack, to have to care about people and have them depending on him to always be there? He stalled for time. "In what capacity?"

A smile curved her lips. She stroked his arm, watching her fingers travel its length. "My Beta? My lover?" Her hand rested on his heart now and she raised her eyes to his. "My…mate?"

Mate. The word had him holding his breath. Beth was…had been…his mate. Taking another had never entered his mind and yet… He hesitated. How do you know when it's time to let go? To move on?

His silence must have unsettled her for she spoke in a rush, her eyes earnest, intent. "If you're worried about the infertility problem, I doubt it will affect me. Since my father mated outside the pack, my genes are more varied and we should be able to have as many pups as we want."

Pups. The word sent a chill through him. He'd lost one child already. What if something happened? The pain would be more than he could bear.

"Damien?" She removed her hand from his chest. "Never mind." She turned her face away. "Apparently, I read more into last night than I should have." She climbed out of bed and began searching for her clothes.

He blinked and pulled himself out of his introspection. "Sam, it's not you…"

"Yeah. I know. It's Beth. You still love her and I can't compare." She tugged on her jeans and pulled her sweater over her head. "It's the story of my life. You. My grandfather."

"It's not about Beth."

"Sure." She grabbed her boots. "I laid my heart on the line, Damien, and you didn't grab it. You snooze, you lose."

"What?" He pushed back the covers and swung his legs out of bed.

"Thanks for last night. It was fun."

"Sam, wait!" He reached out to catch hold of her arm but she evaded him.

"Wait for what?"

"For…" He dragged his hand through his hair, his mind racing, not sure what to say.

She arched one brow, hands planted on her hips. When he didn't continue, a flush appeared on her cheekbones and temper sparked in her eye. "For another screw? No thanks. I can get one of those any time I want." Her lip curled and she flicked a derisive look over his naked body before shaking her head and turning away.

"It wasn't just screwing."

"Could've fooled me." She glanced about the room as if looking for something then gave a shrug and reached for the door.

"Sam!" His heart rate began to quicken, a sick dread filling him as he realized her intent.

She didn't respond. Not even a 'fuck you'. The door slammed shut behind her, leaving him to stare at the marred wooden surface. He could hear her booted feet stomping down the stairs; she didn't slow down or hesitate even once.

Swearing, he strode to the window looking out just in time to see her storming across the street. She got into a nondescript grey car and drove off. If the road hadn't been snow covered, she likely would have squealed her tires in a declaration of her anger. As it was, the vehicle fishtailed slightly when she turned the corner.

Sam had left him.

Chapter 37

Stunned at the turn of events, Damien looked blankly around the room, seeing the bed they'd shared, noting her knit cap lying forgotten on the ground. Bending over, he picked up the cap and stared at it. He couldn't even begin to comprehend what had just happened. They'd been in bed talking about her tattoo and then…

He tossed the cap down. Hell, what had she been thinking, springing a question like that on him and expecting an answer right away?

Grumbling, he got dressed and headed downstairs, not sure what he'd do but needing to get out of the room, away from her scent, away from the memories of last night.

The bar was empty except for Armand. He was morosely staring into a teacup. Damien hesitated and then sat down beside the man. Misery loved company.

"Mind if I join you?"

Armand pushed the teapot his way.

Damien looked at it suspiciously and then shrugged. Why not. He reached over the bar and snagged a cup and then poured some of the steaming liquid. A tentative taste had him wanting to spit.

"What is this?"

"Herbal tea. Pine needles, some roots and bark. My own recipe."

Damien looked at the vile brew. No wonder it tasted like turpentine.

Armand drained his own cup and poured another before finally shifting his attention from his drink to the man beside him. "You look sad, my friend."

He shrugged. Sad? Damien hadn't thought of it that way. Pissed off. Confused. Lost perhaps…

"The woman who came to visit you last night, the meeting didn't go well?"

"It did. For a while. But this morning… Not so good." He took another sip of the tea. It didn't taste so bad, once you got used to it. Or maybe his taste buds had died after the first mouthful.

"Ah! The morning after." Armand nodded wisely. "Regret often raises its ugly head when the sun rises. Many of my customers suffer from this."

Regret? Did he regret making love to Sam?

"You should listen to your inner animal," Armand added. "Many years ago, I did not. I let my lady leave. I thought too long and too hard even though my animal urged me to act."

"What happened?"

The bartender sighed and returned to looking glumly into his cup. "It was too late."

Too late. Damien sipped his drink. Was he thinking too long and too hard?

"If I could do it again, I would have followed her. Demanded that she stay with me."

The bear is correct, his wolf decided. *We should follow her. We've been alone too long. It is not the way we are supposed to be.*

Damien swirled the remains of his tea in his cup. Was he feeling guilty for betraying Beth, or was he afraid to face the future? Hadn't Beth pretty much given him her blessing last night? If their positions had been reversed, would he have wanted Beth to spend the rest of her life alone?

No.

He'd loved her too much to wish that fate on her. So it must be fear that was keeping him glued to his seat. He was afraid to care. Afraid to risk being hurt again.

His wolf curled its lip. *Fear should be beneath us. We don't live our life cowering like a pup. Perhaps I should take control again and do what must be done.*

The animal would try it, too. Of that Damien had no doubt. He'd spent enough years of his life battling the beast inside. The human half might be in control, but concessions to the wolf were sometimes needed. Especially if the wolf was right.

"Thanks, Armand." Damien set down the cup and got to his feet.

Armand looked at him out of the corner of his eye and gave an approving nod. "You are going after her. If you don't return, I will give your things to Ryne."

"Thanks." Damien clapped the man on the shoulder. "I hope you find a replacement for the lady you lost."

The werebear gave a small nod. "I am getting tired of waiting. Soon I will act."

Damien left the bar and got into his small rental. He hated cars, but the winter roads were no place for a motorcycle so he'd left his in storage before heading north.

It had been at least half an hour since Sam had left. Thankfully, there was only one paved road leading into Stump River so it wasn't hard to know which way she'd gone. With any luck he'd catch up with her before she hit a main highway.

The roads were snow covered, not impassable but they required a judicious use of the gas pedal and both hands on the steering wheel. About ten minutes out of town, he caught sight of skid marks veering off the road into a drift. Only the bumper of the car was visible but he had an awful suspicion that…

It was Sam.

Her car was at a 45 degree angle, half buried in a snowdrift, part of the undercarriage showing. He eased his car off the road, his heart pounding with fear. The fates couldn't do this to him.

As fast as possible, he clambered through the thigh deep drifts, each step an effort. An icy crust had formed over the surface and it crunched and crackled as he pushed his way through. Snow seeped into his boots, numbing his toes and soaking his clothing.

"Sam? Sam, are you okay?" He called her name and it echoed across the frozen wasteland. Only the howling of the winter wind answered him with a low, lonely sound. His breath came out in puffs of steam, his eyes watering as the sunlight gleamed off the thousands of sparkling ice crystals.

He imagined her unconscious, slumped over the steering wheel, blood dripping from her head. Was he too late? Was she already…dead?

When he finally reached the vehicle, he hoisted himself up so he could see inside, bracing himself for the worst. He pushed the snow from the window and looked inside.

The car was empty.

For a moment he was shocked, then relief seeped in as he saw no sign of blood, then worried once again as he wondered where she might have gone. He slid back onto the ground and slowly turned in a circle. Miles of nothing stretched out on all sides as far as the eye could see.

Damien tested the air, trying to pick up her scent. His frozen nostrils strained to detect anything in the icy air. He began to move in a circular pattern, constantly widening his search, knowing she had to have gone somewhere. When he finally caught a trace of her scent, it was accompanied by the blurred remains of a set of wolf tracks heading straight down the center of the road.

He cursed.

Hadn't she ever heard that you were supposed to stay with your vehicle in situations like this? What was she planning on doing? Walking all the way to the next pocket of civilization? Did she even know how far it was or which way to go? Had she even thought to check the weather forecast? The temperatures were supposed to drop to near record lows that night.

Climbing back in his car, he began to follow her trail. While his wolf might want to chase her down on foot, it wasn't a smart move. Sam would be cold and tired when he found her and the car would provide some shelter, plus it came with a winter survival kit that included blankets and packets of food.

Eventually he spotted a small white wolf trotting down the middle of the road acting as if it owned the place. As he drove nearer she veered to the side of the highway, no doubt hearing him approaching and thinking the random vehicle behind her would just pass by. He slowed to a crawl, rolled his window down and called out her name.

"Sam!"

There was hardly a break in her stride. If it wasn't for the way her ears twitched and her chin lifted, he might have even wondered if she'd heard him. Little spitfire.

He pulled alongside her. "Sam."

She ignored him.

"Sam, talk to me."

When she still didn't acknowledge him, he gave an exasperated huff, sped ahead, pulled the car to the side and got out. Standing in the middle of the road, he faced her.

"Sam, this is ridiculous. It's miles to the nearest town. You'll be lucky to make it by nightfall and you don't know the terrain well enough to find shelter for the night. What if you stumble upon a regular wolf pack? They won't be happy to have you invading their territory."

The wolf stopped. It glared at him, looked away and then sneezed not bothering to hide its disgust that his words made sense. The air shimmered and Sam stood before him. She didn't say a word, merely stalking to the passenger side of his car and getting in. The door slammed shut after her with sufficient force to make the entire vehicle rock.

He rolled his eyes and got in the driver's seat. Resting his hands on the steering wheel, he waited for her to speak. When she didn't comment, or even deign to look at him, he clenched his jaw and started to drive.

After about five minutes of silence she finally gave in. "Where are we going?"

"Where do you want to go?"

"Chicago of course."

"Good."

"Why? Can't wait to get rid of me?"

"No." He paused and then slid a look her way. "That's where I'm headed, too."

She swung her head around to look at him. He focused on driving, holding back a pleased grin. Now he had her attention.

"Why are you going to Chicago?" She asked the question slowly, tentatively.

He gave a one shoulder shrug. "I hear there's a Beta position open there." He hazarded a glance her way.

Sam studied him for a moment before replying. "Really?" She resumed staring out the window. "I heard the position is no longer being offered."

That was a shock. Had he screwed up that badly? He clenched the steering wheel tightly, wondering what to say. Before he could decide, she spoke again.

"The position has been upgraded to co-Alpha. Provided the right Lycan applies."

The tension began to ease from him. "The right Lycan?"

"That's correct. I'll be holding interviews…private, personal interviews. Quite soon as a matter of fact." Out of the corner of his eye, he noted how her hands were clenched. "Do you know anyone who would like to apply?"

"Perhaps." Thankfully a side road was right ahead. He pulled onto it and turned off the engine. "Do you think I might qualify?" Undoing his seatbelt, he turned to face her. When she didn't answer, he reached out, gently touching her chin. "Sugar?"

"Dammit, Damien!" Abruptly, she turned on him. "What the hell kind of game are you playing with me? I can't handle this blowing hot and cold business any longer. If you're applying for the position, you had damned well better mean it."

"Of course I mean it! I mean…" He paused, trying to gather his thoughts. "Sam… I… We're good together. I feel a connection to you. But a part of me is afraid. Afraid to lose someone I…care…about again."

"Everything in life is a risk, Damien. And just because you're afraid to admit that you…care…doesn't mean the feeling isn't already in your heart. That's what my grandfather has spent his whole life doing."

"Your grandfather?"

"Yeah. He admitted as much to me. Said he'd never dared use the word love even though that's what he felt in his heart." She pulled a face. "I always knew he cared, but without the words I never knew for sure."

"That's why you chose that tattoo."

She nodded. "I don't want to be the kind of Alpha he was. He did his best, what he thought was right, but I want to do even better."

"You will." He stroked her face.

"With you at my side?"

He sighed heavily, staring out across the barren land. Could he do it? Did he really have any choice? Lacing his fingers with Sam's, he nodded. "I'll try."

A wide smile broke over her face. Grabbing his shoulders, she kissed him hard. "Damn well took you long enough. I was thinking I'd have to beat it out of you."

He laughed. "That's my spitfire. All prim, proper, and ladylike." He tried to pull her close, but the console was in the way and he had to make do with an awkward hug. She returned it but then stiffened in his arms. He could sense a hint fear coming over her. "What are you thinking?"

She looked away. "Nothing."

He gently grasped her chin and turned her face towards him. "Show no fear only works when you're fighting. In a relationship you have to open up. Let each other know what you're thinking." He gave a rueful laugh. "I know coming from me that's a bit like the pot calling the kettle black, but it's true."

Sam compressed her lips before giving in with a sigh. "A part of me worries about competing with Beth."

"There is no competition." He brushed her hair from her eyes. "Beth was white daisies and a quiet fire and you're—"

She made a face. "Pizza with extra cheese and a Harley."

"Totally different and incomparable, but each good in their own way." He kissed her and then tried to tuck her close only to curse the console again. Instead, he laced their fingers together. "Three years ago, I was a different person. Beth was what I needed then. But I'm not that man anymore. I've lived hard, experienced things, done things that have changed me. You're what I need in my life now. You're not Beth and I wouldn't want you to be. You're Sam Harper, a very unique, special woman. And if someone doesn't like it, then screw them."

He could feel her relaxing and rubbed his chin against her hair before continuing. "My turn now."

"What do you mean?" She twisted and looked up at him.

"You know I'm a rogue."

She nodded.

"I'm not sure about being part of a pack. I want to be, but I wonder if I'll be able to handle it, day in and day out."

"You were fine when you were with us."

"But that wasn't year after year. What if I get restless?"

"Then you'll hop on your Harley and take off for a road trip for a week or two. As long as you come back."

"Are you sure?"

"Damien, I'm not the clingy type. I'm pretty independent. I'll understand if you need your space. Sometimes I need mine, too. The important thing is that we'll always come back to each other."

He nodded. Reaching out he traced her eyebrow with his fingertip, then the curve of her cheekbone. "I guess the future is full of unknowns, but whatever it holds, I want to face it with you. If you'll have me."

"Well..." She placed her hand on his chest, seeming to absorb the steady thumping of his heart. "Tina once told me men are like motorcycles and you should never buy one without taking it for a test drive or two."

A crooked smile formed on his lips. "And that means...?"

"I want a ride, Damien Masterson."

"A gentleman should never refuse a lady's request."

"Are you a gentleman?"

"No. Are you a lady?"

She snorted. "We're a good match."

"I think you're right." Once again he tried to pull her closer but the console was still in the way. "This is *not* going to work."

"No, we need to find someplace with a bit more room."

He started the car up and made a u-turn. "We'll head back to Stump River. I have some friends there you should meet."

"And a room with a bed." She slid her hand into his lap and cupped him.

"Yeah. Definitely a room with a bed." He grinned over at her, a feeling of lightness that had been absent for years filling him. Driving down the open road, his mate at his side…

Somewhere in the distance he heard a long, low wolf howl. He glanced at Sam but she didn't seem to have noticed. Had it been Beth? Was her spirit wishing him a final farewell? He'd like to think so. It put an end to any final feelings of guilt he might have had.

Putting his hand on top of Sam's, he laced his fingers with hers, feeling her warmth blending with his.

This was right.

This was his destiny.

This was his road to redemption.

Epilogue

Frowning, Sam twitched her leg. Something was tickling it, disrupting her concentration. She was lying on her stomach in bed, laptop in front of her as she finished going over the contract Sinclair had sent her and…

The tickling sensation returned.

Absentmindedly, she reached back and waved her hand in the general direction of her leg again. The deal she'd worked out with Sinclair to lease part of her territory should prove to be financially beneficial to the pack. They'd spent the last three months hashing out all the details, but she wanted to make sure Sinclair hadn't slipped something extra in at the last moment.

Some might say she was over-cautious, but she still didn't completely trust the—

Damn! Was that a fly walking on her or…? With a growl, she swung her hand backwards and promptly connected with something hard.

"Hey!"

"Damien!" She rolled onto her side to find her mate sitting beside her on the bed giving her an affronted look and rubbing his cheek. Last time she'd checked he'd been sleeping beside her.

"Why did you hit me?"

"Why were you tickling my leg?"

"I wasn't tickling your leg. I was blowing on it."

"Technicality. Why?"

"Because the back of your thigh is irresistible, and it leads to other, even more irresistible places." He gave her a crooked grin and she couldn't help but smile back.

Reaching over, she closed her laptop and then settled on her back. The contract could wait. Damien had apparently woken in a playful mood.

"Other irresistible places? I'm not sure what you mean." Sam blinked at him innocently.

A mischievous glint appeared in Damien's eye and she could feel a quiver of excitement starting within her. In the short time they'd been together, her mate had proven to be an adventurous and extremely skilled lover.

"It would appear a demonstration is in order." He rose to his knees beside her and began to unbutton the shirt she was wearing. It was one of his that she'd donned as a nightshirt; she loved having his scent wrapped around her.

As the material fell from her body, Damien replaced it with soft touches and tender kisses. She gave a contented sigh as he murmured against her skin.

"Right here, your cleavage, is very irresistible to me." He licked between her breasts.

"My boobs aren't big enough to have cleavage." She pointed out.

Damien responded by cupping her breasts and lifting them, testing their weight. "They're the perfect size," he declared, kissing the tip of each before sliding lower on her body. "Your bellybutton is fascinating."

"Really?"

"Are you doubting my judgement?" He cocked an eyebrow at her.

"Well…"

Damien shook his head and continued his inventory of her charms. "But this spot…" He nuzzled the crease of her thigh. "Is what I really can't resist." His breath tickled her sensitive skin and she squirmed under his attentions. "I love your scent. Your taste…"

She felt the hot moisture of his tongue as he flicked it over her skin. Anticipation grew within her and she reached down, burying her hands in his hair, guiding him lower.

"And down here…"

He was so close to where she wanted to be touched, to the place that was moist and aching.

Betrayed: Book Two – The Road To Redemption

Suddenly, he sat up. "What about you? Do you find any part of me irresistible?"

A snarl of frustration escaped from her throat. "Damien, that isn't nice!"

"And since when have I ever been nice?" A smirk curled his lips.

"It would seem a certain co-Alpha needs to be put in his place." Abruptly, she pushed him onto his back and began to tickle him mercilessly.

He laughed and attacked back, the two rolling like pups on the mattress. Eventually the game grew sensual and soon they were kneeling, facing each other.

"I love you, Sugar." He urged her to straddle him.

"I love you, Damien." She said the words on a sigh as she sank down on him.

Face to face, equal. It was her favourite position. She wrapped her arms around his neck. He held her hips. Together they began to move, staring into each other's eyes. She loved watching him, seeing the fierceness in his face, the protectiveness, the love.

Her fingers lightly brushed the mark of their blood bond. It was on the opposite side of his neck from Beth's. She hadn't wanted to erase the other woman's memory. Beth had helped make Damien the man he was now.

Sam leaned forward and kissed her mark. Damien responded by quickening their pace. She could feel the need growing within him, and still marvelled at how a blood bond could multiply the pleasure both partners felt. She knew there was a tingling at the base of his spine, that his balls were drawing up, the pressure mounting inside him. It increased her own excitement and she rode him even harder, her breasts brushing against his chest, sweat slickening her skin.

Damien growled in approval. Sam knew he was experiencing her feelings as well. The growing tension within her, the way her heart was pounding, her vision beginning to blur. She hovered on the edge, hanging on to him tightly, her nails digging into his flesh as she tried to prolong the moment.

The tiny pinpricks of pain drove them both beyond reason and with a unified shout they lost all control.

Passion spent, they slumped against each other, hearts pounding, enjoying the afterglow.

The doorbell rang.

"Damn." They swore as one, eyes meeting, equal looks of frustration on their faces.

"We could ignore it." Damien suggested. "Someone else will answer."

"No one else is home except us, and Grandfather and Florence; they're both resting right now." She'd made her peace with the old man—sort of. As Damien had pointed out, you never knew when someone would be gone forever. Holding onto old hurts didn't prove anything.

The doorbell rang again.

"Maybe whoever it is will go away." Damien nibbled at her neck.

Sam sighed regretfully even as she angled her head to allow him better access. "You'd better see who it is."

Damien grumbled but got up and pulled on a pair of sweatpants. "Don't go anywhere. I'll get rid of them and be right back."

"Hurry!" She urged him as he left the room. Another round of lovemaking seemed a lot more interesting at the moment than going over legal notes.

Damien stomped down the stairs. His afternoon delight with Sam was being interrupted and he wasn't happy. He'd arranged for everyone to be away for the day and now some door-to-door salesman was going to ruin everything. Funny how he'd never given much thought to the restrictions a pack placed on an Alpha's sex life. There was always someone around, always someone wanting to talk to you. He and Sam really needed to look at reorganizing the house so they had a wing to themselves. A sound-proofed wing.

The doorbell rang again just as he reached the front entryway. He jerked the door open.

"Yeah?"

"Damien Masterson?" A tall rugged-looking man eyed him up and down. A Lycan. Older, with a scar on one cheek. He looked vaguely familiar.

Damien gave a brief nod. It was probably someone from Lycan Link sent to check up on him. His name might be off the most-wanted list, but he had no doubt they still kept close tabs on him.

"Good." Without warning, the man slugged him in the jaw.

The unexpected greeting had him staggering backwards into the doorjamb and the other fellow grabbed him by the throat before he could react.

"What the f—" Even before he could finish his curse the Lycan replied.

"My name is Stone. Did you work for Deirdre?"

Damien stiffened, wary of the man. Elijah Stone. Deirdre's mystery partner. "Why do you want to know?"

"If you did, I might have to kill you."

"Do you get a lot of positive responses with this warm friendly manner of yours?" Damien quirked a brow, refusing to acknowledge the man's scare tactics. Breathing was overrated anyway, or so he tried to tell himself when his comment resulted in the man tightening his grip.

"Just answer the question."

"You seem to already know the answer, but yeah, I was stupid enough to work for her."

Stone slowly released his grip and stepped back, arms held loosely at his side, his gaze assessing.

Damien straightened and tested his jaw. It wasn't broken, but the man had a damned good right hook. "Interesting way you have of greeting people." Stone didn't react to his snide comment, so Damien tried again. "If you're here to kill me I'd suggest we take this out back. Too many human witnesses." He gestured towards the street.

Stone didn't turn to check behind him. "Deirdre said you'd quit. Why?"

Realizing he couldn't distract the man, Damien sighed and answered his question. "Let's just say I saw the error of my ways."

A sneer twisted the man's mouth. "Poetic, but what the hell does it mean?"

"It means I was fucked up and the whole organization was, too. I finally realized it and left." Damien moved to fold his arms and then thought better of it. He needed to be ready to block another attack. His inner wolf didn't trust the man before them and neither did he.

"Good answer." Stone inclined his head.

"Come again?"

Stone didn't explain, instead seeming to steer the conversation in a new direction. "I've been watching you on and off for the past few months."

Damien frowned, recalling all the times he'd felt he was being watched but had never been able to locate who it was. Stone? But how had the man remained undetected? He hadn't been using a scent mask...or at least not one that left a flowery trail. "How and why?"

"The how is my secret. The why... Like I said, you left. I wanted to find out why."

"Deirdre didn't tell you?"

"We've had a...falling out over the direction our organization developed during my absence. I've spent the past few months tracking down ex-employees and dealing with them. My way of making restitution for any damage they might have done."

"Which means?"

"Some lived. Some died." Stone's eyes narrowed, a deadly look coming over his face.

"Not the best severance package." Damien murmured. He had no difficulty seeing this man enact it. There was a cold, ruthlessness about the Lycan that had been evident in some of the men who worked for Deirdre; men for whom life had no meaning, and killing was as much a part of their daily routine as taking a piss. Yeah, Elijah Stone had that look about him with something extra added in; an air of determination that he'd accomplish his mission no matter what obstacle got in his way.

Not even a hint of a smile curved the corner of the man's mouth. "They got what they deserve."

"And what do you think I deserve?" Damien flicked a glance over Stone's shoulder to the street beyond. Traffic was light, a few neighbours were on their porches. Still too many witnesses for the man to kill him on the spot.

"Damien?" Sam had grown tired of waiting for him. She'd pulled on a t-shirt and yoga pants and, hearing an unfamiliar voice, had headed downstairs to see who was keeping him from her bed.

As she descended the steps it became apparent it was a Lycan. Male. Powerful. Deadly. She slowed her pace as she analyzed the scent emanating from him. Who the hell was this and what was he doing in her territory?

Her inner wolf raised its hackles, preparing to defend the pack against this new threat and by the time she reached the bottom of the stairs she was in full Alpha mode. Damien tried to pull the door shut just as she reached it, but he was too late. She yanked it out of his hand and then stood in the doorway shooting questioning glances between her mate and the strange Lycan. "Who's this?"

"An old... acquaintance." Damien replied, clearly not pleased she'd made an appearance. He tried to step in front of her but she firmly took her place at his side.

"My name is Elijah Stone." The male eyed her up and down then lifted his chin.

"Sam Harper." She snorted at his posturing and put her hands on her hips. This Elijah dude was impressive and, if she didn't already have her own mate, she might have found him interesting. About Damien's height, solid muscle, dominant. But where Damien's eyes sparkled, this man's were deadly serious, almost flat as if he'd forgotten the joy of living; his last name—Stone—suited him. And there was no quirk to the corner of his mouth, no playful sexual aura about him. An order from this man would have most Lycans turning belly up. Good thing she wasn't most Lycans. "What are you doing in my territory? Passing through or reporting in for a prolonged visit?"

Stone didn't answer her, instead casting a look at Damien. "You chose well. She's a good mate for a warrior."

A warrior? She'd never considered Damien a warrior, but it appeared to be Elijah's mindset. It would be easy to picture the man in fatigues and dog tags, a gun slung over his shoulder or a knife in his hand.

"We're good for each other." Sam stepped closer to Damien, bristling at being ignored. "And you didn't answer my questions."

Stone looked at her and inclined his head. "Passing through." His voice was deep, guttural, and she barely held back a shiver at the sound of it.

"And my severance package?" Damien put his arm around her shoulders, holding her protectively close.

Sam frowned, wondering what was going on. While she wanted to ask, she didn't want to let on to Stone that she and Damien had any secrets from each other. Damien's past was something they'd only started to explore. He had a rogue's natural reluctance to share, and she knew it would take time to uncover all the demons that lived inside him.

Elijah shook his head. "No need to worry. What I've observed matches the records I retrieved from Deirdre. You won't be seeing me again."

Damien didn't let his relief show but, because she was pressed against his side, Sam felt the fractional relaxing of his muscles. Whatever this 'severance package' had entailed, she didn't have any doubts that it wasn't good. And knowing Damien, he would have taken off rather than stay and allow danger anywhere near their pack. Thank heaven she wouldn't have to go tracking him down again! Another trip to Stump River wasn't part of her plan. The place was probably still frozen rock solid despite spring being just around the corner.

"And what about the others?" Damien asked. "The rest of the organization?"

"Everyone gets what they deserve in life. I just make sure it happens." Stone's voice was as expressionless as his face, but Sam was sure she saw a hint of emotion behind his flat, black eyes. Was it sorrow? Perhaps the man wasn't quite made of granite. "There's only one I'm still looking for. A man named Dante."

"Dante?" Sam looked at Damien. He hadn't even flicked an eyelash in response to hearing the man's name. Too bad she hadn't controlled her own reaction better for Elijah immediately focused all his attention on her.

"You know him." It was a statement, not a question. Stone narrowed his eyes. "Where is he?"

Damien pulled her protectively closer, a warning rumbling in his chest. "Sam only knows him in passing. Dante came looking for me. And before you ask, we weren't friends and I've no idea where he's hiding his sorry ass."

Stone flicked a look between the two of them, seeming to weigh the veracity of their statement and finally nodding. "There's no scent of deceit about you. I will look for him elsewhere."

Without another word, he turned and left.

Sam remained silent until Stone was out of earshot and then let free the shiver she'd been holding back. "What was that about?"

"My past. For a minute I thought it was going to bite me in the butt."

"I'm glad it didn't." She reached behind him and pinched his rear. "I'm the only one allowed to bite this."

"Really?" Her playful attitude helped defuse the tension she sensed in him and a wicked grin curled his lips. "Perhaps we should go back upstairs so you can check the area out."

She laughed and he swung her into his arms and spun her around. As he turned to carry her inside, she caught a glimpse of Elijah, now nearing the end of the street. There was a deadly determination about the man, but also a sadness.

Silently, she wished him luck. Everyone deserved to be happy in life, even those who seemed to be made out of stone.

~FIN~

A Message From Nicky

Hello readers!

Thank you for reading my book. If you enjoyed it, please leave a review at your favourite retailer.

This story was the sixth story in my Lycan series. I have ideas for several more installments provided my muse cooperates. Daniel and Tessa still need to be sorted out. Armand is pining away and now the mysterious Elijah Stone has appeared! As well, there are several new characters dancing about in my head, all clamouring to be brought to light. If all goes as planned, I will be busy writing for the next several years.

In the meantime, you might want to check out Forever In Time. It was the first original story I'd ever written and has just been revised and republished.

~Nicky

Connect with Me:

Email me at
nicky@nickycharles.com
Or nicky.charles@live.ca

Visit my website:
http://www.nickycharles.com

Follow me on Facebook:
https://www.facebook.com/NickyCharles/

Books by Nicky Charles

Forever In Time

The Law of the Lycans Series
The Mating
The Keeping
The Finding
Bonded
Betrayed: Days of the Rogue
Betrayed – Book Two: The Road to Redemption
For the Good of All
Deceit can be Deadly
Kane: I am Alpha

Hearts & Halos Series
(Written with Jan Gordon)
In The Cards
Untried Heart

Manufactured by Amazon.ca
Acheson, AB